Hold Me Until Morning

A.L. Jackson
www.aljacksonauthor.com

Cover Design by Enchanting Romance Designs
Editing by SS Stylistic Editing
Proofreading by Julia Griffis, The Romance Bibliophile
Formatting by Champagne Book Design

More from

A.L. Jackson

NEW YORK TIMES BESTSELLING AUTHOR

Hold Me Until Morning

NEW YORK TIMES BESTSELLING AUTHOR
A.L. JACKSON

Prologue

MY EYES DEVOURED THE OUTLINE OF HIS PERFECT SHAPE. His big body roiled in sharp restraint and caused a constant wave of strength that battered against me.

He held onto the steering wheel like it might be the one thing that kept him contained.

The only thing grounding him when the world had floated away from us.

Each thirsting for what we knew better than to chase, but right then, after everything that had happened tonight, all rationale ceased to exist.

"You need to stop looking at me like that," he warned in a rough, low voice.

"I don't think I can stop." There I went—a fool who was begging for it.

Heartbreak.

Every muscle in his body flexed, a bristle of repression and a rush of greed. "I'm not sure I can give you what you need."

"You told me last night you knew exactly what I needed."

His tongue stroked out over his lips, and that energy swelled.

Need rose up from the depths to consume.

My thighs pressed together, and his gaze dropped to the action. I squirmed beneath the weight. Beneath the potency that lured me in his direction.

"That's right. You need to come." His words were harsh. A rough scrape of seduction.

"Just once. Tonight."

I thought I could handle it, but I should have known my love for him would grow and he'd become my world.

And him loving me?

It was going to cost everything.

Chapter One

Cody

IT WAS JUST BEFORE SIX WHEN I TOOK THE LEFT INTO MY neighborhood. Rain was pouring down, a deluge from the sky. It was a summer storm that had built for the better part of the afternoon, the clouds gathering high and thick, before it'd finally unleashed its fury just as the sun had begun its descent toward the horizon.

I fucking loved storms.

Loved the energy.

Loved the blinding flash of lightning before the crack of thunder followed.

Loved the way the earth smelled afterward, like it was promising something brand new.

Though I personally preferred watching it with my boots kicked up on the railing of my porch while I tossed back a couple beers rather than to be standing in the middle of it.

So, I was grumbling out a disbelieving, "Shit," when my headlights cut across the U-Haul that sat in the driveway of the house next to mine.

It was parked facing out, and it wouldn't have caused such a stir except for the fact I caught sight of a woman running out of the house and down the sidewalk before she disappeared into the back of the U-Haul.

Racing through the driving rain with her head angled toward the ground like it offered her any hope of not getting drenched.

The place had been empty and posted for rent for the last month, and I'd heard it on good word from the neighborhood gossip that it'd been rented. Never once in the last week had Millie failed to come around to speculate about who might be moving in.

Poor old lady was always sure it was bound to be a serial killer.

It appeared I was about to find out, and not under the best of circumstances.

But hell, it seemed a prick move to pull into my garage and act like I hadn't noticed someone was trying to move their shit in during a storm, which in my humble opinion was a bit on the reckless side.

Like it was offering proof, a flash of lightning streaked across the sky before a crack of thunder followed, and I was huffing again as I pulled into my garage, killed the engine, and climbed out.

I hesitated for only a second before I ducked out into the pelting rain.

A torrent pounding from above.

In an instant, my hair and tee were soaked, the pummeling only getting worse and spreading to my jeans as I jogged across the lawn that separated the two houses.

I rounded to the back of the U-Haul to the trailer and found the ramp was extended out and the rolling door was open. The minimal light that still remained cast a faint glow into the trailer.

Boxes were stacked on furniture, and the woman I'd seen come darting out had her back to me, frantically rifling through the boxes.

She wore shorts and a crop top as she bent over to hunt for whatever she was searching for. The action emphasized thick, lush thighs and the most delicious ass I'd ever seen.

My dick kicked, and my stomach gripped in a fit of lust.

Fuck me.

My new neighbor was perfection.

It was no secret that I loved women. Loved to touch and tease and fuck. But this smack of greed hit me like nothing I'd ever experienced.

I sucked the reaction down because I didn't know a single thing about this woman.

Hell, she could be married for all I knew, and ogling someone else's wife was not my thing. Though if the douche was sitting inside as she was out here in the rain? He and I were not going to be friends.

I hopped into the bed of the truck.

"Hey, there," I called, though my voice was drowned by the rain battering against the metal roof.

Apparently, she wasn't expecting any sort of neighborly welcome because a scream suddenly ripped out of her. The piercing sound ricocheted against the confined walls.

In the same second, she whirled around. Drenched locks of this dark, honey-kissed blonde hair whipped around her shoulders.

The box she'd just picked up toppled out of her hands and thudded to the floor right as these cute, dainty little fists came out in front of her like she was ready to throw down.

A vicious little thing who clearly was prepared to claw my eyes out.

I held back the chuckle that threatened. All I could think was she and Millie might be kindred spirits, only this woman had been sure she was moving *in* next to a serial killer.

I didn't laugh, though. Not when I could feel it—actual fear rolling off her in waves.

I couldn't make out her face in the shadows, but that didn't hide the ferocity that lay beneath it, seeded deep in her bones.

I lifted my hands in surrender. "Whoa, sorry. I didn't mean to startle you, darlin'."

"What the hell is wrong with you? Sneaking up on me like that?" Her voice was low and throaty and skating over my skin.

At the sound of it, a strange sensation pulled at my stomach.

A clench of uncertainty.

A tug of familiarity.

One I couldn't place, like some long-ago memory that scattered like debris.

My brow lifted in disbelief. "What the hell is wrong with me? I was actually popping by to ask you the same question, considering you're out here trying to unload boxes in the middle of a lightning storm."

I tried to keep it light, though there was a part of me that wanted to toss her over my shoulder and carry her to her door.

Being out here like this wasn't safe.

And shit, I might not know her, but I needed her to be.

Safe.

Exasperation huffed from her mouth. It drew my attention to the sound. In the wisping darkness, I could just make out the heart-shaped lips, so plump and full I thought they might permanently look like they were puckered for a kiss.

Which was the dumbest damned thought I'd ever had since I didn't kiss. It was too fucking intimate.

And here I was the moron thinking I might make the exception for her.

I could physically feel the shock of irritation that rolled through her, her tone pitched in a challenge as her shoulders hiked up to her ears. "Did you come to *my* house to tell me when it's prudent for me to unpack my things?"

She crossed her arms over her chest. She probably meant for it to be defiant. A barrier that told me to fuck off. Too bad the only thing it did was drop my gaze to the spot.

Good God, her tits were gorgeous, too.

A beat of that lust rebounded, and a smirk took to my face as my head angled to the side. "I just was thinking you might be able to find a better time, is all. You do seem...a little wet."

Okay, so I still didn't know a goddamn thing about her, but I couldn't help but tease her a bit. Wondering if she'd bite since I was definitely salivating to get a taste.

One delicious hip cocked to the left, though I was getting the message it wasn't to be coy.

Clearly, she wasn't impressed by the insinuation.

I took a step forward into the severity that vibrated the trailer, toward this woman who quivered with a distrust so fierce that it stabbed me in the chest. What the hell could put a chip so big on someone's shoulder?

"I'm Cody. Cody Cooper. I live next door. Looks to me like you could use a hand, and I'm here to be of service."

I stretched my tatted arms out like an offering.

She stumbled a step farther back into the shadows.

"You don't have the first clue what I need," she sneered.

Huh.

Not the usual reaction I got when I chatted up a chick.

She had a man, then. Yeah. That had to be it.

She turned away like she was completely disinterested, and she started digging through the boxes again. "You can go on back to your place. Like you said, it's storming, and I'm sure a man like you has plenty of other things he'd rather be doing with his time."

I was thinking something along the lines of pushing her up against the wall and getting to what was hidden under those short shorts seemed like a good place to start.

She'd likely cut off my dick and shove it down my throat if I even suggested it.

"Nah, I don't have anything better to do. How about you let me give you a hand, instead?"

"I don't need a hand," she grumbled as she stacked three big boxes before she picked them up. She struggled to balance them, but the one on the top slipped.

Lunging forward, I caught it before it hit the ground.

I did my best to ignore the gravity rolling off her flesh, though I could feel it skating over mine when I stepped into her vicinity, the air feeling heavier than it should.

I forced the casual arch of my brow. "Looks to me like you do."

I wrangled the rest of the boxes from her hold, taking two in one arm and the third in the other.

She gasped out a surprised sound. "Excuse me, what do you think you're doing?"

I sent her a wide grin, the one I used that normally won me

whatever favor I wanted. "I'm just doing what my momma taught me to do and helping out a neighbor."

Turning on my heel, I ducked out of the trailer.

Rain pelted from above, the gusts of wind pushing it sideways, stinging my flesh as I hurried up the walkway toward the little house that was almost identical to mine except the floor plans were flopped.

Hers was painted white with blue trim, and there was a porch swing out front.

I could feel her right behind me, aghast, brimming with indignation.

"You can't just come over here and put your nose in my business," she spluttered.

I glanced back as she was trying to shove back the hair that was matted to her face. Her face that I caught the vaguest glimpse of.

Again, that familiarity speared me through the chest, though this time it didn't feel so distant. It was right there. Waiting for me to catch onto it.

"I'm not pretending to know a thing about your business," I tossed out.

I felt her come to a stop behind me, though her voice grew in strength. "I don't need some muscled up cowboy coming around here thinking I'm weak."

I faltered for the flash of a second before I continued on, my boots thudding on the wood as I took the three steps onto the covered porch. I stalked over to the door and dropped the boxes onto the mat.

She was still standing in the rain when I turned around, but it was me who was gasping when I fully was able to take her in.

The goddamn breath knocked from my lungs.

Because that was right when another strike of lightning lit the atmosphere, illuminating her face, and I was getting slammed by the intensity of these giant eyes.

The color of tumbled blue glass.

As distinct as the river that ran through the town.

Bright.

Clear.

Bottomless.

Rimmed in these full, long lashes that only made them appear larger, so powerful they could look right through the middle of you to every secret you'd ever tried to keep.

These eyes? These eyes I knew.

Dumbstruck, I gaped.

"Hailey?" Her name tumbled out like a question. Because the last time I'd seen her she'd been little more than eighteen. Young and innocent and sweet.

And now…now she was…

Fuck me—she was stunning.

Her face this perfect heart, cheeks high and full, and her jaw tapered down to an almost sharp chin, though it was softened with a dimple that sat right in the middle.

Right then, her expression roiled in a crash of turbulence. Violent and chaotic where she stood beneath the power of the storm.

Fierce.

Fiery.

Though there was no missing the way she was shaking.

My chest tightened.

She let go of a patronizing laugh. "What, you recognized me now?"

My brow pinched at the dislike she was tossing at me. "It was dark and…it's been a lot of years."

"Yeah, it has." The fire inside her blazed, the woman wearing it like a shield.

I knew exactly what it looked like to barely be holding the broken pieces together. What it looked like to be holding on so tightly because your world was unraveling.

Hers trembled all around her.

My stomach twisted in a way that it shouldn't. A swell of protectiveness rose from out of nowhere.

It took all my strength to bat it back down into nonexistence because Hailey Wagner was the last person I could care about. The last person I could get close to.

Just standing here talking to her was likely hazardous.

I'd long ago accepted my philosophy on life.

I was happy to lend a hand when I could. Keep it polite. Mind my manners the way my mother had taught me, and my father had insisted.

But other than for my friends and my family? My mother and my two sisters? It ended at that.

I didn't form bonds or attachments. Never got too close or too deep.

I fucked a lot and made sure to please, then I left it at that.

I couldn't take the chance of someone relying on me. Couldn't risk the choices I'd made in my life affecting someone else. Because I didn't know when my luck was going to fail.

It looked like right then, with Hailey staring back at me, that luck might have run out.

The problem was? I saw it written all over her. She'd been. Time and again.

Failed.

I should stay far the fuck away from her, but I couldn't remain standing still. Couldn't stop the slow approach of my feet as I crossed the porch and climbed down the steps.

I kept moving until I was a foot away from her.

A greedy bastard because I reached out and ran my thumb over that divot in her chin, hating that I was the reason it was trembling.

I got struck with it then. The scent of strawberries and cream so distinct that it hit me like a punch to the gut. Memories pummeled me like a landslide. That summer six years ago that had changed everything. I'd done my all to bury those memories, memories I'd do well to leave in the past.

Surprise dropped that pouty mouth open, and the air crackled around us. My voice came out hoarser than I'd intended it to. "From where I'm standing, Hailey? There isn't a thing weak about you. Never has been, and I'm pretty sure there's never going to be."

Before I could contemplate what the hell I was feeling, I turned and jogged back to my house, leaving her standing in the rain.

Chapter Two
Hailey

I REMAINED ROOTED, UNABLE TO MOVE, SHOCK SPEARING ME through and staking me to the ground as I pwatched him jog across the lawn that separated our yards, his giant frame getting eaten up by the raging storm that thrashed around him. A gray mist covered him whole before he disappeared through his garage door that had remained open.

Like a ghost had appeared from out of nowhere and evaporated just as fast.

Except he was no ghost.

He was Cody Cooper.

I stifled the wave of grief that threatened to suck me under. I knew it wasn't wholly because of him.

It was just the memories of this place. The memories I'd worried would be too much, which was the reason I hadn't come back here in six years.

But it was time.

Time to return to myself.

Time to reclaim.

Time to renew a purpose that had been lost somewhere along the way.

Time to stand up and fight.

It was only a tiny hiccup that it turned out Cody was my new next-door neighbor.

No doubt, Karma was laughing her ass off at me right then.

I shucked it down, the twinge of guilt I felt, and chalked it up to coincidence.

Cody was just a flirty bastard who so clearly knew how to get what he wanted. Country charm and arrogance in vats. Just as aloof and self-centered as he'd ever been.

It wasn't a big deal. I could handle it.

Another streak of lightning flashed overhead, and it knocked me from the trance and jolted me into action.

Beneath the pelting rain, I scurried the rest of the way up the walkway and onto the porch. I tossed open the door before I leaned down and shoved the three boxes inside, internally scolding myself for being relieved for even a second that I hadn't had to carry them in myself.

I was not in need of a white knight.

Specifically, one named Cody Cooper.

Slamming the door shut and locking it behind me, I straightened and dragged my fingers through the sopping wet mess of my hair to get it out of my face.

A buzz of satisfaction filled me as I took in the house.

The middle section was done as a great room, completely open.

Airy and letting in a ton of light when it wasn't storming out.

The kitchen was on the left and the living area was on the right.

The floors were done in plank tiles that looked like wood. The cabinets a deep chestnut, and the countertops were a swirl of creams and browns and golds to tie it all together.

It was nice but small.

Modest.

Especially when compared to the extravagance I'd lived in for my entire life.

But I loved it.

Loved the possibility.

Loved this brand-new chance.

I shoved down any thoughts of fear it triggered and started to lean down so I could open the boxes.

"Now *who* was that?" The question hit me from the side.

A gasp left me as my attention whipped that way, and I shook my head at myself when I realized it was Lolly. Only I would jump out of my skin at my grandmother's voice, but I couldn't help being on edge.

I still wasn't sure if this was the most reckless decision I could make. If I was begging for trouble, coming here. Standing out in the open like a sitting duck. But I refused to spend my life hiding.

My grandmother stood at the window with the drapes peeled open so she could peek outside. Her wrinkled face was twisted in something that appeared a little too close to glee.

Awesome.

She'd witnessed whatever the hell that was with Cody.

"No one," I muttered as I climbed down onto my knees to rip the tape free of one of the boxes.

"Oh, I'm pretty sure it was someone. No missing that hulk of a man. That one was pure muscle from his head all the way down to his boots. And those boots were big. Real big. Sex on a stick, that one. Like taking a good lick of candy."

Exasperation had my eyes dragging closed and my head wagging back and forth. Like I needed the reminder of how hot the guy was.

That was somewhere I would not let my mind go.

But I wasn't sure I could expect anything else when it came to my grandmother. I had a mind that her drooling all over my father's employees was half the reason he'd wanted to put her into a nursing home.

"You probably shouldn't be peeping out at the neighbors, Lolly. You're going to catch a reputation."

She chuckled without a trace of shame. "Oh, sweet girl, I've had a reputation my whole life."

"Lolly," I chastised, trying to suppress my grin. The woman did not need to be encouraged.

My grandmother had been married five times. Four divorces before she'd finally met the love of her life when she was sixty. She'd been devastated when he died last year, and I knew she was still suffering from it, even though she always seemed to find a way to smile.

Almost eighty years old and she was still looking to the good. I'd idolized her my entire life, sitting at her feet when I was a little girl, dreaming of being as wild and vibrant and free as she was long before I'd really understood what it meant.

Her laughter was wry. "Maybe you should earn one with that cowboy. Looked to me like he might want to take you for a ride."

"The last thing I need in my life right now is to get mixed up with the likes of that." I wasn't about to admit that I knew him.

Besides, I knew Cody's type of *mixing*. That guy reeked of *player*.

Always had.

Always would.

I went for light, playing the entire thing off. "Besides, have you seen me? I look like a drowned rat. I think he was looking to win some brownie points with his new neighbors."

Some place to toss all that brawn.

Too bad it'd felt like he'd lit a fire when he'd looked at me with those gold-colored eyes. Flecked in reds and browns that licked and danced like flames.

Too bad my lungs had felt hollow, and my stomach had felt too tight as he'd towered at the end of the trailer with the last of the day illuminating him like some kind of tempting silhouette.

Too bad my thoughts were tossed right back to the way I'd felt when I'd first seen him all those years ago.

I blamed his overpowering presence on his sheer size.

He had to be at least six foot three, a pillar of strength. Shoulders as wide as he was tall. I swore that I could have counted every muscled groove and ridge beneath the soaked fabric that had clung to his chest and abdomen.

Arrogant.

Cocky.

The man dripping sex and easy smiles.

He'd aged, though.

The boyish features that I remembered had hardened to something rough and rugged.

Worst of it all? I'd nearly gotten swept away by the undercurrent of something beautifully brutal that had radiated from him when he'd reached out and touched my chin.

Like he was on the verge of understanding.

I knew I looked different. The years have changed me. Inside and out. But I'd just thought…

Shaking off the direction my thoughts were going, I focused on trying to get into the box and did my best to ignore the way my skin tingled in the spot where he'd held me by the chin.

"Have I seen you?" Lolly tsked, taking a couple steps across our still-empty living room. "The most gorgeous girl on the planet?"

I finally got the tape up at the edge and ripped it free, and I gave a roll of my eyes to my Lolly, my voice drifting into a light chuckle. "You have a moral obligation to say that."

"I think you know full well I tell it like it is. No lies come from this tongue. And you could be my twin back in my heyday, and believe you me, I was a looker."

I laughed outright. "Don't kid yourself. You're just as beautiful as you've ever been."

Her smile went wry. "That's right. You and I are going to be the talk of this little town."

Well, it was certain one of us was going to be.

A grin spread across my face when I suddenly heard the clatter of tiny feet rushing up the hallway that ran down the right side of the house, her sweet little voice carrying as she came. "Did you find my Princess Verona?"

I glanced up to see my four-year-old daughter standing just inside the living area, wearing her favorite purple jammies and bouncing on her bare toes.

"I think it might be in one of these."

I'd searched through the trailer for the boxes with her name written on the side that had come from her room.

Madison.

She'd written her name on them herself, all the letters different colors, messy, and upper case. She'd insisted on helping me pack her room, which was how I was pretty sure we'd ended up with a missing Princess Verona, assuming the stuffed animal had been accidentally tossed into a box.

So no, *Cocky Cowboy*, there was not a better time to unload these boxes.

It was bad enough that Maddie had freaked out when she realized she didn't have it. The only way I'd been able to calm her down was I'd promised that Princess Verona was in one of the boxes keeping an eye on the rest of her things, and I'd find her the second we got to the new house.

We stayed at a motel in Hendrickson last night since I couldn't pick up the keys to the house until this morning.

It wasn't in the first, so I hurried to open the second box, and I rummaged around inside. Relief struck me when my fingers brushed over the soft, plush fabric.

I pulled it out, producing the stuffed, purple bunny.

"It's my Princess Verona!" Madison cried. She came running over and slid onto her knees in front of me. "You found her, Mommy! You found her!"

No question, the stuffed animal was a safety blanket for my child. One that gave her comfort when she was afraid. One that made her believe she was always secure.

Finding this bunny? It wasn't close to being frivolous or inconsequential the way that jerk had implied. I passed it to her. "Here you go, sweetheart."

She hugged it tight, swinging her shoulders back and forth as she pinched up her face in the most adorable way. Right then, her dark blonde hair appeared almost brown since it was still damp from the bath I'd given her just before I'd gone on the rescue mission.

The riot of curls springing back to life.

"Thank you, Mommy," she said in her little drawl. Holding the bunny out in front of her, she bounced it around. "We got a new house,

Princess Verona! I think it's going to be our favorite, favorite because we got a yard and a swing set and even a sandbox!"

Madison turned her blue gaze on me. Her eyes were the same color as mine, though hers still shined with awe and innocence. I would give it my all to keep it that way.

"Is it your favorite, too, Mommy? I like it that we got here and now we get to live with Lolly, and we even get to go see Grandpa's horsies, and I don't think you need to be sad here one little bit."

Regret squeezed my chest. I hated that my daughter had seen me in that state. Crying and afraid. But I wasn't going to be that person for a second longer. So instead, I let love invade. The devotion that pumped eternally.

I reached out and brushed my fingers down her plump cheek. "I do think I'm going to like it here. Very much."

"Oh, I bet you're gonna like it here." Pure suggestion filled Lolly's voice, even though there was a wedge of worry beneath it.

Pulling my daughter onto my lap, I sent a playful scowl at Lolly. "Keep it up, and you're going to find yourself in that fancy nursing home in Santa Barbara my dad keeps suggesting."

She waved the idea off with a scoff. "You both wouldn't know what to do without me."

Everything softened, all teasing gone. "Thank you for this, Lolly. I truly don't know what I would do without you."

I'd finally found the courage to leave Madison's father three months ago. I'd run from Austin, Texas to Boston, Massachusetts, unsure of where to go or where to turn, but just wanting to put as much time and space between us and Pruitt as I could.

During that time, I'd lived terrified. Terrified of who he was and what he might do. But I'd come to the resolution living that way was no life, and I'd prayed the threat I'd made him when I'd packed up and left would be enough.

So I'd returned here.

To my home.

To my family.

Lolly didn't know the real reason why I'd left him. I had to keep it that way. At least until I knew exactly what I was going to do.

I'd chosen a place near my childhood home in Langmire, Colorado, though I'd decided to settle in Hendrickson, closer to where I'd gotten my dream job.

My hometown was about an hour from here. That was where my father owned the largest stud ranch in the west, and his Thoroughbred stallions were known to have produced some of the fastest racehorses in the country, though the ranch produced at least a dozen different breeds.

His wealth verged on the obscene.

He'd wanted me to come back to his home and work for him, but I'd known I had to be able to stand on my own. Have my own experiences and chase after my own goals.

Give my daughter the type of life I hoped for her.

Lolly had been living in a wing of his home, and she'd offered to move in with me until I got on my feet.

Help me care for Madison until I found a good preschool program for her.

I looked back at my grandmother. "You knew how much I needed you."

Softness played across her aged features. "Of course, I knew. You and I have always belonged together. Besides, it's time to get out from under your father's roof. My son is constantly flitting around, thinking I'm incapable of taking care of myself, and if I'm not careful, he really is going to send me off to that nursing home. He already has a room reserved and paid for."

My smile was soft. "He just wants what's best for you, but you aren't ready."

"That's right, I'm not. I still have a little purpose here. The dream team is back together."

Emotion thickened my throat and stung at the backs of my eyes.

"Can I be on your dream team, my favorite Lolly?" Madison asked, her voice perking with excitement.

"You already are, sweet child. You already are."

Affection pulsed through my spirit.

God, I'd missed her. I had missed the way she'd stood in the vacant place after my mother had been killed in a car accident when I was six.

I had missed her teasing.

Had missed her belief.

I cleared the sogginess from my throat, forced a bright smile, and patted Madison's thigh. "All right, time to get your teeth brushed. We have a big day tomorrow, and Mommy has to be up early to get to work."

Today had been my first day, which had been comprised mostly of introductions and a few meetings to familiarize myself with the staff and my surroundings.

I knew I was going to love it. I'd found the place where I belonged.

Maddie popped onto her feet, and she swung her bunny around in a circle. "Okay, me and my Princess Verona will go brush our teeth so clean they're gonna be shining."

She scrambled down the hall, leaving me sitting there smiling behind her.

"She's so sweet," Lolly murmured. "So much like you when you were little."

"She's my world."

My reason. My purpose. My everything.

And I would never let anyone taint or threaten that again.

Resolved, I climbed to standing and headed down the hall on the right side of the house where there were two bedrooms and one bathroom.

Lolly had taken the largest one at the end of the hall, and Madison's was directly across from the bathroom in the middle.

I eased in behind my daughter where she was standing on a step stool, eagerly brushing her tiny, gapped teeth, Princess Verona propped on the counter beside her.

"All done!" She beamed those gleaming teeth up at me. "What do you think? Do I have 'em shining?"

"You did a great job," I whispered, wiping the bits of toothpaste she had smeared on her cheek with a hand towel.

She grabbed her bunny and shoved it my direction. "Princess Verona, too?"

A soft giggle pulled free as I swept her into my arms, tickled her, and said, "Princess Verona, too."

I carried her into her room, the perfect weight of her in my arms, hers locked around my neck, the scent of her bubblegum toothpaste all around me. I set her on the bed.

Our beds were the only things we'd had time to bring in and set up before the storm had hit, so her walls were still a stark white and the floors were barren.

I tucked her under the covers.

"Story time!" She grinned as she clutched the top of the blanket to her chest with both hands.

I sat beside her and picked up her favorite book, *Goodnight Moon*, my voice softened as I moved through the story.

My daughter began to get drowsy, lulled by the familiar, comforting words.

When I was finished, I leaned down and kissed her nose. "Goodnight, sweetheart."

She gave a groggy giggle and grabbed me by the cheeks, keeping our noses touching. "Night, Mommy. You better get some big rest so you're not tired at your new job."

My heart swelled.

My sweet, sweet girl.

"I will," I promised before I rose and crossed her room, flicked off her light, and crept back down the hall.

Lolly had already retreated to her room, the light glowing beneath the crack.

I edged toward mine that was on the other side of the house, through double doors on the opposite side of the kitchen.

I'd tried to give the primary to Lolly, but she'd insisted on taking the smaller room.

I stood in the doorway, taking it in. It had the same tile floors as the rest of the house, and the walls were painted a warm beige.

I had to have pulled ten muscles dragging the black fabric

headboard in, but somehow, I'd managed, and now it was covered in a plush duvet that was a rich teal and embroidered with black lilies.

Unease wobbled through me, and I knew what had me trapped in that spot didn't have a thing to do with the new room. It was the energy that swallowed me.

This feeling of compulsion.

Drawn to the window that looked out toward the side of the house.

Such a fool to give into it, but there I was, shuffling across the room as if I had a hook in my chest.

My breaths turned shallow as I pulled the drape back an inch to peer out, all covert and sneaky like some kind of creeper.

It was just as I'd suspected.

My window faced a matching one next door, the houses a mirror, though his curtains were open wide. A light burning from within illuminated his bedroom.

I somehow already knew he'd be there—on full display.

Still, a choked, strangled sound worked its way up my throat.

The man was fresh from a shower, everything bare, except for the towel that was wrapped low around his waist.

Hair damp and dark brown, longer than I'd realized, soft waves curling over his ears.

He moved to a dresser across the room, and his chiseled back was to me as he pulled something out.

Ink littered his flesh, though I was too far away to be able to discern any of the words or shapes. But I thought I would have been able to make out every carved, hewn muscle of his enormous body from a mile away.

Desire climbed out from the place where she'd been dormant, tugging at my belly in a way that made me feel sick.

And I wondered if he knew, if he could feel me, too, when he turned and waltzed all kinds of casual across his room, roughing a giant hand through the wet locks of his hair as he came, nonchalant even though each step felt profound.

An earthquake.

As powerful as the storm that continued to pound.

Because I swore, he smirked before he reached out and quickly dragged the curtains shut.

My teeth ground.

Cocky. Freaking. Cowboy.

I forced myself away from the window, climbed under the covers, and pulled them up to my chin. My eyes squeezed closed, and I whispered around the knot of sadness that suddenly pulsed in my chest, "Brooke...what am I supposed to do?"

Chapter Three

Cody

CAMBREY PINES SPA & RESORT.

The most luxurious, upscale, trendy guest ranch Colorado had to offer. Sitting on a hundred acres, tucked back in the pines at the base of a mountain with Time River running through.

It was the place that was going to change my entire life.

The resort was about twenty minutes outside of my hometown of Time River, and I lived ten minutes east of here where I'd decided to settle in the small town of Hendrickson after I'd started my fledgling landscaping company nine years ago.

Adrenaline pumping through my veins, I drove my pickup truck along the winding road that curled through the endless maze of evergreens. Their spires disappeared into the vast canopy of blue above. Any trace of the storm from the night before had been eviscerated by the sun that already beat down, a heatwave unlike anything we'd ever seen laying siege.

Save for the fresh scent that saturated the air.

After a storm, I always got the sense that the muck had been washed away.

Giving life.

A second chance.

That's what today felt like.

A second chance.

Hell, it was the way I viewed my entire life.

Living each day full and to the extreme. Seeking as much plea-sure as I could because I never knew when it was going to run out.

Before I could get lost in the old dread, before I could spiral in the fear, I clamped them off because I refused to waste even a single second of the time I'd been granted, so with a grin on my face, I trav-eled the mile up the long drive before the woods broke open to the resort in the distance.

The massive lodge sat in the center, four stories high and as fuck-ing posh as it came. A slew of cabins and smaller buildings were situ-ated around the sprawling grounds, surrounding pools and spas and different areas for outdoor activities.

But the pride of the place were the enormous, elaborate stables that sat on the far-right side of the property.

There was already a small group of guests on horses getting ready to hit the trails, a guide ready to lead them out to explore the gorgeous expanse of land, giving them the type of experience they'd never find in the city.

I took a right onto the loop that wound around the stables to the maintenance area that was hidden behind them.

My project manager, Matthew, was already there, idling in his truck. I pulled into the spot next to him, killed the engine, and hopped out.

He followed suit.

The guy was tall and thin and sporting a crop of light brown hair.

"About damned time you got here. I thought I was going to have to head over to your house to drag your lazy ass out of bed." He couldn't keep from smiling when he said it.

Hell, neither of us had been able to keep the cheesy-ass grins from our faces over the last two months.

"And miss out on the best day of my life? I don't think so, brother."

I didn't know if it was luck or derived purely from the blood and sweat I'd poured into the business, but somehow, I'd made it happen. My small landscape company had put in a bid to do a full overhaul and renovation of the landscape and exterior living spaces at the resort. I had gone up against five big companies that'd come in from all over the state, and I'd actually won.

A five-fucking-million-dollar contract.

Not that all of that was going straight into my pocket, but still, it was life changing.

And from where I'd started? The bullshit I'd gone through? The mess I'd gotten myself into and had nearly succumbed to?

Thankfulness got me in a chokehold.

I knew there had to be some sort of luck involved because I shouldn't be standing here right then.

Matthew tipped his face toward the blinding rays of sunlight that speared down through the tops of the trees. "Not sure how this is going to be the best day of my life when there is a fifty/fifty chance that I'm going to sweat my balls off today."

A chuckle rolled out of me, and I clamped a hand on his shoulder and hung off him as we started up the walkway toward the maintenance facilities.

I kept my voice low as I razzed, "With all that cash that's going to be sitting in your bank account from that fat bonus you're getting, that's how. If you sweat them off, you'll have plenty to buy a new pair. You know, like they're doing with dogs these days after they get their jewels cut off. Seems fitting."

Matthew shoved me off, shaking his head as he laughed under his breath. "What the fuck is wrong with you, man? That is not an image I need in my head." He reached down to cover his boys.

"Besides…" He narrowed his eyes. "I'm pretty sure the only dog around here is you."

"Who me?" I lifted my arms out to the sides, playing innocent.

The dude never failed to give me shit about my reputation, like I should somehow feel bad that I chose not to live my life bogged down by chains and commitment and heartbreak. It was hard enough to stay one foot ahead of the game. Running so fast that the demons could never catch up to you.

Unbidden, a vision of Hailey slammed my mind again. The same way as they'd done all goddamn night.

Held in that old ache.

Sticky and tenacious.

It hadn't helped a thing that I'd caught her peeking at me through the side of her curtains.

Through that small space, attraction had blazed.

I swore, everything about her was enticing.

Tempting.

Following me into my dreams.

"Yeah, you," Matthew razzed.

"Well, if I had a wife half as pretty as yours to go home to at night, maybe I would change my wicked ways." I wagged my brows, knowing it'd get a rise out of him, though he clearly knew me well enough to know there wasn't a chance in hell that was going to happen.

"Don't even think about my wife, or you're going to be the one losing his balls today, and it won't have a thing to do with this weather."

Laughing low, I squeezed his shoulder. "Don't worry, man, going after married women is not my thing."

He scoffed. "Like Soira would even look your way."

I didn't try to roast him about the claim. Not when he was a thousand percent right. The two of them were solid. Perfect together. Just like the rest of my crew who'd all settled down over the last couple years.

I was happy for them.

Really happy.

That didn't mean any of that shit was in the cards for me.

We made it to the swinging double doors of the maintenance facility, and I tossed the right side open to the cool air pumping inside.

"I might have to park it right here," Matthew mumbled under his breath. "Take on a supervisory position only. Get one of these nice, cushy offices just for myself."

"Not going to happen. We're going to need every man on deck."

We'd already had to triple our roster with any hope of making this happen.

"Ah, good, you're here." We looked toward the voice coming from the left to find Tyrek coming down the hall.

"It's good to see you," I said, reaching out to shake his hand.

"You, too."

Matthew leaned in to do the same.

Tyrek was the head of maintenance, and he'd be the one overseeing the entire project. He had long black hair that he wore in a ponytail and a short goatee on his chin.

"Got a call from the guys from Hartville Construction. They're running late and will be here in about an hour," Tyrek explained. "I thought we'd get started by walking through the property and plans one more time while we wait for them to show."

We'd be collaborating with the construction company who'd be working on any actual building construction. Plans had already been drawn up and integrated on both sides so we'd be ready to break ground.

The owners wanted the project complete by the end of summer before the winter crowd flocked here to hit the ski slopes. It was bound to be grueling, hard work. Long fucking hours. The pressure set to high.

But I didn't get here by taking the easy way out.

"Works for me," I told him.

I resituated my cap on my head and followed Tyrek out. We treaded up a path toward a grouping of cabins where we were set to begin work first.

Each cabin was getting a new elevated porch with an outdoor fireplace, plus new sidewalks and lit paths that were going to be surrounded by abundant, extravagant flower beds.

Pride expanded my chest. This place might have already been a five-star resort, but my design was only going to elevate it.

"Like we discussed, no guests are booked in this area for the month of June…" Tyrek started to ramble over the details again, reiterating the plan.

I nodded along, following him up the path that weaved through the lush scenery, beneath the enormous trees that swelled above and provided the slightest reprieve from the intensity blazing from above.

We made a circle around the area we were set to begin work first, Tyrek pointing out anything of importance, before we headed back down the walkway toward the maintenance facility that wound around the stables.

My footsteps grew slower when my attention caught on a woman standing by a side door that opened to the rambling stalls.

Her back was to us, and a luxurious fall of blonde hair laced with streaks of maple and honey was twisted in a braid that rolled down her back, topped off with a cream-colored cowgirl hat.

Tight jeans clung to the ample shape of her hips and ass.

When she heard us coming, she shifted to look over her shoulder.

Piercing blue eyes stared back, crystalline, as clear as the river that rolled through the property. The striking contour of her face glinted beneath the rays of light that spiked through the leaves.

My chest tightened and the air suddenly seemed too heavy to draw into my lungs.

Fuck me.

It was Hailey Wagner.

Chapter Four

Hailey

WHAT THE HELL WAS HE DOING HERE?
I tried not to choke on my tongue as I stared at the man who'd stumbled to a stop ten feet away, standing there in all his muscled-up glory, though this time I thought he might be suffering the same kind of shock I'd felt when I'd first seen him last night.

He wore a trucker's hat with brown curls peeking out at the bottom, a tight white tee, and jeans that hugged his massive thighs in the most indecent of ways.

Only this morning, there were no shadows on his face, and he was lit up like he was a magnet for the rays of sun.

Each accentuating the rugged angles of his face, his strong brow and severe cheekbones. A squared jaw that was covered in a short, trimmed beard.

I tried to tamp the reaction I had at seeing him, how my traitor stomach twisted, and I forced a smile when Tyrek kept ambling my direction. He gifted me with the same welcome in his demeanor as he'd had when I'd met him yesterday.

"Good morning, Hailey."

I gulped around the skittering of emotion and turned the rest of the way around. "Good morning, Tyrek. How are you today?"

I tried not to let my gaze slant to Cody as they came closer.

"Great. The big exterior renovations begin today, so we were making another round of the grounds before the landscape team starts doing their thing." He waved a hand at the man whose presence battered relentlessly. "This is Cody Cooper. He owns Cooper Landscaping, so you'll be seeing a lot of him around. And this is his project manager, Matthew."

I couldn't even look at Matthew since I was gaping at the grin that spread across Cody's face.

I bet that grin alone could make all kinds of horrible choices seem like the best ideas you'd ever had.

But it was those gold-colored eyes dabbled in flecks of rusts and earthy browns that took me in as if he were trying to peer into the deepest parts of me that made my pulse skitter and my knees wobble.

Lolly might have thought he looked like sex on a stick, but what he really looked like was a giant dose of heartache. I'd seen it in action myself.

He hadn't even remembered me at first. Why that bothered me, I didn't know. Or maybe what really bothered me was that he was still smiling after everything.

"This is Hailey Wagner," Tyrek introduced.

Cody stepped forward, and the ground trembled beneath his massive frame.

Those lips quirked up farther on the left side as he stretched out a massive palm, acting like he'd never seen me before. "It's a pleasure to meet you, Hailey Wagner."

I stared at his hand like it was a viper and I was about to get bit. With the way my chin had tingled for hours last night in the spot where he'd touched me, I figured it was a valid concern.

Still, it was my first day of work, and I didn't want to appear rude, so I gulped around the reservations and stepped forward, trying not to shake.

I reached out, and he curled his hand around mine, swallowing it in his enormous grip.

The burn of him raced up my arm like a shock of electricity.

I swore, his temperature must have been a thousand degrees.

"It's nice to meet you, too." I lifted my chin, pretending like I'd never seen him, either. Silly, since who cared if we were acquaintances? But something about it felt like a secret. Or maybe like something that should be swept under the rug.

At my response, arrogant mischief twinkled in his gaze. The man was nothing but a tease and a player.

"And you work here?" he asked. His interest drifted over my shoulder to the enormous stables behind me.

I started to respond, only Tyrek beat me to it. "It's Hailey's first week, too. She was hired on as the new stable manager. I hear we were lucky to snatch her up. She came all the way from Boston."

Lolly had let me know about the opening for the stable manager position at Cambrey Pines and encouraged me to apply. I'd been a riot of nerves when I'd sent in my resume, and I'd nearly fallen on my ass when they'd called for an interview.

I'd been so nervous during the Zoom call that I'd worried I was going to word vomit and make myself come across as incompetent rather than highly qualified, but the resort director and the outgoing stable manager had talked to me for all of five minutes before they'd offered me the position.

They'd basically begged me to get here as quickly as I could.

I didn't doubt that my last name had helped. The resort had purchased their trail horses from my father for years.

But that didn't make me any less experienced.

I'd given my entire life to horses, even when the last six years of it had been tainted. Still, I was proud that I'd been offered the position.

"That's kind of you to say," I told Tyrek.

He smiled slow. "I don't think it's any secret that you're an asset to the resort. I'm not sure if you've had the chance to review the plans yet, but there are some landscape elements that are included in the project around the stables."

He glanced at Cody. "Hailey will be your point of contact anytime you're working near the stables. Extra caution is always taken around the horses as their welfare is our first concern."

I swiveled my gaze back to Cody. He was still grinning. Still holding onto me with that giant mitt. "Of course. We've already been instructed we'll be working closely with the stable manager."

Suggestion filled his words.

I refused to let it get to me, and I cleared the roughness from my throat and somehow managed to wrangle my hand out of his so I could pull out the business cards I'd had expedited that were tucked into my back pocket.

I handed one to him.

"Here's my card. Don't hesitate to use it."

Please hesitate to use it.

Wishful thinking. I was going to be stuck working *and* living next to this guy.

Cody Cooper eyed the information on the card like he was reading about the discovery of a new lifesaving drug.

"I won't," he said in that grumbly voice, that grin still plastered on his stupid, gorgeous face.

God, I kind of hated him.

"Right. Good. Well, I need to get back to work."

I looked at his project manager who seemed to be trying to make sense of the awkward conversation, his attention jumping between the two of us.

"It's nice to meet you, as well," I added.

"Same to you," Matthew said.

I tipped a forced smile toward all three of them. "Good luck, gentlemen."

Golden eyes gleamed. "No luck required."

My teeth ground.

Cocky Cowboy.

Turning on my heel, I pulled open the door situated at the end of the stables and stepped inside.

My heart squeezed at the sight.

The Cambrey Pines stables were a bit on the extravagant side, in keeping with the resort.

Long rows of stalls ran both sides. The ceiling was pitched and soaring, the dark-stained wood robust and maintained, the metal gates engraved and ornate. There were always at least ten hands on staff, keeping the floors and stalls immaculate and ensuring the horses were well cared for.

There were a bunch of different guides and instructors for the different trail rides and experiences offered for the guests, plus a full-time vet on site.

Pride welled in my chest.

I oversaw them all.

Smiling at a guide who passed, I moved to the stall three down on the right where I'd left off. I'd spent my morning familiarizing myself with each horse, its name and health and age.

My job might be to manage every aspect of the stables, but the horses were my main concern.

I unlatched the gate of a four-year-old foal named Giselle and stepped into her stall. Her coat was black and shiny, her eyes the color of pitch and brimming with soul.

I swore, horses saw everything. Felt everything.

Knew.

My stomach tightened in a fit of nostalgia, the tiniest bit of grief, but I sucked it down and stepped forward so I could softly run my hand down her neck. I whispered, "Hey, there, beautiful girl. You are gorgeous. Just perfect, aren't you?"

I let my hand sweep down her neck a couple times in hopes of winning her trust.

She snorted and sighed before she shifted her weight into me, and I edged around to her front so I could stroke my thumb between her eyes.

Softly.

Slowly.

"That's right," I murmured.

She chuffed and nuzzled her nose into my cheek. A quick giggle got free, and I leaned in even closer, wrapping my arm around her neck in an embrace.

She was as gentle as could be. Most all the horses here were since we needed them to carry guests of varying experiences, sizes, and demeanor.

I stayed like that with her for the longest time. Getting to know her and letting her get to know me. Each of us giving our trust. Our love. Our devotion.

I froze when I felt the frisson of energy cover me from behind, and a swath of irritation blazed over my flesh when I finally pulled away to peer back at the source.

Cody Cooper was leaned on the inside of the gate, big hands stuffed in his pockets, one boot crossed at the ankle.

Looking like the epitome of a self-loving cowboy.

Arrogant.

Brash.

Too big for his own britches, like my father used to say about the hands I'd been instructed to stay away from. God, should I have listened.

He wore that smirk that forever seemed to light on his face.

There was something different about him, though, the way those golden eyes seemed to glow as they watched me from three feet away.

"Is there something I can help you with, Mr. Cooper?" I asked, going all business.

That grin twitched, and something sly and flirty drifted into his tenor. "So, we're just going to pretend we don't know each other? Don't you remember me?"

There was almost a tease tacked onto the last.

Was he serious? As if I could ever forget.

"I think it's you who didn't remember me." It came out far too snippy. Like I cared, when I didn't. Guys like him didn't deserve the extra attention.

His gaze raked over my body, dragging from my head to my toes and back up again. Far too languid for it to be considered polite.

"I'll admit it was dark last night and…"

He trailed off, leaving the obvious unsaid.

I looked different.

Back when I'd met him when I was eighteen, I used to be rail thin, bare faced, covered in dirt and grime and running around the ranch like I was the same as the hands.

Now I was all curves and had decided I loved a good haul from Sephora.

"...I thought you'd moved away," he added, his voice dropping in caution.

My spirit clutched.

Maybe he did remember after all.

I turned back to Giselle, petting her again, needing something to do with my hands. "I did."

"And now you're back." It rang with some kind of implication before I heard the tease weave its way back in. "And living right next door to me."

An unfortunate complication.

"Apparently so."

"You didn't move back to work on your father's ranch?"

My head shook. "It was time I did something for myself."

I cringed, hating that it revealed too much, that I was opening up to this guy who I knew better than to trust.

"Because you're not weak." He took me back to what I'd done my best to claim last night.

Disbelief punched from my lungs. He didn't know anything about me, and I didn't need him standing there insinuating that he did.

"Fuckin' gorgeous, too."

Desire twisted my stomach. *Do not fall for his bullshit, Hailey.*

"I think you should get back to work, Mr. Cooper, and save the inappropriate comments. From my understanding, this is a big project. That's where you should probably put your focus. I saw the contract, and I think you're being more than well-compensated."

He was making a small fortune.

I refused to look back at him, just kept my regard on Giselle as he stood there like he was shocked that I didn't fall into his hands.

So typical of his type.

He was used to women falling all over him. He used them up for one night, then he left them broken in the morning.

And by whatever energy he was exuding, he had some kind of delusion I was going to be one of them.

Like I would ever betray...

My teeth ground as my thoughts threatened to dive into dangerous territory.

"If you'll excuse me, Mr. Cooper. I'm busy." I could hardly force it out.

He wavered for a moment, the heat of his gaze burning into my back, consuming as his presence swelled in the space.

I felt it when he finally gave, and the metal rattled as he straightened and walked out. I could hear the heavy thud of his boots as he retreated, the man taking the suffocating energy with him as he went.

I breathed out in relief, and my forehead dropped to Giselle's neck. I drew in a bunch of steadying breaths, silently encouraging myself to get it together.

It was ridiculous I was letting Cody Cooper affect me at all.

He was nothing but the catalyst for the worst day of my life.

And I bet he was so self-absorbed that he didn't even know.

Easing back from the foal, I swatted at the one tear that got free, lifted my chin, and got back to work.

I made it through the rest of the day without any more run-ins with Cody, other than catching sight of him in my periphery and in the far distance when he'd been standing over his team, giving instructions.

He'd been holding his cap in one hand and running the other through the messy locks of his brown hair, not that I was keeping tabs or anything.

It'd been a super busy day for me, acquainting myself with the horses, plus I'd called a meeting with the members of the staff under me to review the daily processes and to go over a few changes that I wanted to implement.

I felt both energized and zapped by the time I climbed into my Durango at just after five.

Satisfaction brimming because I knew this was exactly where I belonged. I'd worked for this, and I'd never again allow anyone to try to sway me from my path.

Would never allow anyone to use me.

Delude me into thinking I was serving a good purpose when the only thing I'd been was a pawn.

Starting the engine, I pulled out and weaved down the long driveway of the resort with a smile plastered to my face. I was eager to get home to see how Lolly and Madison had faired today.

My grandmother would be watching her during the day until I got her settled into a preschool. I was so grateful that my daughter was going to have the same time with Lolly as I'd had when I was young.

Sure she would be safe and cherished and loved, plus if I knew my Lolly well enough, they'd get up to all kinds of shenanigans and adventures.

Memories that Maddie would forever hold.

When I got to the end of the resort's drive, I made the left onto the winding two-lane road that ran between Time River and Hendrickson.

This area was mostly desolate other than the turnoffs to a few ranches and massive estates that were hidden in the woods.

Here, the forest was dense and deep, and I settled into the comfort as I drove beneath the hedge of trees that tightly hugged the road.

The sunlight was partially shut out by the thick canopy of branches and leaves, and it created a quiet, secluded vibe.

A vibe that could almost pass as creepy if I didn't know better, so I all but rolled my eyes at myself with the way my nerves twisted when I glimpsed a car in the rearview mirror.

It'd seemed to have come out of nowhere but now remained set back, far enough that I couldn't make out any details other than the flashes of metallic black and the glimmer of glass that struck in the rays that broke through the foliage.

Though there was something about it that set me on edge. The way it seemed to be keeping an exact amount of distance between us.

I accelerated just to prove to myself that I was letting my imagination get carried away.

I was still letting fear win, and I didn't come here to sink right back into the same dread that I'd worn for years.

Only the car accelerated, too.

Keeping pace.

I pushed down on the pedal, and my heart climbed into my throat when the car came even closer.

Thoughts whirled, my mind frantic as I searched for a solution.

An escape route. For a way to make this go away forever.

Because I refused to be afraid.

Pruitt didn't get to control me any longer, and I wouldn't stand down, no matter how much pressure he put on me. No matter the threats.

Relief punched like a shock to the chest when the trees fell away and my path opened to the town of Hendrickson, Colorado.

Businesses sat on each side, stores and restaurants and offices. The buildings were mostly two story and situated close to the road with cobblestone sidewalks out front. Each were painted cute colors with abundant flower beds and pots sitting on their stoops.

People meandered.

Activity all around.

An SUV with Sheriff stamped on the side passed me coming the opposite direction, and I glanced into the rearview mirror to gauge what the car would do.

Only it was gone, no longer visible behind me.

I blinked then looked again.

Shaken.

Confused.

Wondering if paranoia had me making the whole thing up.

Conjuring a danger that wasn't there.

But maybe I was nothing but a fool for thinking that danger hadn't followed me here.

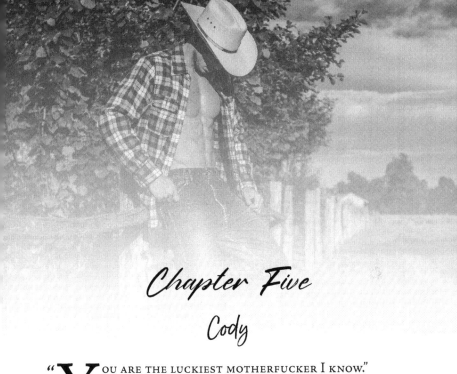

Chapter Five
Cody

"YOU ARE THE LUCKIEST MOTHERFUCKER I KNOW."

I grinned at my best friend's voice coming through the line as I pulled a fresh tee over my head. A shower had been more than required after I'd gotten home covered in sweat and dirt after I'd spent the day tearing out the old decks to make room for the new.

"Come now, Ryder, were they really going to pick anyone else? Have you met me?" I laid it on thick, my cell propped between my ear and my shoulder as I ran a towel through my wet mop of hair.

"Of course not. You go flashing that grin, and women tend to fall at your feet. Who'd you dip your dick in to get your way?" he razzed.

"You wound me, man. That contract didn't have a thing to do with my sex appeal and everything to do with my raw, crazy talent."

Dude had been giving me shit about winning this contract since I'd told him about it two months ago. If I didn't know better, I'd say he was jealous, but really, we just loved to bust each other's balls.

"Besides, you know I don't mix business with pleasure," I added.

I couldn't tell you the number of times I'd been working a job and a housewife had invited me in for *a glass of lemonade.*

Fuck no.

That was a sure-fire way to lose everything I'd built.

Hailey's face flashed through my mind.

Undoubtedly, I'd crossed a line I shouldn't have, seeking her out earlier today.

I'd made the excuse that I needed to take a piss, and I'd slipped into the stables.

There was no question in my mind that I was pushing boundaries.

If she wanted to, I bet she could go to her supervisor and claim I'd been harassing her, and I'd be booted off the property, some fine print making that contract nil.

Buh-bye five million dollars.

And I was the idiot who'd done it, anyway.

Apparently, I was losing my goddamn mind when it came to her.

But there it was, nagging at the back of my mind.

The oldest kind of guilt and want, that time so fucked up that I still didn't know how to process it. I'd done my best to put it behind me, but there it was, luring me to a place that I knew better than to go.

"Besides, I've taken the whole week off from dipping my dick in anyone." I smirked, knowing he could feel it through the phone.

Ryder chuckled low, and I could almost see him scrubbing a tatted hand over his face, all black hair and intimidation. "Such a fucking liar. I was just at Mack's with you two nights ago, and you left with that short-haired chick. Unless you couldn't get it up?"

"Blasphemy, man. I just…forgot about her."

"You forgot about her?" Incredulity dripped from him.

"Can't help it if she wasn't exactly memorable."

Hell, I couldn't even place her face at this point. Not with the one that was currently inhabiting every thought.

"Such an asshole," he mumbled.

"Like you weren't the exact same way until you started dipping *your* dirty dick in my sister."

Truth be told, I had nearly lost it when I found out he and my sister, Dakota, were hooking up. Was legitimately pissed because I knew the trouble he'd had himself in, and I didn't want my sister involved in any of that.

I hadn't found out they were sneaking around behind my back until she was already reaping the consequences of his mess.

As much as it'd broken my heart, I'd honestly thought it was over for me and Ryder. A lifetime of friendship gone because I wouldn't stand for him hurting my sister. My entire purpose in this life was standing for her.

For both my sisters and my mother.

Which was kind of fucking ironic considering the jacked-up decisions I'd made. But I'd promised—promised to provide and protect—whatever that looked like.

Besides, I hadn't understood the way Ryder loved her. The lengths he would go. The way he'd fought to protect Dakota and her son.

It didn't take long for me to see it for what it was, their love something bigger than I had the right to intervene on.

That didn't mean I would ever let him live it down, either.

His laugh was raw. "Now that is memorable."

"Gross, man," I grumbled, though I was laughing under my breath, too.

"Hey, you're the one who brought it up. Besides, I'm not going to deny that I can't keep my hands off her. Speaking of, she's pulling in. I need to run to help her bring in her and Kayden's things. Just wanted to call and say congrats again. I know this was a big day for you."

"Thank you, man. I truly appreciate it."

"Of course. You know Dakota wants to celebrate? Did she text you yet? Girl can't help herself when it comes to the ones she cares about."

It wasn't like I was going to complain.

"Yup, next Saturday because her café has some big gig this weekend," I told him. "She made me swear to put a reminder in my phone."

As if I was going to forget.

"Sounds about right."

"Sure does."

I heard a clatter in the background, the slamming of a door before the voice of my little nephew, Kayden, carried through the line. "Hi, my Daddy Rye-Rye. I home! Come find me!"

"See you then, brother. Take care." The line was dead before I even had the chance to say goodbye, dude so far gone for the both of them he didn't think of much else.

And that? It meant the fucking world.

I tossed the towel onto the bed and walked from my room, dragging both hands through my damp hair, loving the way the tiles felt cool on my bare feet as I walked out into my kitchen.

It was done in light grays and whites with splashes of color since my sisters and my mother had insisted on coming to help me decorate.

Each of them were so damned sweet, doing their best to take care of me when my only true purpose in life was taking care of them.

The rest was fucking fluff.

Extra.

Bonus days that I got to live out because I never knew when my time was going to run out.

I dipped out the front door and into the waning day. The temperature was still warm, though it'd cooled a bit as the sun had begun to sink behind the soaring trees that enclosed the neighborhood.

Twilight tossed those wispy hues of blue and pink through the atmosphere.

Nothing but calm and peace in the air as birds flitted through the leaves.

I headed down the sidewalk toward my mailbox at the end of the drive, making no attempt not to eye the U-Haul that was still parked in the neighbor's drive as I opened my mailbox and blindly reached in to find what was inside.

Wondering why the hell she was back.

Well, mostly wondering why she was living here in this modest neighborhood when she'd been raised in what equated to a palace.

A fist of contempt squeezed my chest as that voice I'd come to abhor flitted through my mind.

Don't think you could ever be good enough for her.

Regret clamped down behind it.

So many times, I'd wished I'd done things differently. Said them differently.

But would it have made a difference?

Changed a thing?

I fuckin' doubted it.

But I'd spent a lot of damned nights wondering if I was to blame.

And I guessed my attention was so firmly rooted in the past that I didn't notice any other activity in the neighborhood until a tinkling voice came flooding from the opposite direction.

"Hi, mister, hi! What's your name?"

I swiveled that way, peering down the sidewalk that rounded the cul-de-sac at the end of the road. My house was the last on this side of the street, and at the very end of the cul-de-sac was a small, grassy playground that took up the lot before the land gave way to the woods.

A little girl with tight ringlets of blonde hair that made her head look three times its actual size was hopping and skipping my way, dragging a tiny wagon behind her, the plastic wheels grinding on the concrete.

An elderly lady trailed close behind.

The child was all pink cheeks and overexaggerated excitement and the brightest damned smile known to earth.

No doubt in my mind the force of it could guide satellites.

Caught off guard, I scrubbed a palm down my face to break up the disorder before I let a slow smile claim it. "Well, hey, there. I'm Cody."

She increased her speed, little legs bringing her up the sidewalk, her free hand lifted above her head in a zealous wave as she approached. "Hi, Mr. Cody. I am Madison Ella, but I got a nickname called Maddie, and this is my greatest grams-gram, Lolly."

Before I had time to respond, another voice hit from the opposite side, one that was throaty and low and dragging like a caress across my flesh. "And you are not supposed to be talking to strangers."

A shockwave of lust barreled straight through me. Fuck, that was the last reaction I should have toward the woman, but the attraction had already taken hold last night, and I wasn't sure there'd be any taming it now.

I looked that way to find Hailey standing there with her arms crossed over her chest, still dressed like the hottest damn cowgirl I'd ever seen. Though she'd ditched the hat and had undone her braid and waves of that ridiculously long blonde hair now whispered around her striking face.

It was those lips that could do a grown man in, though. Set in this endless pout that screamed seduction.

I was immediately pummeled with the vision of wrapping those locks in a fist as she got on her knees and put that delicious mouth on me.

Yeah, that was exactly where I wanted to dip my dick, except the woman was scowling at me so hard I was pretty sure the only *vision* she was having right then was stabbing me.

"Mommy, he was gettin' his mail, and that means he lives right next to us, and we gotta meet our new neighbors if we're goin' to have any friends, and there wasn't even one single kid on the playground." The little girl huffed through her reasoning.

It took me a second to catch up to the fact the child belonged to Hailey.

She was her mother.

She had a kid.

I wasn't quite sure what to make of the feeling that swept through me. Something that was both sinking and swelling.

On instinct, I peered over Hailey's shoulder like I was going to catch some fucker standing behind her in a stance of possession.

My gut twisted, the thought of someone touching her making me sick to my stomach. What the fuck was that? She was the last woman I should want.

Clearly, I needed to keep my distance the best that I could because I was losing my damned mind.

Another voice snatched my attention. "That's right. We must meet the new neighbors, especially this one. No need being standoffish when he's already been so helpful."

The old lady was grinning wry, her stringy gray hair set free and red lipstick staining her lips. "Braving that storm the way he did to help Hailey rescue our Maddie's favorite stuffed animal last night."

"You helped to get my Princess Verona for me?" Madison squealed it as she came to a stop right in front of me, grabbed a purple bunny from the wagon, and held it up for me to inspect.

"I was gonna get another bad dream if I didn't find my Princess Verona because I got to sleep with her always, and she got lost in our big truck that has all our stuff from our old house, and my mommy got super wet trying to find her. Did you get wet, too?"

I felt the exasperated sigh pilfer from Hailey, and my attention swung to her.

Apology on my face.

Because it was becoming clear why she'd been out there in the rain, and I'd given her shit for it when I didn't have the first clue of her intentions.

When I didn't have the first clue about *her*.

Not one fucking idea about her circumstances just like she had accused me of.

I looked back at her daughter. "No, I didn't get too wet. It was your mom who found her. She's the one who gets all the credit. I just helped bring the boxes to the door. No big deal."

"Well, that's good that you didn't think it was a big deal because we might need your services again, big strong man that you are."

Shock was spluttering from my mouth when I realized the old lady was suddenly standing at my side, bony fingers squeezing my biceps as she issued the words.

Hailey gasped, and her voice whipped in a reprimand. "Lolly."

Lolly shrugged. "What? You didn't think I was going to help you haul that couch into the house, did you? I might be spry for my age, but an old lady knows her limits."

The woman winked at me, and I chuckled low before I turned my gaze back on the woman who appeared to be about two-point-five seconds from blowing a gasket.

"You don't have a man to help you?"

Shit.

The question was out before I had time to contemplate the ramifications.

But there was a coil of something inside me that needed to know.

Her arms tightened over her chest, emphasizing those gorgeous tits under her blouse. Her head cocked to the side. "I don't see how that's any of your business."

She said it at the same time as the old woman offered up, "No man around here. Not one for miles and miles."

Hailey shot out another frustrated, "*Lolly.*"

"Are you gonna get our couch for us?" The little girl hopped on her feet, that hair bouncing all around her, beaming up at me, so fucking adorable it speared me in a place that wasn't supposed to exist. "Mr. Cody, that is so very nice."

She turned to her mother. "Mommy, I think we hit the jackpot and got the best new neighbor."

No doubt, I was digging a brand-new grave, but how the hell was I supposed to resist that?

So, I looked straight at Hailey and said, "Well, then, it looks like I'm moving in a couch."

Chapter Six

Hailey

"Um, no, you most certainly are not." I made the mistake of taking the time to send a glare at Lolly, because mark my words, she was in so much trouble, while she stood there with some kind of wicked glee dancing over her face.

She actually had the nerve to mouth, *You're welcome.*

Only it gave the hulk of a man the time to turn on his heel and start striding up my driveway like he owned the place, all fresh tee and damp hair and ridiculously sexy bare feet.

Wearing clean jeans and smelling like cedar and soap and every bad idea that'd ever been had.

I snapped into action, hurrying behind him in an attempt to sway what I was sure weren't close to noble intentions, while my daughter started to trot alongside him, too, having no clue the devil was in our midst.

Because that's what he was.

Tossing out all those smirks and smiles.

Madison clapped her hands as she skipped along and sang, "Yay, we get our couch! That's really good news because the only thing we got to sit on is the floor, and we don't even have a TV."

"Well, you're in luck, Button, because you're about to have one."

Button?

Was he serious?

I increased my pace, growling under my breath, "I told you last night that I do not need your help, Mr. Cooper."

"Who said I was helping you out? I'm doing it for Lolly and Madison. They're the ones who asked nicely." He tossed it out from over his shoulder, that smirk riding on those ridiculous lips, the man dripping sex and salacious schemes.

He rounded to the back of the truck and tossed up the rolling door. Metal grated as it lifted, and he hopped into the high bed like it was nothing.

Exasperation kneaded beneath my skin. Flustered, I tried to think of a solution. How to get this man out of here without disappointing my daughter, but unfortunately disappointment was an inevitable part of life.

"Maddie, go inside with Lolly and make sure nothing is in the way of where the couch is going to go."

How I came up with that as a valid solution, I didn't know. Conceding to him bringing in the couch was a treacherous disloyalty.

But I needed to get her out of there because I didn't want her bearing witness to what was boiling inside me right then.

"On it, Mommy!" She gave me a salute before she turned to Lolly who was slowly making her way up the drive. Excited, she grabbed her hand. "Come on, Lolly! We got to make sure the house is super clean for the couch."

"Good plan, little one. I'll even whip up some tea." Lolly glanced at me, gray eyes gleaming.

God, she was such a schemer.

But she didn't know. I couldn't expect her to. She thought she was nudging me in the right direction when that *direction* was riddled with potholes and dead ends.

I silently counted to ten while they ambled up the walkway, and

I waited until I heard the front door slam before I turned my attention to the man who was currently moving boxes out of the way to get to the couch.

I inhaled a shaky breath, trying to form some semblance of cool when I felt like the foundation I was trying to build was already crumbling beneath me. "I don't know what you think you're doing, Mr. Cooper."

He lifted a box over his head to place onto the top of five others he'd already stacked against the wall. The movement caused his tee to ride up over the waistband of his jeans. It revealed a swath of packed, chiseled abdomen, hip bones peeking out.

It should be a felony for one single man to be that hot.

Me even noticing was the true crime.

"Helping out a neighbor, is all."

I huffed as I hoisted a leg up so I could climb into the bed of the truck. "And I keep telling you I don't need your help. I have movers coming this weekend."

"That's not for four days." He kept moving my things around, freeing the couch that three minutes ago had been buried.

"Which is not going to hurt a thing. We have our beds. That's all we need," I said as I edged deeper into the truck.

He turned on me faster than I ever could have anticipated.

His proximity froze me to the spot. The man towered, so tall his head nearly touched the top of the trailer.

Nothing but a heaping stack of muscle and brawn and cruel intentions.

Only right then, he wasn't sporting that smirk, and something intense dimmed his grin just like it'd done when he'd touched my chin last night.

The same as I'd thought I'd sensed in his voice when he'd been talking to me in the stables.

He angled down, too close.

My stomach twisted and my knees quaked.

"I'm not sure about you, Ms. Wagner, but I'd prefer to keep that smile on your daughter's face rather than disappointing her. Especially when it doesn't cost me a thing to put it there."

I warred, my voice haggard with the way the air had gone dense, the oxygen too thick to breathe.

"She needs to learn that not everything is easy. That sometimes we have to wait. That sometimes things are hard and she's not always going to get her way."

"I'm sure life is going to teach her that lesson just fine." His teeth grated when he said it.

I got stuck there, by the pain that suddenly roiled in those gold-fired eyes, a dam opening and something I was sure he normally kept hidden gushing out.

I wondered if he could see to the depths of mine.

If it was real. This understanding that passed between us.

The truth that I would do anything to protect my daughter from all those things. From the pain and the wounds and the hurts, thinking that maybe I could prepare her for them, and when she understood they were coming, they might not sting so bad.

Or maybe I somehow foolishly thought if she experienced small ones, tiny knicks of disappointment, it would keep her from the gashes that cut so deep they'd never heal.

Maybe…maybe he did because he murmured, "As far as I'm concerned, we take the good when it's presented to us because there's going to be plenty of bad shit to come along. So how about you let me do the simple job of taking this couch inside your house, then you and your kid can snuggle up on it and watch a show tonight."

I couldn't breathe.

Couldn't speak.

I nearly fell on my ass when he suddenly took a step back, like whatever tether had stretched between us had been holding me up and it'd just snapped.

Then that smirk was back in full force. "Unless you want me to hang out for a bit, and once the two of them go to sleep, you can snuggle up on it with me."

There he was.

The player I knew him to be.

Careless and only out for one thing.

I scoffed around the chaffing at the edges of my heart. "You know that's not going to happen."

He shrugged, all kinds of casual as he went back to the last boxes remaining on the couch. "Suit yourself. Just was checking to see if you'd decided to take a little of the *good* when it's presented to you."

"You're awful sure of yourself," I gritted out.

He came my way with a stack of boxes in his hands, and he leaned in close to my ear. "Oh, darlin', you can be sure it'd be good."

Chills skated down my spine and lifted across my flesh. I wanted to be sick at the reaction.

His chuckle was dry as he wound around me and jumped down from the back of the truck, still balancing four boxes and slanting me one of those looks that shivered through my insides.

"And why don't we drop that whole Mr. Cooper bit and stop pretending like you don't know me, yeah?"

Then he turned and strode up my walkway with the boxes in hand, not bothering to look back.

⚯

I was only accepting the good when it was presented to me.

That's what I kept telling myself as Cody Cooper brought load after load into my house.

I had to wonder if he was doing it as some kind of penance.

It was bad enough that I'd given up the fight of letting him bring in the couch, but before he'd brought it in, he'd disappeared back over to his place and returned wearing boots and pushing a hand-truck, which he'd assured me could do the work of three men, and he was going to *knock this job out lickity-split*, before he'd rolled out the ramp and started in like he somehow thought it was his duty.

"That man is something, isn't he?" Lolly sat on that very couch where we'd placed it under the window and facing the wall where the TV now sat. She sipped at an iced tea as she watched Cody disappear back out the front door on what had to be about his twentieth trip.

His shirt clung to the small of his back from the sweat that slicked his skin and those jeans hugged an ass that had to be every bit as ripped as the rest of him.

He was most definitely something and every freaking thing that I couldn't want.

I had to remember that.

Even having him here sparked with betrayal.

Still, there was a gratitude that kept threatening to rupture through the barriers I was struggling to keep intact.

I scowled at my meddling grandmother. "And that man gave up his whole evening thanks to you."

I still wasn't letting on that I knew him. Lolly had to remain in the dark or else she was really going to start needling her nose into places that I couldn't let her go.

She waved an errant hand in the air. "Oh, he's happy to do it."

My gaze narrowed. "And you know this how?"

"All the whistling he's doing and the skip to his step is proof of that. Not to mention he can't wipe that smile from his face every time he looks at you."

"I'm pretty sure that man's smile is permanently tattooed on his face, and it doesn't have a thing to do with me."

Except something about that didn't ring true, and my thoughts kept flashing to the way his expression would dim and all that carelessness would fade away. When he'd suck me down into some kind of darkness that lurked in the deepest part of him, like he too would get caught up in that summer.

Like maybe it had mattered.

But this was Cody Cooper we were talking about.

The man couldn't seem to remain serious to save his life.

"You just go on telling yourself that," Lolly drawled, "but if a hottie like you moved in next door to me, I'd be smiling, too. I bet I know what would make him smile even wider." She wagged her brows.

I refused the visions that wanted to assail me. The ones that had forever wondered what that might be like. If that summer had gone down differently.

That was attraction for you.

Errant.

Inopportune.

No thought of the heart even though that was where you felt the strike of it.

"You're ridiculous, Lolly," I told her, forcing lightness into my tone.

"Nothing ridiculous about it."

"You and I both know it *would* be ridiculous to get tangled in the likes of that. That man would chew me up and spit me out, and then I'd be stuck living next to him for the next God knows how long. My life is too complicated right now. No use in adding fuel to the flames."

Flames that would likely consume, and there was no pretending that Cody wasn't gasoline.

All of it was the truth, not that I would ever let him touch me, anyway.

"Oh, but the chewing would be so nice." Lolly grinned.

I shook my head and stood as Cody came in pushing my nightstand on the hand-truck.

The air shifted the way it did, growing thick and somehow light, like the man was radiating the sun all while casting me in shadow.

"Where's this one go?" he asked, so casual, like his presence wasn't wreaking havoc on the brittle pieces inside me.

"You can leave it right there."

"Already have it inside. No point in that." His mouth tipped up at the side.

"Might as well show him to your room." Freaking Lolly, thinking she was cupid when she had no idea the type of arrows a man like him carried.

But whatever, he'd already forced his way inside. I might as well let him finish the job.

Awkwardly, I gestured toward the primary that was through the double doors on the other side of the kitchen. "Right in there."

"Ah, you've got the same room as mine." That golden gaze sparked in some kind of mischief, a silent affirmation that he'd caught me peeping on him last night.

So freaking embarrassing.

He guided the hand-truck down the little pathway between the kitchen and table before he disappeared through the bedroom door.

I itched, unsure, before I hurried to follow him.

He went directly for the right side of the bed, like he already knew that was the side I slept on, even though it was made.

He moved around to slide the nightstand off the hand-truck, his muscles straining and his tee shirt stretching over the definition of his back as he maneuvered it into place.

Then he straightened to his full height, dragging a massive palm up his face and through his hair as he turned to face me.

"That should do it," he said.

My teeth clamped down on my bottom lip, and I shifted in discomfort.

I couldn't stop staring at him.

A giant in the middle of my room.

Handsome as hell and dangerous to my sanity.

Blowing out the strain from my lungs, I wrung my fingers together. "I honestly don't know how to thank you."

Sure, he'd offered to do it.

Okay, insisted on it.

And even though I didn't want to be indebted to him, appreciation pulled heavy at my chest. It hadn't been an *actual* lie that I had movers set up for the weekend, only the movers were *me*.

"You don't have a thing to repay me for." His voice was gravel. A bait.

Uncertainty shook my head, suddenly unsure if there was a way to put a finger on him. If everything I thought I knew about him was true at all. "You just unloaded an entire truck. By yourself."

A hint of that arrogance curled through his expression, though there was something softly goofy about it, like he wasn't taking himself seriously when he raised his right arm out to the side and flexed it. "What do you think all these muscles are for?"

His stupid biceps bulged, and I fought the way my throat suddenly felt thick.

"I'm sure you get plenty of exercise doing the work you do."

"Among other things." The teasing insinuation was clear.

I bit down on the inside of my cheek.

Cocky. Freaking. Cowboy.

But there was no stopping the heat that crawled up my neck.

His features softened. "I was happy to help, Hailey. It's what any good neighbor would do."

He said my name the way he used to, and his gaze shifted into that soft familiarity he used to watch me with. He peered at me from across the room, the gold of his eyes glinting beneath the light that shined from the ceiling.

The air tugged hard as I stood there in the silence, no clue what to make of him all while knowing I shouldn't be putting in the effort to make anything of him at all.

I needed to stay away from him. Reject whatever old feelings were trying to climb their way out of the vat where I kept them sealed.

"Where's Maddie's father?" He asked it like he had the right to know.

Point-blank.

I choked over the question. Apparently, we weren't going for surface pleasantries.

"I left him three months ago." I forced it out around the lump in my throat, unable to keep the spite out of my voice.

"He's a prick, yeah?"

My laughter was raw, a shot of disgust and disbelief. "You could say that."

Leaving the hand-truck standing on its own, Cody took a step my direction.

Another then another until he was standing in front of me.

The air shivered and lashed, tension binding the space.

I stumbled back until I was pressed to the wall.

Intensity radiated from his flesh.

All the easiness had vanished.

I could almost feel something vicious pulse through his veins.

He leaned in, so close that I could smell him.

Spice and cedar and the earth.

"I can't stand the thought of some asshole doing you wrong." It rumbled from him like a threat.

Shivers raced, and I was worried he could feel the way I was shaking.

I'd been done wrong, but not in the way that he imagined.

"You don't even know me."

"I remember you. Sweet. Innocent. Kind. You had everyone on that ranch wrapped around your finger."

How could he say that after what had happened?

My lungs quaked. "I'm not that girl anymore."

Gold-hewn eyes blazed, and he reached out and touched the divot on my chin again.

A fire lit in my belly.

"Aren't you?"

"You don't know anything about me," I attempted again, the words ragged.

A smile wobbled on his face, somewhere between a grimace and a grin. "Then I guess I'm going to have to get to know you better, aren't I, Shortcake?"

My stomach clutched.

God.

Did he remember?

It didn't matter. It didn't matter.

I shook my head to jar myself out of the trance he had me under.

Defenses locked, I said, "I think it's probably time you went home."

He edged back, just a fraction, enough to memorize every line of my face. Then he went back to the hand-truck, grabbed it by the handle, and began to wheel it toward the door.

Unfortunately, that meant he had to come back my way. He got to within a foot of me, and he paused there, at my side, his voice so low as he muttered, "I'm sorry you lost her."

Without saying anything else, he walked out, while I remained nailed to the wall, unable to breathe or speak or move.

I startled when a shriek of joy suddenly carried through the house.

One compliments of my daughter, her feet pounding down the hall. "Thank you, Mr. Cody, for getting all my very favorite things and putting all the boxes and my desk in my room! And we even got a couch. You are the very best neighbor I ever met, and I'm very glad I got a house next to yours."

Somehow, I managed to stagger to the doorway. It was just in time to see my daughter throw her arms in the air.

Without hesitation, Cody swept her up.

Lifted her high.

Made her squeal and giggle and laugh.

"It was my pleasure, Button." He set her on her feet and poked her in the belly.

She squealed again, shining all her belief and sweetness in his direction as she grabbed at her tummy. "You got me!"

Everything about him softened, and he knelt a fraction as he touched her nose. "Nah, Button, I think you got me."

Then he straightened and pushed out the front door without looking back.

I glanced to the side to find Lolly grinning victoriously, mouthing, *You're welcome*, again.

My gaze slid back to the door he'd disappeared through. Nerves rattling and something else vying for position.

Crap. I was in trouble.

So much trouble.

But I couldn't let a man like Cody Cooper get the best of me.

I would never commit a betrayal that great.

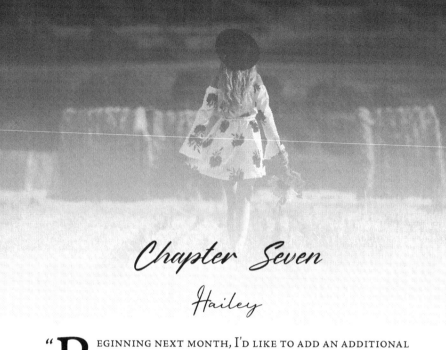

Chapter Seven

Hailey

"**B**EGINNING NEXT MONTH, I'D LIKE TO ADD AN ADDITIONAL fifteen minutes of instruction before trail rides."

Sherry, the equestrian activity coordinator, scrawled the notes on her iPad. We stood in the big, open middle section of the stables running through the typical processes taken with guests when they interacted with the horses and discussing how we might improve systems.

"I know we can't require hours of riding lessons because they're going to grow impatient, but the more training they have, the safer it is for both our guests and horses," I added.

"I fully agree, but Kassandra might have something to say about it." Sherry tucked an errant strand of black hair behind her ear, chewing at the end of her stylus as she studied her notes.

Kassandra was the resort director, and of course, her main priority was the comfort and experience of the guests.

I was certain this lent itself to both their enjoyment and their safety.

"If she has an issue, I'll talk to her about it. Besides, in my experience, most people who come to a guest ranch love the idea of behind the scenes, anyway. So, let's present it as that…getting the inside to the actual workings of a ranch. We'll bring them into the stables and show them around and give safety tips as we do. We can even offer specific activities centered around learning about the care of a horse."

"Oh, I like that idea."

"Great. Get that on the schedule for next month's activity flyer, and I'll go over the details with the guides. Please let me know what Kassandra says."

"I will."

"Thank you, Sherry."

"Of course. I'm excited about the changes you have planned. I think it's going to be a true benefit to the resort."

Pride swelled, but I shored it away, watching as she turned and ducked out the main stable entrance which had monstrous double-metal doors. They were situated right in the center of the building, and they'd been left wide open to overlook the grounds and the lodge in the distance.

A slight breeze whispered in from outside, a balm to the heat that saturated the air, and I could hear shrieks and laughter coming from children who were playing in the pool. The energy was both calm and invigorated.

Peace fell over me, this intrinsic contentedness that I'd made the right choice. Coming home. This was where I'd always belonged, even though I'd been fearful that I might be consumed by the ghosts waiting for my return.

I'd set my laptop on the high wooden table that rested along a metal partition. The table served as the check-in station for guests, and I turned my focus to tapping out a few notes about the meeting with Sherry, so engrossed as I leaned over the table that I could have missed the shift in the atmosphere.

Okay, maybe there was absolutely no chance that I could have missed it.

The way a brand-new tension curled through the space.

An awareness that flashed.

Both suffocating and light.

Like warm streaks of sunlight were spearing into my back and prodding all the way to the soul.

I did my best to act like I didn't notice he was there until a rough chuckle skated over me from behind. "I see you are already whipping this place into shape."

Steeling myself, I looked over my shoulder.

The *steeling* bit didn't work. Not even a little bit.

Because all the air heaved from my lungs when I found him casually strolling my way, wearing another plain white tee that stretched and strained with each step that he took, jeans clinging to those thighs, and dusty boots that promised the man did more than an honest day's work.

But it was that gilded gaze taking me in that nearly did me in. The way the rust-colored flecks seemed to lap like the warming of flames.

He must have shaved since the last time I'd seen him two days ago, and now his strong jaw was covered in a short brown stubble.

His lips quirked up at the side.

So easy.

So casual.

As if the moment he'd left me shaken in my bedroom hadn't occurred—as if there'd been no tension and it hadn't felt like my heart was getting shattered all over again—as he sauntered up with his big hands shoved in the pockets of his jeans.

I finally gathered myself enough to speak. "I'm just going through some of the practices here and seeing where we can improve things."

"Pretty sure you being here is definitely improving things." Playful suggestion filled his voice.

A scowl came unbidden, the natural instinct to protect myself from him. "Don't you have enough to keep you busy that you shouldn't feel the need to come in here distracting me from my work?"

He smirked as he angled the rest of the way up behind me, coming so close that I was inundated with his scent.

Spice and cedar and earth.

"What, you weren't missing me?" He breathed the tease at the shell of my ear.

Chills lifted on the nape of my neck.

Whipping around to face him, I backed up a step to put some space between us. "Now, why would I be missing you?"

I shouldn't even grant him that, but the question was out before I could process the consequence.

Begging for the things that would hurt me in the end.

He hiked a massive shoulder to his ear where those stupidly adorable curls peeked out from under his cap. "Well, I was missing you, so I thought you might be feeling the same."

Exasperation shook my head.

Such a player, feeding me those lines.

"I don't need you coming around here toying with me. I have work to do, the same as you."

"I thought you might want to have lunch with me."

Air huffed from my nose. "I don't think that's a good idea, Mr. Cooper."

His eyes crinkled at the corners. "And why not? Everyone has to eat."

"Because I know the type of games men like you play, and I don't have time for that."

Not the time or the space or the inclination to get my heart trampled. He could. So easily. Just him standing there felt like he was peeling back a scab to reveal a wound. Worst was the way my reaction to him felt like I was committing a mortal betrayal.

He rocked back on his heels, head canting to the side. "And what kind of games might those be?"

I scoffed. "Don't act like you don't know exactly what I'm talking about. I don't do one-night stands, Mr. Cooper."

I froze when I suddenly felt another presence cut into the atmosphere, and I turned my attention to the left to find my father standing in the middle of the yawning stable doors. Protectiveness lined his features as his attention jumped between me and Cody.

Cody followed my line of sight, and the second he saw him, he went rigid, like we were teenagers who'd been caught in a sordid position. He edged two steps back, sucking in a deep breath before he tipped his head my way. "I'll see you around, Hailey."

He waltzed off, heading for the far door at the end of the stalls, though he pulled off his cap and squeezed the brim together as he passed by my father. "Mr. Wagner," he said, voice a low rumble that tumbled through me.

"Cody," my father returned, probably a little cooler than necessary. I could still remember my father's warnings. *Stay away from him, Hailey. That guy is trouble. The real kind of trouble. I mean it when I say I don't want you anywhere near him.*

But I'd been little more than a child then.

Eighteen, though I might as well have been a twelve-year-old suffering a crush. God knew the paltry number of experiences I'd failed to rack up by then.

I didn't realize my stare was stuck on Cody's retreating form until my father cleared his throat.

When I looked his direction, he was standing two feet away.

I could only pray my tongue wasn't hanging out.

I pinned the brightest smile on my face which wasn't all that hard to find. "Hey, Dad. What are you doing here?"

His returning smile was easy as he leaned in to peck a kiss to my cheek. He wore jeans and a striped button-down with the top two buttons undone. His style was always that of polished casualness, oozing power without having to exert it. "I have an appointment with the horse buyer and thought I'd swing by to see my favorite girl first."

I leaned in for a hug, and he wrapped his arms around me, holding me close the way he always did.

"I'm really glad you did," I whispered. God, I loved that I was here. That I was able to have these moments with him again. I didn't realize how much I'd missed it until I was standing right here.

He pulled away, though he held onto me by the sides of my shoulders as he studied me, blue eyes soft as he took me in.

My father was as handsome as they came. Brown hair thick and wavy, only the slightest bit of gray teasing at his temples.

He was also smart.

Determined.

Crazy successful.

I respected the crap out of him.

"How is the new job treating you?" he asked.

I let my gaze wander the stables, again struck with the satisfaction that brimmed. "It's amazing, honestly. I love it here."

"Good to hear." Concern pinched his brow. "They aren't working you too hard, are they? I can have a word with—"

"Absolutely not. I can handle myself."

I swore, there'd never come a day that he didn't think of me as eight years old. The proof of it came in full force when he angled his head down the long row of stalls where Cody had disappeared, voice curling with disgust. "And what the hell is he doing here?"

"He's just a contractor who's working a landscape project. He came to get my approval to start digging out around one of the pastures. I can handle him."

And now I was lying to him like I was sixteen. Pathetic, considering I was twenty-four, had a child, had been married and seeking a divorce.

Maybe lying to my father about men came naturally since I'd spent so much time hiding the truth of my marriage from him. The truth of who Pruitt was. At first, I'd not wanted to believe it myself before it'd become a dirty secret.

A secret I'd been chained to.

One that had festered and decayed.

A rotted pit where I refused to go under.

So, I'd left Pruitt, praying I had enough on him that he would never dare try to touch me, all while feeling despicable that I didn't have enough courage to actually use the evidence against him.

Hold him accountable.

Expose who he was.

Instead, I'd come here, free but a hostage. Captive to this fear. Trepidation and alarm roiling in my spirit. Constantly looking behind me waiting for my choice to catch up, for the veiled threats Pruitt had made to manifest as real.

"Watch out for him," my father said, referring to Cody when he had no idea who was really the danger. "You know I don't trust him."

The warning rang between us, the memory of that summer when Cody had been working on his ranch so distant yet so distinct.

It was a time that was carved in the middle of me like the branding of scars.

"You don't have to worry about me."

Frowning, my father squeezed my shoulders tighter. "I always worry about you." He hesitated, then pushed into the territory that I kept blockaded. "Pruitt called me. He's worried about you, too."

He might as well have driven a blade through the center of my chest.

I bit it back because my father didn't know. I couldn't blame him when I'd kept him in the dark. I did my best to keep it together when I said, "Pruitt doesn't have a right to be concerned about me any longer."

My father's brow pinched. "I still don't understand, Hailey. He is a good man. Provided for you and Madison. Loved you like crazy. And he still does. He's worried sick about you. Maybe you should—"

"Please, don't say it," I cut him off. Disquiet jackhammered my heart, the beating so loud that it roared in my ears, thick as it pounded through my blood.

I wanted to confess it so he would understand. Tell him so he would stop urging me to go back to Pruitt, the way he had been doing since I'd left him.

Pruitt Russel had looked good on paper.

He had put on a dazzling front for my father that he'd been completely blinded by the same way as I'd been when I'd first met him.

Successful.

Rich.

Powerful.

My father had more than approved.

I guessed I'd been enamored, too. Glamoured, maybe. Blinded by the young owner of a gorgeous ranch in Austin, where I'd taken a position to work with horses, who'd taken an interest in me. I'd been desperate for anything that made me feel good after the tragedy that had befallen me here, and I'd all but run away in search of something better.

I'd somehow thought that was Pruitt.

But so many times what looked good on paper didn't take into account what happened behind closed doors. Under the surface. In the secreted places that whispered of wickedness and atrocities.

"I need you to let it go," I whispered.

My father's throat bobbed as he swallowed, and he slowly nodded. "I'm sorry. I didn't mean to upset you. I just want to help you…fix this."

Pain pealed through my insides, the clanging of chains, and I lifted my chin, refusing to look away when I said, "I already did."

He ran his thumbs over my arms where he still held onto me. "Okay, we won't talk about this right now."

I wanted to tell him we wouldn't talk about it ever.

It was dead and buried.

I would never go back to Pruitt.

But I figured I'd take what I could get right then.

"I'm really happy you're doing so well here. That you're back in your element." His gaze was soft as he looked around the stables. "Though I still don't understand why you refused to come and work for me."

"I think it's time I spread my wings a little bit, don't you? Stood on my own?"

"It doesn't have a thing to do with you standing on your own. I'm just jealous Cambrey Pines got the best stable manager in the west." His smile was soft.

Affection swelled, pushing at my ribs. "Thank you, Dad. You really don't know what that means to hear you say that."

"I mean it." He stepped back and ran a hand through his hair. "All right, I'd better let you get back to work. Bring Maddie by soon?"

"I will."

He tapped the knuckle of his index finger on my chin. "Love you."

"Forever," I told him, and he turned and strode down the hall that led to the backside of the stables where the offices were located.

I watched him go, trying to regulate my breathing. To calm the riot that clattered through my being.

Only that riot erupted into chaos when my phone buzzed in my pocket, and I pulled it out to see the message that was waiting.

It was only a number, the sender not in my contacts, but I knew who it was the second I read it.

Unknown: Who said I wanted a one-night stand?

My stomach tightened, and in an instant, my blood felt too hot.

I should ignore it. Block his number. Tell him how wildly inappropriate he was being using my number for personal reasons when that business card had been meant for work purposes only.

But no, instead, I foolishly glanced around all covert-like to ensure no one was around before I tapped out a reply. Apparently, playing with fire was my thing.

Me: And what made you believe I want anything from you at all?

It took all of two seconds for another text to blip through.

Unknown: Do you think I can't feel it? The way every molecule in your body reacts when I get close? Don't fool yourself, Shortcake.

Unbelievable.

He had to be the most arrogant man I'd ever met.

Too bad every single one of those molecules trembled right then.

Me: Believe me, Cowboy, I have zero interest.

I was far too eager waiting on his reply, staring at my phone for so long that when a text did come through, I frowned at what it said.

Unknown: Yeah. That's what I thought.

That's when I felt it. The stir in the air. I followed the enchantment of it, my attention traveling to the far end of the stables. In the distance, I saw him leaning against a stall, one boot kicked back on the gate as he smirked my way.

Thinking he'd caught me red-handed.

My teeth ground and my fingers flew across the screen.

> **Me: I'd suggest you get back to work, Mr. Cooper. You wouldn't want to be caught slacking off, flirting with the staff. It wouldn't look good.**

I put as much spite into it as I could, an undercut of warning, even though there wasn't a chance that I would report him.

I could feel the low roll of a chuckle that was too far away to actually hear permeate the space.

A lure.

A trap.

> **Unknown: You tell yourself what you need to, Shortcake. I'll be right here when you're willing to admit it.**

I wanted to screech or maybe stamp my foot in frustration the way Maddie did when she didn't get her way.

Because the man was infuriating.

I glanced around again to make sure no one was around before I turned back to where Cody loitered in the distance. When I found no one around, I lifted my hand and gave him the finger.

There.

Maybe he'd get the message then.

Only I could see his chest jerk with laughter, amusement shaking his head as he pushed from the gate. He turned his back to me and strode for the doors at the end of the stables.

So tall and overbearing, the ground vibrating below him.

He pushed out, and the bright glare of the sun swallowed him whole as he walked out.

One second later, the door slammed shut behind him, and metal clanked in the distance.

I gritted my teeth to stop myself from making something more of the interaction than I should.

To stop myself from letting my mind wander into what that might be like.

Letting him touch me.

Tingles raced, and I squeezed my hands into fists. I needed to stop that train right then.

Kill the idea before it started.

I looked back at his messages, not knowing if I was more annoyed or aroused.

Block him.

Block him.

It was the obvious, logical choice.

But what did I do?

I tapped on his number and saved him in my contacts as CC.

Cody Cooper.

Cocky Cowboy.

I guessed they both worked.

Chapter Eight

Cody

CODY'S HAND WAS STICKY WITH SWEAT WHERE IT WAS GRIPPED in his momma's.

His heart made a loud thud against his ribs, pound, pound, pounding in time with the echo of his footsteps on the shiny white floor.

His momma paused outside a door, and her face was all soft the way it always got when she looked at him, making his heart that was thundering beat even harder. She reached down and touched his cheek.

"Now remember what I told you. He's going to look a little different than you remember, but he's still your daddy. You don't have to be afraid."

Except Cody didn't think he'd ever felt more afraid than right then, but it was a different kind of scary than when the lights were off at night. He was scared because his momma was so sad, and she kept crying and crying, and he didn't know how to make her stop, so it made him sad, too.

He hadn't been allowed to come for a lot of days, and his momma was gone a lot, but she'd said this morning it was a special day and his daddy really wanted to see him.

He'd been excited until they walked through the doors of the building *his momma called hospice, and it felt yucky inside. Like he was sneaking into a place he wasn't supposed to be.*

"I'm not afraid," he told her, trying to puff out his chest. Maybe if he showed he was big and strong she might not be so sad anymore.

She gave him a shaky nod, then she squeezed his hand again before she swung open the door. They slowly walked inside the room.

It was quiet in there. Too still. And something about it felt dark even though the curtain was open on the window and the sun was shining in.

His belly felt sick and heavy, like on the day he had to stay home from school because he was throwing up, and he thought he might when he saw his daddy on the bed.

The bed was bent so his daddy was sitting up, and he had a bunch of pillows behind him.

His momma used to say his daddy was as big as an ox.

But he looked real skinny, and his skin was the wrong color.

Like the yellow-gray clay he and Ryder played with on the bank of the stream behind Cody's house.

He'd heard his momma whispering to her friend Linda that his daddy's liver was broken and didn't work anymore and it made him super sick, but Cody didn't really know what that meant.

"Hey." His daddy's voice was raspy, though his eyes and his smile were soft when he looked at Cody. "There's my boy. Come see me."

Cody looked at his momma for permission, and she nudged him forward. Cody's feet felt like they were sticking to the floor when he moved forward, like it was hard to move, that thunder in his heart banging so loud he thought his daddy could hear it.

His daddy patted the spot on the bed next to him. "Climb up here."

Cody did as he was told, climbing up and staying on his knees and facing him, keeping real still because he was afraid he might hurt his daddy if he got too close.

His daddy touched his chin. "There's my big, brave boy. And you're going to grow into an incredible man one day."

His stomach wobbled as he stared at his father.

"You're such a good boy, do you know that?"

Cody could only give him a tiny nod of his head.

"*I want you to always remember that—you're a good boy and it's this right here that makes you that.*"

His daddy tapped at the spot where it felt like Cody's heart was going to burst through his chest.

"*You be kind to those around you. Use your manners and help out wherever you can. Be respectful but also stand up for what you believe to be true and right.*"

Cody nodded again, and his eyes felt tingly, and his throat burned real bad.

"*And I want you to always look out for your momma and your sisters. You're gonna be the man of the house now, so you make sure no one ever does them wrong. Take care of them. Protect them with everything you've got.*"

"*Yes, sir, I promise.*" The words sounded garbled when they came off his tongue, and his daddy reached up and wiped away a tear that had gotten free.

"*I know you will stand for them. I'm so proud of you, and I'm always gonna be.*"

My eyes popped open to the darkness of my room. My heart galloped in my chest, no different than it'd done that afternoon when I was six years old. It was the day that was inscribed in me like a brand.

My purpose. My responsibility.

Only that promise had taken me down a road I never should have let it, but at the time, I hadn't thought there'd been another choice.

Maybe there hadn't been, and those consequences had been coming for me all along.

Destined.

Inevitable.

Sweat slicking my flesh, I tossed off my covers and sat up on the side of the bed. I scrubbed both palms over my face before I dragged my fingers through my hair, taking in deep, even breaths like it would hold the power to eradicate the chaos that hunted me.

I could almost feel the wraiths hiding in the corners. On the fringe and in the periphery, murmuring that one day they were going to catch up.

I touched the tattoo on my chest, that permanent reminder that I was living on borrowed time.

A reminder to live hard and full and with everything I had, to always watch my back, to never stumble, to never *fall.*

Problem was, the ground felt shaky beneath me, like I was riding an edge that I knew better than to take.

Slipping off a crumbling, disintegrating cliff.

Pushing past boundaries that I'd set for myself.

A fool who couldn't seem to help himself.

Unease coiled with the interest. This stupid, reckless thing that I couldn't shuck from my brain. It had been following me into my dreams the entire week. Unable to resist it, I pushed to my feet and padded across my room to the window.

I peeled back the drape.

A murky darkness held fast, cut by the bare glow of the half-moon and the billion stars smattering the canopy overhead.

Her window was nothing but a blackened square, but I swore, there was something about it that glowed.

A beacon I should ignore.

A beacon I *had* to ignore because I'd seen what was in her father's eyes when he'd caught me talking with her yesterday.

I should have turned my back, walked out, made an oath to never speak to her again, and instead, I was sending her calamitous texts insinuating something along the lines that I might want something more than a one-night stand.

Motherfucking stupid.

Reckless.

Hailey Wagner was the absolute last person I could seek, even if I ever was in the position to allow myself to fall which was highly un-fucking-likely.

I had to stay away from her.

Problem was, I was terrified there was something about her that promised I couldn't.

The lawnmower whirred as I pushed it in perfect rows up and down the front lawn. Heat already saturated the air even though it was only nearing nine in the morning, sweat soaking my tee and running down from the edges of my cap.

I made the last turn and pushed it up the edge of the flower bed sectioned off by decorative rocks up close to the house, then I killed the roar of the engine when I made it to the sidewalk that cut up the middle of the yard.

The screen on the door clattered shut, and I looked up to the stoop of my childhood home to see my mother step out, a towel in one hand and a glass of lemonade in the other. She watched down on me with that same adoration she'd watched me with my entire life.

"Would you come inside? You're likely to melt out here in all this heat."

Affection bound my chest, and I swiped my forearm across my face to gather the sweat. "You act like I don't spend every single one of my days exactly like this. It comes with the territory."

"Well, you could take a day off of it if you didn't think you had to show up here to mow my lawn every Saturday morning."

I grinned as I started her direction. "And what else would I do with myself?"

"Oh, I don't know…sleep in? Especially considering I know the way you like to spend your Friday nights."

She didn't try to hide the insinuation.

Funny, I hadn't been in the mood for it last night.

I took the two steps onto the porch and leaned in to peck a kiss to her cheek. "And miss out on seeing your beautiful face? I don't think so."

Her scowl was playful as she passed me the towel. "It's not like you won't see it at Sunday breakfast."

I used the towel to mop up the sweat on my face, running it around to the back of my neck, my grin slow. "Saturday and Sunday mornings right here with my momma. Best hours of the week."

She tsked. "Are you trying to flatter your momma? You always knew how to butter me up."

"Speaking nothing but God's honest truth." My smile was wide, and she was shaking her head, though something tender slipped into her features.

In my opinion, there wasn't a better human being on this planet than my mother. Her eyes warm and brown, her hair frizzy, her clothes plain. It sometimes gutted me looking at her because I knew every single one of the lines written on her face were carved of the worry she'd carried for us, with the grief that had knitted itself so deep in her spirit she'd never found a real way of healing.

But she'd taken that grief and weaved it into the love she had for us.

The devotion she'd poured into us.

She'd never wanted me and my two sisters to suffer when our lives had been upended after my father had passed, and she'd worked her fingers until they'd literally bled. I had zero fucking regrets that I'd given it all for her, even though she didn't have the first clue.

Reaching out, she set a hand on my cheek, gaze emphatic as she brushed her thumb over the scruff. "You do too much for me, Cody. You always have. You're young. I want you livin' your life. With everything you've got. I want you to find joy. Love. Your reason."

My throat grew thick, and I reached up and curled my hand over hers, voice gruff when I murmured, "I already have, Mom. It's right here."

And I needed not to fucking forget it.

Chapter Nine

Hailey

It was just after five-thirty when I hopped into my Durango that Friday evening.

A sigh of contentment fluttered past my lips as I turned over the ignition.

It was hard to believe I'd already been working at Cambrey Pines for two weeks. Those two weeks had been productive. Both exciting and terrifying, the hope of freedom whispering around me while a piece of my spirit still toiled and warred.

Seized by the dread of the choice I had made, constantly worrying I had done this all wrong, the rubbing at my soul urging that I was taking the easy way out. Guilt clotting the flickers of joy I'd already found here.

But I hadn't heard a word from Pruitt, not since my father had mentioned him, and I was standing on that.

I just had to make sure my daughter was safe first, then I would make the choice of how to proceed, how to handle the burden of this knowledge.

As if I didn't have enough to fret over, I'd spent an inordinate amount of time trying to ignore the presence of my new neighbor that seemed to follow me everywhere, both at my house and at work, the man's aura so distinct that I swore I could sense his footsteps wherever he went.

He was always tossing out easy hellos. Texting me to ask if I was okay and if I needed a hand. Acting like we were long lost BFFs and he owed me the time and the effort.

It would be a whole lot easier to dismiss the man if I wasn't subject to the energy he emitted whenever he was in his house, this magnetism that'd had me peeking out my window too many times to count, then feeling guilty the second I'd give in.

The way my eyes couldn't help but search him out whenever I roamed the grounds of the resort, drawn to an entity that would destroy.

Cody Cooper was nothing but a black hole.

A stupidly hot black hole that threatened to suck me in.

Shaking it off, I backed out of my parking space and took off down the long drive that wound out of the resort.

A ton of cars passed me coming in. The resort was booked to capacity for the weekend, which was typical since people flocked here for weekend getaways.

I was halfway down the drive when my phone rang from my Bluetooth speakers. A surprised smile stretched across my face when I saw the name on the screen.

Eagerly, I touched the button on the dash to accept the call, my voice full of wonder, "Oh, my goodness, if it isn't Paisley Dae."

She shrieked from the opposite end of the line. "Tell me it's true, and your gorgeous ass is back in Colorado."

Warmth flooded my chest. "I'm here!"

I made it to the end of the drive and carefully made a left, Paisley's excitement in my ear. "Oh my God! I can't believe you're actually back. I heard some murmurings going around town, but I had to call to find out for myself."

"The rumors are all true." I grinned.

"Huh, who'd have known that rumors could be good?" she teased.

A tiny sliver of laughter rumbled out.

"And you're back in town, too?" I asked.

The last I'd talked to her, she was moving to Arizona with her boyfriend. That was years ago, and we'd lost touch after that.

Honestly, I hadn't known her all that well, the two of us more acquaintances than friends, though that's what I really had considered her.

A friend.

Someone who shared my same interests when my best friend had been terrified of horses.

My spirit clutched with the errant thought of Brooke. A sheering of sadness. I squeezed my eyes closed for a beat to block the vision that tried to take possession of my mind.

I forced myself to listen to what Paisley was saying, refusing the way my thoughts kept threatening to spiral.

"I've been for almost two years now. Back home and engaged to the love of my life," she said.

"Jeremy?" I hoped she couldn't hear the way I cringed when I asked it. I'd only met the guy once, but I couldn't be considered a fan.

Paisley exaggerated a gag. "God, no. My fiancé's name is Caleb and he's the hottest man alive. Wait until you see him. But don't look too close because that man is mine."

Mirth covered every word, and there was no stopping my giggle. Paisley Dae had a way of spreading joy wherever she went.

I'd met her on my father's ranch when she'd come to purchase a couple of his horses when she'd been starting her own training facility in Time River. I'd only been sixteen at the time, and she was a couple years older than me. She'd strutted in, wearing cutoffs and boots and a cowgirl hat, so confident and wild and free that I couldn't help but want to be just like her.

"Don't worry, I won't look too close," I ribbed, then sobered. "It's so good to hear you're doing well and are happy."

"What's *good* to hear is your voice. I'm sorry it's been so long." I could almost see her pout from across the line.

"Don't even apologize," I told her. "Life has a way of doing that, and I'm sorry we lost touch, too. But I am back and living in Hendrickson with my little girl and my grandmother."

Paisley squealed, her words a ramble that flew out of her. "Oh my God, you're a mom? I'm a mom, too! I mean, my fiancé has a little girl, too, and she's absolutely mine in my heart, if you know what I mean? How did I not know this about you?"

"Oh, I don't know, probably since we haven't talked to each other in like six years?" I said, completely droll.

She laughed. "Well, that is never going to happen again, Hails Bells."

A soft chuckle rolled out of me at the old nickname she'd given me. "Oh God, I haven't heard that one in a long time."

"Well, get used to it because you're going to be hearing it a lot. Are you married?"

I tamped down the agitation that wanted to rise, and I somehow managed to keep my voice even when I said, "I'm in the middle of a divorce."

I just wished it was that simple. Something that could be stamped and stowed away, a mistake that never had to be thought of again.

"Oh, no, I'm so sorry." She paused for only a second before she rushed, "Come out with me and my friends tomorrow night. We obviously have a ton to catch up on."

"I'm not sure—"

"Don't even try to say no. We're going out to celebrate my bestie's brother getting a big job, and it's the perfect chance for you to meet everyone. Then another time we can get our girls together."

She stated it like it was already done.

"I…" I hesitated.

In my pause, she demanded, "Say yes!"

Honestly, I could use it.

A distraction.

A night out.

Fun.

Friends, even.

My chest tightened. I'd thought I'd never want to have them again.

Had thought it would hurt too bad to even think about putting my heart on the line that way. I'd isolated myself for years.

I imagined that was part of the reason I'd been so blinded by Pruitt. Needing a connection while denying the type that had caused so much pain.

So lost in my own world that I hadn't realized what was happening right in front of me.

But I'd come back to Colorado to make a change. To reclaim who I was or maybe discover who I wanted to be.

Hiding out in my house wasn't going to help that.

"Fine. I'll come as long as my grandmother doesn't mind watching Maddie for a little while."

"Heck, yes, baby! This is going to be a blast. I can't wait to see you. We're going to Mack's in Time River. Be there at seven."

Hesitation suddenly bubbled up, and I bit down on my bottom lip. "Are you sure your friends won't mind?"

I didn't know much about Paisley's personal life since our topics of conversation had always centered around horses. Our experiences. Different training techniques. Our dreams surrounding them and our goals for the future.

"Are you kidding me? They will love you. Believe me. Just come."

Where I thought I might feel reservations, I felt...excitement. There was something about being here that felt...healing.

"Okay, I'll be there."

A squeal reverberated through the line and basically shook the cab of my SUV. "Wear your dancing boots, Hails Bells. We're about to get our party on."

Oh lord, what did I get myself into?

"I'll see if I can find them in the mountain of boxes I still need to unpack."

"Just look at it as motivation to get through a few of them," she drawled, her voice sly.

There was no containing my grin. "That'll probably do the trick."

"Good! Okay, I'll see you tomorrow. Be prepared for the best night of your life!" she sang before the line went dead.

I laughed out loud at the whirlwind that was Paisley Dae.

She was someone I hadn't even expected might come back into my life. Anticipation thrummed, a gratitude that she'd taken the initiative to reach out, and I thought this might be the start of something great.

Ten minutes later, I pulled my Durango into the angled drive of my little house.

My gaze drifted over our home. It was painted white with blue eaves, and there was a manicured lawn out front in a kidney shape, lined by rocks to give it extra texture and design.

A bed of pink and white flowers ran along the walkway and swinging pots containing the same flowers hung from the porch.

Pride welled in the depths of me, though it thudded with something deeper.

No. It wasn't anything extravagant. Not even close to the type of excess I'd lived in my entire life. Both at my father's ranch and at the estate I'd shared with Pruitt outside Austin.

But it was what this house represented that made it magnificent.

Freedom.

Goodness.

A safe, untainted place for my daughter to learn, live, and grow. A place that would be filled with love and belief and joy.

I sat in the magnitude of it for a few moments, let it enfold me, the determination that I would do whatever it took to give her all those things swilling. Bricks building to conviction.

I would never let my fear sway me.

I would stand.

No matter what that looked like. No matter what it cost.

Resolved, I turned off the ignition and snapped open my door.

A rush of awareness slammed me. Coming at me like a barrage of arrows I had no time to deflect.

No way to divert or dodge the intensity.

It muddled my mind that something so severe and stark still managed to stir the heavens into tranquility.

A slow warmth stretching out and wrapping me in a fuzzy embrace.

I looked to the left to find Cody sitting on his front porch. He was rocked back in a chair, his legs kicked up on the railing, one boot crossed over the other at the ankle.

A patter of something I shouldn't entertain skipped through my body. A reckless beat of anticipation.

Steeling myself, I stepped out.

He tipped the neck of the bottle of beer he was nursing in my direction, the sun all around him, bathing him in a golden glow.

"How's it fair one woman could look so damn good after she worked all day in the stables?"

My instinct was to scowl at him. The way he let his attention drift down my body, like he was reveling in the sight of the tight jeans that I wore, the legs flaring out to accommodate my boots. I'd paired it with a black, western sleeveless top, embroidered with turquoise accents with black pearlescent buttons running down the middle.

I had to resist the urge to cross my arms over my chest.

All his cool and casual was back.

That smirk so easy.

No question, it was dangerous to my sanity.

He chuckled low like he found some kind of twisted pleasure in poking at me.

"How has work been treating you?" Those penetrating eyes creased at the edges, like he was trying to peer all the way to the middle of me. Like he might truly care about the answer.

"It is actually…great." I couldn't help but be honest with him.

"That's good to hear," he murmured.

I should have excused myself and hurried inside, but I stood there in my driveway, the breeze rustling through my hair as I stared at this guy I needed to ignore.

Just looking at him conjured a wave of guilt.

Unfortunately, he had this magnetism about him that I found hard to resist. "How are things going for you?"

He grinned, words rolling like seduction from his mouth. "It's going great."

"I'm glad to hear that."

"Yeah, the project is running smooth." Then his head cocked to the side as one of those flirty smiles took to his handsome face. "And you can say my view has gotten really good."

That gaze swept over me again. Devouring me where I stood.

A shiver curled down my spine and my stomach twisted in attraction.

I tried to gather up my defenses, to put up some boundaries, and I lifted my chin as if it could possibly be enough to shield myself from the onslaught of his heat. "You should probably look somewhere else."

"Now why on earth would I want to do that?" He took a lazy pull of his beer, his thick throat bobbing as he swallowed.

He slung a muscled, tattooed arm up so it was hooked behind his head, and he rocked back farther in the chair. So smooth and easy and so damned good to look at that I swayed to the side.

It took me a second to realize I hadn't said anything for at least a minute and was standing there mute, rooted to the spot. Staring through a lulling calm that still thrummed with energy.

He was conflict and peace.

Disorder ushered in by a warm spring breeze.

A paradox.

Clearing my throat, I tightened my hold on the strap of my bag, clinging to it like it might be an anchor. "I should get inside."

He dipped his chin so casually. Like the interaction was trivial when the man was nothing less than an earthquake. "I'm sure I'll see you around, Shortcake."

There was that Shortcake again, and my chest clutched, the memory of him sitting beneath that tree with his boots stretched out in front of him, the man so distraught as we'd shared that cake.

It was the first time he'd allowed me to see him. To see deeper into the intricate layers of his depths. To see more than the careless player I had to believe he was.

Shuttering the thoughts, I hurried up the walkway, put the key into the lock, and swung open the door.

Any tension I'd felt a second ago drained when I stepped inside to find Lolly and Maddie gathered around the coffee table in front of the couch, a game of Candyland spread out between them.

Maddie was on her knees on the floor, and she threw her arms into the air when she saw me. Her plump cheeks dimpled when she gave me that adorable smile that wrecked me every time.

My heart was hardly able to hold the magnitude of my love for her.

"Mommy! You got home so fast. You gotta come play with us. I already beat my Lolly like a hundred times, and she needs your help super bad. She's real terrible at this."

Madison's expression pulled in mortified disappointment.

Lolly chuckled and slanted me a knowing glance. "Little one's too smart for me."

"Well, then I guess Lolly and I are going to have to form a team, aren't we?"

Lolly's smile was soft. "We've always been the best kind of team."

"That's right," I told her, sitting down beside her and squeezing her knee. "The best one there is."

Maddie beamed from across the coffee table, those curls wild and her innocence stark. "Hey, I'm on your team, too. That's gotta mean we all win, right, Mommy?"

I squeezed Lolly's hand.

Yeah, that had to mean we all won. And I was set on the prize being *this* life.

Chapter Ten

Hailey

IT WAS A FEW MINUTES AFTER TEN THAT NIGHT WHEN I WAS in the kitchen, unloading a few boxes.

When I'd fled to Boston three months ago, I'd furnished the small apartment I'd rented the best that I could, hoping to give Maddie any semblance of normalcy. Ripping her from the only home she'd known and dragging her across the country with only the clothes on our backs and her Princess Verona she'd been sleeping with when I'd left that night hugged to her chest.

I imagined that was when she'd formed the attachment to it, when it'd become a safety net, something she could count on always being there to give her comfort.

I'd brought all our things from that apartment with us because I didn't want to fully upend her again, though she'd flourished while we'd lived there, the child coming alive in a way she hadn't in Austin, as if her spirit had been tamped and tamed there, too, and that sweet spirit had only seemed to soar even higher now that we were in Colorado.

It was the right choice, coming here. I knew it all the way in my soul. The way the ground seemed to be a little more solid beneath our feet each day, even though the man next door seemed to be doing his best to disturb it.

I was still shaking from our interaction from earlier when I'd gotten home from work.

Refusing to contemplate it, I turned back to place a stack of teal-colored plates into the cupboards with the glass doors that ran above the countertop.

Affection pulled at me when I heard Lolly shuffle into the kitchen from behind, and I tossed a glance at her from over my shoulder.

"Is she asleep?" I asked.

Her smile was sly. "Out like a light…that is only after reading her favorite book fifteen times over."

"She knows exactly how to wrap you around her finger."

"Well, I didn't get to spend a whole lot of time with her for a lot of years, so I think a little spoiling from her Lolly is in order."

"Just don't spoil her too much. She'll have you convinced there is no harm in both of you trying the monkey bars out back if you let her," I teased.

She'd been eyeing them since we moved in, but I kept telling her she wasn't big enough to give them a go yet. Of course, she'd looked right to Lolly to see if she might have something different to say about it.

Lolly pulled out a stool at the island and sat down. "You aren't implying I'm too old to take a little jaunt across the monkey bars, are you?"

"The only thing I'm implying is if you get hurt over here, my father is going to have something to say about it. Hell, he'd have you on the first plane to Santa Barbara." I raised an eyebrow at her.

She waved it off as inconsequential. "My son doesn't get to tell me how I spend my days. Bossy, that one, I tell you. He might think he gets to toss around all the orders, but I go right on like I didn't hear a word."

I sent her a soft scowl. "He just worries about you."

"Just because that man thinks he knows what's best for all of us doesn't mean he's right." She folded her arms on the counter. "God knows, he's made plenty of mistakes."

"We all have, haven't we?" I hummed.

"Yeah. The only thing we can do is hope we learn from them."

I got the sense she was trying to give a gentle prod in the direction of Pruitt, the horrible choice I'd made to stay with him for as long as I had.

"Can I get you a cup of tea?" I asked, changing the subject.

"That sounds nice."

I went about filling two mugs with water and setting them in the microwave before I moved to the pantry where I'd placed a variety of tea bags. I picked out a nice chamomile for us both.

By the time I made it back, the microwave dinged, and I set the cups on saucers, tucked the tea bags under the cups, then slid one across the counter toward her. "There you go."

"Thank you, sweet one."

Standing on the opposite side of the island, I unwrapped my tea bag, eyeing my grandmother, hating that I was feeling any nerves at all. "I need to ask you something."

Interest tipped her drawn-in brows toward the ceiling. "And what might that be?"

"I need a favor."

I didn't know why I was so nervous to ask. Probably because she was already watching Maddie for me during the days.

"What kind of favor?" she asked as she dunked the tea bag into the steaming water.

"An old friend called and asked if I wanted to go out with her and her friends tomorrow night. I don't want to take advantage—" I rushed behind it, knowing I was asking a lot.

Maddie might be the cutest thing that had ever come into existence, but I'd be a liar if I said she couldn't be a handful.

Something devious creased every wrinkle on Lolly's face. "If that means you might go out and earn yourself a bit of a reputation, you know I'm game for it."

Rolling my eyes, I took a sip of tea. "There will be no earning a reputation. I thought I'd go have a couple drinks, meet her friends, and plan to be home and in bed by ten."

Disbelief left her on an exaggerated gasp. "Well, that's no fun. I won't agree to it if you don't stay until closing. And you'd better dance your cute little booty off while you're at it."

"Lolly." Her name was nothing but an exasperated sigh.

"What?" She shrugged a shoulder to her ear. "I'm just trying to help a girl out. If I were a few years younger, I'd come with and help you scope out a little trouble."

"I'm sure you would."

Her chuckle was wry before a vat of softness swam into her features. "I'd be more than happy to watch her. You need to get out. Have a little fun. Sow some oats now that you finally got rid of fuckface."

Tea spewed out of my mouth.

"Lolly." I choked her name around the bit of tea that I'd inhaled.

She laughed, no shame. "He was a fuckface if I ever met one. Nothing but a snake."

"He wasn't a snake." The rebuttal wobbled on my tongue. "We just…didn't work out."

Her gaze narrowed. "You don't need to tell me everything, Hailey, but I sure don't need you to lie to me. I know there was something more going on over there than you ever let on."

I couldn't form any words as I stared across at her.

She gave me a tight dip of her chin, my silence an affirmation. "Good. Then we're clear about that."

Standing from the stool, she picked up her cup and rounded the island. She reached out and set a weathered hand on my cheek. There was so much love behind her touch that a wave of comfort rippled beneath the surface of my skin.

"It's time for your joy, Hailey, because I know you didn't have it in Austin. I see you struggling. Still trying to hide. But it's time to come out from behind it. Time to come out and shine. And believe me, it's going to be my pleasure getting to witness it."

Turning, she shuffled back across the kitchen and into the great room, heading for the hall that led to her room at the end. She paused to look back. "And if that comes in the form of a too-hot cowboy, then so be it."

Surprise hefted from my lungs. She had a way of leaving me speechless. Delving deep, dipping into the profound, before she turned right around and tossed snark right back in my direction.

Because I knew exactly which *too-hot cowboy* she was referring to. Too bad there wasn't a chance of it. Too bad no real joy could come from him. The man was heartbreak wrapped in a big, flirty bow. So easily doling out the devastation without a second thought.

Uneasiness quivered through me at the thought, something shaky in that judgement that I'd kept trying to cast. How sweet he'd been last Tuesday, offering himself freely, the words he'd given to my daughter, the way he'd whispered his sympathy to me, as if he might understand.

How could he, though? And how could I be so vile that I would even consider giving him the chance?

But the man had needled his way beneath my skin a long time ago, though it'd become stagnant in the years I'd been away, when I'd be quietly consumed by grief and sorrow and the regrets that built with each day that had passed.

Shucking it off, I took my own cup of tea and wandered into my room to get ready for bed.

I plugged my phone into the charger on the nightstand before I moved into the en suite bathroom. It carried the same theme as the kitchen, brown cabinets so dark they were almost black, the countertops a swirl of creams and browns and golds.

Tossing my hair into a ponytail, I washed my face then changed into a pair of silky teal sleep shorts and matching tank.

So yeah, teal was my signature color.

Massaging night cream onto my face, I wandered back out into my bedroom and sank onto the side of my bed. My attention drifted to the window, errant thoughts traipsing to the man next door.

Wondering if he was there or how he spent a Friday night.

I rolled my eyes at myself.

I knew full well how someone like Cody Cooper spent his Friday nights. Hell, it was likely how he spent most every night of the week. Giving someone all those smirks and teases and dishing out the type of pleasure I was most certain he had to offer.

I refused the urge to peel back the edge of the blinds to peer out—just to check—and I reached over and flicked off the lamp on the nightstand. I slipped under the plush covers and relaxed into the comfort of the mattress.

I thought I must have already been drifting to sleep when my eyes popped back open, the sound of my phone vibrating on the wood pulling me from the promise of blissful sleep.

Groaning, I reached out and grabbed it, and I squinted through the darkness at the message.

CC: You didn't even text to say goodnight. And here I thought we were friends.

My heart rate accelerated. A brimming of excitement and that clawing uncertainty that skimmed beneath the surface of my skin. A heatwave of warning.

The attraction that had never been extinguished through the years and the betrayal that gnashed at my insides for even giving it consideration.

I needed to put a barrier between us. Build a fifteen-foot wall.

The endeavor seemed doomed since he was in my face all the time.

Brow pinched, I tapped out a response, making sure to imbue all the accusation into it that I could muster.

Me: Are you watching my window?

His response neared instant.

CC: Tell me you weren't watching mine.

Me: I have absolutely no reason to be watching your window, Mr. Cooper.

I fired it back just as fast, my breaths coming a little too shallow.

CC: Such a sweet little liar. And I thought we established it was Cody? Cody, baby. Let me hear you say it.

How easily he tossed out the tease and the taunt. It wound around me in a knitting of greed. Another text came in right behind it.

CC: I've never been so good at hiding what I want, so yeah, Shortcake, I was watching your window, wondering when I was going to catch you sneaking a peek at me again.

The air fled from my lungs, the oxygen growing too thin. How many times had he caught me peering out the window toward his in the last two weeks?

The stupid impulse to seek him out coming back to bite me in the ass.

It suddenly felt as if the temperature had risen by fifty degrees. My skin grew sticky with sweat.

Feeling suffocated by it, I threw off the covers and sat up on the side of my bed.

The draw I felt toward him was mad.

He was arrogant and brash and every-single-thing that I didn't need in my life right then. My life was incredibly complicated, and it would be insane to toss another wrench into it.

More than that, it was our history that branded him as off-limits.

None of that seemed to make a difference, though, since desire was pounding through my bloodstream like the warning blare of a freight train.

Me: I can't help it if our windows face each other and I need to pull back the drape to make sure the window is locked. It doesn't mean I was looking at you.

CC: Is that right?

Me: That's right.

Lies.

So many lies.

> **CC: You think I don't feel those eyes on me? You think I don't know what you're imagining? You think I don't know what you need? I've been trying to ignore it for the last week. Can't do it any longer.**

My teeth grated.
Cocky. Freaking. Cowboy.
But there went that desire.
Sailing.
Surging.
Making me stupid as my fingers flew across the screen.

> **Me: And what exactly is it I need?**

I was asking for it. Just asking for it. A slew of messages came through, one right after the other.

> **CC: What you need is someone to show you how gorgeous you are, inside and out.**

> **CC: What you need is someone strong enough to hold you up so you can let go for a little while.**

> **CC: What you need is someone who knows how to bring you the kind of pleasure you've been aching for.**

> **CC: I can feel it radiating off you. How bad you need it.**

> **CC: An escape.**

> **CC: I'd fuck you so good, Shortcake.**

A wildfire raced across my flesh, and I couldn't breathe by the time I'd made it through them. My stomach coiled with the exact kind of ache he was describing, my thighs tingling and my core throbbing.

I couldn't formulate a response. Didn't know how to answer when every single one of the thousand words that spun through my head conflicted.

God.

I couldn't breathe.

Could barely even read when the next text came through.

CC: You want to see how bad I need you, too?

No.

I absolutely did not.

Me: Yes.

The response was out before I could stop myself.

A glutton on my knees.

I feasted on the picture that popped into the thread.

The image was shadowy. Grainy in the bare light that seeped in from the side. But it was bright enough that I could tell the man was laid out on a bed, wearing only a pair of tight black briefs.

Sculpted body and bulky, defined muscle.

Every inch of the man was chiseled and packed and rippling with the kind of strength that should be impossible. Ridges and caverns and grooves.

His flesh was littered in ink, though the designs were obscured in the duskiness, shrouded where he held the phone high.

But honestly, I couldn't focus on anything else, anyway.

My mind had glazed over at the sight of his cock pressed against the thin fabric of his underwear. The outline was perfectly defined and angled off to the side, his massive length stone, the bulging head barely contained by the waistband.

One second later, words followed it.

CC: That's how damned hard I am for you. What is it about you, Shortcake? What is it that's sitting in my memory like a shadow? Something haunting me?

It was Brooke.

It was Brooke.

The thought of her sent reality crashing back into the forefront.

This was wrong.

So wrong.

Frantically, I pounded at my phone to get out of the text app, hands shaking out of control, then I took it a step farther and held the button down to fully shut down my phone.

I couldn't be trusted with it.

Couldn't be trusted with whatever *this* was.

Because this?

It was dangerous.

Dangerous to my resolve.

Dangerous to my purpose.

Dangerous to who I was and who I wanted to be.

Dangerous to her memory.

And disregarding that memory?

It would destroy me.

And that meant I needed to stay as far away from Cody Cooper as possible.

Chapter Eleven

Cody

Mack's was packed like it always was on a Saturday night. The bar swollen to the gills.

The upbeat country band playing on the elevated stage at the very back of the cavernous building drew a slew to the dance floor that sat smack in the middle of the huge space.

Those who weren't shaking their thing were crowded around the high-top tables that surrounded the dance floor on three sides or were tucked into the secluded tables and low chairs that lined the walls. Others gathered in a horde around the two bars where the bartenders fought to keep up with the demand.

I shouldered my way through the crush of people who were making the best of their Saturday night, laughter and voices elevated, the vibe one of carelessness and letting go. One of chasing down a bit of pleasure.

Smokey vapor caught in the strobes of light that flashed from over the stage, twining and twisting as it climbed toward the soaring, arched ceiling before it disappeared.

I could almost taste the lust as I wound through that haze. Could scent it in the darkened atmosphere.

Any time I was here, which was pretty damned often if I was being honest, my pulse always beat a little faster. Body prepping for what the night might bring.

The thrill of the hunt.

Wondering who I'd end up going home with once last call was made and I stumbled out these doors to give myself over to the craving that never seemed to abate.

I always found a willing partner. A hot body who hungered for the same thing I did.

It was my release.

My gratification.

My living free and to the fullest.

The last couple weeks that feeling had been all off, though. The anticipation scraping with something I couldn't quite pinpoint.

An edge that blurred into confusion.

What bullshit.

I knew exactly what it was.

It was all about the woman who was close to driving me insane. Right out of my godforsaken mind. This heedlessness that I couldn't tame getting loose of its chains.

Wanted to kick myself in the damn head for sending that picture last night.

I'd fucking tried to keep it friendly.

The scrape with her father had reminded me why I had to.

But seeing her through the week had whittled that conviction down to shit.

And there I'd gone, pushing her in the direction that she kept saying that she didn't want to go.

Problem was, the way she looked at me told an entirely different story.

I'd nearly lost it when she'd gotten back from work yesterday evening. A crack running right down my middle when I'd seen the way she'd sat in the cab of her SUV staring out the windshield at the house as if she were coming home for the first time.

Like she'd finally stumbled on where she belonged.

Then she'd stepped out and I'd been slammed by her aura.

Floored by the sight.

So fucking pretty in that western outfit that it'd taken every ounce of willpower I'd possessed not to toss myself right over the railing to go striding for her, but there'd been no stopping the truth of my words from sliding out.

I'd always had a thing for cowgirls.

But with her? It was something more. Something that should send me running but instead had me contemplating foolish things.

I mean, fuck, this was Douglas Wagner's daughter we were talking about. Not that I blamed him, but the dude fucking hated me and could have me by the balls if he wanted to.

He was the one person who'd discovered what I'd been involved in.

A desperate man getting mixed up with corrupt people often had a catastrophic effect.

And believe me, it'd been fucking catastrophic.

I still had no goddamn clue how I'd walked out of the wreckage still standing. Still breathing.

And there I was, the fool that kept crawling back in that same direction.

I'd hit a breaking point last night when she'd flipped off her light and the window had gone dark.

Visions assaulted me.

Fantasies.

Ones of her on the other side of the wall.

In her bed.

Naked and spread out.

Fuck me, I wanted to disappear into the curves of that lush, tempting body.

Dive into the clear, endless depths of those eyes.

Fuck her out of my mind because the obsession I was forming was getting out of control.

But I knew that wasn't going to happen.

I didn't do attachments, and she'd made it more than clear she didn't want a fling.

I mean, what kind of scumbag was I? This was a mom, and she clearly wasn't up for messing around, and I was sending her half-fuckin'-nudes like a horny teenager who was hoping to get a nip shot in return.

But holy shit, would I like to get a good look at those tits.

Scrubbing a palm over my face to break up that train of thought, I angled through a group of guys who were getting rowdy tossing back tequila shots, and I wound around them in the direction where my crew always sat on the right side of the bar and up close to the dance floor.

They were already there, a riot of energy buzzing around them, their laughter just a little louder than everyone else's.

Paisley was holding court the way she always did, standing at the side of the two high-top tables they had pushed together, arms waving and demeanor animated.

She was all long white hair and over-the-top sass, wearing a white emblazoned tank that sparkled beneath the lights, red boots, and the shortest pair of cutoffs that I'd ever seen.

Her fiancé Caleb was sitting on the stool closest to her, basically drooling his ass off watching her.

Ezra was snuggled up with his girl, Savannah.

And my little sister, Dakota, was sitting on a stool, her back to me where she sat angled to the side with her legs draped over Ryder's lap.

It was Ezra who noticed me first. He lifted a plastic cup brimming with beer over his head. "Ah, there he is, the man of the hour."

Everyone turned.

A round of cheers went up, and my chest tightened with the welcome.

These were people who I'd do absolutely anything for. Lay down my life. Give it all.

Without paying attention, I cut through two chicks who were standing in the middle of the aisle, only then realizing that one of them was *familiar*. She ran a hand up my chest as I tried to squeeze past.

"Hey, Cody, is there a party tonight?" Her voice was all kinds of coy and interested.

I should be interested, too, but the thought of her soured in my stomach.

"Hanging with my family and friends tonight. If you'll excuse me." I shrugged her off as I took the last couple steps toward my group.

Ryder's grin glinted beneath the flashing of lights, asshole instantly catching the interaction. "Already scoping out who you're going home with tonight, I see," he taunted above the raucous din of the bar.

"Nah, man, just got held up in traffic," I punted back as I pulled the cap from my head and tossed it to the table.

He chuckled low just as Dakota swiveled her legs off him and hopped from the stool. She came beelining my way, and she threw her sweet arms around my neck.

"You're here! Congratulations!" she sang as she rocked me back and forth.

I hugged her tight.

Dakota was so much like our mother.

Fucking sweet and giving.

Kind and modest.

She poured that sweetness out on everyone she met, using her restaurant, Time River Market & Café, to share her love.

The entire town was better for it.

"Thank you, though you didn't need to throw another celebration. I think you've been celebrating me enough."

Aghast, she swatted at my shoulder. "There is no such thing as too much celebrating, Cody. We need to take the time to recognize everyone's achievements, big and small. And this one is big."

She squeezed my biceps like she was comparing the size.

She was right. It was big.

Astronomical.

Something I'd never imagined would come my way.

And somehow, I kept losing sight.

"We know what's big," I said, you know, just because it was me. It wasn't like I could pass up an opportunity like that.

"Eww." Dakota's nose curled.

"Your freaking head, that's what," Paisley piped in. "And now he's got money, too? Lord help us, he's not even going to be able to fit in the room."

I chuckled as I released Dakota and rounded the table to pull Paisley into my arms. I picked her up and swung her around a bit. "Don't worry, I'll make sure to come down off my throne to hang out with you suckers every once in a while."

I settled Paisley onto her feet and sauntered toward Savannah who was draped across Ezra's lap.

"Ah, if it isn't the gorgeous Savannah Ward. What are you doing hanging out with this giant oaf?" I gave a playful jut of my chin toward Ezra who had a massive arm possessively looped around her waist.

He grinned, all teeth, though there wasn't a brutal bone in the guy's body.

Ezra had one of those hearts of gold, the town Sheriff who did his best to make this a safe place for everyone. Good through and through.

"She doesn't want to be anywhere else than right here on my lap," he tossed out, pulling her closer and nuzzling his nose in the locks of her blonde hair. "Isn't that right, Little Trespasser?"

"That's right," she murmured back.

I wrangled her out of Ezra's paws and gave her an enormous hug. "Good to see you, Savannah. How are you feeling?"

She just found out she was pregnant a couple weeks ago.

"Amazing, honestly. I still can't believe it."

"All the good things coming to you," I murmured.

"Yes. The same as they're coming to you. I'm so proud of you."

Emotion tugged at my spirit.

This gratefulness that kept getting tainted by the memories I suddenly couldn't seem to keep at bay. "Thanks, sweetheart. Are you taking care of this guy?"

She peered back at Ezra, her expression soft. "Always, the same as he takes care of me."

"How are the kids?" Ezra had three kids from his previous

marriage. A marriage that I'd had no idea had been wrought with lies and betrayal and had come to a tragic end before he'd met Savannah.

Now, she and Ezra were raising them together, and they were going to add another. I was so happy for them.

"They're the best thing that's ever happened to me." Awe filled her voice.

"And I know they adore you, too," I told her before I released her and turned back to the table. I smacked my hands together. "I'm going to hit the bar. Can I get anyone anything?"

Standing, Caleb polished off his beer and set the empty onto the table. "Nah, man, we're celebrating you. First round is on me. What can I get you?"

"Surprise me."

"Someone knows my man has good taste," Paisley drawled, glancing at Caleb.

His gaze raked over her. "The best taste. I'm going to remind you of what that means later."

"I'm going to hold you to that." She dragged her fingers down the front of his shirt, gripping it in a fist at the bottom as she leaned in close. "Why don't you grab a pitcher of margaritas while you're at it? We have a few more coming."

My little sister waved the martini glass that swam with the last dregs of her favorite bright-pink concoction. "This girl needs another cosmo, too."

"Do I look like I have ten arms?" Caleb tossed out.

"I'll help." Ryder drained his whiskey and slammed it to the tabletop before he grabbed my sister by the back of the neck and kissed her hard. "Be right back."

"Hurry," she returned, voice breathy.

I scrubbed a palm down my face.

Bunch of loved up motherfuckers, the lot of them.

Ryder and Caleb disappeared into the fray, and Paisley hopped onto a stool, glancing between Savannah and Dakota. "So, like I was saying before Cody showed up, I haven't seen her in like eight years and haven't talked to her in six. We weren't besties or anything—"

"Good, I wouldn't want to have to stab her." Dakota spouted the razzing.

Paisley laughed. "Don't worry, Doodle-Boo, no one could ever replace you. But I think you both will really like her. There was something about her that always drew me in, probably since she loves horses almost as much as I do. She's a little younger than me and crazy beautiful. Super genuine and sweet. She'd moved away out of the blue, and I never got the whole story behind it, but I found out she was back, so I decided to invite her tonight. I didn't figure anyone would mind."

"Of course not. We're always excited to meet new friends. Family we didn't know we had." Dakota glanced at Savannah when she said that.

I swore, my sister always made the effort to ensure those around her knew how important they were.

Appreciation deepened Savannah's features, and she lifted her copper mug. "To family we didn't know we had."

"And you…" Paisley suddenly pointed at me just as I was sliding onto a free stool.

My brow lifted for the sky as I slung back in the seat. "Yeah?"

"I want you on your best behavior."

I let a smirk slide to my mouth. "Come now, Paisley-Cakes, I'm always on my best behavior."

I tossed the nickname my sister had called her for her entire life back at her. The two were ridiculous with the names they gave each other.

Eyes narrowing, she jabbed that finger harder in my direction. "And that right there is exactly the kind of *behavior* I don't want to see. I haven't seen Hails Bells in years, and I don't want you chasing her off by trying to get into her pants."

Hails Bells? Case in point. But damn, I had to admit, it was kind of cute.

I lifted both hands in surrender. "Now why would I go and do that?"

"Oh, I don't know, because she's stunning and you are…you." Paisley gave a snarky tip of her head. "You'll turn on all that charm and take off with her, and then she's never going to talk to me again since you'll ditch her before the sun comes up."

"I would never—"

Dakota cut me off with a disbelieving laugh as she polished off the last gulp of her drink. "Cody Cooper, don't you dare say you aren't guilty of that every single weekend."

"Well, I can promise you I'm going home alone tonight." It flew right out like truth.

Because I truly wasn't in the mood. Normally, I'd already be making the rounds, scoping out the crowd, waiting for someone to catch my eye.

"Really?" Paisley challenged, her brow shooting for the sky.

"Really." I said it like an oath.

Signed and sealed.

Dakota reached out and placed her palm on my forehead. Clearly, she was lacking any real concern since she giggled when she asked, "Are you sick, big brother?"

I swatted her hand away, only half annoyed when I said, "I am not sick."

Though maybe I really was coming down with something because nothing was sitting right.

My stomach coiling in knots and my thoughts residing in a place they completely shouldn't be.

"I don't know…you feel a little…feverish." My sister drew the jeering out.

I rolled my eyes while Dakota's own brown pools danced, though I could tell she was trying to actually look deeper, delve down into the parts of me that I kept buried beneath the smiles and easiness. Down to the places I'd never let her see.

She'd hate me if she knew.

"I see you all invited me out to give me a hard time rather than actually celebrate my accomplishment," I said, keeping the roughness out of the retort.

"Who else is such an easy target?" Savannah asked.

Ezra chuckled from where he'd been silently watching the

exchange. "Yeah, and we all know the way you *like* to celebrate. What's up, brother? Someone finally knock you down a peg?"

Yeah. Someone had knocked me down a peg.

Right onto my fucking knees.

But I sure as shit wasn't going to admit that.

"Hell, no. I just feel like blessing my family with my complete attention tonight." I set my palms out like I was offering a gift.

Amusement rolled through Ezra's expression. He wasn't buying it for a second.

"Oh, there she is." Paisley's shouting pulled my gaze back to her. She had her arm lifted overhead and was waving it frantically as she bounced on her stool. "Hails Bells, over here! Over here!"

I followed her line of sight, through the roiling crowd that writhed within the dusky shadows of the bar. Lights strobed, faces flashing in time with the music that thrummed over the speakers.

I caught a glimpse of the movement, of the woman who was making her way through the crush. Flickers of lush blonde hair woven with honey and maple. The hint of a profile, cheeks full and chin sharp.

The pucker of a sexpot mouth.

Energy flash-fired, careening straight through my nerves.

It took her one more second to fully break through.

I realized I hadn't caught Paisley's friend's actual name. Hadn't made the connection that it was very likely Paisley had been out at Wagner Ranch sometime in the past, even though I didn't know the two of them had ever met.

But there she was.

Hailey Wagner standing there in this short as fuck, glittering silver dress that clung to every luxurious curve of her body.

No doubt about it.

The woman's shape was the definition of my perfection.

My fingers twitched, and I didn't know how I remained sitting as my gaze gulped down the sight of her.

The dress's neckline plunged deep between her breasts, those enormous tits barely concealed in narrow swaths of fabric that were held up by thin spaghetti straps that bared soft shoulders. My stare roved, riding down the curve of her legs to the pair of sky-high ankle boots she wore.

Also glittering silver.

The woman was a motherfucking beacon.

I could hardly get my lungs to cooperate as I was struck with a lightning bolt of heat.

Blood boiling in my veins and sweat slicking my skin.

Instantly suffering from that fever I'd just denied.

Hails Bells.

I was in trouble.

Chapter Twelve
Hailey

"OVER HERE! OVER HERE!" PAISLEY'S VOICE WAS STILL carrying when I fumbled to a stop three feet away from her party. Two high-top round tables had been pushed together and a bunch of stools were arranged around them. Paisley sat on the opposite side of where I stood, along with a few other people I didn't know.

But it was the man sitting closest to me that made me feel as if I'd slammed face-first into a brick wall.

My eyes colliding with that golden, fiery gaze that staked me to the spot.

Breath punching from my lungs as if I'd gotten the wind knocked out of me.

Cody Cooper.

The sight of him was sweet mayhem where he was rocked back in a stool.

Delicious as always, wearing a tight black tee that stretched across those broad, imposing shoulders. Tatted arms crossed over his chest, stubble thick on his indecently handsome face.

His tongue stroked over his bottom lip, and a rush of that desire he'd gripped me by last night trembled through my body.

His words.

That picture.

It didn't matter that I'd avoided my phone at all costs today, refusing to even turn it on until after noon. It was emblazoned in my mind.

Carved into my consciousness.

All that rugged, masculine beauty that I recklessly wanted to reach out and touch.

And there he was, a solid, hard manifestation of every fantasy I'd given myself over to for a few reckless seconds last night.

I was snapped out of the trance by Paisley who was suddenly in front of me and throwing her arms around my neck. "Oh my God, I can't believe it's you! I wasn't sure if you were going to show or not, and I thought I might need to have my Sheriff friend over here do some reconnaissance and get your new address..."

She tossed an errant hand at a man sitting next to Cody.

"Okay, sure," she rambled, "I know that is illegal and all and it would put his job on the line, but it would absolutely be worth it so I could go to your house and drag your gorgeous ass over here. And when I say gorgeous ass, bullocks and ball-sacks—Look. At. You."

Edging back, she held me by the shoulders and blatantly inspected me. "I mean, you were so pretty before...but like kind of cute and adorable, you know? But now? You are a freaking smoke show. What are we even supposed to do with you?"

Self-consciousness slicked through me while at the same second I glowed.

Paisley Dae had that power about her, and God, it felt amazing to see her again.

Even though right then I was a little terrified of the cost.

She knew Cody.

Why would I have thought otherwise?

I should have assumed it. They were both from Time River, and it wasn't like most didn't stumble into their neighbors at some point in a small town this size.

But I'd never imagined they'd be friends.

"This is coming from you?" I finally managed when I got my emotions far enough under control that I could speak.

I just needed to remind myself that Cody didn't matter.

He was an acquaintance.

A memory.

And like I'd told my father, I could handle him.

Paisley tossed back a curled lock of silvery hair. "Well, I do admit I look pretty amazing tonight, but you in that dress and those boots? I'm afraid this place might go up in flames. Combust. Go boom!"

She made an exploding motion.

Only I wasn't the one who was lighting a fire.

It was him.

Because there was no mistaking the flames licking softly across my flesh. So palpable I could have sworn they were physical.

I peeked to the side, no resisting the lure.

Cody sat there without saying anything, though he didn't need to.

All that masculinity he was radiating spoke for itself.

She yanked my hand and started to haul me to the table. "Come meet everyone."

I fumbled on my too-high heels to keep up with her, Cody's aura inundating me as I staggered deeper into his space.

"Everyone, this is my old friend I was telling you about…Hailey Wagner, better known as Hails Bells."

She exaggerated a wave like she was showcasing a prize before she started tossing out introductions. "This is my bestie, Dakota."

She pointed at a woman who was maybe a year or two older than me. She had brown hair that was the color of toasted chestnuts pulled into a high ponytail, and she wore a floral dress.

She didn't hesitate to stand to pull me into a hug. She squeezed me tight in the sort of welcome I wasn't expecting, oozing the type of warmth you could sink into.

"It's so nice to meet you, Hailey. Paisley was just telling me how much she adores you and is excited you're back in her life."

"It's great to meet you, too." My chest felt both heavy and light, buoyed, while a whisper of loss pulled in the deepest recesses of me. I'd been so hesitant to open myself up to relationships. To friends after what I'd done.

After what I'd caused.

The pain of it almost too much to stand beneath.

But is that what Brooke really would have wanted? For me to remain stagnant? Frozen in the mire?

Paisley continued, pointing as she introduced me to Savannah and Ezra who were engaged and expecting a baby and as adorable as could be before she gestured at Cody. "And this is Cody. Cody Cooper. Dakota's older brother."

Ah.

There was the connection.

It was strange how one person could inhabit so much of your mind, could take up a page in your history as if they held the utmost significance, and you knew next to nothing about them.

I swore Paisley shot daggers at him.

The hulk of a man just smirked in return. The sight of it tumbled through my belly, and a ripple of intensity rolled through the air when he sat forward, as if he'd single-handedly taken possession of the atmosphere.

"No need for introductions, Paisley. Hails Bells and I are acquainted." He drew out the last, a scrape of seduction and amusement.

Paisley's attention swung between us. "You've met?"

"I worked at her father's ranch way back when, and I somehow got lucky enough that now we're neighbors."

He said it at the same time as I blurted, "He's just doing some work at the resort where I'm running the stables."

Paisely gasped. "You're working at Cambrey Pines? That's why we're here…celebrating Cody and the big job he's doing right now." Then her eyes narrowed. "Wait, and you're neighbors?"

"Right next door." That grin was in full force when Cody issued it.

Paisley pointed at him, words slashing like razors. "Don't even think about it."

She turned back to me. "I already warned him I'd stab him if he gave you any trouble. He's to be on his best behavior tonight. Aren't you, Cody? Even if you two already know each other."

I got the sense it was always like this between them.

Teasing.

Easy.

Comfortable.

Except there wasn't a thing that felt *comfortable* when Cody set one of those big hands on his chest. "My very best behavior."

The words were low and rough and pulsating with that over-the-top arrogance.

A warning blared at the back of my mind.

Yeah, I knew what his type's best behavior entailed. The evidence was currently sitting on my phone.

"Famous last words," Dakota tossed out with a chuckle.

Her attention swept to me. "Don't believe a word that boy says. He might be cute, but there are nothing but lies that come out of his mouth."

"Wow, even my sister has no issue busting my balls, and on a night that's supposed to be celebrating my amazing achievements." He didn't seem all that offended. "And don't worry, Hailey here seems to know exactly what she wants."

His focus was fully on me when he said it.

The flecks of red in his eyes simmered beneath the shadowy light.

A wave of uncertainty ripped through my consciousness.

Unsure if I should stay or if I should run.

I'd resolved to keep as far away from him as possible.

And here I was, drawn into his gravity again.

He patted the stool next to him, that smile turning sly. "Come over here, darlin', and sit next to me. I promise I don't bite."

Dakota was right. The man might be cute, but he was nothing but a liar.

⌒⋇⌒

Laughter and voices rang over the loud din of the bar, and the upbeat tempo of the country band thrummed in the air. It spun the energy into something alive and palpable.

A buzz that held fast and covered you whole.

I took another drink of my margarita. The sweet and sour concoction slid down my throat and pooled in my belly. Each sip chased away a little more of the nerves I'd been riddled with since the second I'd come in and found Cody sitting at the table.

Maybe I should have been concerned that an easy comfort glided through my veins.

Concerned I'd settled into the mood.

Into the casual support of this group who cared so deeply for one another that their lives had become intrinsically intertwined.

But I wasn't concerned because it was a gift to witness. To get to experience it.

People who loved each other this way.

Some related by blood.

Others not.

It didn't seem to matter. The connection was there. Solid and real and forever.

Unbreakable.

It was strange to feel a part of it, as if maybe I'd been sitting here all along and I wasn't meeting most of them for the first time. The way they included me as if I weren't an outsider but an integral piece of the building blocks of who they'd become.

From where she sat next to me, Dakota knocked her shoulder into mine, making sure to include me in the conversation since they'd all been sharing stories about their kids.

"Wait until you meet little Evelyn," she said, referring to Caleb and Paisley's daughter, a little girl I'd learned Caleb had gotten custody of after his sister had been killed a couple years before. Now, he and Paisley were raising her as their own. "She is the sweetest little thing you'll ever meet. I bet she and your Maddie are going to be the best of friends."

"Of course, they're going to be besties," Paisley shouted over the din. "How could they not? Evelyn is obsessed with horses, and when she finds out her horse Mazzie came from your father's ranch? She's going to lose it. We have to get them together next weekend. Why don't you bring her to our place for a playdate?"

Warmth spread through my chest. "She would love that."

"Ah, I bet she would." The grumbled words brought attention back to the man who sat beside me. The one I kept trying to ignore.

Impossible when I was getting consumed by the heat he emitted.

Leaning forward, he rested those tattooed forearms on the table, and he swung those golden eyes in my direction before he spoke to the rest of the table. "Little Madison is nothing but a button. Cute as can be. Can only imagine she and my Evie-Love will hit it off. First time I met her, she was out at the park hunting for friends."

My stomach twisted in a fit of that attraction that I couldn't tame.

The man might have been wicked hot, but I thought most dangerous was how sweet he was proving to be.

I had to remember to keep up my guard. Barriers. The most Cody could ever be was a friend. I'd just have to get used to the attraction.

"We've moved twice in the last three months, so she is definitely itching to find a friend," I added.

"Then you have definitely come to the right place," Paisley said. She turned to Savannah. "You should bring Olivia, too. Actually, bring all the kids. We'll make a whole thing out of it."

"I'm game." Dakota lifted her glass.

"It's a party then," Paisley said.

With a slow smile, Caleb slung an arm around Paisley's shoulders. "This one is always looking for an excuse to throw a party."

"That's because this life is worth celebrating," she shot back.

"That's right," Savannah agreed.

"Speaking of..." A sly grin quirked up on Paisley's face when a cocktail server showed up at the table with a tray of shots. "We are definitely celebrating tonight. I ordered shots."

"Are you trying to kill me?" Dakota whined as the server began to pass out the little glasses filled with a yellow liquid and rimmed in sugar.

"A lemon drop never hurt anyone," Paisley said, nudging one her direction.

"Yeah, all except for my pride," Ryder grumbled as he wrapped a tattooed hand around the tiny glass.

Paisley sent him a glare. "You need a little sweet in all that sour."

Ryder tugged Dakota closer to him, and he ran his nose along her jaw. "Believe me, I have all the sweet I need."

Cody groaned next to me. "There you go with those dirty paws all over my sister."

I tried to contain a giggle.

It was cute how Cody kept trying to maintain a façade of annoyance that his best friend and his little sister had gotten together, though I couldn't feel an ounce of true irritation rolling from him whenever he mentioned it.

It was warmth, instead, his love stark and obvious, even though I was pretty sure he thought he was pulling off that casual indifference he wore like a brand.

"Give me a few minutes, and they're really going to be all over her." Ryder prodded it, needling it in.

"Do you see what I have to put up with?" Cody grumped as he elbowed me softly. A streak of fire ripped down my spine.

"Brutal," I told him, glancing his way.

I shouldn't have.

I should have remained with my attention focused on the rest of the group. Because he was so close, and there were only two inches that separated our noses.

Every sharp, rugged angle of his face right there, the warmth of his breath mingling with mine.

His scent all around.

Spice and cedar and earth.

My fingers itched with the need to reach out and trace every inch of his face.

His brow.

His jaw.

His lips.

My brain was right back on that image he'd sent me yesterday, my throat going dry and my thighs clenching with the need I shouldn't feel.

A tease of a smirk played over that delectable mouth, like he knew exactly what was running through my mind.

"To friends…"

Paisley's voice pulled me from his trap, and I tried to clear the ball of need stuck in my throat as I reached for a shot glass.

"To family," she continued. "To this group of amazing people. People I could never express just how thankful I am to have them in my life. And to Cody, of course."

She winked at him, teasing him like he was an afterthought, even though it was clear they all adored him.

A grin spread over his face, the mountain of a man ridiculously gorgeous as he sat back in the stool.

Everyone leaned in to clink their glasses together, Savannah's a virgin since Paisley refused to leave anyone out. "To us! And to Cody, of course."

Laughter rang as everyone tossed back their shots.

Everyone except for Cody who shifted his focus my direction.

I could feel those eyes on me as I pressed my lips to the sugared rim before I tossed the lemon drop back.

Could feel them as I swallowed the intensely sweet concoction down, one that left a burning wake of fire in its path.

Could feel them as a full-body shiver tore through me.

I squeezed my eyes closed as I was hit with a thousand different sensations.

The rush of alcohol swept through my system and spun my head a fraction, a buzz washing me through, but I had to wonder if it had more to do with the man sitting next to me than anything else.

Intoxicating.

Overwhelming.

All-consuming.

His voice was rough when he leaned in to whisper in my ear. "Can't help but wonder if that is your exact expression when you come. Because you, darlin', look like ecstasy."

Shock popped my eyes open.

I attempted to play it off like I was unaffected. Like he didn't make me quiver with this lust that I'd all but forgotten existed.

Too bad every inch of me was trembling when I turned to him.

The world faded around us, the sound of the room a drone as I stared at him.

"I thought I told you that you'd do well to look somewhere else?"

"I can't help it if you're the most interesting thing in the room. I'm finding it hard to look away."

I searched around in myself for defenses and found them lacking.

Reserves close to depleted.

Still, I tried, though the words were wispy. "The only reason you think that is because I'm a new face. Don't worry, I'm sure you'll get bored soon enough."

He was just...studying me. This strange emotion crawled through his features that I couldn't put my finger on.

I glanced at the shot in front of him to distract myself from the intensity. "Aren't you going to drink that?"

"Nope. I have someone special to get home."

My teeth raked against my bottom lip. "And who might that be?"

"I think you might know her well. Gorgeous as hell, as sassy as she is sweet, shares strawberry shortcake with strangers under a tree when she sees they're having a bad day."

He said it nonchalant.

Like it didn't matter. Like we hadn't shared that moment. Like it hadn't changed everything.

Though there was something in his gaze that went deeper.

Sucking me under.

That remembering right there, pulling between us like a dream.

"Who said she needed a ride home?" It was raspy.

Protectiveness ridged every angle of his being. "Tell me you didn't drive here."

"No. Lolly dropped me off, and I planned to get an Uber home."

"You realize there are like two Uber drivers in Time River and there isn't one who's going to want to drive all the way out to Hendrickson?"

I blanched.

Right.

This wasn't Austin, and I hadn't fully thought that through.

"Exactly as I thought. I do need to get someone special home."

I could feel myself drifting toward him. Getting caught in the web of charm and looks and this feeling deep inside me I couldn't shake.

Something old and precious.

Twisted and wrong.

"It's my jam!" Paisley's shout broke into the trance Cody held me under. "Get those booties on the dance floor, my babes!"

She hopped off her stool as the band jumped into a new song.

I felt half disoriented when I tore my attention away from Cody, no way to float back down to reality.

Paisley pointed at me. "I told you to wear your dancing boots, Hails Bells. Let's go show them what that means."

Dakota slipped off her stool, and she looped her elbow in mine and gave me a tug. "Just go with it. She's not lying when she says she will drag your butt out there."

"Because what else would a good friend do?" Paisley hiked a shoulder.

Taking Savannah by the hand, Paisley pulled her over to where Dakota and I stood. Without hesitation, she looped her elbow through mine and her other through Savannah's, making the four of us a chain. "Leave poor Hailey here with your brother drooling all over her? I don't think so," she tacked on the tease.

Giggling, Dakota turned to whisper so only we could hear. "Um, yeah, I think my brother might be enamored by his new neighbor."

Paisley started weaving us onto the dance floor. "He's like a freaking dog. I was worried he was going to start humping your leg."

"I'm not really sold that she'd mind all that much." Savannah angled around, smiling too wide, like she'd been sitting there reading every salacious thought I'd had running on a circuit through my mind.

I shook my head. "Uh, no...I'm not in the place for a fling right now."

Dakota tucked my arm a little closer, leaning in as she whispered conspiratorially, "Then stay far, far away from my brother."

Right.

He was a player.

I knew it.

I knew it from then, and I knew it now.

Hell, he'd made it clear in those texts last night.

And I was the fool who couldn't stop myself from looking over my shoulder to find that molten gaze staring back.

Chapter Thirteen

Cody

"**D**OWN BOY."

I turned to find Ryder grinning from where he sat like a tatted king on his stool. Dude was the smuggest asshole I knew.

"No clue what you're talking about."

Disbelieved laughter rolled from Ezra, and he sat forward and propped his elbows on the table. He took a pull of his beer as he eyed me. "Seems clear who it was that knocked you down a peg or two. Tell me you didn't already try to hook up with her?"

Caleb turned his attention to the dance floor where the girls had gotten in line with about half the other people in the bar.

This was Paisely and Dakota's favorite thing.

Line dancing.

Letting go.

Giggling as they moved through the choreographed moves and tossing every single care aside.

They'd taught Savannah since she'd come into our group last fall, and she was keeping up just fine. But it was the woman stuck between Paisley and Dakota who stole my damned breath.

The sight of that glittering silver beacon out there running straight to my dick.

Every movement she made was smooth.

Sexy as fuck.

Hips and shoulders rolling, each shimmy and twist roiling with rhythm and seduction.

It was her face that got me, though. The way she was laughing with the rest of the girls, easy and without all the restraint that'd been radiating from her when she'd first stumbled upon the table.

Like she'd realized in an instant that she fit. That she meshed, like she'd always belonged.

I liked it.

Fuck, I liked it.

Too bad she was the last fucking woman on earth I should be catching feelings for. I shouldn't—not with anyone.

But with her?

Unease rippled my spirit, slithering through that ugly place inside me that whispered of every mistake I had made.

Every sin I'd committed.

"You don't actually think he *didn't* try to hook up with her, do you?" The razzing came from Caleb. "Dude probably tried to climb straight through her window."

If he only knew...

Ezra chuckled, half his attention on us and the other on his girl. "She's probably already had security bars installed."

"Haha, fucking hysterical, assholes. Besides..." I shrugged like this was no different than any other woman I'd been interested in for a night. "I didn't know she had a connection to Paisley. No biggie. I'll find someone else to keep me occupied."

Ryder's gaze narrowed. "Yet you just promised Paisley you weren't going home with anyone tonight. Wonder why that is? Seems like a whole one-eighty coming from you."

I went for indifference. "Work was brutal this week. I'm pretty wiped, if I'm being honest."

"Code for he's having trouble getting it up." Caleb flashed his straight, white teeth.

Chuckling, I shook my head. "This coming from the oldest of our crew. Wouldn't be rubbing that in too deep, brother. You don't know when that's going to come around and bite you in the ass."

"Doubt that's going to be a problem when it comes to Paisley. I'll be ninety and still wake up hard for her."

Ryder gagged. "Gross, man. I did not need an image of your shriveled up dick in my head."

Laughter rolled through our table, that easiness gliding through.

Our regard was out on the raucous line of four women.

Each of them fucking knockouts.

Paisley was hamming it up the way she always did, adding extra flair with every turn, and Dakota laughed nonstop as she fumbled around considering she'd been tossing back those pink frilly drinks the whole night and she was feeling *extra light*.

Savannah kept continually peeking over at Ezra like she couldn't wait to get back to him, and Hailey…Hailey was laughing, too.

Though she had a hand wound in those honeyed locks, twisting up the length to get it off her neck.

She spun, her backside fucking spectacular, hips swishing from side to side.

And her calves.

Fuck me.

They were thick and muscled and rock hard, emphasized by the height of her boots.

Why was that so damned hot?

I had the intense urge to get her alone, take her by the ankle, and run my tongue all the way up the back of her leg until—

The smack to the back of my head came from out of nowhere. "Yeah, that's what I thought," Ryder said.

"What? She's hot. You can't blame a man." I said it casual. Just like me.

"She's gorgeous. No doubt about that." Ryder took a sip from his tumbler.

He was only stating the obvious. His eye would never stray from my sister. Still, something irrational tugged hard at my gut. A possessive thread that could never be mine.

The upbeat song ended, and the mood shifted to slow, the new tempo instantly dragging the atmosphere into something erotic.

Ryder drained his whiskey and slammed the empty to the table as he pushed to standing. "That's my cue."

"Yup," Caleb agreed at the same time as Ezra stood.

From behind, Ryder reached out and grabbed me by the shoulder. He leaned in so only I could hear. "Judging by the way you're itching like a fiend, I'd say that's your cue, too."

Couples were pairing up, the lights dipping to dark, a bare glow that filtered the air into a gilded haze.

Caleb, Ezra, and Ryder strode through the crowd, and they headed in the direction of their girls who'd already turned like they'd felt them coming.

While Hailey seemed surprised for a second as everyone broke apart.

Disoriented.

Having so much fun she was jarred by the shift as the rest of her friends got swooped up by their men.

Discomfort rolled from her for a single beat, and she peeked side to side, before she came to a quick decision and started to angle through the bodies, though she was winding through toward the back of the bar rather than in my direction.

I was already on my feet, moving that way.

I cut her off about two feet before she made it off the dance floor.

I pinned the biggest grin to my face as I pulled her straight into my arms, one arm locked around her waist and the other taking her by the left hand. "Where do you think you're going, gorgeous?"

Surprise billowed from her on a gasp, and I was struck with the sweetness of her presence. With the heat of her body. With everything that this girl possessed that was driving me straight out of my mind.

Nothing seemed rational when it came to her. Just this innate feeling like I needed to get close to her.

Her surprise dwindled into uncertainty that was all fronted by the fire that lifted her chin. "What do you think you're doing?"

I started to move in time with the music, leading her along the floor in an easy two step.

"Dancing with the prettiest girl in the club," I told her.

Crystalline eyes rolled. The blue depths tossing diamonds beneath the slow strobe that rolled over the crowd. "You are nothing but a flirt, Cody Cooper."

"Ah, a Cody coming from your mouth. I like it."

"I bet you do." Something both timid and teasing touched the edge of her decadent mouth.

Greed fisted my stomach.

"I'd probably like to hear it in a different context even better, though you can be sure that you'd still be in my arms."

Her exasperation was lighthearted, and the girl peeked up at me as she tried not to laugh. "You have no filter, do you?"

"Well, I can promise you that picture wasn't *filtered* last night."

Redness climbed from her chest and up her throat, splashing her full cheeks in this pretty glow that tugged somewhere behind my ribs. "You are a whole lot."

"You bet I am." I winked before I spun her. When I pulled her back close, I sobered. "I want to apologize for sending that picture. It was inappropriate after you'd made it clear you didn't want to go there with me."

Blue eyes dipped, those lashes so long as she looked down and off to the side for a second before she returned her gorgeous face to me. "I nearly begged you to show me."

"But you regretted it," I pressed, not even phrasing it a question.

Her nod was slight. "Wanting you makes me feel…" She winced as her confession trailed off, a murk rising up to clot out the brightness she'd been glowing with. Phantoms of memories swirling around her in a cloak of darkness.

I wanted to press her, but she beat me to the punch. "My life is…"

She paused, unsure before she looked up at me with this sadness that stabbed me right through the heart. "It's complicated, Cody. And I don't do one-night stands, and I sure don't have time for a fling. But I think I'd really like to be your friend."

I shifted her, taking her by the chin and tilting her face upward. "I think that could be arranged."

The riot of need that blazed around us was probably less than friendly, but it could be ignored.

Controlled.

Beat into submission.

At least I fucking hoped so since I nearly came unhinged when this cowboy prick came sauntering up like she and I weren't having a moment, all kinds of cocky as he barely glanced at me and claimed, "Excuse me, brother, I'm gonna have to cut in."

Really fucking brave considering I was two times his size and I'd snap him like a twig.

Every instinct in my body screamed to make a claim.

The idea of someone else's hands on her made me feel like I was the one who might *snap*.

But Hailey and I had already established a boundary.

Made a pact.

And I really needed to get away from her if I was going to maintain it.

So, I sent her a half encouraging half regretful smile as I released her and stepped back.

A piece of myself felt like it was getting hacked off when I did.

I guessed that was always what caring about someone had been about.

Sacrificing.

Putting their needs before your own.

It wasn't always intuition for me, only showing its face for those who were closest to me, but I think I got it right then.

The truth that this girl could come to mean something if I let her.

She had then, hadn't she? But I'd tucked the memories of her right into my album of mishaps. My corruption and delinquency. Did my best to forget her when she had touched my spirit in a way no one ever had before and no one had since.

Funny when our interactions had been…innocent.

All except for that energy that had thrummed between us. A connection that had forever strained taut even though I'd believed I'd snipped it.

I started to turn on my heel to give her some peace, only Hailey reached out and wrapped one of those sweet hands around my wrist to draw me back.

Fire raked like claws down my back.

"Wait," she said, her voice barely breaking above the music that blared from the speakers.

Dickface stepped in front of me, anyway, trying to block me out. It wasn't until then that I noticed he was sloppy drunk, the way he pushed in and wrapped an arm around her waist and started to rock her back and forth, attempting to guide her deeper into the crowd.

"I don't feel like dancing."

The prick turned her so she lost hold of my wrist.

"Sure you do, baby," I heard him say.

Regret clapped me across the face. I never should have stepped away from her.

In a heartbeat, I was right behind him. My hand clamped down on his shoulder because he wasn't going to get away with this bullshit.

I leaned in real close to make sure he got the message. "The lady said she doesn't want to dance. Respect that, yeah?"

"Screw off, asshole," he slurred through a laugh like he wasn't about to get torn to shreds, turning back to Hailey whose expression had tinted with disgust.

Motherfucker.

Rage billowed, and I gritted, "I'd suggest you step away from her before you don't have the capacity to do so."

I'd hoped to keep my voice even.

Instead, the words whipped out like bullets. Cracks of fucking lightning that reverberated through the bar and would send a wise man running.

124 | A.L. JACKSON

This bastard?

He wasn't wise in the least.

Because he turned and threw a fist.

It came at me from out of nowhere, catching me so off guard that he clocked me in the mouth.

That wasn't what bothered me, though. That tiny sting that was brought on by a split lip.

The problem I had? He'd caught Hailey in the jaw with his elbow when he'd done it.

A swill of shock and pain rushed the river of those eyes, and her hands shot up to protect her face, but there was no protection for this little prick.

Because I fucking *snapped*.

Chapter Fourteen

Hailey

A BLUR BROKE OUT IN FRONT OF ME.

One second my eyes were wide with the surprise of getting hit in the jaw, and the next, the guy was on the floor and Cody was on top of him.

Cody cocked back an arm and pulled the guy up by the neck of his shirt with the other.

"You hurt her, motherfucker? You're going to pay for that." Cody didn't wait for an answer before that fist flew. It smashed into the guy's nose.

Blood burst at the connection.

A shriek ripped out of me, and I felt frozen to the spot as Cody started to pound the guy's face.

A storm of fury whipping the chaotic atmosphere into disorder as Cody threw his fist again and again.

Once.

Twice.

Three times.

Screams broke out and the couples split apart, a scattering of feet and bodies across the dance floor to get away from the mayhem while a whole slew of new people rushed forward, making a circle around the mess Cody had just thrown himself into.

The music clanked off, and his shouts ricocheted through the cavernous room.

"You piece of shit. You hit her. I'll end you for that."

He hit him again.

Finally, the sense came back to me, and I surged forward and pleaded his name, "Cody!"

I thought to jump on his back to stop him from being the stupid one, only Ryder came busting through the crowd, a dark cloud that descended in a flash. He wrapped both arms around Cody's waist and hauled him back onto his feet.

Cody tried to break free and go back for the jerk who was moaning on the floor, covering his face with his hands as he cried, "That asshole broke my nose."

"Yeah, and I'm going to break a whole lot more." Cody struggled against Ryder. "Let me go, Ryder. He hit her. This dickbag hit her."

"Cool it!" Ryder shouted, yanking back harder before he leaned in and said something in his ear that I couldn't make out.

Cody finally shook himself off just as Ezra came running up. "What the hell happened here?"

"This drunk fuck hit Hailey in the face with his elbow." The accusation was abraded gravel.

"I didn't touch her." The guy writhed on the ground, and Ezra glanced back at Cody and gave a tick of his head. "Get out of here. I'll take care of him."

Cody hesitated, clearly contemplating diving back for the jerk.

"Now, Cody." Ezra's voice was a low warning, and I knew if Ezra hadn't been there, Cody would likely be heading to jail right about then.

Paisley came through the crowd. Shock colored her expression when she saw the scene, and she rushed over and slid her arm around my waist. "Oh my gosh, what happened? Are you okay?"

"I'm okay." I was barely able to say it, and I was suddenly thankful she had an arm around me to keep me steady when Cody shifted and took two steps in my direction.

His bottom lip had a small cut, and a droplet of blood was already drying into a scab. Every line of his face was riddled with ferocity, with an apology, with the truth that he didn't regret it all except for the worry that he might have hurt me in some way.

Ezra dragged the drunk guy onto his feet and pushed him through the crowd, and the band struck back up and people hit the dance floor like this was a routine event, which I supposed in a bar like this it probably was.

People getting unruly and rowdy.

Alcohol suppressing inhibitions.

In my experience, it was always when true personalities came out, usually amplified, good or bad.

But nothing about this felt routine to me.

It felt like a shift.

A crack right down the middle.

"Get out of here, Cody." Ryder repeated what Ezra had instructed, though it was urgent with a warning.

I stood surrounded by my new friends, flanked by Dakota and Savannah, and Paisley's arm was still solidly hooked on my waist as the crowd moved around us like we weren't standing still in the middle of them.

Cody's attention slanted to me.

That apology grew deeper.

Severe.

Stark.

Before he shook his head like he'd come to some conclusion, like he'd suddenly seen himself as the problem, and he turned away from us and started to carve himself through the disorder that roiled on the floor.

"I'll get you home," Paisley told me, just as Ryder roughed a frustrated hand over his face and said, "I'm going to go check on him."

I swallowed around the thickness in my throat. "No, let me."

A frown cut into Paisley's brow. "Are you sure? He's a lot when he's upset. You might want to let him cool down."

"I'll be fine," I promised.

In reluctance, she wavered, before she dipped her chin. "Text me later?"

"I will."

"Okay."

I weaved through the crowd, heading in the same direction Cody had gone.

Through the toiling bodies that writhed on the dance floor and the groups who'd grown thick around the tables.

I kept weaving through, following the wake of heat.

I pushed out the main door and into the summer night.

The deafening volume coming from the bar was cut in half the second the door clanged shut behind me.

A few people dotted the packed parking lot, their voices distant but distinct with the quiet that echoed in the air.

My attention drifted to the right, to the bluster of energy that pulsed, heavy and hot.

Cody stood facing away, a giant in the night, eyes on the ground and his shoulders heaving in spastic quakes.

I took a couple tentative steps toward him. My voice was barely a whisper when I spoke. "Are you okay?"

The shake of his head was harsh, and I could almost see the aggression still lining his muscles. All the easygoing casualness he normally wore had gone completely missing and in its place was a frisson of volatility.

"It's not me I'm worried about, Hailey."

"I'm completely fine, Cody. You didn't need to do that."

He peered back at me.

Golden eyes flashed beneath the dingy light that hung from the side of the building. "You don't think I'm going to stand aside and let someone I care about get hurt, do you? I never should have let you go to begin with."

My chest panged.

I never should have let you go.

But he would. He'd already made it clear. And standing there right then made me sure him walking away would break me.

Still, I pushed out the jagged words. "It was just some jerk who had too much to drink. He barely caught my chin. I'm completely fine. It's you he attacked, though I doubt very much he anticipated the retaliation you inflicted."

Sighing, Cody scrubbed one of those big palms over his face. "I lost it, and I'm sorry for that. I just…"

He trailed off like he didn't know what to say. Or maybe he was scared to admit it.

"I ruined the night," he settled on.

"You didn't ruin it. It's one of the best nights I've had in a long, long time."

"Until the end."

"It's not over yet." I attempted to play it a tease, but it came out all wrong, and I knew immediately where his mind had gone. That unflinching gaze flamed, and my stomach twisted, and God, this was getting complicated.

"I think I'm ready to go home, if you are?" I managed.

A rough chuckle skated up his throat. "I doubt much I'm welcome in Mack's right about now. I'm lucky Ezra was here."

"He knows you were protecting me."

"He also knows I can be a bit of a hothead." He looked away for a beat before he returned his attention to me. "But I won't regret standing up for you. It's just the way I am, Hailey. I protect those I care about. I take care of them. Whatever the cost."

A warning was woven in the words, and I knew this man went much deeper than the careless smiles and smirks. I thought if I looked close enough, I might be able to see the ghosts that gathered around him, phantoms that played in the night.

I was worried every single one of them might be a partner to mine.

"You say that like it's a bad thing," I murmured.

"It is if you knew the lengths I'd go."

That warning had gone dark.

I wanted to press him. Push him to open up. But the door clattered open behind me, and I shifted to look at a group of people who came stumbling out, laughing and breaking the moment.

When I turned back, Cody had stretched out his hand. "Come on, let's get you home."

Tentatively, I walked toward him, taking one step, then two.

The power of his presence grew the closer I came.

A shiver rushed through me when he pressed the hand he had extended to the small of my back and began to lead me toward the parking lot.

Heat blazed at the bare connection.

A fire that leapt.

I tried to keep my breathing even, but I was pretty sure there was no way he'd miss the way my pulse was speeding.

The bar grew quieter and quieter the farther we traipsed down the row of vehicles, and the darkness gathered thick. He led me to where his truck was parked about halfway down, his boots crunching in the loose gravel as he guided me to the passenger's side.

The lights blinked when he clicked the locks, and he opened the door. "In you go."

A short gasp left me when he reached down and curled a hand around my side to help me into the high seat.

A low growl echoed from behind me. "That dress should be illegal, darlin.'"

I settled onto the seat, trying to ignore the path of his attention. The tingles that rushed and raced as his gaze traveled over me where I was propped in the seat of his truck, hungry eyes riding down over the glittering fabric and fluttering like fingertips down my bare legs.

"I think it's pretty." Why I answered, I didn't know.

"Oh, it's pretty, all right. Now get yourself buckled because I'm going to shut this door and pretend like I don't want to set you back on your feet, turn you around, and push that skirt up around your waist so I can get to the deliciousness hiding underneath."

Before I could say anything, he slammed the door in my face.

My mouth dropped open because this man truly had no filter.

He rounded the front of the truck, and I couldn't look away as he went. He was right back to oozing all that cool as he strode to his side, tossed open the door, and hopped in like he hadn't left the ground shaking under my feet.

I was swept in it, his aura as he buckled himself and pushed the button for the ignition.

Spice and cedar and earth.

He put the truck in reverse and pulled out, then stopped as he shifted into drive, right before his attention swung to me. A deep frown carved into his brow when he saw the way I was just sitting there staring at him, my hands under my thighs to keep myself from doing something stupid like reaching out to touch him.

This man would destroy me. Chew me up and spit me out.

What Lolly had said was undoubtedly true.

The *chewing* would be so nice.

But it was my conscience I would never survive.

My jaw unlocked again when he suddenly leaned all the way over the seat, the oxygen gone as he pushed into my space, his unrelenting stare pinning me to the spot when he reached around and pulled the buckle across my front.

Surprise jutted my chest.

Crap. I'd been too busy ogling him to take the time to remember to buckle myself.

I couldn't think straight.

Couldn't move.

The buckle clicked into place, and he never looked away when he rumbled, "I guess I have to do everything myself, don't I?"

There was a gleam to those eyes then, sparks of gold and flickers of light right as that smirk edged up at the corner of his mouth. He was nothing but a toil of charm and mayhem. An easy, tempting danger that would be so easy to slip into.

I hoped I wasn't panting when I peered over at him as he pulled out of the parking lot and out onto the road.

This burly, mountain of a man who drove beneath the cover of night.

"You seem to be taking care of me a whole lot," I murmured into the wisping darkness of the cab.

He sent me a wicked grin. "It's my pleasure to take care of you, Shortcake."

Suggestion flooded the words.

Cocky Cowboy.

A country station played softly from the radio, and the stars were heavy and dense where they hung from the blackened expanse of sky, surrounding us like a fuzzy blanket that we might be wrapped in too tightly together.

We made it through Time River and took to the twisting, two-lane road that wove through the forest and led to Hendrickson.

Soaring evergreens hugged us on each side and the stars glinted overhead, the engine a low hum as we traveled. We were held in this tranquil peace that still had knitted me into disorder.

We chatted about inane things that still seemed to matter.

How my first couple weeks of work had been and vice versa. The project he'd been surprised to win the contract to, how he'd tossed in his bid thinking it'd be a long shot and how proud he was of his team, and for the first time, there was a deep humbleness that penetrated his voice.

I couldn't look away from him the entire trip. My intent focused on his face. On his jaw and his brow and his nose, his strong profile that I thought would forever be emblazoned in my mind.

I cherished every shift and intonation of his voice.

Rapt on his words.

His flirtiness.

His kindness.

"You're a beautiful man, Cody Cooper," I finally whispered as he was making the left into our neighborhood.

Inside and out.

I realized he let very few people see the inside, but I thought maybe he'd allowed me to all those years ago.

He glanced my way, and a dark chuckle rolled up his masculine throat and flooded the space. "You should probably stop looking at me that way if you want to remain friends, Hailey. Not when the only thing I want to do is reach out and touch you."

His face was illuminated by the bare light that glowed from the exterior lamps of the houses we passed, and those eyes raked over me where I'd turned to press my back to the door so I could see him better.

Greed filled the cab. So intense that I felt it coil through the air and crawl across my skin.

Like those hands were tapping out a rhythm on my flesh.

Exploring.

Needy and hot.

I pressed my thighs together, hoping it might be enough to assuage the ache that had been building all night, desperate for the type of pleasure I knew only a man like him could give.

The first person who had ever made me long.

Ache and want.

And I wondered…

Cody groaned and his jaw ticked, his knuckles whitening as he tightened his hold on the wheel. "Yeah, you really need to stop looking at me that way."

He pulled to the curb in front of my house. Here, it was dark, his face in the shadows, his massive body a silhouette. My eyes devoured the outline of his perfect shape.

His big body roiled in sharp restraint, this constant wave of strength that kept battering against me.

He continued to hold onto the steering wheel like it might be the one thing that kept him contained.

The only thing grounding him when the world had floated away from us.

Each thirsting for what we knew better than to chase, but right then, after everything that had happened tonight, all rationale was erased.

"I don't think I can stop." There I went—a fool who was begging for it.

Heartbreak.

Because this man had already broken me a long time ago, and he didn't even know it. Self-reproach writhed, a murmuring that howled from the abyss of my misdeeds and mistakes, though the shout of it was drowned out by the need that howled.

Every muscle in his body flexed, a bristle repression and a rush of greed. "I'm not sure I can give you what you need, Hailey."

"You told me last night you knew exactly what I needed."

His tongue stroked out over his lips, and that energy swelled.

Rising up from the depths to consume.

My thighs pressed together again, and his gaze dropped to the action. I squirmed beneath the weight. Beneath the potency that lured me in his direction.

"That's right. You need to come." The words were harsh. A rough scrape of seduction.

"Just once. Tonight."

I could handle that.

Could handle the shame.

The regret that was sure to come.

But right then, the only thing that mattered was getting to experience what it was like to have this man's hands on me.

Then I would go to sleep and pretend it was all a fantasy.

And tomorrow...tomorrow we'd be friends.

A disbelieving scuff blew between his plush lips.

He clearly was on to me. He knew exactly how my brain had processed through everything. How I was rationalizing this disastrous choice.

"And you're going to be fine with it come morning? And here I thought we were going to just be friends?" Irony filled his tone.

"We are." It barely made it free on a breath. "This is just...tonight."

That's all it could be.

"You sure about that?"

"Yes." It wobbled on the tremoring air.

He released his seatbelt, and he pushed a button on his door that sent his seat gliding all the way back. He patted his lap. "Then get that sweet ass over here."

"Right here?" Incredulity jetted from my tongue. I didn't think I'd even fit.

"Right here, darlin', because if I take you to my bed, I'm going to want to keep you there."

My fingers were shaking out of control, and I fumbled to release my seatbelt, my limbs trembled, unsteady with the way those eyes were locked on me.

Intent.

Fierce.

They flamed in the darkness.

Golden sparks.

A fire that lit all the way down in the depths. In that hidden place where I'd always kept him.

He waited like he fully expected me to change my mind.

I crawled to him, over the soft leather that felt cool to the touch. I had to look ridiculous, so awkward in the confined space.

"So fuckin' gorgeous, you on your knees crawling for me." Cody rumbled it like he'd heard my insecurities. A low reverberation that skated far and wide.

I shifted to straddle his lap, keeping up high on my knees as my fingers sank into his shoulders. It was tight where I was wedged between him and the steering wheel, the space enclosed, his temperature close to a thousand degrees.

The skirt of the dress bunched up high, and it barely covered the very top of my thighs.

At the brush of our bellies, he grunted, and a big palm came to curl around my side.

My stupid heart thrashed against my ribs so hard that I knew come tomorrow morning it'd be completely battered.

His hand smoothed up and down my side, both calming and inciting, and his other wound up in my hair as he stared at me.

"What is it about you, Hailey Wagner?"

He searched me in the shadows, eyes flicking all over my face, as if his thoughts were racing back to that time, everything about it digging too deep.

Reaching into the places I needed to keep him from.

The blood careened through my veins, and I lifted higher on my knees.

Electricity crackled when my chest brushed against his.

"Touch me," I begged.

The hand in my hair tightened. "Where's it you want me to touch you, darlin'?"

I wanted to tell him everywhere.

That I wanted his hands and his mouth and that body on me, except I'd lost the capacity for speaking when he angled my jaw back and pressed his mouth to the sensitive flesh of my neck.

He kissed there, up and down the column of my throat, lips suckling and tongue licking along my pulse point.

Heat streaked down my spine, a tumble that pulsed and spread, stretching out to saturate every cell.

Desire lit like a spotlight behind my eyes.

His hand cinched down on my waist, and he dragged me against his body. The throbbing, sweet spot between my thighs rubbed at the stony planes of his abdomen.

The most embarrassing sound got loose of my throat, and my fingers sank deeper into his shoulders. One big hand slipped around to my bottom and splayed out to cover an entire cheek.

He guided me, rocking me up and down, and his enormous cock that I'd been blindsided by last night hardened to steel beneath our movements. Pressing huge and heavy at his jeans.

My hand slipped down his muscled chest, the black fabric stretched wide over his bulging pecs, before I glided south over his trembling stomach. I eased back enough so I could get to the button of his jeans.

The coarse chuckle he released was needy and pained, and he grabbed me by the wrist and drew my hand back to his shoulder. "Only thing we agreed on was me touching you, and I think you might need to hold on for that."

"You don't want me?" It gasped out, my thoughts disoriented, need so intense that I couldn't process anything but the desperation to feel him inside me.

Filling me full.

Taking me over.

"I think it's plain just how damned bad I want you." He ground my center against his dick. "Already told you last night how bad I do. But I don't want to complicate things."

Right.

He didn't want to complicate things.

I should probably be concerned that I felt very, very complicated right then.

But he was right, if we were going to wake up tomorrow and just be friends, then this needed to be a quick release.

This wasn't intimate.

It wasn't anything but feeling good.

I started to tell him that I only wanted to touch him, but my mind stopped functioning when he smoothed his hand down my leg to my knee before he rode back up, though this time his hand slipped beneath my dress when he got to the hem. He pushed it up higher until it was completely bunched around my waist.

I thought to be self-conscious. My thighs thick and trembling where I straddled him, my legs completely bare.

I thought of looking out the windows to make sure no one was watching us. But I was too enraptured by the growl that rolled up his throat, by the way that ravenous gaze slid over my body.

"How's it I have a Goddess sitting on my lap?"

Every inch of me quivered and rocked.

An earthquake.

He nudged me up a fraction, and he dragged the tip of his thumb over the satiny fabric of my underwear.

Sparks flashed, and he'd barely touched me.

"Look at you...needy and wet."

I choked over the tightness that bound my throat. "Did you expect me not to be?"

"Oh, I expected you to be. I could smell you..." He ran his nose down the slope of my neck before he kissed across my collarbone. "How fuckin' bad you need it."

He nudged my underwear aside, and he dragged his thumb deep between my lips.

I gasped at the sensation.

At the heat.

At the flames.

I writhed and whimpered, not even caring that he probably thought I was pathetic. The mere brush of the tip of his finger nearly setting me off.

"Fuck. If I thought that dress should be illegal, then those sweet little sounds coming out of your mouth should be a felony."

He rumbled it, running his thumb back and forth, barely brushing over my clit with each pass.

"Cody."

"That's right, honey. That's exactly what I want to hear. My name on your tongue. Give me one minute, and you'll be chanting it so loud that I'll have to gag you."

"Cocky Cowboy." It wheezed out as he rolled his thumb over my throbbing clit.

A chuckle reverberated from deep within his chest, the man enjoying this far too much. He had his face tipped up toward mine, our lips a breadth apart.

I was breathing his air.

The scent of him all around.

That spicy aura drugging me, leaving me desperate for a taste.

"Kiss me." I begged it.

Something flashed through his expression.

Terror it looked like.

Fear or regret.

But it was gone before I could process it, and surprise was squeezing from my lungs when he had me pressed against the passenger door so quickly that I hadn't even realized he'd moved.

My mind spun with the disorder that was this man.

A riot.

Peace.

Complete anarchy.

A sweetness that was so hazardous that I felt the truth of it twist like a dull knife in my guts.

Because in an instant, I was spread out for him, one leg bent and pressed to the back of the seat and the other draped out across the floor.

Cody leaned over me, gold eyes glinting in the muted dregs of light.

He took me by the knees and spread me wider. "Look at you. So fucking gorgeous you could make a man weep."

I arched from the door where I was propped, unable to process it, the sensation and the need and the electricity.

The man enthralling.

Entrancing.

Knocking me free of any sense.

Inhibitions slayed.

He planted one hand on the seat and rose up higher, his attention intent on my face as he slipped his hand between my thighs.

He'd never seemed so enormous than then.

Hovering over me like a leviathan in the cab.

A shield of protection.

A shroud of depravity.

He drove two fingers inside me, and my walls clenched around them. I gasped at the fullness.

"Yeah, knew you'd have a sweet little cunt," he rumbled.

He started driving his fingers in and out as he rolled his thumb over my clit. Swirling and pressing and spinning me into a frenzy.

My hips started to move, jutting up to meet each thrust.

He was right. It took all of a minute for me to start chanting his name, pleasure winding and curling and tightening to a boiling point.

"I—" I couldn't speak.

Emotion broke free of where I'd kept it trapped, shackles that vied to be released. Warmth spread, a dark cascade of memories that wound through the recesses of my mind and penetrated to the spirit.

Did he remember?

Did he know?

"You feel that, Hailey? Just my fingers and you're lighting up like the morning. A little fire that's been begging to burn."

"Cody."

He drove his fingers faster, that golden gaze locked on my face, refusing to look away.

Bliss gathered, a rising tide in the cab. A tornado erupting from the bottom of the sea. A whorl of energy. An unfurling of need.

My fingers sank into his shoulders as I levitated beneath the power of his touch, sure I was going to drift away, lost to the flood. "Cody."

"Do you feel it, Hailey? Do you get it yet? How I see you? How gorgeous you are, inside and out? Do you know how bad I've been dyin' to touch everything that you are? All this beauty that's been tapped? Let go, darlin', the way you've been needing to."

His praise swarmed me, the gruff of his voice spurring me farther, as if he truly knew how badly I needed to hear it. The way I'd been living without it for so long. In a darkness where I'd remained hidden. He pushed up higher, hovering right over me as he pumped deeper, his thumb working magic, but I thought it might have been the expression on his face that threw me over. His words tipping me right over the edge.

"That's right, Shortcake. Let me feel you come all over my fingers. Let me hold your pleasure...just this once."

Ecstasy splintered me apart.

A shockwave that barreled through my body.

I writhed and jerked as sensation raced, every nerve ending firing and alive.

Wave after crashing wave.

Cody stroked his fingers in time, leading me through, and I thought the orgasm might go on forever as he eked out every drop of pleasure that he could coax from me.

Ridge after rising ridge.

Trembles rocked me, and I shivered as the intensity flickered then ebbed.

Cody's jaw was clenched the whole time, his body rigid, though his eyes went soft while I sat there panting and trying to catch my breath.

"I was right…it was the exact same expression when you come. Don't think I've seen anything so beautiful as that."

"I already told you that you're the beautiful one."

My fingers quivered with the need to trace every rugged, handsome line of his face.

Commit him to memory.

So I gave in and let my fingertips trail the contours and lines of restraint that hardened his stony features, before my hand glided down his neck and over his chest until I was cupping him through his jeans.

The man so big.

Heavy and hard.

"Shortcake," he warned, his stomach jolting as I stroked him over the fabric.

"You got to touch me…it's only fair."

A growl got free of him, and harsh rasps panted from his mouth as I jacked him over his jeans. He burrowed his face in my neck, groaning before he forced himself back, his hand hot as he curled it around my wrist to stop me.

Only he lifted it between us, hesitation brimming from him before he brought the inside of my wrist to his lips.

A buzz burned at the connection.

So damned sweet that I thought my chest would cave.

And God, I had the urge to beg him to kiss me again. To push this farther. For him to take me right there.

But I think we both somehow knew where that would lead. This already felt far more significant than it was supposed to. Like merging spirits and twining hearts.

He affirmed it when he said, "You touch me like that, and I promise, we aren't going to be friends tomorrow."

That was all it took for the guilt I'd tried to suppress to spring up from the recesses of my mind, from the dark corners where grief lived. For a beat, I squeezed my eyes closed like I could protect myself from it, and I silently whispered, *Oh, God, please forgive me*, to that ghost that lingered in my head.

It was wrong, doing this. Letting him touch me this way. Leave it to Karma that it would feel so damned good.

Punishment.

A tease.

Everything that I couldn't have.

Sitting back on his knees, Cody readjusted my dress and pulled it down to cover my thighs.

I still felt wholly exposed.

He canted me one of those easygoing grins like he might be immune to the energy that crackled in the cab. "Let's get you inside, Shortcake. It's late, and I'm betting that sweet little Button is going to have you up at the crack of dawn."

Then he pushed away, popping open his door and sliding out. He strode all kinds of casual around the front of the truck, while I was barely able to get my body to cooperate enough to sit upright by the time he swung open my door.

Confounded.

Body weak and sluggish while my mind started to spin.

He held out the same hand that he'd just touched me with, and the man had the audacity to wink.

"This didn't happen," I finally said, voice still haggard.

I needed to erect a wall. Guard myself from the feelings that were threatening to sprout. Hell, they'd been there all along, and I'd just drenched them in life-giving water.

The edge of Cody's mouth ticked all the way up, that smirk back in full force. "Whatever you say, darlin.'"

Reluctantly, I took his hand and let him help me out, and he reached out to steady me when I swayed the second my feet hit the ground. "Whoa, there. I've got you."

He shut my door and guided me onto the curb, and he rested his hand lightly at the small of my back as he guided me up my driveway and around the sidewalk that led to the porch. He followed me all the way to the door.

I didn't realize how badly my hands were shaking until I fumbled with the zipper of my little purse, how I couldn't stop the quaking of my insides when I retrieved my key and tried to get it into the lock.

Cody reached out and set his hand on mine, his movements controlled as he helped me slide the key into the lock and turn it. The latch gave, the knob twisted, and the door creaked open to the darkness of my house.

I went to step inside, only Cody's mouth went to my ear as I passed. "You might want to pretend that didn't just happen, but believe me, Shortcake, the sight of you coming is going to be imprinted in my mind for the rest of my life."

Then he backed away, stuffing his hands into his pockets and wearing one of those flirty grins, and said, "See you tomorrow...*friend.*"

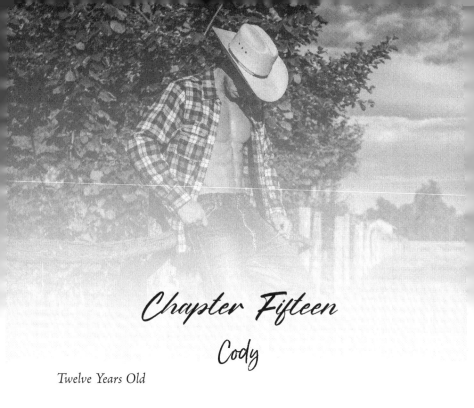

Chapter Fifteen

Cody

Twelve Years Old

"BEAT YOU BY A LANDSLIDE, SUCKER!" RYDER SHOUTED AS he jumped onto the bottom step of Cody's front door stoop. Cody came barreling to give a shove to Ryder, pushing him off the step and planting himself there, cracking up as he claimed, "Doesn't look like you won to me, now, does it?"

"Ah, you jerk!" Ryder pushed him back, hard enough to send Cody toppling to the grass. "I totally got here first, and you know it. You're such a cheater, Cody."

Cody grabbed Ryder's arm and sent him falling, too, and in an instant, they were wrestling around, the race forgotten in favor of being the one to get the pin. It didn't take much for Cody to get on top, his arm across Ryder's chest to keep his back glued to the lawn.

Ryder might have been crazy fast on his long, skinny legs, but Cody was at least double the size of his best friend, so in wrestling, Ryder wasn't close to being his match.

Cody shouted, "One. Two. Three," as he smacked his free hand in time against the ground considering it only took one of them for

Cody to keep hold of Ryder, counting down as Ryder thrashed below his hold, struggling to get free.

"Pinned." Cody boomed it. He jumped onto his feet and threw his fists in the air, pumping his arms as he showboated his victory. "I am the champion."

Ryder kicked out, catching Cody at the ankles, dropping him right to his knees on the ground. That time it was Ryder's turn to howl with laughter. "Got you, asshole."

"Freaking cheap shot."

"No different than the *cheap shot* you took. I totally kicked your butt in that race."

Cody couldn't help but smile, and he climbed to his feet and stretched out a hand to help Ryder pop onto his feet. "Like I even had a chance of keeping up with you. Pretty sure when you get on the track team, you're going to break every record ever set."

Ryder shrugged a little. "Maybe. At least you're allowed to play football. My mom said no way because I'm gonna get crunched."

"I woulda protected you," Cody said, swiping the dirt off his pants since his mom scolded them every time they came in the house dragging in mud, and the last thing Cody wanted was his mom working harder than she already did.

Cody was bummed Ryder wasn't allowed to be on the team, but they'd already tried to talk Ryder's mom into it, and she wouldn't budge.

"It's fine. I'm going to be going to Seattle to visit my cousin Caleb, so I would have missed a bunch of games, anyway."

Cody threw a light punch to Ryder's shoulder. "Lucky ass."

Ryder shrugged again, smug, saying, "Don't need to be jealous," as he tossed open Cody's front door.

They were struck with the scent of sugar and dough and warmth.

Ryder inhaled, his black eyes going wide. "Chocolate chip cookies. My favorite."

Dakota was always in the kitchen, baking up a storm, and Cody had half a mind that the only reason Ryder came over was to get a taste.

Case in point: Ryder beelined across the living room and disappeared through the arch to the kitchen without looking back.

Grinning, Cody trudged down the hall toward the bedrooms and dumped his backpack on his bedroom floor.

He stepped back out into the hall to head for the kitchen, though he paused, unease skittering over his skin when he heard muffled sounds coming from his mom's bedroom.

Soft sobs that were buried in what he was sure was a hand.

A ball of rocks lodged at the base of his throat, and he quietly edged that direction, pausing where his mom's bedroom door was barely cracked open. He peeked in through the slit and saw his mom sitting on the side of the bed holding onto a piece of paper, tears streaking hot down her face.

Sadness blasted him, like a furnace he was standing next to right in the middle of the summer, and that spot in his chest pressed hard. The spot that kept getting bigger and bigger every time he heard his mom crying like this.

He pushed open the door, and the old hinges creaked.

His mom's head popped up, and she swiped frantically at the moisture soaking her face like she could hide that she'd been crying.

But Cody knew.

He could hear her at night.

Could hear her during the day when she thought no one was listening.

Or maybe he just felt it. Sensed it down in that place where he'd tucked that promise that he'd made his father.

He crept up close to his mother. He already knew what she was looking at. The rest of them were spread out on her mattress.

Bills and bills.

Lots of them marked in red.

"I'm fine, Cody. Go on and give me a minute."

His mom's face was splotchy and red, the color of her eyes almost as drab as the brown of her hair. It made his stomach sick that she looked...old.

Like the years were going too fast.

"Stay right here, Mom. I'll be right back."

"Cody," she called after him as he hurried out of her room and into his. He dropped to his knees on the ratty carpet and looked under the dresser where he kept the box. He grabbed it and jogged back into her room.

He lifted the lid. "There's a hundred and fifty dollars in here."

He'd been mowing lawns for the last year and saving up. It was supposed to be for a new bike, but he already had one, and he knew his mom needed this money way more than he did.

It was selfish to keep it for himself.

Grief curled across his momma's face, and she cried harder. "Oh, Cody, my sweet, sweet boy. You don't have to worry. I'm going to figure this out. It's not your responsibility."

His father's voice echoed through his mind.

You're a good boy. Take care of your momma and your sisters.

"I'm going to take care of you, Mom. Always."

Sorrow blistered, and she set a shaking hand on his cheek. "Cody. I'm your mom and I'm the one who's supposed to take care of you. I'm sorry you saw me like this. It's not a big deal. I've got it covered. I just…got a little stressed."

He glanced down at the sheet she'd been holding.

It was the sheet he'd brought home from football practice with the cost of the uniform. He was supposed to bring the money to tomorrow's practice.

His stomach sank.

Hit the floor like a big boulder.

Because he knew what he had to do.

Chapter Sixteen

Hailey

"**M**OMMY, MOMMY, MOMMY!"

An avalanche of excitement collided with my slumber, a violent jostling of the bed that jarred me from sleep.

From where I was lying face down and wrapped around a pillow, I cracked open an eye to find Maddie waving her arms in the air and her little feet bouncing on the mattress a foot away from my head. "You have to wake it up right now because me and my Lolly is making you the best breakfast you are ever gonna eat in your whole life because Lolly said today is extra special."

I tried not to wince at the stabbing of light spearing in through the window, and my voice was craggy when I asked, "What's so special about today?"

"She said you are finally earning a reputation." Maddie flapped her arms so hard I thought she might take flight, and I groaned and buried my face back in my pillow.

Crap.

Had Lolly known I was out there with Cody last night? I couldn't even allow myself to contemplate it. My behavior risky. Verging on treacherous. I did my best to cram the surging of emotions back down. To keep them contained.

Deteriorating into a puddle of panic over my actions last night did not seem like the best way to begin the morning. But it was right there, bubbling beneath the surface.

Fear.

Guilt.

All mixed with the wash of warmth that skimmed across my skin as my mind flashed to the memory of the way those golden eyes had watched me last night. The way he'd touched me. The way it'd felt.

How he'd felt against my hand.

I squeezed my eyes against the assault of it.

One time.

It was one time.

And I was chalking it up to a fantasy.

I couldn't allow myself to dip my toes any deeper into the treacherous waters I'd already been waist deep in last night. I could already feel the sharp scrape of shame dragging across my conscience.

Maddie reached down and yanked at my hand, trying to haul me straight off the bed. "Come on, Mommy! It's already eleven and it's almost afternoon and you are a lazy butt."

"What?" I shot upright. "It's already eleven?"

My attention bolted to the clock on my nightstand.

Eleven o' one.

Crap. I hadn't meant to sleep that long. Had planned on being up first thing in the morning and acting like last night had never transpired.

Maddie moved to get directly into my line of sight. "It was the time Lolly said I had to wait to before I was allowed to wake you up, but it took one whole minute to get all the way in your room, so I'm very sorry I'm late."

Inhaling a deep breath, I tried to gather my nerves.

To focus on my daughter.

On what was important.

And that definitely wasn't the man next door.

The sweet smile Maddie gave me was full of love and belief.

The impact of it dumped directly into my chest.

A squeezing of devotion and loyalty.

A consummate reminder that she was the reason.

My purpose.

I reached out and tucked a wild lock of her warm blonde hair behind her ear. "I'll be out in a second, okay?"

"Okay, Mommy, but you have to hurry. Breakfast is already all done, and it's going to be my second breakfast and you can't miss this one." The words poured from her mouth as she jumped back to her feet, waving those arms again before she hopped off the side of the bed.

She raced across my bedroom and out the door, untamed curls flying behind her as she shouted, "She's hurrying, Lolly! Pour her a cup of coffee because you know she is gonna need it!"

Affection bound my chest, and I blew out the strain and forced myself to toss off the covers and get out of bed. I tiptoed to the bathroom, gasping a little as a tremble of last night's greed vibrated through my body each time my thighs brushed.

It wasn't like I was sore or tender, but I could still feel the markings of Cody there. Like he'd scored himself on my body.

Written himself deep with those massive fingers.

And there I went, spiraling again.

I flicked on the light and stared at my reflection in the mirror. My hair was matted, knotted and mussed, and my skin was still flushed.

God. I doubted I'd ever be able to erase the man from my consciousness.

But that'd been a risk I'd been willing to take.

The selfishness I'd given into.

The need to feel him once.

It was a need I'd carried for so long. Now that I'd sated it, I prayed it would finally begin to fade.

I splashed cold water on my face and twisted my hair up into a haphazard twist, then I inhaled a steeling breath and walked out into the great room like nothing had changed.

Lolly watched me from where she was pulling biscuits out of

the oven. A cunning glee gleamed in her eye. "Well, good morning, sunshine."

"Good morning. You shouldn't have let me sleep so late. I guess I really was tired after the long week of work. Sorry about that."

There.

The perfect excuse.

Lolly chuckled, and her brows lifted in suggestion as I slipped onto a stool at the island across from her.

"I take it you found a ride home last night?" she asked.

I gulped. "Yep, got an Uber. No big deal."

"Hmm…that Uber sure looked familiar. A big, shiny truck fit for a big, hulking man."

Crap. Crap. Crap.

I sent her the best glare that I could find. "Tell me you weren't being nosy and spying on the neighbors again? Because I was in a car. A little white car. An electric one. I was home by eleven. You must not have heard me come in. The car was super quiet. Stealthy. You know, like me."

It came out a muddled ramble, cracking on the end, and I awkwardly pointed at myself with both thumbs.

Yeah, I was the worst liar ever.

Amusement shook Lolly's head as she transferred the steaming hot biscuits onto plates then doused them with sausage gravy, the scent sweet and savory filling the air.

My stomach rumbled.

She knew they were my favorite.

"Well, that's too bad." She slid a plate in front of me then winked. "I thought you might have worked up an appetite."

"Gettin' a reputation, Lolly?" Maddie peeped as she clambered onto the stool next to me, her little elbows propped on the island and her grin beaming at both of us.

"That's right, little one, I thought your mommy might be earning a reputation." She placed a plate in front of Maddie, then picked one up for herself and started around the island. "But apparently she doesn't know how to have any fun."

I tried to hide my breath of relief, only she paused at my side just as she was rounding the island. Reaching out, she rubbed her thumb on a sensitive spot where I realized it was raw from Cody's scruff. "Only I think you might have a little reputation...right here."

All the craps.

Lolly was never going to let me live this down.

⌒⋆⌒

"Mommy, watch me!" Maddie climbed the ladder to her slide for what had to be the hundredth time. We'd been out back all afternoon, soaking up the sun, relaxing, playing, enjoying this freedom we'd been given.

I sat on the top step of the back porch, watching my child, my chest stretching full with the hope of this life.

With the hope that we could leave the past behind. That we could flourish here. Find the true joy of safety and security.

Of love and devotion.

The chains still rattled at the back of my mind, a constant threat, but I knew this was the true risk I'd had to take.

The one that was worth it.

I couldn't allow fear to reign. Couldn't succumb to the pressures that had been given.

The bright blue of the day had faded into a misty hue of pinks and grays, and the sun slipped far behind the trees, the night barely creeping up on the cloudless sky. A single star blinked to life, and the air had cooled a fraction, enough that we'd left the screen doors open to the house.

I'd done my best throughout the day to ignore the lure I could feel emanating from the house next door. To ignore the way I could feel his big body moving through the space, as if each step he took within his walls sent a bolt of seismic activity into the ground and trembling into me.

Which was insane and obsessed, and I was not that girl, so I'd done my best to push all thoughts of one Cocky Cowboy out of my mind.

I inhaled a deep breath, holding in the joy that surrounded me as I watched my daughter get to the top of the slide. "I'm watching you," I called.

"Good. Don't even look away for one single minute or you're gonna miss it. Count 'em down, my Lolly!" she shouted to my grandmother who was reading a book from a rocking chair on the far side of the porch.

Lolly was happy to oblige. "Three, two, one, go!"

Maddie threw her arms high as her little body flew down the slide.

"Look at you go!" Lolly whistled.

Maddie planted her feet when she hit the bottom, angling her arms back like she was sticking a dismount in gymnastics class. "What's my score, Mommy?"

"A 9.9, at least."

"Whew. I knew it was a really good one. Did you see how fast I went?"

"So fast," I told her.

"Like a rocket, right?"

"Even faster."

"One more because I have to get a 10." She darted around to go for the steps again.

That was right when the doorbell rang, echoing from within the house.

"Are you expecting someone?" Lolly lowered her book, which was one of her favorite smutty romances, to look at me from over the top.

A tiny bolt of unease rippled through. "No. You?"

"Unfortunately, I can't say I have any hot dates on the books. Though maybe you're about to get yourself one." She grinned, and I shook my head, getting ready to tell her to drop the pushing since she'd tried to corner me twice during the day to get the *dirty deets* from last night, her words, not mine, when the doorbell went off again, twice in a row.

Huffing, Lolly arched a brow. "Someone's impatient."

A frown pulled tight between my eyes, that unease lifting, and I pushed to standing. "Watch Maddie for a second?"

"Won't look away," Lolly promised.

I entered through the back screen door and hurried across the house to the front. The exterior light had just flickered to life, illuminating the front porch, though I couldn't see that anyone was standing on the other side of the screen.

Disquiet clamped around my chest, slowing my steps as I edged forward, my mind starting to whir.

It's nothing, it's nothing, I silently chanted. I had absolutely nothing to be afraid of.

Except it was fear that smacked me across the face when I took the last step up to the screen door and caught sight of the man who lingered just off to the side, facing away with his hands planted on his waist.

Fear that drummed my heart and thinned the air, the oxygen becoming so thick I inhaled it like an oil slick.

Pruitt was here. Standing on my front porch.

Sickness curled in my stomach and bile climbed up my throat.

But he didn't get to control me any longer. He had no bearing on my happiness. On my joy. On my daughter's safety.

I refused to be afraid of him, which was kind of comical since I was terrified.

But I wouldn't let him see it. Wouldn't let him wield his manipulation.

So, I flicked the lock and lifted my chin as I stepped out into the descending night and prayed to God my knees would hold.

Darkness rained down and the air felt cold, as if it'd dropped by fifty degrees.

"What do you think you're doing here?" I gritted my teeth to keep the words from shaking.

Pruitt shifted around, and a shockwave of that cold gusted. A squall that battered against my body.

Pruitt was tall and lean, and I'd once thought he had to be one of the most attractive men I'd ever seen. Brown hair and green eyes. Clean cut and high bred. I'd just failed to notice the wickedness that soaked him through.

Bitterness filled his voice. "I thought I should pay a visit to my wife."

"I'm not your wife." I spat it.

He laughed a condescending sound. "You promised your life to me. Don't you remember?"

"And you turned out to be a man I didn't know." I wouldn't back down or cower. Wouldn't pretend.

I just tossed the truth out between us, the words toppling to the wood planks like jagged, pitted stones.

There was no missing the threat that was etched into them.

"You think you know me, do you?" His head cocked to the side. His own warning.

Ice slicked down my spine, and I forced myself to remain upright, to keep from slumping in the fear that wanted to overtake. The vision of the depravity I knew he was capable of flashed through my mind.

My hands clenched and unclenched at my sides. "I know exactly who you are, and the rest of the world is going to, too, if you don't get off my property."

Cruelty spilled out with his laughter, and he was across the porch before I could prepare myself, no defense before he had my back plastered to the wall and his hands planted on either side of my head.

Foulness spilled from his spirit and dripped from his mouth as he whispered his venom close to my ear. "Do you think to threaten me, Hailey? Do you think I'm afraid of you? Do you realize how easily you could cease to exist?"

"What do you want from me?" My eyes squeezed shut, and there was no stopping the trembles that rattled my voice.

Agony blazed a path through my insides and ripped at my spirit.

The only thing I wanted was to be free. To raise my daughter right. To turn my back on everything that he was. It was bad enough that I was allowing him to get away with what I knew.

But for my daughter...

"You know what I want." The words dropped lower, gnarled and dark.

"I'm giving you two seconds to step away from her before you don't have the ability to."

We both froze at the low growl of words that curled through the air, coming from the direction of the steps. They were almost the exact same words as Cody had issued last night at the bar.

Though they were delivered even more menacing than last night. Shards.

Broken glass.

A knife that was clearly ready to impale.

Only Cody didn't know the type of man we were dealing with. Pruitt wasn't some drunk guy who didn't know when to keep his mouth shut or his hands to himself.

Pruitt was calculating.

Devious.

Precise.

I didn't know why he hadn't come for me sooner. I should have known that he would. Should have known he would never let me be.

Should have known I'd never truly be free.

Pruitt slowly shifted to look over his shoulder, though he didn't move an inch from where he held me hostage against the wall.

"You'd do well to turn your back and walk away, hick," Pruitt hissed, like Cody was trash.

Inconsequential.

A bluster of energy blew through the air, coming from every direction. Colliding in the middle.

An aggression so intense I gagged on it.

A clash of Pruitt and Cody.

Neither of them were going to back down.

"It's fine, Cody. Go back to your house." Each word croaked.

"You should know that's not going to happen, darlin'." He softened his tone for me.

His words from last night flooded my thoughts.

"I won't regret standing up for you. It's just the way I am, Hailey. I protect those I care about. Take care of them. Whatever the cost."

"You say that like it's a bad thing."

"*It is if you knew the lengths I'd go.*"

I had a hunch he would go far right then. Dive right into brutality.

But I couldn't ask him to stand in the line of fire for me. Get involved in something he didn't understand.

Pruitt would destroy Cody and take pleasure in it when he did.

"I'm fine." I somehow managed to force it out, though I knew it was rasping.

Cody took another step up the porch stairs. Slowly, though there was nothing hesitant about it. "Yeah, you don't seem so fine to me, so I think I'm going to have to stick around."

"Leave, now, before you regret it." Indignation poured from Pruitt. Disbelief that someone would dare stand against him.

"Nah, I'm pretty sure it's you who's going to regret it if you don't get the fuck off Hailey's property. Now step away from her before things get ugly. Trust me, they're about to."

Cody took the last step onto the porch.

The man was enormous where he stood towering in the night.

A massive shadow that vibrated with an aggression that thirsted to be unleashed.

Pruitt wouldn't stand a chance against him if it got physical. Pruitt's tactics were always more insidious.

Undercut.

An attack that came out of nowhere, quiet and stealthy, and you were finished before you knew what hit you.

I pleaded with my eyes for Cody to leave, my heart heaving with desperation.

Walk away. Walk away.

I would handle this. I had before. I would find a way…

Cody took another step, his boots thudding on the wood, a low rumble of thunder that promised violence approached.

Rage blistered in Pruitt's green gaze, though I could feel his reservations, the fear that skittered across his skin.

He knew Cody was about to bring him pain.

Taking a slow step back, he released me.

I sagged against the wall, relief slamming me even though I knew better than to feel it.

This was temporary, one battle in a war that had just begun.

Pruitt's attention swung between me and Cody, his jaw clenched in outrage and offended disbelief.

"This isn't over, Hailey." His words were darts, pinpoint and emphatic.

"Oh, but it is," Cody said, massive hands in fists where he stood, refusing to back down.

Pruitt hesitated for one second more before he lifted his head like he wasn't the one cowering, his ego taking a hit, something I knew he wouldn't forget.

He wound around Cody, clearly trying to maintain a show of dominance when he appeared pathetic next to the man who pulsated power.

"Don't come back around here," Cody spouted at his retreating form.

When he stepped down onto the walkway, Pruitt turned, glaring back. The smile that stretched across his face smug and terrifying. "Ignorant fool. You have no fucking clue."

"That you're a prick? Yeah, I think I do," Cody taunted.

Indignation puffed from Pruitt on a heave of air, and he spun and stormed down the walkway and hopped into the black, shiny car that was parked on the street, the tires squealing as he peeled out from the curb.

I knew deep down it was the same car that had been following me the first week I'd been here. When I'd thought I'd found sanctuary and peace. When I'd thought I was letting paranoia settle in when I should have known my ghosts would always catch up to me.

Cody didn't move until the taillights disappeared down the road. The second the sound of the engine faded in the distance, he turned, a hurricane that flew across the porch.

"Are you okay?" He begged it.

A shiver rolled through my body. "I'm fine."

I kept saying it, again and again.

I'm fine. I'm fine.

I was desperate to be.

Cody reached out and ran his thumb over the cleft in my chin. Warmth spread.

A comfort I shouldn't allow myself to feel. But how could I not when this brute of a man stood over me like a shield?

A tower of safety.

But he couldn't be. I knew that, even though with him standing there, I wanted to dive into the hope of it.

He studied me, golden eyes flaming beneath the bare light that flooded from the lamp hanging next to the door.

"You're not okay, Hailey. I can see it." He whispered it softly, though it was underscored in severity. "He's hurt you."

"I'm fine," I repeated on a shaky exhale, another lie I kept trying to believe.

"Oh, darlin', I see you're not. But I promise that you're going to be."

Something passed through Cody's intimidating features.

A steely determination that rumbled the ground beneath my feet.

"Go inside and lock the door. I'll be back in five minutes. Don't open it until I return."

"I—"

His face dropped close to mine, expression fierce. "Just do it, Hailey. For me. Please."

Warily, I nodded, logic still blurred by the shock of finding Pruitt outside my door.

Cody spun on his heel and strode across the porch, taking my breath with him as he went. I finally got my senses together enough that I pushed myself upright and called his name, trying to stop him from whatever was going through his brain.

He just sent me a smile from over his shoulder and said, "You don't worry about a thing."

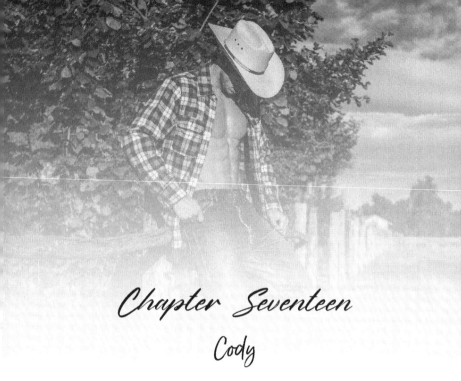

Chapter Seventeen
Cody

RAGE BLISTERED MY INSIDES, FLAMES FUCKING EATING ME alive as I stormed into my house where I went directly into my room and started tossing things into a duffle bag.

Activity was required because if I didn't do something with my hands, I'd give in to what I really wanted to be doing with them—strangling the life out of that fucking little fucker who'd had Hailey pressed to the wall like he owned her.

Swore, I'd tasted it, her fear that had infiltrated the air when I'd stepped out my front door.

I'd planned on drinking a beer and watching the rest of the day melt away, keen on sitting outside beneath the stars. Sit in that dusky peace for a little while and let my mind wander, which I was pretty sure it would wander straight back to when I'd made her come so hard on my fingers that I'd nearly split apart myself just watching it.

The whole damned night had been spent fantasizing about the fucking hottest chick I'd ever met who somehow was worming her way into the places I didn't allow anyone to go.

Not one.

I was worried she might be the one person who had the power to weave herself right in there anyway.

What twisted, ironic shit that she was the most dangerous woman on earth I could give myself to.

Only when I'd stepped out, there'd been no peace.

There'd been a dark cloud of wickedness. Thick and sticky and coating the air. Clotting out reason and sight.

Had nearly lost it when I'd rounded her house and saw that bastard towering over her. Had nearly come unglued when I'd heard the way her voice had trembled.

Fucking *terrified.*

I knew she'd been, and I knew she'd been trying to play it off like she wasn't. Doing her best to send me away like I'd pretend that I hadn't just witnessed her being manipulated and bent. Her gorgeous being that was so full of fire and life dwindling beneath his shadow.

It was not going to happen.

It didn't matter if it made me a masochist to be in her space. Begging for destruction.

She was worth it.

I shoved two more tees into the duffle, stormed into my bathroom and tossed in my toothbrush and toothpaste and some shit from the shower, then I was back out the door and in front of hers.

It'd taken less than three minutes.

I pounded at the door at the same time as I shouted, "Open up, Hailey, it's me."

She must have still been right on the other side because she flew through the lock and opened it. "I'm sorry you—"

I cut off whatever apology was getting ready to spill from her mouth by pushing through the door.

A frown pulled to her gorgeous face when her attention dropped to my duffle bag. "What do you think you're doing?"

"My house was feeling a little empty, so I figured I might spend a night or two here." I tossed it out casually, like my insides weren't knocking so hard it was a wonder I wasn't splintering apart.

I wound around her and started deeper into her house.

"Cody, that's not—"

I spun, cutting her off again, hating that her eyes went wide when I came her direction. I dropped the bag to the floor, and my hand came out to cup the side of her face.

Fire sparked at the connection.

Fuck me.

This girl with the power to burn me alive.

Her eyes widened further, and I brushed my thumb along her cheek.

"I would never hurt you." The promise scraped free, and I angled in closer. "And yes, it is necessary. I'm not going to leave you and your daughter and your grandmother here by yourselves after that creep showed up here."

She didn't need to tell me he was her ex. I might not know his name, but it sure as hell was written all over him. Asshole thought he had some claim on her.

"You can't get involved in this. He's…" She trailed off, gnawing at that plump bottom lip, eyes dropping as she bit back whatever she'd been going to say. Rage made a rebound, and my bones rattled with the overwhelming need to hunt the cocksucker down.

My hand tightened on her face, words close to a snarl. "I want you to finish that sentence, Hailey."

I needed to know.

Needed her to admit it.

Her brow dented in a pain that was scarred somewhere deep, and she blinked like she might be able to hide the horror that swam in the depths of those crystalline eyes.

"He's what?" I demanded, voice grating. I hated that I was probably coming off as a prick, too, but I couldn't handle it. The wave of protectiveness that was spinning me into chaos.

Because I knew what she'd been getting ready to say.

He was dangerous.

Volatile.

"He's nothing," she said instead, lifting her fierce chin like she could make it so.

"But he doesn't think so, does he?"

She hesitated, wary, before she barely shook her head with the admission. "No. He thinks I belong to him."

I forced myself to swallow some of the intensity, and I backed away like I wasn't rattled to the bone. Like I didn't want to gather her up and hold her close and promise her I would never let that asshole touch her again.

Instead, I played it as blasé. "Well, I guess I'll have to stick around for a while until he gets the clue that you don't."

I turned and moved deeper into her house. The match to mine except there were toys littered everywhere. The space warm and cozy and singing of life.

Hailey seemed pinned to the spot where I'd left her before she suddenly flew into action. "Wait, what?"

I tossed my bag onto the floor next to the couch. "I just think it would be a good idea for me to hang out for a couple days, that's all."

"Oh, no, no, no, that's not necessary." Hailey rambled it, her hands flying all over the place. "We'll be just fine."

I spun to find her right there. I took her by both wrists, and I gently pressed them together between us. "I told you I won't stand aside and watch someone I care about get hurt, Hailey. No matter the cost. I meant it."

Her throat bobbed as she swallowed. "I can't ask you to get involved."

"You didn't."

"Cody..."

I tugged her a little closer by those wrists, bodies drawn, needing to get deeper into her space.

God, she was so damned pretty.

Heart-stopping.

Mind-bending.

Shout at the heavens kind of gorgeous.

But none of that had any bearing right then.

"I'm not going anywhere, Hailey."

"It's only going to enrage him further if he thinks you're staying here."

"Good. Let him think we're together. Let him think you're mine."

Oxygen left her lungs on a puff that I wanted to inhale. Blue eyes flicked all over my face.

"You want to provoke the devil?"

"What better way to get rid of the bastard than for him to think he's competing with me?"

I went for light when I knew what was riding on this. The importance. This wasn't some fucking game that I was playing.

She was worth it.

Worth it.

Uncertainty played through her features, and she was nibbling at that plump bottom lip the way she always did when she was unsure. A million secrets playing out that she struggled to keep concealed.

"I don't think you understand who you're dealing with."

Reaching out, I brushed the pad of my thumb over that lip that drove me wild. This girl something that I couldn't shake. "Doesn't matter, Hailey. It doesn't matter who he is or what he's capable of. You're worth it."

We froze like that, so close that I was inhaling every panted breath that she released.

She nearly jumped out of her skin when the back screen door clattered open then slammed shut as an excited screech came ringing out, "Mr. Cody! What are you doin' here?"

I turned to find Hailey's little girl come bounding our way, a mess of frizzy blonde curls framing her adorable face. Cheeks chubby and denting in these adorable dimples.

I glanced at Hailey, almost asking for permission, before I turned back to her daughter. "Ah, well, my hot water stopped working, so I asked your mom if it would be okay if I hung out here for a few days until I get it fixed."

Seemed a viable excuse for the kid.

Maddie came right up to my side and took my hand. My chest tightened. God, she was cute.

"Well, I think that is a very good idea because we got to be neighborly, and when our neighbor has a big problem, we gotta help them with it."

Warmth streaked. Different. This coil inside promising I would do whatever it took to protect them. To keep them safe.

I shifted to look at Hailey. At this woman who needled even deeper.

I knew better. I'd dug my grave a long time ago, and I'd been waiting for the day that I finally got dragged into it.

But maybe I had a chance to do something right. Stand for beauty when some monster was trying to rip it apart.

I squeezed her daughter's hand, heart getting battered by the amount of emotion slamming into me.

I couldn't look away from Hailey when I murmured, "That's right, we have to help our neighbors when they have a big problem."

And I'd be willing to give everything to solve hers.

Chapter Eighteen

Hailey

THIS WAS A DISASTER.

My thundering heart clobbered the base of my throat like a bass drum, my nerves so uncontrolled I could barely walk a straight line as I moved to the linen closet in the hall that was nestled next to the bathroom Maddie and Lolly shared.

I ripped open the door and frantically dug around for a blanket and pillow.

Flustered.

Agitated.

Shaken to the core by Pruitt showing up here. The truth that he didn't seem to care about what I had hanging over his head.

His threat lingered over me like vapor that swirled and spiraled and loomed.

Do you think I'm afraid of you? Do you realize how easily you could cease to exist?

It wasn't the first time he'd said something like that.

For years, it'd kept me stagnant.

Static.

Unable to move.

Somehow, some way, I'd found the courage to leave anyway, and I'd been so close to believing that we might actually be okay.

How ignorant I'd been.

I didn't know if Cody showing up here had made it better or worse. This comfort that I wanted to sink into that I knew could only be fleeting. Respite for what was sure to come.

It was stupid to allow him to stay here, to do this pretending thing out in public like he seemed set on, but I hadn't known how to argue when he'd been standing there looking at me like that.

So freaking resolved with my daughter's hand wrapped in his, the child jumping at his side, emitting all her joy without a single clue of what was coming for us.

Pruitt was here.

Nausea swam in my stomach, clawing its way through my insides and festering in my spirit.

Pruitt was here.

I had to figure something else out. Find a way to stop him.

Fully and completely.

My mind raced to the proof I kept hidden in a locked box beneath my bed.

But what then? What would it do to my dad? My father had been selling him horses for years. The thing was, he had no idea what was really happening with those horses, what they were being used for, the lawlessness that Pruitt embodied all while keeping a squeaky-clean name.

It'd taken me two years of living in the middle of it to discover his sins.

But I knew exposing it was the one thing that would stop him. It was the single power I possessed. I just needed to figure out how to wield it correctly.

Finally, I managed to tug free the big blanket I was looking for and dumped it on the ground then went in search for an extra pillow.

I gasped when a hand reached out and grabbed me by the elbow, and I whirled to find Lolly standing there with the most salacious grin on her face.

It slid right off when she saw what must have been written on mine.

Worry knitted her wrinkled brow.

"What is going on? I thought you were going to be happy that mountain man came knocking at your door, pushing his way right in, but I don't see a lick of happiness right now."

She almost tried to phrase it a tease, though I heard the concern.

The knot in my throat refused to lessen, and I took a painful, gulping swallow around it, looking over her shoulder to make sure no one was listening.

I dropped my attention back to her when I heard Cody laughing at something Maddie said from the kitchen.

"It wasn't Cody who first showed up here."

Surprise jarred her features, her dull gray eyes narrowing. "Who was it?"

My tongue darted out to wet my dried lips. "Pruitt."

Horror heaved from her lungs. A bout of anger rushed in behind it. "Are you kidding me? I can't believe that man had the nerve to show up at your door. I'd have thought he would have gotten the message that you don't want anything to do with him by now?"

"Pruitt has never been so good at taking no for an answer."

Only my grandmother didn't know how deep that really went. I'd never given her details, and she'd assumed that he'd strayed.

Cheated.

How sad I wished it were true.

"What does he want?"

A haggard laugh rolled up my throat. "What he's always wanted… me."

Under his thumb.

Submissive.

Playing the pretty prize to be paraded.

And you could say he'd never been much of a sport when he didn't get his way.

I should have seen it when he'd set his sights on me all those years ago, but I'd been too blinded by my grief to realize what was happening.

So desperately needing to be loved that I'd allowed him to catch me up in a whirlwind.

"Well, he can't have you."

"No. He can't." It was a breath.

A heavy chuckle echoed from the kitchen, and Lolly gestured in that direction. "And just how did that cowboy show up here?"

"He must have heard me arguing with Pruitt."

Except our voices had been so low there was no chance that he had. And he'd appeared from out of nowhere, manifested from thin air as if he'd been summoned by my fear.

"And now he's staying here?" Her tone drifted into suggestion. She couldn't help herself.

I rolled my eyes. "He's staying here because he's a nice guy. For one night. That's it."

Because I couldn't handle him rambling around under my roof. Especially after what had happened with us last night.

Letting him touch me had been just as big a mistake as letting him stay here was going to be. But honestly, I was shaken enough—worried enough for my daughter—that I didn't have the strength to disagree with him tonight.

"That's awful nice of him." Lolly drew it out.

I found the pillow I was looking for and dragged it out from between the towels where it was wedged. I leaned down to grab the blanket and held the stack against my chest.

"Don't get any big ideas in that head of yours."

"And what kind of ideas might those be?" She pressed her hand to her chest, completely innocent.

"You know exactly what I'm talking about."

"Well, I do have the best ideas…and I'm pretty sure it doesn't require an extra blanket and pillow. Your bed is plenty big enough."

"That is absolutely not going to happen." I angled around her to head back for the great room.

"And why would you deny yourself something that you know is going to be so good?" she urged from behind.

I turned to her, my heart close to bleeding out onto the floor. "Because I've had enough trouble in my life, Lolly, enough hurt, and my daughter needs stability. I need stability. And you and I both know that man is not going to give me that."

Tendrils of guilt flailed out of the black hole inside me. How could I even consider wanting that from him?

But I'd be a liar if I denied a piece of me did.

Sadness cut into every line in her expression. Her touch was gentle on my arm, all traces of mischief vanished.

"I just want you to be happy, Hailey. It's the only thing I've ever wanted for you. And I cannot tell you how proud I am that you left that scheming sleazebag."

Surprise at her accusation had a frown carving me in question. Her directness severe and sharp. Did she know more than she'd let on or was it just obvious that Pruitt was scum?

I didn't have time to ask before she forged ahead, her voice curled in ardent earnestness. "So proud of you for standing up for what you deserve. The only thing I've wanted is to see you and Maddie safe and happy. And you're going to be, Hailey, you're going to be, just as long as you remain strong. Strong and fierce the way I know you are."

She paused then emphasized, "I know that deviant changed so much of your perspective. That he hurt you. I just hope the wounds he left don't make you so guarded that you don't allow yourself to live."

"I am living, Lolly. For the first time in a long time, I am. And I won't let anyone steal that from me. I promise you."

I wouldn't allow any one person to hold my happiness.

Not ever again.

⌒⊷⌒

"Thank you." Cody's voice was as quiet as the shadows that babbled in the room, lulling and peaceful as he glanced at the blanket and pillow that I'd left for him on the couch.

I'd tucked Maddie in a half an hour before, while Cody had

plodded around in the bathroom next to her room, setting me off-kilter the entire time, trembles rolling and energy pulsing.

Now he stood in the darkness in front of me, a giant in my living room. A man I didn't really even know but somehow trusted to be there.

I shouldn't.

It was a fool's game, whatever the hell this was.

The only thing I knew was I was going to lose in the end.

"You're thanking me?"

That smirk tugged at the edge of his mouth, far gentler than it should ever be. "I'd fully come prepared to sleep on the hard floor, nothing but a dog. It seems you're doing me a favor."

"I think it's you who's doing all the favors." The words were wisps.

"It's my honor to be here, Hailey."

Silence danced around us, the questions radiating from him so profound that I could almost see them hovering in the room. I itched in them, unsure of how to respond. What to give him and what he expected.

A warning is what it should be. A true one. One that told him to run as far as he could. Turn his back. Act like he'd never met us before, and sure as hell not dive into this headfirst the way he was suggesting.

In discomfort, Cody roughed a hand through his hair, staring at me through the night. "Think we should talk about your ex."

Right. There they were. The questions coming.

"We probably do."

"Maddie's father?" he pressed.

"Yes."

His nod was tight. "How long have you been apart?"

"Three months."

"And it's safe to assume you were the one who did the leaving?"

"Pruitt collects things. Possessions. He doesn't like when he gets them taken away."

Cody flinched, his voice a scrape of animosity. "Seems like a solid douche to me."

I fiddled with my fingers, gaze dipping away before it drifted back up to him.

I needed to lay this out. Make him see.

"He's someone you don't want to mess with, Cody."

The heap of a man stilled, a frozen boulder of heat, like he was afraid to trust himself to move. The protectiveness I'd felt from him earlier lapped against me in warm, dragging waves.

"Already told you the bastard can come at me, Hailey. He's going to find out really quick I'm not someone you want to mess with, either. Especially when it comes to you."

It was scored in dark aggression. The mark of a man who didn't shy away from destruction.

He always came off as carefree.

Heedless, even.

Almost reckless in his detachment.

But that wasn't close to who was standing in front of me right then.

"You don't owe me anything." I nearly begged it, knowing I should put a barricade up between us. Send him away. Stop this before he got any deeper.

But my spirit leaned his direction.

He reached out like he could touch it, and he set one of those big palms on my cheek again. The brush of his thumb was achingly tender as he ran it back and forth along the hollow of my eye.

"That's what friends do, Hailey. They share the load, and it looks like yours just got a little too heavy to bear."

Threads of guilt curled around my ribs and tightened around my heart. What kind of friend was I, doing this? Allowing him to invade my space like this? Touch me the way he had last night when I knew the trouble it would bring him? More so, with the way Brooke had felt about him?

But that was so long ago, and this…

Intensity blazed as he traced my face with his eyes, as if he sought to memorize every line and divot and curve. His caress soft and adoring.

I felt beautiful beneath it, the way this man saw me. The way he made me feel. But he didn't have the first clue what he was signing up for.

"I can handle Pruitt," I forced out.

"Of course, you can, but that doesn't mean you have to do it alone. Let me be strong enough to carry some of it," he murmured. "Let me be there. For you. For Maddie. Let's chase this fucker off, then you can get on with your life the way you so clearly need to do."

"Why would you do that for me?" My head barely shook, trying to understand.

"Because there's something special about you, Hailey Wagner. There's always been." Then he cracked a grin like he didn't think either of us could endure the weight that sagged the room any longer. "That and I really like the sound of my name on your lips when you come."

I didn't know whether to laugh or cry with the heat that flooded, pulsing between us.

In an instant, that tether of energy writhed and thrashed.

"We agreed last night that was a one-time thing."

I forced myself to take a step back before I did something stupid and reached for him again. Got to my knees and undid his belt so I could...

I didn't realize my attention had drifted to the enormous bulge in his jeans until he cleared his throat. I jerked, my eyes flashing back up to his.

A challenge pulled across his ridiculously handsome face. "Is that the way you want it?"

Gathering all my resolve, I said, "We're just friends, Cody. That's all we can be. It will only complicate things."

I repeated his defense from last night.

"And maybe I've come to realize I'll welcome any complication if it means getting close to you."

That arrogance resurfaced, the man nothing but a taunt, and he reached down to the hem of his tee and peeled it up and over his head like he'd done it a thousand times in front of me before.

My mouth dropped open, and I swore, the world canted to the side.

Annihilated by the sight.

I was pretty sure it was the result he was going for since he let one of those smirks free, the kind that did a little slaying of its own.

I couldn't form a coherent thought or word, stupefied as I stared at him through the moonlight that flooded through the window.

There'd been no question that he was made of muscle and brawn. A fortress of strength. A mast of power.

But I nearly crumbled at the sight of him like this.

Skin bare and glowing, like the sun breaking on a dreary, gloomy day. A golden, coarse stone, ruggedly chiseled and shaped. A sculpture of tenacity.

Shoulders obliterating view, wide and hulking, that power reverberating beneath the flesh stretched tight across his packed, quivering chest.

It rippled down his abdomen, his stomach engraved in sharply cinched divots and lines, his hip bones jutting out from above the waist of his jeans.

Where I was soft, he was hard, forged of slate.

Designs covered his left arm and scrolled up over his shoulder to his pec, bright colors that gleamed in the night.

But what caught my attention was where the mosaic lines opened to a clock that sat right in the middle of his chest.

Prominent and emphasized like it'd become the focal point of who he was.

An emblem that was drawn to appear rustic like the man, rusted metal or bronzed iron, the teeth heavy and gnarled as it ticked through time.

Though the hands of the clock were bent, jagged where they forever rested at eight-seventeen.

He winced for one beat when he realized what I was fixated on, then he jarred me out of the trance he had me under when he tossed his shirt over to the couch. "You don't mind, do you? I mean, it shouldn't be a problem for you to see me like this considering we're just friends, yeah?"

It was pure provocation.

I blinked a bunch of times.

Damn it. He was distracting me from the point of this conversation.

"You need to reconsider—"

A finger was pressed against my lips, stopping the words from spilling out. "I'm doing this, Hailey, and I promise you, I won't have a single regret."

Why was he proving to be so sweet? So good and right?

"Cody." It was barely a whisper, and I wished I could divulge all the information so he could make an actual educated choice.

But I couldn't give him that.

Not yet.

It wasn't safe.

"Mean it, Hailey. You don't need to worry about me."

"I think I already do."

"Well, we are friends after all." He winked, back to light, as if the weight of my world hadn't just suddenly been placed on his shoulders.

I fidgeted, warring, before I gave.

Accepted his gift.

"Let me know if you need anything."

He smiled. "You might not want to know what it is I need, Hailey."

Heat flamed.

"Right…okay." Awkwardly, I tossed a hand behind me toward my bedroom. "I'm going to bed."

I couldn't get my feet to cooperate, and Cody kept grinning like he was somehow making a good time of this. Standing a foot away. That big body so close and on display.

I finally forced myself to turn, and I rushed across the floor, though I paused when I got to my bedroom door to whisper, "Goodnight, Cody."

He was still standing there, watching me. "You sleep well, darlin', because I'll be sleeping light. You can rest assured that no one is getting by me."

How was he so different than I'd imagined or expected him to be? Or maybe he'd been a different man when I'd met him that summer.

A player who probably didn't have the first clue that that way-ward smile had crushed two bleeding hearts.

One to never beat again.

"Thank you. For everything." I meant it.

With all of me.

"It's what I'm here for."

I could only give him a small nod, deciding it was no use to argue with him that we weren't his responsibility any longer.

He'd already chosen that we were.

It was on me to make sure it didn't bring him harm.

On me to be the one to chase Pruitt away before Cody got in-volved any deeper.

Maybe it was time to be brave enough to do what I'd been threat-ening all along.

Apprehension prickled in my consciousness, and fear whispered terrors into my mind.

Swallowing it down, I forced myself the rest of the way into my bedroom and snapped the door shut behind me.

Cody didn't move until I'd clicked the lock, then I pressed my ear to the wood and listened as his boots thudded across the floor. Listened to the rustle of fabric and the steady cadence of his breaths.

Resigned, I peeled myself out of my clothes and changed into my favorite teal sleep shorts and matching tank then climbed under the covers.

I sank into the warmth.

And just like all the nights since I'd moved in, I felt the pull of his presence.

His aura profound.

Only it didn't echo from the window.

It echoed from the other side of my door.

Chapter Nineteen

Cody

Sixteen Years Old

"No, Cody, I can't accept this." His mother looked at the stack of cash he set in her hand, eyes wide, moisture making the brown pools swirl and swim.

His chest tightened in a fist. "You need it."

Grief puckered her brow while adoration spun through the tight clench of her expression. The love she had forever watched him with poured out of her like a sieve.

Still, she tried to argue. "You're sixteen. You're supposed to be off having fun. Playing sports. Being wild."

Cody grinned. "Don't worry about that, Ma. I'm sowing plenty of oats."

A soft huff puffed from her lips, and she tsked as she shook her head with tender reproach since the truly *fun* things were the ones she didn't relish hearing about. "Cody."

He grinned wider. "Only said it so you'd know I'm not lacking on the sweeter things in life."

"But that's the thing. I want you to be happy. To thrive."

Reaching out, he curled her hand around the money.

He'd taken that lawnmowing job he'd started at twelve and turned it into something that was actually producing. Working at least three hours after school each day and on the weekends. He'd told his mother he was saving for a car, and he'd bought an old beat-up pickup truck that would suffice.

The rest was for her.

For his sisters.

"I am thriving, Ma. And taking care of you...of Dakota and Kayla...that's what makes me happy."

The moisture in her steadfast gaze built to tears, and one streaked down her cheek. "But this money is supposed to be for you."

His head shook in denial. "No, Ma. It never was. It was always for you. And I promise, I will always take care of you. I know you pretend like you're just fine, but I see you struggle. I feel it right here."

He pressed her free hand to his chest.

Misty, brown eyes peered up from his mother's adoring face. "You were never supposed to take on that burden."

He was, though. He'd promised his father. He knew his mother did her best to hide her financial troubles from him and his sisters, but it was blatant.

Obvious and glaring.

Things were crumbling around them.

And he wouldn't stand aside and watch it destroy his mother.

Not when she'd lost so much. Not when she'd sacrificed everything for them. Working three jobs and then coming home to take care of them, cooking and cleaning and showering them with love when he knew she didn't get more than three hours of sleep at night.

He could chip in this little bit, and one day, he would get to the place where he could finally take her burden away.

Permanently.

"This isn't just your struggle. We're a team. A family," he told her.

She pulled her hand from his chest and set it on his cheek. "How could I ever deserve you?"

"I'm the one who got lucky. So just let me give this little bit, yeah?"

Because he would always, always take care of her. No matter what it took.

Chapter Twenty

Hailey

TINKLING LAUGHTER NUDGED ME FROM SLEEP. CONFUSED, I pushed up on my elbows where I'd been sleeping face down, and I squinted at my pillow as I turned my ear to the sound that echoed in the distance.

Maddie.

I'd be able to identify her sweet laugh in a crowd of a thousand people, though this morning it was muddled, coming from somewhere outside the house.

Alarm raced through my veins when I came to the swift realization she wasn't inside, and I tossed off my covers, flew out of bed, and fumbled through the latch on my bedroom door. My feet smacked against the hard floor as I raced to the back door, my heart in my throat and fear churning through my senses.

She knew she wasn't supposed to go outside alone.

Especially after Pruitt had shown up last night.

Only I skidded to a stop, my hands shooting out for support and my nose touching the glass panes as I stared out at the scene.

Cody was facing away and kneeling on one knee, sifting through the disorder of plastic pieces of Maddie's playhouse that were dumped out on the lawn. Maddie was dancing around him, on her toes, clapping her hands and talking nonstop, though I couldn't make out her words from inside.

Only I was sure they were a form of her sweet manipulation that she'd used on him.

Inhaling a steeling breath, I opened the door and stepped out onto the back porch.

It was still cool enough, though the sun climbed its way from the horizon into the sky, the vast stretch above pinked with the first light of morning.

A slight breeze wisped through the trees, birds flitting and chirping and rustling through the leaves.

I eased toward the end of the porch and somehow managed to find my voice. "What's going on out here?"

From over his shoulder, Cody swiveled to look at me, grin tweaking wide. "Good morning, Shortcake," he said, rather than answering.

"Hi," I barely managed.

Though Maddie clapped and jumped, all too happy to fill me in on the details. "Guess what, Mommy? Mr. Cody said he bet he could put my playhouse together since you already said it was so many pieces and there was no way on this godforsaken earth you were going to be able to put the damned thing back together."

I cringed.

Maddie'd overheard me mumbling it yesterday afternoon when I'd been out there in that exact same spot as Cody was now, riffling through the pieces and having no clue where to even begin. I'd made the mistake of taking it apart when we moved, and I didn't have the instructions to put it back together.

"Mommy didn't mean for you to hear that. I was going to figure it out," I explained.

"I think Mr. Cody is probably *way* better at it than you."

Yeah, I thought he probably was, too, but still, I was reprimanding, "Cody isn't here for you to swindle him into doing jobs for you, Maddie."

"Sure I am. Why would you want to go and waste all of this?" He actually flexed his arm, his biceps bulging out.

Maddie laughed like she thought the man was hysterical. "See, Mommy, Mr. Cody is really strong and has really big muscles and he's going to put this sucker together, lickity split."

It was Cody's turn to cringe, likely only then realizing my daughter would proudly repeat every vulgar word that might drop from his mouth. I could only be thankful the word that had come off her tongue didn't start with an *f*.

A wry chuckle rumbled from the side. I shifted to find Lolly was out there, too, quiet as a mouse while she watched the exchange.

Okay, more like sly as a cat since she hiked a shoulder, smiling at me in her lacy nightgown with red lipstick smeared on her lips.

"Now *why* would you want to go and waste all of that when he can take care of it, lickity split?" she parroted, though her tone was painted in suggestion.

I sent her my best glare.

She shimmied her shoulders.

Good lord, what was I supposed to do with these people?

I returned my attention to my daughter and Cody.

Cody stared at me from over his shoulder, frozen to the spot, the intensity of him billowing on the morning air.

It wasn't until then I realized I hadn't taken the time to dress. I'd flown out here wearing my favorite pajamas—super short satiny sleep shorts and the matching tank in that teal color I loved, my legs bare and my boobs spilling out the top. Hair wild and untamed.

I shifted on my feet. It was one thing having him take me in on Saturday night. It'd been dark, and well...I'd felt sexy and beautiful in that dress.

It was an entirely different story when I was standing lit in the spotlight of the sun, and I was sure I looked a disaster right then.

I tried to clear the discomfort from my voice. "Cody has work this morning, Maddie, and I'm sure he needs to get ready, the same as I do."

Cody pushed to his feet, and he dusted off his hands before he ruffled one through my daughter's hair.

Affectionate.

Tender.

Slow.

"Yeah, your mother's right. I should probably finish getting ready and get to the job site before my partner thinks I'm slacking, but I think I can knock this out this evening if you help me out while I'm gone and put all the big pieces in one pile and all the small ones in another. How's that sound?" he asked.

"I can definitely help you so much, Mr. Cody. Look it, I got muscles, too." Maddie flexed both arms.

Amusement rippling from him, he tapped the tiny lump. "Those suckers look like they could bust right through a brick wall."

"I bet so. Wanna arm wrestle?" she challenged.

Cody laughed, this low, rolling sound that tumbled through me. "Maybe after we get this thing built."

"You'd better be ready," she told him. "You won't even know what hit you."

His attention slid back to me, and he slowly started back across the yard, his boots taking the lawn before he climbed the steps to come to stand in front of me.

Towering and tall.

Overwhelming and right.

So gorgeous with the backdrop of the sun lighting behind him.

The man sanctuary and warmth.

But I couldn't allow myself to settle in it. Couldn't allow myself to get too cozy before that blanket was ripped away. Most of all, I couldn't let Madison get attached. I could already see her slipping, enamored with the man, which I was realizing was an easy place to be.

Enamored.

"You don't need to do that, Cody," I mustered, tipping my head back to meet the magnitude of his gaze.

"I want to."

"It's not your responsibility."

He glanced back at Maddie. "I'm not doing it out of obligation,

184 | A.L. JACKSON

Hailey. I'm doing it because your daughter is amazing." Then he leaned in close and murmured so only I could hear, "Just like her mother."

He straightened like he didn't feel the roll of the ground vibrate beneath us, and those big boots thudded across the porch before he swung open the back door. "Now hurry up and get that cute butt ready. We need to leave in fifteen."

It took me a second to process what he'd said, and still, I wasn't fully gathering his meaning. "What?"

"You heard me. You're riding with me."

Then he stepped inside and let the door slam shut behind him.

Chapter Twenty-One

Cody

NOPE.

Little Button was right.

I most definitely didn't know what had hit me.

Didn't know what the hell had come over me.

Getting close to people when I'd sworn I'd never do it. But there didn't seem to be any choice in the matter when it came to Hailey and Madison.

Hell, to Lolly, too.

It struck me like an arrow when Hailey finally stepped out her front door twenty minutes later, wearing tight jeans and worn cowgirl boots and a coral-colored top that scooped way down low on her chest.

A mass of blonde hair twisted into a long braid with those locks of honey and maple weaved through it. Thick and heavy and perfect for fisting.

Lashes long and lips pouty and those eyes both wary and intense as she ambled down the steps and took the walkway to where I'd pulled my truck up to the curb. It was sitting in the exact same spot as it'd been on Saturday night though facing the opposite direction.

She slowed the closer she came, brow furrowing in speculation. "You don't have to drive me to work, too, Cody. This is ridiculous."

I was leaned back against the front side-panel, a boot kicked up on the tire and my hands shoved into the pockets of my jeans. "I don't find a thing about it ridiculous."

Air heaved from her nose, and she glanced around, no doubt checking for the bastard I itched to hunt down.

It had taken every ounce of willpower I possessed to play it cool last night. To stop myself from demanding a name so I could track him down and put an end to any bullshit he might think of bringing to her door.

Since I doubted much that she'd be too happy if I made good on it, I figured standing as a barrier in front of that door would have to suffice.

Frustration heaved from her lungs. "I'm not weak, Cody."

"Never implied you were."

"Yet you think you need to sleep on my couch and drive me to work."

A wave of protectiveness swelled. "It's not what I think of you, Hailey, it's what I instantly knew of him. One look and I knew that fucker would gladly hurt you if you didn't cave to what he wanted. And there you stood, brave and refusing to give, even though I knew you were afraid. Afraid of who he is and what he's capable of."

Part of me wanted to press her for the details. Demand to know what he'd done to put that look on her face. The other part wasn't sure I could hear the atrocities and remain a sane man.

Besides, I sensed she was shuttering.

Keeping a piece of herself veiled.

But I needed to get there. To that place where she could trust me with her demons.

Let me hold them.

Fully.

"So no, I don't think you're weak," I continued. "I think you're in a bad position brought on by a creep who will force you into what he wants if given the opportunity. I'm simply not allowing him that opportunity."

I crossed my arms over my chest.

A war went down in her brain, curling through the depths of those crystalline eyes, and her head slowly shook as she whispered, "I keep trying to warn you that he's trouble, Cody."

That was what was fucking me up. The way she went cold when she said it.

Dread slithering like ice beneath the surface of her skin.

A secret she held that she wasn't quite ready to let go of.

"Without a doubt. But you're worth that trouble, Hailey. I thought we already established that?"

Emotion flooded her face, her reserves dropping to show off this well of goodness.

I'd recognized it then.

I was even more sure of it now.

"And what if you're worth it to me?" she asked. "What if I don't want you involved because I don't trust the lengths he would go if someone got between him and me? What if I don't want to see you hurt?"

Pushing from the truck, I took the single step that separated us and moved into her space.

Severity throbbed, a thrash of that energy that compelled.

Girl a magnet that I kept trying to resist.

I set a palm on the side of her striking face, letting her warmth glide through me.

"I'm already there, Hailey, between you and him. Use me up. I'll be your shield. Until you figure out how to deal with this guy, I'll be right here, and we'll let him think you've already moved on."

With me.

Fuck. Right then, I wished it could really be that way. That I could give it all when I'd already given it away.

Because what kind of person would I be if I asked her to go from one monster to another?

I watched her struggle, unsure if she wanted to argue or agree.

188 | A.L. JACKSON

My thumb brushed the plump angle of her cheek, and that feeling swept through me.

A whisper.

Old and familiar and somehow distant.

"I remember the evening I left. I couldn't stop from going to you, Hailey. I saw how sad you were. I wanted to wrap you up and make it better. Kiss away your pain. But I couldn't. I wasn't worthy. I was lost to my own bullshit, caught up in my life, so I turned my back. I won't make that mistake again." The words were hoarse when I released them.

She gasped at my words, and I could feel the shock roll through her.

Neither of us had mentioned it. I guessed both of us had spent the rest of our lives pretending that time didn't exist.

Tiptoeing around the past.

It was time we brought it to the forefront.

Blue eyes flicked all over my face like she was looking for a lie only it was her truth that came riding out. "And I was the fool who wanted you to."

I got lost there for a beat. How sweet she'd been. The way she'd made me feel something different for the first time.

Like maybe I wanted—

I cleared the memories before I got lost in them and slanted my regard back toward the house.

To what was important right then.

"Are they going to be okay here? Not sure I like the idea of leaving Maddie and Lolly alone."

Indecision curled through her features, long lashes dipping with the turmoil before she seemed to settle.

"I honestly think he'll try to get what he wants through me first."

"But what better way than using Maddie against you?"

Regret pulsed through her demeanor. "I think he thinks Maddie sees him as some kind of hero, and he won't want to taint that if he doesn't have to, even though I know her little soul knows."

She glanced back at the house, sorrow in her voice. "I've seen it. Her fear. Like she sees deeper than the surface."

She turned back to me. "I hate that I exposed her to that."

"You're doing the best you can, Hailey, and you being here? Making the change? Being brave enough to leave that bastard to give you and her a better life? That's what counts."

"I just want to be a good mother. Give her peace and safety and the knowledge that she is safe."

And my hand was still there on her sweet face, my heart stuck like glue in my damned throat, every oath I'd made to myself going haywire.

Getting crossed.

My voice deepened. "There is no chance you could be anything other than a good mother, Hailey. I've seen it, and I promise you that little girl knows how much you love her. I've never seen so much joy shining out from a child than it does in her. Makes my own heart burst every damned time I look at her. And she's going to be safe. You and I are going to make sure of that."

"Cody." My name was a breath.

Before I got stuck in it, I cleared my throat. "Come on, let's get you to work."

Her nod was shaky. "Yeah."

I set my hand on the small of her back and led her around the front of the truck to the passenger side. Fire stroked through my insides, guts a tangle of greed, that little connection nearly too much to take.

Fuck.

I wanted her.

Wanted her in a way I didn't think I'd ever wanted anyone in all my life. It was a terrifying, unsettling fact, but one I was going to have to learn to deal with.

I opened her door and helped her in. "Fuck me, Shortcake, those jeans should be illegal, too."

I cracked the tease because I didn't want her to spend the day washed in dread. Besides, her glorious ass was in my face and my mind was treading to alternate things.

She popped onto the seat, and the smallest smile kissed the edge of her mouth when she reached out and grabbed her buckle and pulled it across her body. She exaggerated the action to prove she was fully capable of doing it herself. "What, you think all my clothes should be illegal?"

I pushed in closer and took her by the chin. "That's right. I'd much prefer if you weren't wearing anything at all. You should have seen the way I wanted to burn that little number you came waltzing out in this morning. Trying to drive a man straight out of his mind."

A rush of air escaped Hailey's lips, though this time it was needy.

Hot and pulsing between us.

Fuck, I had the urge to kiss her.

That should be my warning right there because kissing was something I didn't do.

Never had.

That intimacy something I didn't give into. Funny, I'd wanted to kiss her then and that unfortunate fact still remained true. She was the one person who'd ever made me contemplate it before.

Look where that had gotten me.

Still, there I was, playing a dangerous game, some kind of twisted Russian Roulette.

I stepped away before I got lost in it, shut her door, then hustled around the front and jumped into the driver's side. I pushed the button for the ignition.

I could feel the depth of those blue eyes washing over me.

Devouring me from the side.

My spirit fisted, and I reached out and squeezed her hand. "I'm going to protect you, Hailey. You and Maddie. I won't let that bastard get near you. Whatever it takes. I promise you that."

I'd end him before he ever got the chance.

Chapter Twenty-Two

Hailey

"THERE WE GO, GIRL. YOU ARE GORGEOUS, AREN'T YOU?" I was in one of the exterior covered corrals that ran the backside of the main stable, gently running my hand down the neck of the filly that had just arrived this morning, whispering love and peace into her ear.

She was a blue roan, a perfect melding of white and black, her coat appearing almost gray though her face and mane were dark.

She had those soulful inky eyes, which this morning were just a little on edge since she'd made the trek from my father's ranch to Cambrey Pines.

Five new horses had been purchased to be delivered throughout the month to keep up with the demand of the resort, and I planned to ease them in slowly.

Get them accustomed to their surroundings.

Make sure each was comfortable here and came to know this as their home.

"That's right, you are doing just fine," I murmured, rubbing that spot between her eyes and gazing at her, letting her know she could trust me.

"She is a beauty, isn't she?" The voice that came from behind brought a smile to my face, comfort wrapping me like a hug.

I swiveled to find my father on the other side of the metal railing, his arms draped over the top as he watched me interact with the horse.

"Why am I not surprised to see you here?" I almost teased. He might have been a savvy businessman, but he loved his horses. I thought he mourned a little bit each time one of them left his ranch.

"I had a couple beautiful girls I thought I'd better come check up on this morning."

His gaze was tender as he looked at me, and affection wound through my chest. I caressed down the mare's neck. "I think we're both doing pretty great."

I saw the second his expression dimmed in worry, as if he had a reason not to accept what I said.

"Is that true? You're really doing fine?" he urged.

My stomach clenched, and my teeth ground in an attempt to prepare myself.

I already knew what was coming.

Still, I played oblivious. "I shouldn't be?"

"Pruitt's in town." His voice sounded of an apology.

Incredulity coursed through my system.

Of course, Pruitt would go to my father.

Play the victim.

He'd blinded my father just as thoroughly as he'd blinded me, though my father hadn't been around enough to see the veil being peeled back.

He hadn't been exposed to the shady side, only seeing the pieces that Pruitt presented.

Part of the reason I was afraid to expose Pruitt was I didn't know what it would do to my father. If my father would somehow be implicated since he was the one Pruitt purchased his horses from.

Plus, my father would just be devastated all around.

Believing in someone that way. Supporting them. *Trusting* them.

Then they turned right around and drove a two-foot blade through your back.

I released some of the dread I'd been carrying since last night.

At least now I knew how Pruitt was playing this.

For the time being, he was going to manipulate and twist and coerce rather than attempt to force.

I found some comfort in that. It bought me time. Time to figure out what I was going to do.

"He came to the house," I said, voice flat.

"He wants to see Maddie." There was my father, the peacekeeper.

Disbelief shook my head as I stepped away from the horse, and there was no keeping the spite out of my words that time. "Dad, he doesn't care a thing about Maddie."

"How could you say that? He's been a mess since you left."

I bet he'd been a mess since he could no longer use me as a cover. My name on those papers. It made me sick.

"I know you think you know him, and I know you only want what's best for me and Maddie, but trust me when I tell you that Pruitt is not the man you think he is."

Apprehension creased the edges of my father's eyes. "I'm not sure I know what you mean by that."

"It means he isn't the man for me, and I don't want anything to do with him, and I sure as hell don't want him around my daughter."

"I know sometimes successful men can be difficult, Hailey. Selfish. And I can only imagine he spent a lot of time away from home, and you likely felt ignored and neglected, but—"

"This isn't a lonely housewife issue, Dad, and I need you to drop it because you don't understand."

"He's your husband, Hailey."

"He's not my husband," I defended.

At least I didn't consider him that, and I was praying to push through the divorce as quickly as possible.

He kept right on like he wasn't hearing me. "Times get rough, Hailey. That's all this is—a rough patch. And it's time you pick yourself up and fight through your problems the way I taught you to do when you were young. Stand by your commitments."

Hurt impaled my chest, and a harsh breath heaved from my lungs.

Taking the horse by the reins, I moved to the gate and opened it.

My father still rested right there beside it, concern deepening every line on his face. "I am fighting, Dad. I'm fighting for the life I want," I told him.

I saw the war go down in his spirit.

He wanted to support me, all while remaining staunch in what he believed to be right for me.

When my mother had died in a car accident when I was young, he'd been crushed.

Devastated that he couldn't give me the perfect life that they'd imagined.

Somewhere along the way, he'd turned to hoping for that *perfect life* for me.

"I think you need to hear Pruitt out," he pushed.

"He's said everything he needs to say." With that, I tugged at the reins, and I turned my back to him as I led the filly around the side of the stables to the entry at the far end.

A power tool whirred up the way, carried on the breeze, the sun blazing down from the endless expanse of blue sky and covering the scenery with glittering light.

My heart that had been pounding with regret and anger sped in a completely different way.

I slowed, stumbling to a stop.

Unable to look away.

Cody stood over his crew who were digging a long trench to put in a new watering system, and he pulled the cap off his head and dragged his fingers through his hair as he pointed at something and gave instructions.

Even in the distance, I could see the sheen of sweat that glistened his golden skin, his white tee dampened with the exertion. His big body towered like a sanctuary I had the foolish notion to run to.

He must have felt me staring because he shifted to look back at me.

His promises from earlier pummeled and bashed into my consciousness, battering in the sweetest way.

His oath to be there for us. To stand as a hedge of protection.

I kept worrying that would only make matters worse.

Inflame a situation that was already volatile.

At the brink of imploding.

The presence bristled beside me, and I turned to find my father glowering with loathing, hatred rolling.

Wave after wave.

"Please tell me you aren't acting a fool and messing around with that loser." His teeth gritted as he released the words.

Arrows of affliction speared through my spirit.

I struggled to get a breath of air in around the barbs of pain my father inflicted.

"I don't see how that's any of your business."

Horror creasing his face, he grabbed me by the wrist as I went to pass. "Tell me you wouldn't do something so reckless and stupid."

Air wheezed from my lungs.

"What I do is none of your concern. I know you think you know what's best for me, but I'm a grown woman, and I don't need you or anyone else to tell me what I need."

It wasn't like Cody and I *were* anything. But that didn't mean I was going to allow my father to debase Cody's name when he didn't know anything about him.

"Now, I need to get back to work." I wrenched my arm free of his hold and started down the path.

"Hailey." In an instant, my father's voice had changed, my name becoming a plea when he realized how offensive he was being. "Hailey, I'm sorry, I just…don't want you making mistakes you can't take back."

"I think this conversation is over."

He vacillated behind me, clearly wanting to continue, to apologize, to mold.

And how could I really blame him that he would never truly get it, but I'd chosen that. I'd chosen to keep him in the dark.

But I could blame him for judging. Judging a man like Cody when he was so much better than the garbage dressed as prestige that was Pruitt Russel.

Soon I might have to shed light on the secrets that I'd been keeping like a festering wound. A weight that made me sick to carry, guilt eating away at my conscience.

Soon, my father might really see.

"I love you, Hailey," my father murmured before he finally relented and strode back up the pathway to where he would have parked his truck on the other side of the stables.

He might have tried to hide it, but there was no missing the storm that raged around him.

Unease twisted my stomach when Cody caught the action, his giant body rigid as he watched my father leave.

And this mess I'd dragged him into? I was sure it'd just gotten dirtier.

Chapter Twenty-Three

Cody

"WHAT ALL DO WE NEED?" I ASKED AS I PUSHED THE cart through the double sliding doors and into the grocery store. In an instant, the heat of the summer was squashed by the cold air that pumped from the AC in the small store in Hendrickson.

I'd felt like I'd been being burned alive the entire day, and the temperature outside didn't have a thing to do with it.

It was this woman ambling along at my side that made me feel like I was getting singed.

"I just need to grab a couple things for dinner and some milk for breakfast in the morning." She walked ahead of me, guiding me into the produce section.

"And what are we having?" I asked.

It was a wonder I didn't knock into the displays around me considering I couldn't look away from her ass. That lush, ripe peach swaying with each step that she took.

Hailey sent me a playful scowl. "What, you think I'm going to feed you, too?"

"If you have a problem with it, I'll be happy to cook for you."

Her brows arched, mischief playing on her face. How she managed it after dealing with that prick last night and whatever bullshit her father had clearly been spewing at her this morning, I didn't know.

But I somehow got that she'd spent enough time being dejected and she wasn't going to allow it any longer. She was going to rise above her circumstances, enjoy the good of each day.

"You cook?" Her question rang with speculation.

"I *am* a bachelor. How else do you think I survive?"

"Pizza?"

"That's a little cliché, isn't it?"

"Is it? Who doesn't love pizza?" She leaned over and started to inspect the broccoli spears, the ones she approved of going into the bag as she bent over the display.

I salivated at the *real display*, that ass pert and so tempting it rendered a man stupid.

I edged up so I was standing right behind her, drawn by that gravity. Unable to stay away.

When she turned around, I was right there. Invading her space. Wading closer.

A frown pulled across her pretty, pretty face, and she whispered around the surprise and need emanating from her sweet soul. "Cody."

Unable to stop myself, I pulled her against me, an arm around her waist, bringing us chest to chest.

"What are you doing?" she asked with tremulous words.

God, I loved the way she smelled, like strawberries and cream and the most delicious thing.

I wanted to bury my nose in her hair.

Put my mouth to her flesh.

Drink her up.

Devour every inch.

"Just double checking that you're real because it should be impossible for someone like you to exist."

Her fingers twisted in the fabric of my tee like she was searching for support, the girl swaying as she peered up at me, knocking me off my damned feet with those icy eyes that slicked through me on a fiery chill.

"Cody," she warned, though my name fell from her softly, hitting me like a caress that would be so easy to lean into.

"Hailey," I razzed back, letting the words go as a ravenous tease, doing my best to keep my head above the sea thrashed waters that kept threatening to drag me under, like it was completely normal for me to be holding her like this when we were just supposed to be friends.

"You are nothing but a heap of trouble, Cody Cooper." Redness splashed those cheeks, and she couldn't contain this timid, affected smile when she pulled away.

That's the way I wanted her.

Smiling.

Unafraid.

"You have no idea," I told her, and I took her hand and threaded our fingers together before I lifted them to brush a kiss across her knuckles. "Honestly, Hailey, I needed to check that you're real and whole and safe. Touch you to make sure you're right here with me."

Hailey got stuck there, staring up at me, before she seemed to gather herself, clearing her throat as she unwound her fingers from mine.

"Come on, let's get what we came for. I want to get home. I miss my daughter and I'm starving and want to change out of these clothes. It's been a long day."

A grin pulled to my mouth as I thought of that little Button who'd be waiting for us to return. "Yeah. We'd better get back. I still have an important job to do."

Hailey moved to the onions, going through the pile in search of one that suited her. The whole time, I watched her itch. Disquiet spinning her into unease, reservations vying for a way to be released.

"It looks to me like you have something to say, darlin."

She inhaled as she put the onion into the cart before she turned her attention to me.

"I need you to be careful with her, Cody. She's…" She paused as she considered her words. "Her heart is wide open, but it's fragile, too, and I'm worried she's going to get attached to you. I don't want her to get confused by you being around so much."

She hesitated, teeth clamping on that plush bottom lip, before she looked up at me from beneath those lashes with those bottomless eyes. "Just...don't make her promises you can't keep."

"I don't intend to."

"But it's easy to get caught up in something, to start to believe it's going to end one way when there's no chance that it really could."

I wondered which of us she was really warning.

"And sometimes we end up exactly where we're supposed to even when we never believed for a second it could be a part of our destination," I told her.

She looked away. Without a doubt, she was terrified of believing what I was saying.

Fuck, guess I was, too, but I was having a harder and harder time envisioning walking away from her in the end.

I had to.

I knew it.

But that didn't change the way I felt.

"You know we can't, Cody." It was the softest rejection that still clanged in our ears.

"Excuse me." A voice came from the side.

I jolted out of the spell this woman had me under, turning to find an older woman written in sheer irritation as she waited to get to the potatoes I was blocking with the cart.

"Sorry," Hailey rushed, flustered that we were so caught up in each other that we'd gotten lost to anything around us.

She grabbed the end of the cart and hauled me along as she hurried deeper into the store. She basically went to ignoring me as she grabbed the few things she needed.

Bread.

Steak.

Milk in the dairy section.

Five minutes later, she was heading up to the register and got in line.

I nudged her out of the way, loaded the items onto the belt, then dug into my back pocket to get my wallet so I could take out my card.

"What do you think you're doing?" She whispered it again. Harsh even though it was quiet. It was the same thing she kept asking again and again.

It was a prudent question.

What in the ever-loving-fuck did I think I was doing? Whatever it was, apparently, I couldn't stop.

I put my mouth to her ear. "What does it look like I'm doing? I'm taking care of you."

Because people who cared about someone took care of them.

In any way they could.

We loaded everything into two bags then I carried them out to my truck.

Hailey scrambled along at my side, trying to keep up with my long strides.

It was still hot out, just after five-thirty, the summer in full force.

I clicked the locks and the running lights flashed, and I opened the back passenger door and placed the bags on the floorboards.

Just as I was ducking out, the hairs lifted on the back of my neck as a bolt of awareness streaked through the atmosphere.

It covered me in a cloud of that same vile contempt that I'd been struck with last night when I'd felt Hailey's fear from across our yards.

Only this time, it was directed at both of us.

Hailey must have felt it, too, because she froze where she was standing facing me.

She paled.

Gorgeous face going a pasty white.

Fear so distinct it clotted the air and weaved its way down to saturate my lungs.

Hatred spun me into disorder.

I couldn't stomach that one person could have the power to put that look on her face.

I scanned the lot. It didn't take me long to pinpoint where the source was coming from.

A little café down to the right where a few tables were situated under red umbrellas outside the front.

Pruitt sat at one of them, slung back like a pompous prick wearing a button-down and slacks. Sipping from a tiny cup that was likely a reflection of the size of his dick.

Even in the distance that separated us, there was no mistaking that his dark eyes seared into us.

Hailey was stock-still and staring my direction, not wanting to look over her shoulder to confirm that he was there.

Like she didn't want to contemplate if he'd followed us here or if it was just bad fucking luck that we'd ended up in the same place.

It wasn't like Hendrickson was all that big of a town. If he was sticking around, we were bound to cross paths, but I had a hunch this dickbag was going to be popping up from out of nowhere.

Only solution was getting this bastard out of here sooner. Giving him the damned clue that he wasn't welcome here. That there was no fuckin' chance that he could have her.

"Do you trust me?" I muttered, a secret between us.

Hailey hesitated for only one second before she gave.

"Yes." The word was so tiny but still struck like a bomb in our atmosphere.

Maybe it was me who shouldn't trust myself.

Because I could feel all my reasoning slip away when I wound my hand in the length of her braid and cinched it up tight.

Could feel the ground falling away when I looped my other arm around her waist.

Could feel all rational thought take flight when I spun her around so her back was to the truck and she was concealed by my body.

Becoming the shield between her and Pruitt that I'd promised her I would be.

I wanted to be.

Fuck, I wanted to be.

But the reason for it got distorted when I tugged her closer, became mangled and deformed when I inhaled her scent.

It left me altogether when I leaned down and captured her mouth with mine.

Sweet. Fucking. Heat.

Her eyes went wide for one shocked second before she melted into me when I wrapped my arm tighter around her and pulled her flush. She sighed into the kiss like it was the one thing in this world that could offer her respite.

Somehow, I knew that was exactly what it was for me.

Respite.

Bliss.

Motherfucking heaven.

I kissed her deeper, and she opened to me, and her tongue stroked out to meet with mine.

Strawberries and cream.

I pulled her so close that I lifted her off her feet as I kissed and kissed her, my other hand yanking harder at her braid as I devoured her mouth.

Lips and tongue and teeth.

Greed and lust and something else that hovered around us like the utterings of a lost dream.

So fucking *intimate*, so damned close, that I thought this girl might become an intrinsic part of me.

I drank down the whimper she exhaled, and I nearly got knocked to my knees when she wound her delicate arms around my neck and pressed her tits to my chest.

Then she had to go and whisper my name against my lips. "Cody."

No one had ever once said my name like that. Or maybe it was the first time I was listening.

Possession wound me in a fist, ribs clenching around my heart as the single word thundered through my mind.

Mine.

He couldn't have her.

I wouldn't let him.

Fuck, what was happening to me?

I forced myself to slow because I knew I was cracking, one mistake from splintering, from completely losing control.

Setting my hands on her waist, I peeled my mouth away and dropped my forehead to hers, knowing we needed space but there wasn't one goddamn molecule in my body that could fully let her go.

Both of us were panting for the air that'd gone missing, and Hailey gulped as she tried to orient herself. At least thirty seconds must have passed before she finally asked, "Is he still there?"

Rage blustered through me when I forced myself to look over my shoulder, ready to take on anything that was to come, only the bastard was gone.

"Nah, we got rid of him."

If only it were permanent. I doubted much that he was going to get the message so easy.

Pulling back an inch, she blinked as she tried to process what the hell had just happened. Her fingertips were still nailed into my shoulders, confusion and need whipping her into a puddle.

"What are we doing, Cody?" The words were haggard.

"We're showing your ex that he can't have you." It scraped up my raw throat.

Her teeth raked her bottom lip that was still plump and glistening from the kiss. "I'm afraid we might only be making it worse."

"We'll figure it out. Together," I promised.

I couldn't help but think she was likely right.

The fucker was going to be pissed, his ego ripped to shreds.

And I was the asshole who thought it might be worth it because I didn't think I'd ever felt anything better than this.

Chapter Twenty-Four
Hailey

Eighteen Years Old

HAILEY RAN THE BRUSH DOWN THE MARE'S BACK.

Rhythmically.

Methodically.

The horse was due in a couple weeks, and Hailey had taken to giving her company each day, soothing her, letting her know she was safe.

Besides, the stables were her favorite place in the world.

She didn't want to be anywhere else, and she knew this was the way she would spend her life.

She settled into the calm of it, the cadenced sound of the brush whispering over the mare's dark black coat, a silence all around, her thoughts drifting into the solace.

"There you are."

She nearly jumped out of her skin when the voice hit her from behind, and she whirled around to find her best friend poking her head over the top of the gate.

"What is wrong with you, Brooke? You scared the crap out of me."

Brooke's brow shot so high it was a wonder it didn't touch the arched, soaring ceiling. "I scared the crap out of you? I'm the one who had to wander down here to the stables to find you, and you know how I feel about that."

Brooke overexaggerated a shiver.

Hailey giggled. "These horses are harmless."

It was a little ironic Hailey's best friend was terrified of horses, and Brooke never let her forget it since she was spending the summer here with Hailey before she would leave to attend college in South Carolina.

They were always glued to each other's sides, and they wanted to spend as much time together before Brooke left.

Wistfulness dampened Hailey's mood, though she kept it concealed.

It was going to be rough, being separated from Brooke that way.

She was her person.

The one she was constantly with.

Her confidant.

The one person who she was ever truly open and honest with, especially after Hailey's Lolly had gotten remarried again and moved two hours away, and Hailey had again found herself living alone in a mansion with her father.

Hailey and Brooke were basically opposites. Hailey was verging on shy and unquestionably plain, hoiden through and through, jeans and tees and messy braids, and Brooke looked like she should be gracing the cover of a fashion magazine.

"Are you kidding me? I just saw a beast over there in a pen that clearly was gunning for me. Rearing back then pawing at the earth."

Hailey giggled again. "Um, yeah, you'll want to stay away from that one."

The stallion knew he was surrounded by mares, and he didn't take too kindly that he was cooped up behind metal, and he had a bad temper because of it.

"You don't have to worry about me going anywhere near that monster. No thank you. And there you are, in there with one of those things. Gross." Brooke curled her nose playfully.

Covering the mare's ears, Hailey scowled at her best friend. "Shh. You're going to hurt her feelings."

"The only feelings that thing possesses is a thirst for murder."

"So dramatic."

"Hello. I am going to be a drama major. Do you expect anything less of me?"

"It's definitely fitting." Hailey's smile was wide.

"So, are you done in here, or what? You've been out here for hours, and this girl is bored."

A sigh pilfered between Hailey's lips. "Sure, I can be done. What did you have in mind?"

"A little fun." Brooke shimmied her shoulders.

"I'm not sure I'm up for the kind of fun you have in mind," Hailey drawled. Brooke was always dragging her into trouble, far more out-going than Hailey ever would be. Hailey's experiences were nil compared to when she was standing next to her friend.

"Sure you are."

She gave the horse another pat before she put her tools away and headed back for the gate, slipping out and making sure the latch was secure. "Fine. Take me away from my first loves."

Brooke weaved her fingers through Hailey's and started to guide her down the long aisle of stalls within the enormous stable. "But you love me most."

A soft giggle got free, and she knocked her shoulder into Brooke's. "You know I do."

They pushed out through the main door and into the sunlight that covered the ranch.

Wagner Ranch was tucked deep in the woods beneath soaring pines, and there were four different groupings of stables, one for the stallions, two for the mares, and another for the horses that were for sale but hadn't been purchased or delivered yet.

The ground was a dark soil, damp and covered in leaves, and the two of them tromped up the trail that led to Hailey's house in the distance. It was a rambling, rustic cabin that most considered a mansion, even though Hailey found it warm and cozy.

Home.

"So what do you actually want to do?" Hailey asked.

"There's a party tonight out in the cove."

A scatter of nerves rattled through Hailey.

She'd been trying to stretch her wings.

Attempt new experiences.

But she felt more comfortable covered in dirt or on horseback rather than being surrounded by a bunch of strangers.

Brooke sensed her hesitation, and she shifted to link their elbows together, angling in conspiratorially. "It's time for my bestie to let loose. Dress up and test out the waters."

Hailey groaned. "And what kind of waters might those be?"

"Hot ones. Steaming hot." Brooke wagged her brows.

Hailey laughed, trudging up the trail, though she felt herself slowing.

Tripping on something that changed in the air.

A charge.

An awareness.

One she couldn't pinpoint because she'd never felt anything like it before.

Her gaze collided with someone who was off to her right, digging a hole with a shovel on the far side of a corral.

A boy.

Okay, a man.

One she'd never seen on the ranch before, but it wasn't like hands and contractors weren't constantly coming and going.

He was crazy tall and scarily wide, a trucker's cap on his head and a worn tee stretched over his massive, oppressive frame.

She couldn't quite make out the details of his face, the sun glinting down through the trees and striking over him in a glare that blinded, though she swore she could feel the piercing of his eyes.

Eyes that cut and slayed and flayed her wide open to some secret place that she hadn't known existed.

Her stomach twisted and her heart was suddenly beating manic.

"Oh my God," Brooke was suddenly whispering in a thrill. "That's him."

Jarred out of the stupor, she looked back to Brooke. "Who?"

"The guy I was telling you about. The one I fucked in his truck the other night. Talk about hot." She drew it out, her dark chocolate eyes widening in emphasis.

"Oh." It wheezed out of Hailey.

And she hated that it sounded like disappointment.

Brooke took it all wrong. "Don't worry about me. I mean, I know he's way older and that he comes with a reputation of being a player, but I can totally handle that wild boy." Then she leaned in closer to Hailey's face. "And I fully intend on taming him."

A peal of laughter sprang from Brooke as she shifted and started to race up toward the house, tugging at Hailey as she went. "Come on, we need to get ready. This girl needs to look her best."

Chapter Twenty-Five

Hailey

WHAT THE HELL DID I THINK I WAS DOING?
Playing games with Pruitt was dangerous. I knew it all the way down to my soul. But the problem was I was having a hard time discerning what was real.

How I'd gone from promising myself that I'd never in a million years allow Cody Cooper to touch me because what kind of horrible person did that make me to him giving me the best orgasm I'd ever experienced Saturday night.

How I'd gone from him insisting on staying here for one night to make sure Pruitt didn't come back around to him kissing me like he'd actually meant it in front of the very monster out in that parking lot.

How I'd gone from hating my new neighbor to him out in the backyard putting together a playhouse for my daughter while I finished dinner inside.

Whatever game it was? I knew I was playing it with fire. A crackle in the distance that warned those flames were gathering strength. A few moments more and they'd make it over the ridge and completely consume.

So lost in my thoughts, I nearly jumped out of my skin when the back door burst open and a clatter of energy ripped through the air, though my smile was easy when I found my daughter racing into the kitchen, flapping her arms overhead.

"Mommy! We did it! We got my playhouse all the way done because Mr. Cody is so very strong and has the biggest, most giantest muscles I ever seen, and it's ready and we got the biggest surprise! You need to come see!"

The crash of words tumbled from Maddie, my little whirlwind grinning so wide as she jumped in place, all dimples and chubby cheeks and innocence, wild locks of blonde curls framing her sweet face.

She grabbed my hand and tugged. "Come on, you have to come see right now!"

True to his word, the second we'd gotten back, Cody had gone directly into the backyard and started putting her playhouse together.

"Okay, okay, give me one second and let me turn off this burner so we don't burn the gravy."

I flipped off the knob while Maddie kept tugging at my hand. "Right now, Mommy! Hurry!"

I laughed as she hauled me along. "Someone is excited."

"I'm the most very excited ever." She dragged me across the room and out into the descending night.

The air was grayed and cooled, the heavens colored in sweeps and swirls of fading color as the darkness wisped across the sky.

Maddie turned to face me as she led me down the porch steps. "Close your eyes, it's a surprise."

"A surprise, huh?"

"A really good one."

I peeked over at the playhouse that had been set up beneath the big oak tree that stood on the far end of the yard, its branches stoic and its reach wide.

Madison's playhouse was made to look like a cottage, the plastic shaped into planks of wood with a gray door and white-framed windows that were missing the glass.

She bounced all the way across the lawn until we were in front of it.

I knew the ceiling was basically only high enough for Maddie to stand in, so I was giggling when she threw open the door and demanded, "Keep your eyes closed all the way, Mommy, and follow me all the way inside!"

Trying to keep them closed, I got to my knees to crawl inside, squeezing through the narrow doorway as I patted my hands on the ground to guide myself.

When I made it through, Maddie shouted, "Open them!"

I was on my knees when I did, and a soft gasp escaped when I opened them to take in the scene. Blankets had been spread out on the floor and little twinkle lights were strung up on the ceiling, casting it in a soft, warm glow.

Her Princess Verona bunny and a couple other dolls were set up on the right side at the little table that extended from the wall.

And Cody...Cody had somehow wedged himself inside, the heap of a man curled up in the left back corner with his knees pulled to his chest and a fake pink pearl necklace around his neck.

"Surprise! We're having a party!" Maddie threw her arms up again.

"A party?" I barely mouthed as I looked to Cody, an apology in my expression.

"That's right," he rumbled in that dark voice, his rugged face so handsome in the shadows that played through the confined space. "We're having a party. I even got dressed up."

He gave a soft tug to the necklace around his neck.

"And we have to eat in here because it's a dinner party and I even got drinks but it's not wine because I'm not old enough." Maddie lifted a plastic teacup that brimmed with water, sloshing it over the side in her enthusiasm.

"Wow, this is amazing," I drew out, sending Cody another apologetic look when I said it.

He just smiled one of those easy smiles.

Like this was no big deal. Like he wasn't single-handedly wreaking havoc on my sanity. Or maybe he was just tweaking that sanity into something brand new.

My insides tumbled. God, what in the world were we doing?

That gaze shined, and beneath it, my lips tingled with the vestiges of that kiss.

That kiss that had wrecked me in the best way possible.

Made my knees weak and my head spin and sent my heart clamoring toward something that had felt so fundamentally right all while being intrinsically wrong.

That kiss that I needed to remember was only meant to send Pruitt a message.

"We have to go get the food now," Maddie ordered, tugging at my hand again, trying to urge me back to the tiny door.

"I think a dinner party sounds really fun, but where is Lolly supposed to sit?" I teased.

"She's gonna sit right here." Lolly's ragged voice suddenly echoed from the other side of the plastic. Disbelief hit me when I realized she had to be leaned against the outside wall of the playhouse.

"Is my grandmother actually sitting out there on the ground right now?" I all but demanded.

Maddie looked at me like I was clueless. "Well, of course she's got to sit on the outside because she's got a bad hip and there's no way she's gettin' all the way in here without breaking it."

Maddie nodded when she finished her spiel, proud of herself for issuing what was likely the exact same words Lolly had given her when she'd tried to get her inside.

Aghast, I moved to pop my head out the window. Lolly was sitting on the lawn with her back leaning against the playhouse, just as I'd suspected.

"Lolly, what in the world are you doing? You don't need to be sitting on the ground."

She sent me a droll smile, lips painted a bright pink today. "Well, now that I'm sitting here, I'm not sure I'm going to be able to get back up."

Maddie scrambled over to my side and tried to poke her head out, too. "Don't worry, my Lolly! We got Mr. Cody, and he's got the muscles, so he can pick you right up."

"Well, I do like the sound of that," Lolly tossed right back.

Flustered, I looked to Cody who was quite literally backed into

214 | A.L. JACKSON

a corner. Only he let go of a coarse chuckle, amusement riding all over his handsome face.

"You just tell me when," he hollered.

"After dinner," Maddie proclaimed.

"Anytime, anywhere, I'll be right here waiting for you," Lolly said at the same time.

I inhaled a deep breath, searching for the best solution that wasn't going to ruin the excitement that blazed from my child and get my poor grandmother off the ground. "Why don't we have our party drinks right now, and then we eat our dinner on the patio table so we're close to your playhouse? That way Lolly can eat with us."

"Great idea, Mommy!"

Thankfully, Maddie didn't seem all that disappointed, and she hopped back to the table where she had the teapot and teacups. She poured another one to the brim and carefully tried to balance it as she brought it to me, even though she spilled half of it on her way.

Cody already had his, and he picked it up from where it sat on the floor next to him, mirth covering him whole.

Maddie moved back toward him in the confined space and lifted her cup. "To the best party ever, and to the best Mr. Cody ever, since he built my playhouse so super fast."

She clinked her teacup to his, then I put mine in the center, too, and whispered, "To Cody."

Those golden flecked eyes twinkled back at me when I clinked my cup to his.

Lolly suddenly pushed her teacup through the window. "Now I will drink to that."

⌒✳⌒

"Goodnight, my very favorite Mr. Cody!" Maddie hollered toward the ceiling. She was in her bed and Cody had just unclicked the lock on the bathroom and stepped out into the hallway.

I wasn't able to see him since I was kneeling beside Maddie's bed, tucking her in, but I could almost feel the weight of his smile as he edged forward a little to come stand in her doorway, the weight of his presence pushing in on me from behind.

His aura profound.

That warm energy that felt like a refuge rippling through the air.

"Goodnight, Button. Thanks for throwing the best party I've ever attended."

I finally swiveled to peer at him from across her room, and my breath hitched at the impact.

Freshly showered, his hair darkened to a deep brown since it was wet. He'd pulled on a clean tee and a pair of black sweats, powerful and gorgeous.

Looking like a sea of temptation and a barrel of regret.

Maddie hugged Princess Verona closer to her chest and wiggled beneath her covers. "Do you really think so?" she asked him.

Cody lifted a tattooed arm and leaned it high against her doorframe.

So casual, though the movement hit me like pure devastation.

"Oh, yeah. I've been to a ton of parties, but never one quite like that."

Pride filled Maddie's face, and she shifted her head on her pillow so she was looking directly at me. "I think it was a very good idea that we came here, Mommy, because I think Mr. Cody was lonely and needed us to be neighborly, and now we get to go make even more friends on Saturday and I love it here the best. I don't ever want to go back to Texas."

Her expression dimmed, though hope lit beneath it.

My spirit cramped.

That ache that knew she hadn't been immune.

I brushed back a wild curl from her forehead. "I have no intention of ever going back, either."

I wanted to state it with confidence. Make her trust in it, to claim it like an oath. Still, my soul shook with the terror that lingered at the edges of my mind, lingered right outside the door, far closer than I'd ever wanted to allow them to be.

Maddie's voice went soft like a secret, uncertainty dimming her blue, blue eyes. "Texas is bad."

Dread swept in. "Why do you say that?"

Maddie hesitated, then hid her mouth beneath her covers when she confessed, "Because that's where my daddy lives."

My heart clutched. "And you think your daddy is bad?"

I was treading carefully, not wanting to shut her down but also not wanting to inject my own vitriol into the situation.

"Only when he whispers at you like he's really mad."

Those whispers echoed through my mind.

"You really think you can just leave?" Pruitt had hissed, his hand at my throat as he'd had me pressed to the hallway wall. "You keep forgetting who I am."

"Mommy?" I'd looked to the right to find Maddie standing at the end of the hall, her rabbit held to her chest, eyes wobbling with tears.

"It's okay, Maddie. Go back to your room and go to sleep. I'm fine."

How long had I been saying that?

I'm fine.

I'm fine.

I felt the floor shift as the man slowly approached, like he couldn't remain at bay for a second longer, persuaded by the sudden call of my daughter's fear. Or maybe he'd been compelled by mine, too, because Cody slowly eased to kneeling beside me.

After dinner, I'd bathed and changed into sleep shorts and a tank, and one of those big hands went to my waist, his fingers dipping just beneath the fabric while his other hand splayed out wide over my daughter's chest from over the blanket.

A covering.

A shield.

"You don't have to worry about that any longer, Maddie. I'm right here, and I'm not going anywhere." Cody grunted it in that low voice.

Don't make my daughter promises you can't keep.

I looked up at the man, so solid, so firm.

Impenetrable.

Immovable.

His gaze traveled to mine. "Mean it."

My nod was shuddery, and his was succinct.

The promise sealed.

Then he leaned in and lightly tickled my daughter.

"Cody, you got me," she squealed.

"Nah, Maddie, you got me."

Emotion crushed down.

A tumble of possibility.

A landslide of worry.

A lifetime of regret.

"Now get some sleep, little one." He leaned forward and pressed a tender kiss to her temple.

She gripped the tops of her covers, beaming up at him. "Okay, my very best Cody."

Affection radiated from him, so distinct it filled the room.

I kissed her cheek and whispered, "Goodnight, Maddie. I love you so much."

"I love you, Mommy."

I remained floored as Cody pushed to standing.

Rising to his full, towering height.

Nothing but strength and fortitude.

He stretched out a hand.

I looked at it, divided, somehow knowing what it would mean if I accepted it.

But I did.

I let him enfold my hand in his, and he helped me to stand to my feet.

He watched me as he began to walk backward, leading me out.

I felt the ground shift, the earth canting to the side.

My heart no longer knew the safest way to beat.

I trudged through it like he wasn't destroying my resolve, like I didn't ache at the sight of him, like my belly wasn't in knots and my spirit wasn't in an uproar.

He eased all the way out the door, and I reached out to flick off

218 | A.L. JACKSON

Maddie's light. It tossed darkness over the house and triggered the small nightlight out in the hall to flicker to life.

I pulled Maddie's door closed a fraction.

Still facing me, he kept edging down the hall.

A lure.

Temptation.

Gravity.

My feet shuffled along the bare floor, and our breaths were shallow and too loud, as if they'd become an entity of their own. The air crackling though it was smooth and slow.

I finally spoke when we'd made it out into the living area with the faint illumination of the lights under the cabinets in the kitchen whispering around us. "Thank you."

It was the only thing I could say, the only truth I was brave enough to admit.

A gentle frown carved Cody's strong brow. "And what are you thanking me for?"

My huff was half awe and half disbelief. "For…everything. For putting that playhouse together and then going along with my daughter's imaginings. For making her feel…special."

"I've got news for you, Hailey…" He murmured it in that low, growly voice before he reached out and ran the pad of his thumb across my bottom lip. "Your daughter *is* special."

My heart nearly leapt out of my chest. Was nearly crushed. Was nearly freed.

I tried to shake myself out of the stupor, to knock myself out of the trance he held me under.

Hypnotized.

I jumped when my phone buzzed in my pocket, and Cody carefully watched as I shakily pulled it out.

Pruitt: You're going to learn what happens when you toy with me.

Alarm coiled like a snake, and a frown pulled deep between Cody's eyes. "What is it?"

When I found I couldn't make myself form the words, Cody

gently pried my phone from my hand, and his eyes dipped to the message before they bore back into me.

"What that motherfucker is going to learn is that he can't have you, Hailey."

My throat was tight, and the fear I'd been running from erupted, breaking free of its barricades.

"I don't think I know what I'm doing," I admitted.

Cody tossed my phone to the couch before he took my face between two massive hands. He leaned in close, his lips a breadth from mine. "You're fighting."

I curled both hands around his wrists. "I want to be strong enough."

"You are, darlin'. You are. You've always been."

I gulped, and the air was too thick. Dense and heavy. Pulsing with that energy that in that second felt far more powerful than the demons that hunted me.

And his name rolled off my tongue, nothing but a desperate plea. "Cody."

Chapter Twenty-Six

Hailey

THE SECOND I SET IT FREE, HE HAD ONE ARM WOUND around my waist and the other gripped onto the back of my neck as he pulled me flush against him.

Gold-flecked eyes danced in the muted light, a second of searching before he murmured, "I don't want to fucking pretend that I don't want you, Hailey. Don't want to pretend like there isn't something more to this."

There was no hesitation after that. His mouth crushed against mine, urgent and as desperate as I felt.

This kiss? It was fevered.

He spun me and spun me, never breaking that kiss as we fumbled our way across the living room and kitchen toward my bedroom, hands gripping and mouths searching and hearts thrumming.

We banged through the opening, and the second we made it inside my room, he pressed me to the wall next to the door.

I gasped against his lips.

A hand weaved into my hair that earlier I'd let free of its braid, and he tugged my head back as he pulled back for a beat.

Hunger blazed in his eyes.

It left no question I was about to be devoured.

I wanted it. I wanted to be consumed. Consumed in a way I'd never been before. In a way I knew only this man could do.

"Fuck me, Shortcake. What have you done?" Cody grated it as he reached out and quietly shut the door with a soft snick.

Glancing at me, he flipped the lock. The tiny metallic sound bounced through the room like a promise.

A covenant.

Inciting.

Provoking.

Instigating a disruption that couldn't be contained.

He dove back for me, and his tongue stroked into my mouth to lick against mine.

It was a tangle of greed.

A snaring of lust.

Desire sparked with each crucial lash, a life-beat that spread through my body and pumped through my blood.

I drove my fingers into his soft, damp hair, and I hung on as he kissed me into oblivion.

As reality fell away and the only thing that mattered was this moment.

"Cody."

"I've got you, darlin'," he rumbled into the manic kiss, my feet barely touching the ground because I was already floating away.

I wanted to feel him everywhere, and I searched him in the shadows of my room, palms riding over his shoulders, fingertips exploring his chest, his stomach, his hips. I dragged them back up his thick throat so I could explore the lines of his rugged, handsome face.

Tracing.

Touching.

Memorizing.

The way I'd wanted to do from the first time I'd seen him. The way I'd felt the impact of his presence like a thunderclap.

Like an awakening.

I should have known something so powerful could only mean death.

Cody groaned, and his hands slid down my sides, taking greedy handfuls as he went. "Love these fuckin' curves. Got me fucked, Hailey."

He spread them out over my bottom and pulled me hard against his rigid length.

Need left me on a pant, and I clung to him tighter.

"You feel that?" The possessive sound was close to a growl. "What you do to me? Do you get how fucking hard I am for you? How badly I want you? I don't think there's been a time in my life when I've wanted anything as badly as this. You're the kind of temptation that makes a man do stupid things. Kind of temptation that drives him right up to the edge."

A whimper crawled up my throat as a flicker of pleasure sparked where we connected because he had me there, too.

On the edge.

Doing stupid, stupid things.

Cody grabbed me by the backs of the thighs, and he hiked me up like I weighed nothing.

My arms shot out to curl around his neck and my legs wrapped around his narrow waist.

There wasn't anything I could do to stop myself from rubbing up and down the perfect shape of his chest and abdomen.

"Look at the way you fit in my arms, Hailey. Like you were meant to be there. Making me lose sight."

I couldn't find it in myself to care that I was making these embarrassing sounds, my need for him verging on manic. "It's you who's made me lose reason. You who's making me need things I don't understand."

I kept kissing him without sense, and he stroked his tongue against mine as he carried me across my bedroom.

A gluttonous sound got free when he tossed me to my bed, and I bounced on the mattress, pressing my thighs together since I no longer had the stony planes of his abdomen to grind myself against.

From where he stood at the side of my bed, he smirked down at me. No doubt, he was reveling in the fact he had me spun up so fast that I was close to begging.

"Don't worry, Shortcake. I understand exactly what you need."

"Cocky Cowboy." I wheezed it as my hips arched from the bed.

A rough chuckle skated the heated air, and those big hands came to take me by both knees.

Heat flash-fired, and Cody let that grin that was close to pain right then tweak higher as he slowly pried them apart, the expression on his face ravenous.

Eyes molten, burning me up.

"Have you been thinking about me, Hailey? The way I've been thinking about you?"

"Yes." I saw no point in denying it any longer, even though I was sure it was going to crush me in the end.

"And what exactly have you been thinking?" His voice was a tease edged in possession.

God, I'd never met a man like him. One so easily arrogant who still oozed this power that made me weak in the knees.

One who made me both want to run because I was terrified of what he might come to mean all while knowing I would sell half my soul to stay in his space.

"I haven't stopped thinking of you having me like this since you touched me last weekend."

What I wouldn't admit is I'd thought it for years.

Since that summer.

Fantasies of him that I'd kept like a dirty secret that had only piled on the shame.

"I don't want to go to sleep tonight without you touching me. One more time. Show me what it would be like. If it was real."

Each word was a ragged pant, and he kept taking me in from where he stood hovering at the edge of my bed.

So big in the night. A tower that shrouded.

"One more time, huh?" He prodded it, like he already knew no matter how many times I had him, I was going to want more.

"Yes. Once more." It was the last defense I had. Because I was the foolish girl who already felt herself falling.

Falling for a man who was so out of reach I knew I could never really touch him.

"Don't you fret, darlin', I plan on taking care of you. I'm going to make you come so hard and so good that I'm going to have to gag you so Lolly doesn't hear you screaming."

There was that arrogance, but I couldn't find it in me to be offended by it right then. Not when what he was suggesting sounded so damn nice.

"Please."

Cody ran his hands up the inside of my thighs, spreading my legs wide as he went.

Flames ignited in their wake.

Shivers rolled.

Alive.

My heart a thunder in my chest.

His silhouette was massive where he hovered over me in the swirling dimness of my room.

Both hazard and asylum.

I whimpered a needy sound when he leaned all the way over me and ran his lips along my jaw, his short beard rough and sweet and probably leaving a mark.

Lolly was going to have a field day tomorrow.

But I couldn't find it in myself to care. Not when those hands raked down my shoulders and over my breasts before he sat back enough so he could grab the hem of my tank. He slowly peeled it up.

I shivered as he went, and I angled up to make it easier for him.

My nipples pebbled into the hardest peaks when he pulled it all the way over my head.

I sank back to the mattress while Cody remained standing. Gaze afire and his teeth plucking at his bottom lip.

"Fuck me, darlin.'"

He dragged the knuckle of his index finger over my left nipple.

Fire zipped through my middle and sent shockwaves shooting between my thighs.

"Been dying to get a good look at these tits. Not sure I'm ever going to be the same."

He bunched both of them up, my breasts far more than those big hands could contain, and he dipped down and licked one hardened tip and then moved to do the same to the other.

I squirmed, bucking up as my fingers clawed at his chest. "Cody."

"Don't worry, darlin', I know what you need," he mumbled at the sensitive flesh, and then he was easing down, kissing a path across the soft flesh of my belly.

Desire streaked far and wide, and I breathed out toward the ceiling when he hooked his fingers in the waistband of my sleep shorts and dragged them down my legs.

Leaving me shaking and bare.

He hissed.

I didn't know if I wanted to be shy or bold. If I should press my knees together to cover myself or spread them wide so he'd touch me again, the way he had the other night when he'd sent me flying.

He made the decision easy, taking me back by the knees and rubbing circles on the inside with the pads of his thumbs as he took me in like I was a picture to be admired.

His tongue stroked across his lips. "Look at that pink, perfect pussy, dripping for me."

I whined, mad with lust.

Delirious with what he'd awakened. This part of me that'd gone dormant years before.

"Do you have any idea the number of times I pictured you like this?" he rumbled from somewhere deep in his chest. "Lying right here in this bed? Naked and glorious. Just the way I knew you'd be."

"You think I'm the beautiful one?" I rasped it. Because he left me dumbfounded, his rugged, raw beauty stealing my breath.

Cody shifted his attention to my eyes. There wasn't a trace of the tease he normally wore. "Yeah, Hailey, I do."

Then he slipped his arms under my legs, and he dipped between them and dragged his tongue through my center, all the way up to suckle my clit.

He nearly sent me soaring with the first lick.

My fingers dove into his hair as my shoulders arched from the bed.

I mewled a desperate, "Cody."

He eased back, so freaking smug as he lifted his head to look at me where I writhed. "Didn't even take a minute to have you whimpering my name. Give me a second, and you'll be screaming it."

"I didn't invite you in here to taunt me, Mr. Cooper."

He cracked a grin. "Ah, we're back to Mr. Cooper, are we? Seems awful formal considering your pussy is in my face."

"Shut up." It was a choked laugh, and I was unable to contain the smile because the man was so much, pure joy and light and warmth, then I was moaning when he murmured, "Gladly," and dove back in again.

He tucked his shoulders between my thighs, his tongue hot and perfect as he rolled it over my clit.

Pleasure sparked behind my eyes, and in two seconds flat, my entire body was vibrating. A feeling sweeping through, pinpricks that promised what was to come.

I mewled and whined and tried to keep quiet, but I was whimpering his name like the lyrics of a song.

Cody quickened, swirling, lapping, teasing and taunting, his voice a grumble against that sensitive nub. "Yes, Shortcake. That's it. Let me hear you. Want to hear you come undone as I eat your delicious cunt. Have wanted you on my tongue since the second I saw you."

Bliss gathered quick, from the outermost edges of my body and mind. I writhed and jutted, begging for more, and my fingers yanked at the soft curls of his hair.

Cody pressed two of those big fingers into the well of my body, or maybe it was three, because it felt so good, the way he filled me.

So much.

Not nearly enough.

The incredible pressure as he pumped, driving me right toward ecstasy.

His fingers thrust deep as he intensified the sweep of his tongue.

And it grew and grew—this light that illuminated inside me. This man who was so kind and giving once you peeled back the layers.

His arrogance sweet.

His goodness great.

And what expanded in my chest became overwhelming.

Joy.

Warmth.

The unfurling of something brand new.

A rebirth.

I should be terrified of it. The way it swelled and inflated and billowed through my spirit while the magic he whipped me into gathered to a pinpoint.

My belly tight, each brush of his tongue driving me to a place where I'd likely want to exist forever.

It was reckless, going there, but I was already climbing toward that destination.

He pushed his fingers deep, turning them as he used his other hand to press down on the lower part of my belly. He raked his fingers somewhere deep as his tongue swirled and licked.

I splintered then.

A shattering of pleasure as I blew.

I came apart like rays of sunlight spearing into the sky the second the sun breaks the horizon.

Gold, glittering streaks. Fireworks of pinks and blues.

I throbbed around his fingers as bliss streaked through my body.

Rolling and rolling and rolling.

He slowed though he didn't stop, the man dragging the orgasm out because he knew exactly how to take care of me, just like he'd promised.

I chanted his name, no sense to be found, only the bright light that sparked behind my eyes and the sensation that swept me away.

Rapture.

Release.

A bittersweet sort of heaven that I knew would soon be ripped from under my feet.

We both had to know this wouldn't last.

Before I could make sense of it, he crawled onto the bed and planted both hands on either side of my head.

He hovered over me as he angled down and took my mouth in a mind-bending kiss.

It was rough and demanding and in an instant had me spun up again.

He swallowed the needy sounds that continued to crawl up my throat as I continued to vibrate beneath him.

Ripples of pleasure that tingled and danced.

He kept me there until the aftershocks wore off, then he started to peck little kisses to my mouth.

"I told you I was going to have to gag you." He left the tease all over my lips. I could feel his smile woven underneath.

And my chest expanded again, and I knew it was affection sprouting and looking for a place to take root.

It would be a mistake, falling for him.

But God, how was I supposed to stop myself when he eased back a fraction to gaze down at me, his hand soft where he set it on my cheek?

Tender as he whispered, "So fucking gorgeous, Hailey. I don't think you know. I don't think you have the first clue what you're doing to me. The way you're making me feel. The way I think you always have."

A hint of uncertainty pulled to his strong brow, like he was trying to place where this feeling had come from.

I ignored the guilt that pressed at my ribs and brushed my fingertips down the scruff on the side of his face. "I think it's you who's ruining me."

He smiled in that playful way. "Oh, darlin'…you're all wrong. You are something I never expected."

He took my hand and kissed across my knuckles.

My heart ached.

There was no question I was letting this go too far. This emotion that wound me in a fist and prodded me toward the type of pain I couldn't take.

But I couldn't let him go, either.

Not yet.

Not when he was looking at me like that.

I urged him up to sitting then climbed to my knees, totally bare and not even caring. I eased up between his legs that he had bent with his feet planted on the mattress.

Cody grinned as I reached for the hem of his shirt. "Just what do you think you're doing?"

His voice was all mischief and seduction.

"I figured since I am naked, this is only fair."

Except it wasn't fair at all. Not when I peeled his shirt up and over his head and the man was sitting there with his chest bare, all those colors and designs dancing over the bristling muscle that ticked and flexed underneath.

The man so powerful.

Want trembled my thighs.

But he was more than this gorgeous exterior.

More than I'd imagined.

I'd thought him shallow.

A jerk.

So careless in his actions that he didn't care who he hurt as he barged through his days seeking pleasure.

But I knew he was more than that. I could see it in his eyes and feel it whispering through his spirit.

I think I'd known it then, too, but I'd been so riddled with guilt that I couldn't see through the pain.

I reached out and ran my fingertips over the clock that rested over his heart.

The disfigured hands set in a mournful cry that I couldn't quite hear.

"Why does this sing of sorrow?"

If I wasn't paying such close attention, I might not have noticed the way he flinched. The misery the connection caused.

I'd thought he'd retreat from it.

Deny it.

Only instead of pushing me away, he gathered my hand and pressed my palm flat over the tattoo.

His eyes swam in affliction.

"It's not sorrow, Hailey. It's choosing a path, wrong or right, and following it because you know it's the only thing you can do. It's making a choice for someone else. Giving them peace or joy or maybe *time*, even when it might mean the loss of yours."

My spirit tugged in anguish for him, at the loneliness that was suddenly staring back.

I wanted to ask him what he'd meant, but he kept gliding my palm downward, over the rippling muscles of his abdomen.

My breath went shallow as I glanced down at where he was heading—toward his cock that was outlined by his sweats, pressed up high, so fat and thick.

Only the thin fabric separated us when he set my hand over his hard, steely length. Flames licked up my arm, and he moaned a seductive sound as I fisted my hand around him.

Greed banged against the walls, rebounding and reverberating, sending the heat soaring again, though his voice curled with that easiness. "Careful, darlin', or you're going to make me embarrass myself."

"I don't think there's a thing you have to be embarrassed about." I pumped his massive cock over his sweats.

Lust radiated from his flesh, and he fiddled with a lock of my hair as he looked across at me with eyes that no longer were just molten but flamed.

"How's it possible you are right here in front of me?" The words were ragged rasps. "Meant it when I said it should be impossible for someone like you to exist. There shouldn't be a treasure so great. A beauty so abstract. You had me the second I stumbled on you in that trailer, Hailey. The way my guts curled with lust at the sight of you. I haven't been able to get you out of my mind since."

That's what this was, wasn't it?

Lust?

Except there was something bigger suspended in the air. Something that beat profound and whipped around us, a gravity that I knew better than to slip into.

Only I was getting drawn there, careening his direction.

I angled up high on my knees, letting my chest brush against his as I continued to stroke him.

"I've wanted you since that summer. You're the first man who ever made me desire."

I should keep my mouth shut.

Tie the admissions where they bubbled on my tongue.

But I didn't know how to stop the confession from bleeding free.

He winced again, and a grimness clouded his expression. "When I was with her."

He didn't form it a question. He already knew. And my heart was twisting, and I knew I was in the wrong, that this was a betrayal, and it was going to hurt.

Because everything I felt went so much deeper than this could ever be, knitting up in mayhem, and I should have been smart enough to know how it was going to end.

I was setting myself up to get shredded.

My stupid heart smashed.

But in that moment, I didn't care.

I wanted it.

I wanted it all.

I wanted to be selfish and take and take.

I wanted to feel something brighter than I'd felt in years.

In so long.

In ever.

Since the moment I'd run, gutted by grief, and instead had collided with something so much worse than I ever could have anticipated.

So, I reached down and shoved his sweats down his hips. He lifted to wind out of them, and I pushed them all the way down so he could kick them off his ankles.

A wave of dizziness slammed me when I freed his dick.

Massive and jutting, the head engorged and throbbing with need.

I ran my thumb over the dripping tip before I stroked him once again as I moved to straddle him, my palm gliding down his smooth flesh.

Surprise rasped up his throat, and his hands shot to my waist.

"Shortcake." His voice shook with the warning.

Dark and low.

A warning that echoed against the walls.

Mine matched it when I leaned in and whispered an inch from his lips, "Please, don't question it. Just fuck me."

Chapter Twenty-Seven
Cody

HAILEY'S DEMAND CLEAVED THROUGH THE ROOM, A BANG right in the middle of me.

I should stop this before it got carried away, before there was no going back, before I put the final stake in my grave.

But I was trapped by the torrent that swilled in her eyes. That blue sea drawing me deeper, crystalline and clear. Dark and mesmerizing.

A place I knew I'd never been before.

The heat of her blistered our flesh, burning us both. It incited a frenzy there was no chance I was strong enough to resist.

I twisted a hand up in the soft, lush locks of her hair. I yanked her head back as the rest of her bowed forward, and the hard peaks of her gorgeous tits scraped at my chest.

Fuck me, this woman was nothing but illicit.

A crime I should know better than to commit.

So goddamn hot I couldn't think straight.

"Is that what you want, Shortcake? You want me to fuck you?"

"You promised you'd do it so good." She threw the text I'd been an idiot to send that night back in my face. On the night when I felt like I was going to lose my mind if I didn't have her in some way.

But if I didn't have her right then?

I was going to fully disintegrate.

I was ruined anyway, so I saw no point in not giving in.

"I've always said to be a man of my word."

"I hope you are."

A grin cracked the edge of my mouth while I felt like my insides were splintering apart.

My Shortcake was a spitfire.

I loved it.

Loved every fucking thing about her, and I knew that was the real problem in all of this.

Too late now to consider any of that.

I curled my hand up in those honey-swept tresses until I was holding her by the back of the head, my words going soft as I murmured, "You sure that's what you really want?"

Something that looked a little too close to insecurity passed through her gaze. "Do you?"

"Oh, darlin', I think you can feel just how damned bad I want you." I nudged the tip of my dick against her entrance. "Think I might die if I don't get inside you."

At the contact, she let go of a needy rasp.

"But you're going to have to make that decision," I told her.

Me?

I was already all in. Ready to give it. Whatever it took.

But I knew she wasn't close to being there yet. Maybe she'd never be, and I sure as hell didn't want to be a dirty regret.

Rather than booting me from her bedroom the way she probably should, she wound those sweet arms around my neck and plastered herself against me.

The confession came soft from her lips when she burrowed her face into my neck. "I want you."

Her heart ravaged against mine, thrashing a riot.

"Do you have a condom?"

She blinked like she was just then realizing we should probably be covered, the chaos that bounded around us making us both reckless. She leaned over enough that she could get into the top drawer of her nightstand and pulled one out, the woman close to frantic as she peeled it open.

I hissed when she sheathed my length, a flashfire igniting at her touch and tugging at my balls.

Gripping her by those lush, indecently delicious hips, I stared up at the woman who panted her sweet breaths against me, swallowed them down and let her invade. "Well, if you want me, darlin', then I guess you'd better take me."

Hailey choked a needy, disoriented laugh before she slowly began to sink down, the woman hugging my cock in a fist.

Her walls throbbed and clutched as I slowly fitted myself in her cunt, spreading her wide.

Pleasure sped up my spine and lust prowled through my insides, body already hunting for release.

Hailey trembled as she clung to me, and her breaths turned ragged as I filled her so full that she was clawing at my back.

"Fuck me, Shortcake, how could one woman feel so good?" I rumbled it at her temple, holding her there for a second and letting her adjust.

Because shit—she was so fucking tight, and her pussy kept clenching as she seated herself deep.

"You okay?" I finally asked when her breaths evened out.

She nodded, words breaking when she spoke. "More than okay."

A gluttonous laugh tumbled around in my chest, and I dragged my fingers down the elegant curve of her back.

Chills scattered across her flesh, and she was shaking all around when I said, "When I'm finished with you, okay isn't going to remain in your vocabulary."

She eased back, a little of the sass she'd been wearing earlier riding to her striking, unforgettable face.

No doubt, the sight of her right then was going to be emblazoned in my mind forever.

The girl sitting on my cock with those thighs wrapped around me, her hair mussed and her cheeks flushed.

Lips pouty and swollen from my kiss.

It turned out, kissing her was my favorite thing to do.

"Is that so?" She phrased it coy, a tease that pierced straight into me.

She squealed when I picked her up from around the waist without withdrawing and stood from the side of the bed, then she was gasping as I pressed her back to the wall and pinned her arms over her head.

Her legs clutched around my waist, and I withdrew real slow then thrust back in.

Hard and so fucking deep.

Surprise ripped up her throat as I filled her to the hilt, and she arched from the wall. "Oh my God...Cody...I..."

I couldn't help but smile. "You said you wanted to be fucked, darlin', and I'm not here to disappoint."

I started rocking into her, each stroke possessive, driving into her over and over.

Her body crawled the wall, rising and falling with each thrust, her tits brushing my chest each time I plunged into her.

Nothing but warm, slick paradise.

Her breaths fluttered, the scent of her enthralling, and her tongue kept chanting my name.

I devoured it, that sweet little tongue, ate up her words that she released.

"More...harder...I need...I need..."

"I know what you need," I rumbled back.

Pulling her from the wall, I placed her on her feet and spun her around.

She gasped again, having a hard time keeping up.

The walls spun around us, and energy crackled in the space.

I planted her hands on the bed before I gripped her by the hips.

Her full ass was in the air, and her slit glistened with her arousal.

I dragged my fingers through her pussy and up to her clit.

I tugged at it, making her moan, then I lined my dick up at her center and drove back home.

I nearly blacked out at the feel of her gripping me tight. Her needy pussy sucking me deep.

"This sweet cunt, Hailey. Think you're the one who's fucking me so good." I pulled out all the way to the tip.

Her lips throbbed, greedy for more.

I rocked back in.

"Yes," she rasped.

"Fantasy, Hailey. That's what you are. A goddamned fantasy. Never could have dreamed of something as good as this."

I started fucking her just like she'd asked, picking up a hard, reckless rhythm.

That cascade of hair whipped around her, and those hands curled into the covers as I wound her fast.

She drove back to meet me, thrust for thrust.

"Look at you, Hailey…your pussy is so needy. You're such a good girl, baby. The way you take my cock."

Fingers kneading into her ass cheeks, I spread her wider, pumping deeper, unable to look away from where we were joined.

Captivated by the point where I was consuming her.

Possessing her.

Wrecking her.

But I was sure it was this woman who was really doing all the wrecking.

Destroying me brick by brick. These walls that I'd had up for years. I should have known she'd be the only one who'd hold the power to demolish them.

I slipped an arm around her and pressed my chest to her back.

My bucks turned erratic as I began to play my fingers over the swollen nub of her clit.

She started whimpering, louder and louder with each demanding thrust.

Pleasure swelled, static that cracked in the air.

Suffocating.

The woman became the only oxygen I could breathe.

"Cody...I...please..."

Her head thrashed back and forth, and I could feel that she was getting ready to blow, the way her tight cunt cinched around me in a heady clutch that nearly sent me sailing.

I drove harder. Harder and deeper and faster.

She exploded, and I could feel the force of the scream that was rolling up her throat.

I grabbed the edge of the comforter and shoved it into her mouth just as it was tearing free.

The shout of my name was muffled in the fabric.

Oh, but I heard it. I heard her call, and I followed her lead.

Pleasure splintered, fracturing out from her pussy and climbing into me, and the girl hurled me right into her ecstasy.

I erupted, my cock pulsing and throbbing as I dumped into her. Bliss streaked up my spine and tremored down the backs of my legs. I buried a shout in her hair, my heart battering so fucking hard I thought it was going to claw its way out of my chest.

"Paradise." It grunted from my lips, my face in her hair. "Paradise, Hailey."

She whimpered into the fabric stuffed in her mouth. Aftershocks ticked and rolled, her flesh alight, a full-body glow.

I wanted to hold onto it forever. That light. An embodiment of this emotion that made me feel like I was right where I belonged for the first time in my life.

Like maybe I'd stumbled on a new purpose.

Or maybe it'd been waiting out there for me all along.

I slowed, easing, before I fully pulled out, instantly wishing I could be right back in the fist of her again.

We both went limp and slumped, though I eased to the side so I wouldn't crush her, and when I got myself together enough, I pulled her up onto the bed so we were lying chest-to-chest.

I ruffled my fingers through her sweat-drenched hair, stared at her through the shadows that played in the night.

She brushed the tips of her fingers softly over my lips.

And I knew it then.

I'd been missing a piece inside, and it was exactly in the shape of Hailey Wagner.

Chapter Twenty-Eight
Hailey

W E LAY IN THE DUSKINESS OF MY ROOM, SILENT AS WE gazed at each other across the three inches of space that separated us. Our breaths had evened, and our hearts were quieted, the only sound the contented hum of peace that whispered through the night.

It curled and enveloped and washed, heightening each time Cody brushed his gentle fingers through my hair. I wondered if I'd ever felt as satisfied at any other time in my life than I did right then.

With the warmth of this man covering me like an embrace.

With my body sated.

With my daughter and grandmother sleeping across the house.

Safe and secure.

And I wondered if that's exactly what this felt like.

Safety.

Security.

A promise.

A place I could just *be* without the fears of what was to come. Without the questions and worries about where this might lead.

Without the guilt.

Most terrifying was knowing Pruitt was scared and backed into a corner. I'd hoped it'd be enough to keep him at bay forever, what I was holding over his head, a millstone that would sink him straight to the bottom of the ocean if I exposed who he really was.

It was the coward's way. Holding onto his ugly truth like a vapid threat all while knowing what he was capable of. Knowing what I was allowing to continue.

I knew it was an affliction that would haunt me for all my days if I kept it secreted inside. Where the depravity would fester and rot before it spread out to corrupt every part of my being.

Cody reached and rubbed the pad of his thumb over the crease that pulled between my eyes. "You're thinking awful hard there, darlin.'"

Unsure, I chewed at my bottom lip, trying to push it aside and fall into the easiness that Cody emanated. "I just…I didn't think the two of us were going to end up here like this."

It was a whole lot safer to let him think I was in a stir about the fact that I'd given in than to expose what I was really thinking about.

His brow arched with a tease, his sweet arrogance twisting into the rugged lines of his face. "Seems strange to me since I knew we were heading this direction all along."

It wasn't so hard to find a grin. "Easy for you to say when I'm sure you end up naked with some girl half the nights of the week."

His thumb kept tracing, and for a flash, his expression dimmed before a fierce softness came rushing back. "Not one of them like you."

A blush crept to my cheeks, and I tried to remember that this man was a player. A pro. He knew exactly how to turn a woman to putty.

Maybe I was just a stupid girl who'd fallen right into his trap.

Dumb love.

But I couldn't detect an ounce of dishonesty in him right then.

Hell, I hadn't detected a trace of it since I'd come here.

I thought he might be the most genuine person I'd ever met.

Still, I attempted the razz, though the words were coarse. "Only because I didn't give in the first time you asked. You thought me a challenge. How do you feel now, Cocky Cowboy? Is your ego stroked?"

A chuckle rumbled in his chest, and he kept watching me with those tender eyes where he stared at me through the flickering night. "Oh, something was stroked, all right."

He nudged his cock that still sat at half-mast against the front of my bare thigh.

I tried to smother a whimper.

Impossible.

He sobered and spread his palm across the side of my cheek. "You want to know what I feel like right now, Hailey? I feel like a king who's just been offered the greatest treasure."

My heart fluttered in my chest, and still I was going for light. "You think I'm a possession, huh? I think I've already been in that role, and I didn't like it all that much."

The last went hoarse, a confession that came from out of nowhere. I blamed it on the fact the man had left me goo.

A puddle of bliss.

I didn't have a lot of fortitude left.

No way to keep him out of the places he kept pushing into.

His palm twitched on my face, his hold both fierce and soft. "I hate him, Hailey. Hate that that bastard could ever make you feel that way. I want to destroy him just for the fact that he would ever try to tamp or trap the beauty that you are. I would never fucking do that. Would never hurt you. Would never use you. Would never think of you as any less than the fiery, sassy, strong, unforgettable woman that you are."

Affection slipped through my bloodstream, a soft whisper that spread out to touch every part of me.

This spirit that ached to meet with his.

I should be afraid.

Cody might not ever hurt me the way Pruitt had, but I knew how he easily could inflict wounds. Wounds that would scar so deep because they'd be the kind derived of vulnerability and trust. He'd gained the position, taken a piece of my being that he now held in the palm of his heated hand.

And there I lay, a glutton begging for the pain, wishing there was a way to give it to him.

Cody warred, and I could feel the storm build around him. Darkness called from every direction. A severity that blistered and writhed and shivered him to the bone. "Did he put his hands on you?"

You'll go, Hailey, and you'll do exactly as I tell you. You don't want to find out what happens if you don't.

I could almost smell the foulness that had leached from Pruitt as he'd stood behind me and threatened it so quietly at my ear.

Could almost feel the way my heart had shattered when I'd realized what he was asking me to do.

What he was forcing me to do.

It had taken me two years to realize what I'd unknowingly become. Blinded. A fool who didn't have a clue. Then another four to gain the courage to rip free of the chains.

My tongue swept out to wet my dried lips, and I fought to find a suitable answer to give Cody, my spirit screaming at me to let him in and the rest of me knowing I couldn't. Not until I knew for sure how I was going to handle this.

I was already putting him at risk—having him here. Having him stand for me the way that he was.

A ball of razors lodged at the base of my throat. "No. Pruitt was more about manipulation and control than the physical. Always trying to force me to be the wife he wanted, mold me into who I wasn't, sure to let me know when I wasn't up to his standards."

At least that was true.

A crack of aggression split through the air, and Cody drew me closer, those big arms holding me as if I were fractured. "I won't let him get near you, Hailey. Not you or Maddie or your grandmother."

"I keep warning you that you don't want to get involved. I'm going to get rid of him, Cody, once and for all, and I'm not sure what that's going to look like."

"It's going to look like me doing it by your side, that's what." His voice scraped with determination.

"Cody." Anxiety riddled my conscience all while I fought the urge to fully sink into him.

"You're stuck with me now, darlin.'" Cody issued it like banter, though there was something ferocious seeded in its depths.

He took my chin between his fingers. "Tell me how you got wrapped up in him."

A tumble of nerves skated through, and a sigh pilfered from my nose. "After I left…"

Cody flinched, both of us jarred right back to that time.

When Brooke died.

I gulped around the sorrow that thickened my throat, around the lash of guilt that cracked across my conscience like the scourge of a whip.

"You'd told me you didn't have plans to leave. That you were going to be going to school in Langmire so you could continue to work on your father's ranch since that was your dream."

Agony pulsed, and my tongue stroked out to wet my dried lips. "I couldn't stay here after what happened. I couldn't be on that ranch. Not with her ghost lingering there. I felt…"

Tears blurred my eyes.

Cody just pulled me tighter.

"So I packed my things and left for Austin. There was a ranch there that I knew about. My father had sold some horses to them over the years. I got a job there. The year before that, Pruitt had inherited it from his father."

"And one look at you, and he wanted you," Cody surmised.

My teeth clamped down on my bottom lip. "I was so blinded by pain that I couldn't see who he really was."

"And who was he?"

He pushed me closer to the edge. To that surrender. The guilt that haunted me was only a vague blip in the back of my mind.

"You can tell me anything, Hailey. I'll hold it."

"I know you would, Cody. But I…I need to figure out what I'm going to do with this information. With what I know. I can't drag you into that until I have a definite plan. But you need to understand he's dangerous. Really dangerous."

Awareness dimmed his features, and that stubbled jaw clenched. "And these things you know, you're holding them over his head?"

I gave him a jerky confirmation. "I told him I was going to go to the police if he ever came anywhere near me again."

Disgrace bit down. "But I'm not brave enough to do it. Afraid of what really might happen. Of what he really might do to me. And I'm over here pouring gasoline on the fire."

"He'll die before he gets near you."

A wave of brutality undulated beneath his flesh.

Reaching out, I touched the hollow beneath his eye, running my fingertips over the fierceness that blazed. "And I'm afraid neither of us really know what he's capable of."

Cody took my hand that was tracing his face and pressed my palm to his lips, golden eyes flared beneath the dull, muted light. "We'll find a way. I promise you."

"I'm trying…trying to figure out how to do this right. Without putting my family in danger. He made me sign these papers…" My throat closed off with a breath of hate. "Papers that look like I'm a part of things. Papers that look like I involved my father and his ranch. I think it was Pruitt's way of assuring himself that I would never leave."

An old kind of foreboding rushed through Cody's fierce features.

One second later, he solidified, a resolution building like bricks. He shifted and pressed his palm to my cheek. "How could anyone ever fucking believe that you would do something wrong, Hailey? It'll come out. The truth."

As if the heaviness was no longer in the room, he squeezed my hip with his big hand. "You wait right there."

He pushed to standing, and I watched him waltz across my room and flick on the light to the bathroom.

Buck naked.

That was all it took for the reservations that kept trying to re-surface to be obliterated.

For the guilt and the worry to fade away in the recesses of my room, disappearing into the vapor of this dream—this fantasy—I was momentarily living in.

The man was nothing but a heaping stack of muscle and brawn and this unfound beauty that could never have been expected.

He trembled the ground below him.

An earthquake that rattled me to the core.

His back rippled with strength, his shoulders so wide I wasn't sure how he didn't have to angle to the side to make it through the bathroom doorway.

The globes of his perfect, round ass flexed with each step he took.

My stomach knitted in a knot of greed.

I had to press a pillow against my mouth to stop the needy sound from escaping.

Of course, Cody had to go and catch it, and he was smirking in that way he loved to do as he glanced back. "Are you ogling me, Shortcake?"

"Who me? No, never." How I'd gone from drowning in his intensity to giggling, I didn't know.

Apparently, he'd driven me to delirium.

His amusement grew as he turned around and stretched himself out across the doorway, hands going to either side of the frame as he leaned my direction, no shame as he put himself on display.

God, the man was full of himself.

I was going to have to give him a pass. He'd earned that arrogance.

Every rugged, brutal inch of him was immaculate.

"No fibbing, darlin'. You think I can't feel those eyes on me? Not that you're going to find me complaining."

"Do you think I could look anywhere else?" I gave up on the teasing and welcomed the wash of need that swelled from the secret place I'd kept for him. "I can't think straight when I'm looking at you. And seeing you like this…"

I trailed off, not sure how to admit the way he made me feel but knowing I needed to touch him again.

A growl got free of his vibrating chest. "You should really stop looking at me that way, Shortcake."

"What am I looking at you like?"

"Like you're mine." The words scuffed through the air.

Snares to inflict.

Like you're mine.

I was in serious danger of falling into that spot. Of falling for a man who kept making me imagine things that I knew better than to dream about.

He wouldn't stay. He'd get bored. He'd stray.

He'd broken me once and he didn't even know it.

And Brooke...how could she not hate me?

I'd promised...I'd promised. And still, I was shifting around to sit up on the side of the bed before I slowly rose to my feet.

Powerless.

Addicted.

I wobbled. Weak to his presence.

I inched across the room.

Gold-flecked eyes consumed me as I approached, and I saw the tremor roll through his body. His muscles ticked and jumped in vicious anticipation.

"What if I was?" I whispered, a masochist, begging for that breaking.

None of it seemed to have any bearing right then.

I watched his partially soft shaft harden to stone.

"What if I told you I was yours tonight?"

"Then I'd say get on your knees, darlin', because I want to fuck that sweet mouth."

I didn't hesitate, I lowered to the floor, and I stroked my hand down the velvet stone of his shaft as I peered up at him.

He towered, nearly touching the ceiling.

Pure, chiseled strength.

Harsh cuts and lines with that softness in his eyes.

He rushed a thumb over my bottom lip. "Think you might be my match, sweet girl."

Then he pressed the tip of his dick to my lips.

Desire throbbed and I licked out over his head and swirled my tongue around the fat, engorged tip.

His stomach trembled and he jolted forward. "You are trying to ruin a man, aren't you? Knew it from the second I saw you. I'm not going to be the same."

He fisted a hand in my hair, and he edged me back for a second, both of us held in a moment's anticipation.

Intensity boiled around us.

A bubbling of greed.

Then he nudged his cock a little deeper.

"Suck me, Shortcake. Show me what you've got."

Need pumped through my veins, and I felt powerful, beautiful as I drew him in as far as I could take him, sucking as I drew him to the back of my throat, even though I barely could take half of him in.

Cody groaned, and he tightened his hold in my hair. The other hand went to my face as he ran his thumb along the edge of my lips that were stretched wide with him. "If you could see what you look like right now. My cock stuffed so deep in that sweet mouth. Suck me, darlin'. Show me how much you mean it."

He kept going from rough to soft, the man a whirlwind that had completely swept me away.

No rhyme.

No reason.

Just this.

Just us.

I wrapped both hands around the base of him, and I drew back. I swirled my tongue around his fat, throbbing head, and I gave him a good suck as I plunged back down.

Cody grunted.

I picked up a rhythm. I wanted to give him exactly what he'd asked for. To show him that I meant it.

Even if I couldn't say it, even if I could never accept it, even if this was all going to fall apart tomorrow, I meant it.

I meant that he'd come to mean something. He'd infiltrated the places of my heart that had ached for years. The places that were vacant and hollow.

I wanted him to know it meant something that he'd stood for me.

It meant something that he'd healed and given me hope.

Cody began to snap forward, taking me deeper with each stroke, fucking my mouth the way he'd warned he would do.

I liked it. Liked the overwhelming feel of him. Because I could barely take it and I wanted more.

Lust swarmed.

A cloud of desperation.

Desire sparked in my middle.

I rubbed my thighs together, seeking friction.

A needy grunt ripped out of Cody, and he took my face in both of those massive hands. "Touch yourself, baby. I want to see you go off at the same second I come in this delicious mouth."

Reaching between my trembling legs, I whimpered when my fingers brushed my tingling clit.

Pleasure flickered and flashed, and I shivered as Cody rocked in hard, fast strokes.

"Good girl. That's right. Touch yourself as I fuck this sweet mouth. Let me see you."

I rolled my fingers, and short gasps vibrated up my throat. I knew Cody could feel them, the way he moaned and jutted and jerked as he started to fuck faster.

"Nothing as beautiful as this, Hailey. You on your knees for me. But it's me who's on his knees. That's where you've got me. On my fuckin' knees."

I was gone. Lost to the disorder of this man. To this insanity that I knew was going to burn us in the end. But this was what we both needed right then, so I fully let myself go.

The bliss grew and grew, and I let my hand that had been stroking the base of his cock wander deeper behind his thighs until I was tugging at his balls, my fingertip scratching at the backside.

"Just like that. You know exactly what to do to me. How I want it."

Groaning with the praise, with the glow, I swallowed him deeper.

The vibration rolled through us both.

That was all it took and Cody exploded.

A shout wrenched from his mouth. Far too loud. Banging from the walls and plundering the night.

It plucked the pleasure out of me, too.

An orgasm ripped through my body as he poured and pulsed in my mouth. His hands clung to my face as I whimpered and he groaned, the two of us gone as I gulped him down.

Flying.

Soaring.

My head spun with a dizziness that I felt all the way down to my soul.

In places that were forbidden.

It didn't matter because I knew he was already there.

We both slowed and stilled, our breaths panted, the energy a slow crackle that pulled through the air.

Cody's hands were still framing my face when he pulled out of my mouth, and I reached up and swiped the back of my hand over my lips.

Then I smiled his way, feeling as smug as he could be. "It seems to me someone else needed to be gagged. I think you woke the neighbors."

His chuckle was low. "I'd apologize but I wouldn't mean it."

I gazed up at him, feeling a brittle place inside me crack. "Don't apologize, Cody. Not when I've wanted to see you like this for half my life."

Every molecule in his being went tender. "I won't. Won't apologize for the way you make me feel. Won't deny it any longer."

Without giving me warning, he scooped me up and carried me into my bathroom and perched me on the sink. He kept tossing wayward grins at me as he warmed a cloth under the sink and swiped it across my lips.

"This fucking mouth, Shortcake."

Shifting, he gently pressed the heated cloth between my perfectly sore thighs. "This body."

He leaned in and pressed a kiss to my temple, whispering there, "This mind."

Then he splayed a massive palm over the thunder ravaging my chest. "This heart."

Don't fall.

Don't fall.

I silently chanted it like a prayer.

A fleeting one.

"Knew you were something so fuckin' special, Hailey. Knew it all along. Wish I could be that way for you. Perfect and good and right."

He scooped me back up, my legs around his thighs and my arms laced to his neck. Our naked flesh pressed flush to the other, an aching burn that simmered with something bigger than it should be.

He carried me to my bed and laid me down in the middle. I could see the battle wage in his mind as he hesitated at the side.

I reached for him because I couldn't bear to let him go.

Not yet.

Not when I didn't want this night to end.

"Stay with me." I begged it like a secret.

Cody crawled in, the bed squeaking with his weight, and wrapped me in his arms. Heat blistered, his brutal strength wrapping me whole. I set my head on the steady beat of his heart.

"Hold me until morning," I whispered there, to that clock frozen at eight-seventeen.

He brushed his lips across my forehead and held me tighter. "Don't worry, darlin'. I'm not going to let go."

Chapter Twenty-Nine
Cody

THE FAINTEST GLIMMER OF MORNING PUSHED AT THE window, streams of glitter and dust that played through the room nudging me from sleep. I inhaled, filling my nostrils with the scent of strawberries and cream, and I couldn't help but smile when I realized my nose was burrowed in Hailey's hair.

I tightened my hold on her where she was already tucked into the well of my arms, the way she'd been the entire night, her head rested on my chest.

Her spirit all around as her breaths remained even and long as she slept.

Peace.

I wondered how I could feel even a flicker of it when I knew I was nothing but a monster for taking her. It wasn't like my circumstances had miraculously changed, although it felt like everything was different.

A cosmic shift taking place somewhere in my consciousness.

Got the sense my being no longer fully belonged to me.

It'd been fractured.

Fragmented.

Those jagged pieces given to someone else.

I eased back enough that I could gaze at her precious face. Long, full lashes shadowed her cheeks, and her eyes twitched beneath her pale, delicate lids like she was long lost to a dream. Those plush, full lips were softly pursed, like my name still rested there.

Fuck me, she was pretty. Pretty in a way that shifted orbits because her beauty was so big and deep there was no fucking chance it wouldn't seep all the way out.

Shine like the sun.

A gravity that compelled.

It stole my goddamned breath every time I looked at her.

Punched me in the gut.

Twisted me up in some kind of elaborate origami until I became something else.

Hers.

My chest tightened with the force of it.

This awareness...this need.

This *purpose*.

Leave it to Karma that it'd be Hailey Wagner who'd confound me this way. Knock me clean from my foundation. Make me turn on every oath I'd ever made.

I was an idiot for thinking I could touch her and this wouldn't end badly, but it didn't fucking matter.

She was worth it.

Before I allowed myself to get consumed by another bolt of lust, I carefully eased out from under her and settled her onto her pillow, doing my best not to disturb her since there was no question she was spent.

I crept around her bed, trying to keep my footsteps quieted, though there wasn't a chance my weight wouldn't make the floor creak.

I glanced back at her as I pulled on my sweats where they were in a ball on her floor. The woman was so gorgeous where she lay lost to the abyss of sleep with the kiss of gold skittering across her flesh.

My damned heart clutched.

Thrashed in my chest.

Blowing out the strain, I tugged my shirt over my head then slipped to her door. Carefully, I cracked it open and peered out.

A stilled silence echoed back.

Thank fuck.

I slinked out, just as cautiously, and I clicked the door shut behind me before I started to tiptoe across the floor toward the couch where I'd left the blanket tossed aside last night.

"And just where do you think you're sneaking off to?" I nearly hit the roof with the voice that suddenly broke the silence.

A shout got free, aggression whipping a stir into my bloodstream, and I whirled toward my right.

My hand smacked down over my heart like it was going to keep it from jumping out when my fumbled brain finally came to the comprehension that it was only Lolly.

The old woman let loose a knowing grin. Her lips were already painted red, and she wore a satin floral robe as she sipped from a mug where she sat at the small round table under the window that overlooked the front.

"Someone's jumpy," she said, so damned sly.

"Yeah, that's because you nearly scared the pants off me," I grumbled.

Sure, I was relieved it wasn't an intruder I was going to have to take down first thing in the morning, though that relief wasn't lasting long with the way she was watching me.

My pulse thundered, and I scraped a shaking hand through my hair that had likely dried sticking up all over the place since Hailey had been tugging at it last night.

I dug around in my brain for an excuse. It wasn't like I hadn't been caught sneaking out of a woman's door or window a time or two in the past, and I always managed to come out unscathed.

But I didn't think I'd ever felt as exposed as right then. Like I'd been caught doing something illicit all while feeling like holding Hailey was exactly what I'd been created to do.

Lolly's eyes gleamed. "I'm surprised you're wearing them."

Agitation lit me up, and I shifted from foot to foot. "I was just…"

I swept a flustered hand back at Hailey's door.

"Oh, I doubt it was *just*. It sounded like a whole lot of something to me."

A penciled-in brow arched toward the ceiling as she sent me a challenge, daring me to deny it.

Well, shit, this woman wasn't about to tiptoe. She was just laying it out.

Blowing out a sigh, I shook my head like it could break up the disorder and changed paths. I headed into the kitchen where she'd been hiding out.

The woman was stealthier than a panther.

I leaned back against the island, chewing at the inside of my cheek, wondering what the hell was protocol in this sort of situation. It wasn't like Hailey was a child, but I also didn't want to come around here showing disrespect.

"I don't think you were supposed to hear that," I settled on.

She took a sip of her coffee. "Probably not, but I think the whole town might have heard."

How was I supposed to respond?

Sorry, Lolly, it couldn't be helped. Not when your granddaughter was blowing my mind.

She laughed at my discomfort, playfulness edging her features as she studied me where I itched. "I'm not here to judge. I've been trying to get my granddaughter to step out and have a little fun myself."

Then her gaze narrowed. "And while I'm all about it, I am not sure *fun* is really in her makeup, and I feel I may have been pushing her in a direction she isn't ready for, though it's clear you are well-versed in the act."

There was no missing the implication. What she was pushing at.

I was a player, good for a fuck, and Hailey was so much more than that.

Possession bound me at the thought. Regret crushing down because *this* felt different for the first time in my life. The connection I had with Hailey.

I had no idea how to hang onto it, but God knew, I was going to try.

"I have no intention of hurting your granddaughter."

"No?" Speculation lifted her brow, the woman searching me like she could see right through to my secrets. To every wrong I'd ever committed. To every lie I'd ever told.

"No."

She hesitated, calculating, gauging whether I was being honest or not. Deciding if she could trust me.

She seemed to come to a conclusion, and every bit of the impishness she normally wore vanished.

Her voice dropped lower than the stillness that echoed around us. "She needs a man who isn't going to be afraid of standing for her and her daughter. Someone who's not a coward. Someone who can support her when he finds out—"

Whatever warning she was giving me cut off when a flurry of energy suddenly banged down the hall.

Maddie came running out, her hair a wild mess of warm blonde ringlets and that little bunny she carried with her everywhere hugged to her chest.

"Good morning, my Lolly and my favorite Mr. Cody! Are you makin' breakfast? I am the hungriest and so is my Princess Verona!"

In unease, I shifted to look back at Lolly, to demand to know what she was talking about.

My hate for that bastard Pruitt had grown so fierce I thought I would choke on it. The truth that this was more than getting rid of a scorned ex.

The fucker was dangerous, but I'd already known that. Had felt it. Knew this was going to be a fight.

The graveness Lolly had been wearing had shifted, and she was smiling wide as she stood from the table.

"How did I know you were going to be hungry so early in the morning?" she asked as Maddie came barreling into the kitchen.

Maddie beamed. "Because you know all the important things about me, Lolly, and you love me with all your whole heart, right?"

My chest tightened in a damned fist.

Caught in the affection that bulged in the room. The devotion that banged against the walls, a gonging that claimed.

Warily, I watched the two of them, unsure where I stood, but somehow knowing I couldn't move.

Lolly ran a tender hand through the little girl's hair. "That's right. With my whole heart. And that heart says we'd better get you fed, hadn't we?"

"And don't forget my Princess Verona!" Maddie held the stuffed bunny out in front of her, flopping it around.

"Never," Lolly told her.

The old lady started to shuffle into the kitchen, but I pushed from the island. "You sit. I'll handle breakfast."

Surprise expanded her eyes, shrewdness lighting her expression, with this knowing as she reached out and curled her hand around my bicep. "Ah, I think that I might have been right about you."

"That he's the strongest, most tallest man with the biggest muscles in the whole wide world?" Maddie piped in from the side.

"That's right, Maddie…" Her gaze twinkled. "He might just be strong enough."

Disquiet gusted.

A sense coming in from the recesses of my mind, from the instincts seeded in my spirit.

It warned things were nastier than imagined.

Hailey had let me peek through the barriers last night, though the details were still vague and distorted to the sordid secrets that thrashed behind the barrier where she kept them concealed.

She'd given me a peek behind the veil last night, but I knew firsthand how depraved those kinds of souls went.

Regret throbbed from the vat of immorality I'd kept inside myself.

My own dirty secret.

Was I any fucking different than that monster who was hunting her now?

Maddie took my hand and looked up at me. "Do you know all the important things about me, too, Mr. Cody?" she asked.

Shit.

I fucking had to be.

Had to prove I was better. Be fucking better.

Because it was my whole heart that clutched as the little girl looked up at me with so much trust it grounded me to the spot.

Made me sure I was purposed to be right there.

I squeezed her tiny hand back. "Not yet, Maddie, but I'm going to do my best to learn every single one of them."

Chapter Thirty

Hailey

MY EYES BLINKED OPEN TO THE GLITTERING LIGHT THAT streaked in through the window and to the sound of muted voices echoing from the other side of my bedroom wall.

A low, rumbly drone, another that was high-pitched and precious, and the hoarse rasp of my grandmother's. The quiet conversation was intermingled with the sporadic giggle that flooded through the air and nudged me from sleep.

I inhaled a deep breath and stretched out like a kitten in my bed, the covers still warm from the heat of his body.

My limbs were heavy, leaden with satisfied, satiated exhaustion, though my stomach and chest were light.

The quivering of wings that flapped and fluttered and flitted.

My senses awash in ripples of comfort.

With this rightness that could so easily sink all the way to my bones and become part of my marrow.

A shriek of laughter penetrated the atmosphere, and I forced myself to climb out of bed.

Redness skimmed my flesh as I pulled back on my underwear

and pajamas that were tossed about my room on the floor. I could almost still feel his hands on me. My body marked where he'd gripped and touched.

There was no *almost* about it where I was sore between my thighs. The man was written there like a tattoo, a brand that I was forever going to carry.

Inhaling a steadying breath, I moved to the door, opened it, and shuffled out. I hadn't expected the way my breath would get snatched from my lungs when I saw what was playing out in my kitchen.

Lolly was at the island, drinking from a mug of coffee, and Maddie was on the other side of it, propped up on the counter with her legs swinging as she giggled and laughed and chatted incessantly with the man who was whipping some kind of concoction in a bowl.

He wore the same sweats and tee he'd had on last night, his hair slept in, sticking up from my pillow where he'd been snuggled against me.

Those big, sexy feet bare.

Affection.

It hit me like a rogue wave.

Slamming me from out of nowhere.

His head swung my way when he felt me standing there staring, and he let that smirk ride to his obscenely handsome face, though this morning the grin was slow and close to adoring.

It filled me up to overflowing, this welling of affection there was no chance to contain.

"Mornin', Shortcake."

The words roughed over me.

A tingling of seduction, though I was pretty sure what was being seduced right then was my stupid heart.

Because it beat out of time, to a rhythm that I never could have expected would be mine.

"Shortcake?" Maddie's little voice broke into the trance he had me under, and her nose scrunched up in confusion as she looked at Cody who stood right beside her to make sure she was safe where she sat on the counter.

He tapped her nose. "That's right, Button. I like to call your mom Shortcake."

"Because you like desserts that taste like strawberry?" she asked, so innocent.

Cody's attention was back on me. He didn't even try to hide the suggestion. "That's right, Maddie, I really like desserts that taste like strawberry."

I nearly choked.

Lolly guffawed.

"Me, too, but my favorite is *punkin* pie with a whole can of whipped cream," Maddie said, completely oblivious to the energy that thrummed in the space.

Thank God.

Cody looked back at her. "Is that right?"

"Yup," she said with an emphatic nod.

"Well, that is good to know. I'm storing that away under all the most important things to know about you." He tapped her nose again.

Giggling, she flashed that smile I was pretty sure could win her the keys to any kingdom. Swindling her way right into hearts because she was too freaking cute to be resisted. "Because I *am* really important?"

I thought he'd make a joke.

Keep teasing.

But everything about him intensified.

Became fierce and stark and so tender that I thought I would melt right there.

"Yeah, that's right, Maddie, because you are really important. And we have to cherish the most important things in our lives."

Strike that.

I did melt.

Nothing but a puddle on the floor.

"You're looking a little peaked this morning, Hailey. Did you not get enough rest last night?" This from Lolly who sat there snickering like she could see Cody written all over me.

Discomfort had me shifting on my feet.

262 | A.L. JACKSON

Was I that obvious? Did she know that Cody had spent the entire night behind my door?

Lifting my chin, I tried to play it off. "Oh, I'm completely fine. You know I need my coffee to get me going in the morning."

"I'll bet something got you going," she mumbled into her own mug.

Cody chuckled, though his smile was soft. "You sit. I'll pour you one."

"You don't need to—" I started to argue before he cocked his head and ordered, "Sit."

My teeth clamped down on my bottom lip.

"You might as well listen to the man," Lolly said as she gestured to the stool beside her. "It seems he's set on spoiling us this morning. Not that I mind a bit."

"That's because he's looking for all the important things, Mommy," Maddie told me before she turned her adorable attention on him. "My mommy's important, too, right, my Mr. Cody?"

Cody didn't diverge or divert.

He just looked at me as he murmured, "Yeah, Maddie, your mommy is important, too. I hope she realizes just how much."

I couldn't speak because he was stealing words and clarity and sound mind, my knees weak, and I forced myself to round the island where I pulled out a stool and sat next to my grandmother.

Cody filled a cup full of coffee and passed it to me from over the top of the island, his big body reaching all the way across. He set the creamer and sugar beside it, that grin pulling at his mouth while he watched me shifting uneasily on the seat. "There you go, Shortcake."

"Thank you," I whispered.

"Oh, darlin', it's my pleasure."

A blush flamed at his tone, my cheeks heating with the flash of need that pummeled my body.

I dropped my head to shutter the reaction.

Lolly leaned in close to my ear and muttered under her breath, "Now don't go tryin' to hide it, Hailey. That reputation looks really good on you."

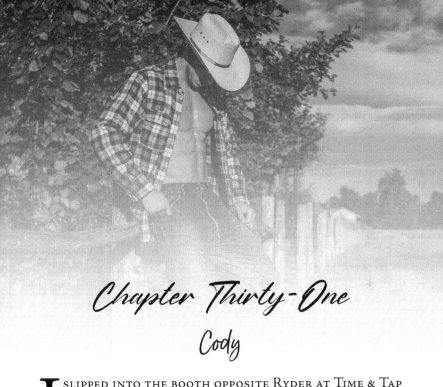

Chapter Thirty-One
Cody

I SLIPPED INTO THE BOOTH OPPOSITE RYDER AT TIME & TAP Tavern.

It was just off the main drag in Time River, and the small bar was a place he and I had come to for years whenever we felt like catching up by ourselves.

The vibe was mellow, country music playing from the jukebox and patrons tucked up to the horseshoe bar that took up the entire middle of the place. The two side walls were lined with elevated booths, seven on each side, and a few tables sat on either side of the door up front.

The lights were dull, swinging from the ceiling over each table.

Ryder was slung back in the booth, already sipping from a tumbler of whiskey when I arrived.

Five minutes late because I'd spent extra time kissing Hailey outside her house before I'd finally pried myself away.

He canted me a smirk when I plopped into the seat. "About damned time. You texted to meet up and here I've been sitting by myself like a poor fucker who was about to get stood up." His expression darkened. "I was worried something was wrong when you texted me."

I cracked a grin. "What, I can't want to hang out with my bestie on a Tuesday night?"

Ryder's sharp brow arched. "Bestie?"

The guy might act like a hard-ass, but I knew he loved it, so I took it upon myself to rub it in.

"That's right. You're my BFF. My bosom buddy. My ride or die." I drew them out, making each more ridiculous than the last, going for whatever nonsense Dakota and Paisley always spewed about each other.

He balled up a napkin and threw it at me. I tried to dodge it, but it hit me in the temple. I feigned outrage. "How dare you, Ryder? Why always so violent?"

Amusement crawled over his face. "Not sure I can be considered the violent one. Not after what you pulled on Saturday night." His tone turned emphatic, head tipping to the side. "You want to tell me about it?"

God, Saturday felt like a lifetime ago. Like the world had been flipped. Every-fucking-thing I knew changed.

I shrugged like it wasn't a big thing while the *violence* threatened to work its way back to the surface, escaping from where I was barely managing to keep it tapped. "Asshole got sloppy and hurt some girl. I was simply reminding him of his manners."

Ryder let go of an incredulous chuckle. "Poor fucker got the message delivered to him in blows. Think he pissed his pants. Ezra had to call his *wife* to come and pick him up to take him to the ER."

Irritation blustered through my consciousness. What a fuckin' prick. Dude deserved to get his ass beat. Unfortunately, there were worse deviants we were dealing with right then.

Speculation in his eyes, Ryder pressed deeper into the topic he was hinting on. "And *some girl?*"

I itched, not sure why I was agitated since I'd been the one to call him here, really needing to talk about that very girl, the *one* girl, but I wasn't quite sure how to broach it. Not when I was so out of my element that I had no idea what the hell I was doing.

Treading thin.

Ice cracking below.

The fractures splintering out, five seconds from a collapse.

No question, the frigid waters were right there to drag me to the bottom.

I scratched at my beard, thankful for the distraction when a server stopped at our booth. I ordered a beer on tap, then turned back to Ryder who was watching me carefully.

"Something's up with you," he said the second she was out of earshot.

I sighed. "Think I'm in trouble."

I could sense the flash of worry that sped through him, though he kept his voice casual and cool. "And what kind of trouble might that be?"

I gnawed at the middle of my bottom lip before I finally confessed, "The kind where I actually *like* that girl."

He looked far too entertained by the news, relieved that this was the only trauma we were talking about.

If he only fuckin' knew.

"Ah, a woman has finally gotten under your skin. Wasn't sure I was ever going to see the day, though it was pretty damned apparent from where I was sitting on Saturday night that she had you in knots."

I scraped a flustered hand over my face and blew out a sigh as I sank back on the booth seat. "She doesn't have me in knots, man. She has me in fucking chains."

Disbelief rocked through him, and his eyes the color of pitch gleamed. "That's how it is, huh?"

"Think so." I was reticent to admit it. The server walked by and set my beer in front of me, and I muttered a quiet, "Thank you," as she walked away.

Ryder slinked back farther in the seat, that shock of black hair flopping to the side. "I'm not sure why you look so disturbed by it, brother. I know you've been chasing your next hookup ever since I can remember, but I promise you, when you find the one, you aren't going to feel like you're missing a thing. You never fucking get bored because each time you touch her, you only want more."

Ryder thought I was afraid of commitment, which there was no goddamn question that I was, but it wasn't bred of the reasons he imagined.

It wasn't because I was scared of getting locked down, worried I'd forever be wondering if the grass was greener on the other side.

It was that I was afraid of what I was bringing to the table. The mess I'd created that would only taint and destroy.

The truth that I would never be good enough for the woman who I'd left at her house after kissing her wild on her porch. The whole time, I'd felt like I was getting a piece of myself ripped away when I forced myself to get in my truck and drive to Time River to meet up with Ryder.

Every instinct demanded that I stay by her side.

Funny thing, Hailey thought she was the one bringing the baggage while I came barreling in loaded like a fucking freight train.

I figured no one else could understand quite the way that Ryder would be able to.

I shook with the truth that I'd been keeping from him my entire life, a hypocrite who'd secreted my mistakes away, all while I'd been demanding that he keep away from my sister because I'd known he'd had himself entangled in some shady shit.

But what I'd done, I'd done for my family.

For Dakota and Kayla and our mother.

Because they were worth it.

Because I would give anything for them.

Because I'd *promised*.

And still, I didn't know how to admit to him my true concerns.

"I want to be good enough for her, Ryder. Right for her and her daughter. Make their lives better rather than become a cloud that darkens their path."

He took a sip of his whiskey, and he pointed at me from where he had his hand curled around the glittering glass. "That right there is a choice, Cody. Whether you make their lives better or worse."

I barely nodded, even though it wasn't quite the truth. I'd given up that power a long time ago.

I pushed out the one thing that I could give him. The first obstacle ahead of us that I wasn't going to just hurdle, but tackle head-on.

Fucking raze it to the ground.

"Her ex is sniffing around…trying to get her back. Rich kind of prick who thinks the world owes him something and everyone should get on their knees and bow when he's coming. He doesn't like it that Hailey isn't yielding."

Darkness rolled through his expression, and he slowly set the glass on the table, the brutality that was Ryder coming out full force.

Mine rolled inside, the warning rumble of an earthquake before the entire goddamn thing split apart.

"Does he know about you?" Ryder asked.

A morbid chuckle rolled out when I thought to the way I'd kissed Hailey in front of him that night, playing this whole thing as fake when the second my mouth had touched hers, I'd known I'd never experienced anything as *real* as that.

"You can say I took it upon myself to make sure the fucker knew she wasn't sleeping alone at night."

Ryder let go of a cynical laugh. "I bet you did."

I shrugged, bringing out the innocence. "I couldn't help myself." Then I sobered. "Think he's seriously bad news. Dangerous sort who's involved in seedy shit. She won't tell me exactly what because she's afraid of saddling me with the truth…thinking she's going to make it worse."

"What are you going to do about this little problem?"

"Whatever it takes." I said it simple.

"Good." Ryder sat back with mischief playing on his face. "So, I'm guessing I'm here because you're wondering if I'm going to have your back?"

"You're the last person I'd call if I needed backup. Look at you… nothing but a stick." I gave him a taunting grin, trying to hold back the laugh.

The dude was deadly, all lean, hewn muscle, a viper who would silently strike. No question about that. But I still loved to rub that shit in.

"You wish, asshole."

I waffled, trying to figure out what I really needed to say. Trying to sort through the mess we were wading in. "I think I called you here because I want to make sure everyone in this family knows what she's up against. I want her to know she's important. To all of us. That she has this crew to rely on if it comes to that."

That *importance* throbbed from within. This feeling that I wanted to gather both Hailey and Maddie up, curl them in my arms, and never let them go.

"You can count on that. Of course, brother. You've come running every time I've ever needed you. Besides, the girls claimed her." Affection pulled to his lips, that soft spot he had for my sister so damned distinct. "Pretty sure Hailey isn't going anywhere."

"That's the way I intend it," I said.

Disbelief pulsed across his face before he seemed to settle on something. "Love looks good on you, man."

That single word pierced me.

Is that what this was?

This thing that made me feel like I was going to lose it if I didn't get back to her?

The itch that prodded me into action?

"I think you're getting ahead of yourself," I said rather than trying to process the magnitude of it. If I could possibly be worthy of it.

Ryder laughed. "Nah, Cody, you're just lagging."

He drained the rest of his whiskey then glanced at his phone. "Listen, I need to call it. Kayden made me promise I'd be home in time to read him a story before bedtime."

Yeah, dude loved the hell out of them.

"Thanks for meeting me."

"I'm glad to talk my *bestie* down any time." Sarcasm rolled through his words, and he leaned forward so he could take his wallet from his pocket.

I waved him off. "I've got it. Go on before you break my nephew's heart."

Ryder grinned. "Never, man." He pushed from the booth then he came around and set his hand on my shoulder. His tone turned serious.

"Don't let fear stand in the way of what your heart needs, Cody. I did it for a long damned time, and the only thing it did was cause more pain in the end. And for the record, you are good enough for her."

Regret burned like a bitch.

Because he didn't know, and I honestly didn't know if that was true. Still, I forced a nod. "Thanks for that, Ryder."

"Always."

Turning, he strode through the bar, weaving through the few people who were mingling around, and he pushed out the door into the descending night. I sat there in my thoughts, polishing off my beer, then lifted my hand to the server as she walked by.

"Is that it for you?" she asked.

"Yeah, I need to get home."

Home.

I'd always considered myself a wanderer. A piece of this small town while forever being detached. Knowing not to hang on too tightly because it would eventually be ripped away, and the thought of losing it then was all the more painful.

Resolve rode in to seize every orifice of my chest.

I made the decision right then and there that I wasn't going to let my past catch up. I was going to do whatever it took to finally put it to bed. Because I didn't want to let go. I wanted to hold on.

I stood from the booth, dug into my wallet, and tossed two twenties on the table to cover the bill, then I pushed out through the single door and into the heat of the summer night.

The deepest gray curled through the vastless canopy above, and a smattering of stars had started to dot the sky.

I shoved my hands into my pockets as I followed the walkway around the side of the bar to the parking lot. My truck was on the far end, facing the building. The drone of cars up on Manchester echoed through the heavy air, though this area was pretty serene.

Through the stillness, I edged that way, rounding to the driver's side as I clicked the locks.

The running lights flashed, and I reached out to pull open the door.

That was when the serenity disintegrated.

Awareness prickled the fine hairs at the back of my neck and the energy shifted to ominous.

A flash of depravity.

I didn't have time to turn around to find where it was coming from before pain splintered across the side of my head.

Searing, splitting misery nearly knocked me from my feet.

I struggled to remain upright as glass shattered and rained around me.

Agony spiraled, and I blinked and fought for the air that I couldn't seem to bring into my lungs. Everything felt like it was caving.

A crushing kind of affliction that fought to wipe me out.

The only thing that kept me standing was the fury that burst in my consciousness. Jumping right into my bloodstream and careening through my veins.

Inciting a riot that whirled me around to face the pussy who'd attacked me from behind.

The second I did, a fist pummeled me in the gut. So hard the last of the air ripped out of me on a rasp. I roared, squinting as I tried to focus through the blur that clouded my eyes.

Dizziness spun through my brain and made it impossible to process sight.

Or maybe it was the hot streams of blood that I realized were pouring down my face from the wound at the side of my head that kept me from seeing straight.

Blinking through the disorder, I staggered forward, and I threw a fist at the vague figure that lurked in the encroaching darkness. The silhouette stepped back, out of my reach, and I was unprepared for the next blow that seemed to come from out of nowhere.

A fist that slammed me up high on my cheek.

Pain blistered out, all of it too much, and I fell to my knees.

My head dropped between my shoulders as I rasped, "Motherfucker...you're going to regret that."

A low, menacing laugh rolled through the air, and I could feel the presence cover me from above. I tried to lift my head to it, to confirm the attacker because the hatred that toiled inside promised I knew exactly who it was.

But the pain kept me on my knees.

The dizziness.

The onslaught too much.

"I'm afraid you're wrong." The scum leaned in closer, spewing venom near my ear. "It's you who's going to be filled with regret. You get one chance. If I were you? I'd run."

Chapter Thirty-Two
Hailey

I PEEKED AT MY PHONE FOR WHAT HAD TO HAVE BEEN THE fifteenth time since Cody had said he'd be back by nine.

This was exactly what I got, wasn't it? Giving in the way I had?

A needy obsession that left me antsy and in a toil of nerves. Wondering where he was. If he was okay. If I'd been a fool and believed something in him that I shouldn't have when there'd been so much proof that he wasn't the type of guy who was going to stick around.

I deserved it, didn't I? Deserved it for casting the type of betrayal I had last night. The same as I'd done last Saturday when I'd begged him to touch me. The one thing I'd sworn I'd never do.

But it felt like he would.

Stick.

Become a piece of the molding.

A brick that perfectly fit even when I wasn't supposed to allow him to.

I tried to act as if I wasn't a deranged mess where I lounged on the couch watching an old episode of *The Voice* with Lolly.

She had her own unhealthy obsession with Blake Shelton.

"Look at that man." She tsked like it was a shame. "If I were only forty years younger...I looked just as good as that Gwen back in the day. And I sure can sing, too."

I held back a chuckle. "I'm sure you would have gotten on that stage and completely stolen the show."

I took another furtive peek at my phone, frowning when the last text I'd sent him remained unread.

Me: You okay?

"Don't pretend like I don't know you keep looking at that thing on your lap or that I don't feel that you're tied up in stitches."

My head jerked upright to find Lolly peering at me from her side of the couch, her expression knowing.

I blew out a sigh. "He just...said he'd be back by nine. That was almost half an hour ago."

Okay, fifteen minutes.

He wasn't even that late, and I was already spinning circles.

"I'm sure he knows how to take care of himself."

I flinched. Is that what I was worried about? That he was taking *care* of himself?

"There you go, twisting yourself up even farther. You don't watch out, you're going to wind yourself so tight you're going to squeeze the life out of the roots that have just sprung." She said it like she'd known exactly what I'd been thinking.

I rubbed my finger at the corner of my eye to try to ease some of the tension. "I know. It's stupid. I either need to trust him or not, but this whole thing is brand new, and that's what we need to be about—building trust between each other—and he's already taking a chink out of mine."

Guilt flailed in my conscience. The hypocrisy of what I was keeping from him. But it was too soon. Too early. Too dangerous. If he knew, it would shackle him. Make him an accomplice of what I was hiding. I couldn't do that. Not when I still hadn't figured out how I was going to handle this.

274 | A.L. JACKSON

"You should probably give a person the benefit of the doubt before you go jumping to conclusions and thinking the worst of them."

That would be all fine and dandy if people didn't typically default to the *worst*.

Maybe Pruitt had ruined me in some way, made me cynical and suspicious, because I sure as hell hated what I was stewing in right then.

This unease that grew and toiled in the pit of my stomach with each second that passed. A sense that left me off-kilter.

Worried and dripping with dread.

I guessed I'd rather think something bad *of* him rather than think that something bad might have happened *to* him. Because there was a speck of alarm that stewed in the periphery. A warning that flared.

I nearly bolted off the couch when headlights finally cut through the night and lit up behind the front windows.

Relief heaved from my lungs, and Lolly chuckled a low sound as she pushed from the couch. She turned and set her hand on my cheek.

Her gaze went soft and sincere. "Demand respect from him, Hailey, always, but keep your heart open. I know that jerk did a number on you, and I don't want you missing out on something great because you're scared of a repeat."

"I think I'm scared of everything right now, Lolly."

Her thumb traced over the apple of my cheek.

Warmth spread with the same love and care she'd covered me with over the years.

The way she'd always been there for me. Taking care of me like a mother, filling the spaces that could have remained hollow and turned bitter, but instead, she'd turned them into beautiful memories.

"You're fighting, though, and that's the one thing that matters," she said. "Fight against the chains. Fight against what's cruel and wrong. Just don't fight against the things that might bring you joy."

Setting my hand over hers, I leaned into her touch. "Thank you. For everything. I don't know where I'd be right now without you."

Her grayed eyes swam. "You'd be just fine, that's where, but I sure am glad I get to be here to experience all of this with you."

The lights cut out from the front, and she sent me a slow grin.

"I think that's my cue. I'll be in my room if you need me, though that man seems to have things handled."

I shook my head behind her as she shuffled for the hall, my heart aching and full, and I whispered, "Goodnight, Lolly. I love you."

"I love you more, sweet child."

Once she disappeared into her room, I stood from the couch, far too eager to see the man who'd only been gone for a couple hours.

I slowly edged to the front door when it seemed to be taking him far more time to come inside than it should have.

Tendrils of that worry spread, vines that slithered across the floor to wrap around my ankles and curl up my legs.

I hesitated for a few seconds before I gathered my courage and told myself to suck it up because I was being ridiculous.

Unlocking the door, I slowly opened it.

The lamp that hung on the wall sent a yellowed glow over the porch, and I frowned when I found Cody sitting on the white wicker loveseat that sat against the exterior wall on the right.

He was leaned far forward with his head drooped between his shoulders.

"Cody?" I whispered it.

Anxiety bottled my senses.

Something sticky that slicked over my skin in a flash of awareness.

Something wasn't right.

I could feel it.

Taste it.

He lifted his head.

A gasp ripped up my throat.

Blood was smeared across his face, streaked where it looked like he'd used his shirt to try to wipe the evidence away. No chance of that since it was dried and caked and matted in his hair.

Golden eyes burned in the night, so wide, filled with rage and hate.

"Oh my God." The shock finally wore off enough that I jumped into action. I rushed across the porch and dropped to my knees in front of him. "Who did this?"

Frantic, I searched for injuries, eyes racing, my heart manic because I already knew.

I already knew who'd done this.

I'd dragged him into it.

Brought danger to his feet.

"Cody," I whimpered.

Agony whipped through my spirit and cast me into a sea of torment.

"It looks worse than it is, darlin'. I just didn't want to go storming in the house looking like death if Lolly and Maddie were still awake."

He had a gaping cut on his right upper cheek and that side was beginning to swell. But it looked like most of the blood had come from a wound at the side of his head where it still trickled from his hairline.

"I'm so sorry." I croaked it. "I'm so sorry."

"Shh…" Cody reached out and took me by the jaw. Softly. Tenderly. Though I could feel the aggression that ticked through his muscles. "It's okay. It's not your fault."

"You know that it is. Pruitt…" I choked over the vileness of his name.

Cody let his hand drift down to the side of my neck. He held me there. His eyes flaming and alive.

"Pruitt is a gutless fuckin' coward. Sneaking up on me from behind and catching me unaware. But you can be sure that's not going to happen again."

"Because you're going to stay away from me." The ball of razors in my throat was so big it was a wonder I could even speak. The pain in my heart too great.

I'd known better, hadn't I?

The risk I was running?

He cracked a grin. So sweet where the rest of his face was covered in blood. With the evidence of my foolishness. Misery squeezed my chest.

"The one thing you can count on, Hailey? It's that I'm not going anywhere."

"Cody, I can't let you—"

He cut me off with a kiss. A hard press of his closed lips.

I could taste the copper tinge of his blood, and I inhaled it, inhaled him.

He held me that way for the longest time before he finally edged back, his thumbs back to brushing comfort along both sides of my jaw. "Whatever you're trying to keep me out of, there's no use in it, because I'm already there."

"Cody." My voice was a breath.

Affection and fear.

Devotion deepened his expression, the masculine lines of his face as inflexible as stone.

"I'm not going anywhere, and I promise you that I'm not going to let that asshole get to you. I wasn't sure what we were dealing with before, but now I know."

He didn't though.

He didn't know the despicable depths.

On shaky knees, I pushed to standing and stretched out my hand. "Come inside. We need to get you cleaned up."

Cody didn't argue.

He stood.

Towering.

Menacing.

Protecting.

I could feel the haven of it as he loomed over me, and I turned and began to lead him inside. He followed behind, his boots thudding on the wooden porch, the race of his heart bashing against my spirit.

I slipped through the door, and he clicked it shut behind us, his action pointed as he turned the locks. Then we quietly moved through the house and into the bathroom within my bedroom.

"Sit." I angled him for the toilet.

He somehow managed a smirk. "Bossy."

Exasperated, I rolled my eyes, every molecule in my body haggard with the knowledge of what had happened. "You seem set on taking care of me. I think it's only fair if I take care of you."

"This isn't a tit-for-tat thing, Hailey. You don't owe me anything."

I reached into the long cupboard beside the sink, pulled out a washcloth, and ran it under hot water. Then I edged back in his direction, the air heavy with implication. With this connection that crackled.

Both soothing and inciting.

My lungs filled with it, almost to the point of pain, like I might burst apart looking at him where he'd been battered because of me.

I gently reached out and pressed the cloth to the wound at the side of his head.

"Isn't it, though?" My words were so quiet they barely broke above the hum that wisped through the small room. "Isn't that what this is, Cody? Giving and taking? Receiving and sharing?"

A big hand clamped down on my hip, and he tipped his marred face up to mine.

I wanted to weep.

Wanted to hold the power to wipe it all away.

"You don't get it, Hailey. Getting to be in your space is enough reward for me. Getting to stand for you is a prize. A fucking honor."

Hesitating, his gaze dropped away for a beat, his expression filled with an old, old grief when he looked back at me.

"I haven't always been the best man, Hailey. I've made bigger mistakes than you could know. I've always known I didn't deserve happiness. Not the true kind, at least. But I'd had this sense coming for a long, long time that maybe…maybe I was meant for something different. For something more. And now I know I was meant for *this*."

My brow furrowed. "We aren't a moral obligation."

"No, you're not, Hailey." He gathered up my free hand and splayed my palm over where the tattoo was seated in the middle of his chest. "I think you're my heart's obligation."

I blinked, trying to process through what he was saying.

Part of me wanted to dive into the safety of it. Get lost in this incredibly kind man who seemed ready to surrender it all.

The other part urged me to run.

Terrified that falling into it would only be asking for more trouble. Everything at risk. On the line.

It was so much and so soon, and I knew he wanted to be there for us, but I didn't think he had the first clue of what that really was going to mean.

Hell, neither did I. There was no certainty of what we'd be facing.

I'd been hoping that Pruitt was here to play the victim. Going to my father and acting the good guy when he was nothing but a villain.

Deranged.

Drunk on power and money.

But I couldn't rest in the hope of that any longer.

And I didn't know how to fix it. Where to go from here. I'd been set on facing this head-on, but I wasn't sure if I was strong enough.

Brave enough.

I wanted to be.

I wanted to stand like Cody and claim the one thing that my heart was aching for.

Because I did feel it. I'd felt the power that had pulled between us since the first time I'd turned to find him standing in the moving truck. Had felt it all those years ago, even though I'd buried it in a grave of sorrow and shame and remorse.

I pulled my hand away from where he had it pinned to the raging at his chest, and I started dabbing at the wounds on his face again, gently cleaning the blood away, my heart cracking further when I forced myself to whisper, "I'm wondering if maybe I should take Maddie away from here. Someplace where Pruitt is not."

I might as well have been dragging a dull blade across my flesh as I said it.

Tormented at the thought of walking away from here.

Walking away from him.

Cody had me pinned against the wall so fast I didn't even realize what had happened.

A raging fortress that towered over me.

Eclipsing reason and sight.

Big hands gripped me by both sides of the face, and he leaned down, his voice near to a growl. "You want to run, Hailey? Then I'll run with you. You want to fight? Then I'll fight for you. But what I'm not willing to do is let you go. Not when you're doing it out of fear."

"I've been afraid for years, Cody. For years. And now—"

"And now you have me."

He swooped down and captured my mouth, stealing the terror from my lungs. Swallowing it as he kissed me deeper, those hands on my face holding me firm and sure.

His tongue stroked over mine.

A demand.

An oath.

Lightheadedness swept through my head, and my knees went weak.

I was overwhelmed.

Taken.

Destitute.

Found.

"You're hurt," I warned between the necessity of his kiss.

"Don't care," he muttered as he gripped me by the back of the neck to control the angle.

There was nothing I could do. No way to resist. No way to stop this.

I dropped the washcloth to the floor and held onto his wrists, silently begging him to hold me up.

Which was such bullshit when he was the one who'd suffered because of me.

He'd taken the brunt.

And here he was, this man who I'd once thought so selfish who was pouring every ounce of who he was into me.

Beauty and light and belief.

Offering it.

Giving it.

Energy lashed, and that connection pulsed and pulled, seeking a way out from the fractured places inside me.

Ribbons that weaved through the cracks and wound within.

Filling the cavities and depressions with a paradigm unlike any I'd ever known.

"Fuck, Hailey. I think I forget how to breathe without you," he rumbled between the frenzy.

His lips passion.

His touch devotion.

His tongue greed.

I was so close to falling over the edge. So close to this heart sitting fully in the palms of his massive hands.

Hands that slipped down my back until he was taking me by the backside and dragging me against the solid planes of his body.

Flames erupted at the contact, and I gasped.

Cody only kissed me deeper.

Harder.

Possessive in his consuming.

He pulled me from the wall and walked me backward out of the bathroom. He peeled my shirt over my head as we went, and I did the same, my fingers racing up his abdomen, his chest, careful as I worked the ruined fabric over his head.

He didn't wince, he only groaned as he urged me farther into my room.

He jerked at the buttons of my jeans, then he was shoving them down. I was quick to work the rest of the way out of them, kicking them off my ankles as I tugged at his fly.

He stepped away long enough to wind out of them, then he was pushing me back onto the bed, gone for the flash of a second as he grabbed a condom from the drawer before a second later he was climbing over me.

Cody Cooper was normally the brightest light. Warmth. The sun.

Tonight, he was a storm.

Shadows and desperation.

A frenzy as he wound himself between my thighs.

No hesitation before he drove into me.

Shock ripped from me on a needy moan, and my back arched from the bed as my nails sank into his shoulders.

A fevered grunt rolled up his thick throat as he seated himself deep.

The man so big my nails raked across his flesh as I struggled to adjust to him all over again.

In an instant, he began to work me.

There was no playfulness to it the way there'd been last night.

This was dire.

This was need.

This was a confession.

One arm fully curled around me to hold me against him as he pumped and stroked and fucked. The other hand was pressed to the mattress to hold us up.

He rocked in frantic thrusts.

Intense and extreme.

I lifted my hips to meet him, thrust after brutal thrust.

Bursts of pleasure sparked in my body and projected from my mouth.

He swallowed them with impassioned kisses.

With his need that I could feel swill around us. Rising from the depths of an unfathomable sea. Sinking down from the darkest heavens.

All around.

Everywhere.

No walls.

No boundaries.

I clawed at his back while he took me as if I were his to take.

Forever.

Branded.

Our spirits melded and our hearts thrashed and the energy that had bound us from the beginning wrapped us in steel threads.

Those shocks of pleasure grew and built, spreading out to leach into every surface of who I was.

Cody angled just right, and his mouth went to my ear, his words gruff and low. "You're mine, Hailey Wagner."

I came apart at the command because that's exactly what it felt like.

A command.

A claim.

A reckoning.

Cody buried a roar in my neck, his body pulsing and vibrating as he came.

Our orgasms rushed through us.

Liquid flames.

An inferno where we were trapped.

A flashfire where we were both consumed.

Burned beyond recognition.

Incinerated.

Ash.

We floated there, in the rubble of who we once had been, in the darkness as we clung to each other.

I didn't know how much time had passed, but Cody had me fully wrapped in his arms, breathing me in, our hearts thundering against the other.

Finally, he pulled away so he could look down at me, and I stared up through the dimness at his marred, beautiful face.

He ran the pad of his thumb along the edge of my cheek. "I mean it, Hailey. I'm here, standing for you. No matter what, I won't walk away."

Reaching out a trembling hand, I scratched my fingers through his beard and whispered, "I trust you."

Chapter Thirty-Three
Cody

Twenty-Four Years Old

THE SUN BEAT DOWN AS CODY HEFTED THE WOODEN POLE to place it into the slot between the two supporting posts. He'd been hired to put in fences around three pastures at Wagner Ranch, a place that had to be the most gorgeous property in Colorado.

Deep in the recesses of the woods, the dense thickets of soaring trees shrouded the area, giving it a quiet, secluded vibe.

He was already slammed for the summer, but he'd taken the project on, needing to stock away some extra cash since he was making his landscaping gig official. Applying for a business license and insurance and all that shit that would make him legitimate.

Allow him employees and expansion and a way to chase down those dreams that hovered just outside his reach.

Hoping to finally pay off his mother's house so he might one day be able to afford his own.

He grabbed the drill and began to drive the huge screw through the log to adhere it to the wooden pole, sweat dribbling down his back as he did.

He stilled, though, when he felt the presence.

When he felt the severity of those eyes that had been haunting him for the last two weeks snag on him from behind. Eyes that continually watched, peeking out from corners and peering through the expanse.

Crystalline eyes that speared him through.

He shifted enough to find her coming down the path toward the stables where she went every day.

Blonde hair braided into two pleats at the side of her head.

Not a lick of makeup, as pretty as could be, though she had that innocent vibe that he normally strayed away from because he didn't mess with that.

He romped and fucked and had a damned good time, but he had no interest in taking anything farther than that. He had his mother and sisters to worry about, a business to build, and he couldn't afford to get distracted.

And she looked like a *farther* kind of girl.

Besides, she was the ranch owner's daughter.

As off-limits as they came.

First thing the ranch manager had told him when signing on was to keep at least a hundred feet between himself and Douglas Wagner's daughter, and he'd heard the rest of the hands making jokes about the knockout girl that would get you lost in a shallow grave if you dared to even glance her way.

Forbidden fucking fruit.

Sweet fucking fruit, though, he'd bet.

He couldn't avert the power of her aura, the way it slipped through the air, infiltrating the oxygen.

She kept coming closer, though she wasn't alone. That chick Brooke he'd hooked up with at the river a few weeks back was at her side.

His stomach fisted.

That was a mistake.

She'd seemed totally on board that night, agreeing she wasn't looking for any attachments when he'd told her he was a solo-kind of guy, but he'd be game for a good time if she was interested.

He should have heeded the warning that spun at the back of his mind when she'd gone for a kiss as she'd been riding his dick in the bed of his truck. The way she'd pouted when he'd told her no. That he didn't kiss because it felt too damned intimate.

He'd had instant fucking regret when he'd seen her here on the ranch a couple days later, and she kept coming around, clearly looking for a repeat.

Guilt thickened his throat. He hated to be an asshole. Hurt someone.

But he'd been upfront and clear, and it seemed she was the one who wasn't being honest. Not with him or herself.

Brooke grabbed the other girl's hand, tugging at her and whispering something as she giggled, before she came dragging her through the field before they were standing on the other side of the fence he was building.

"Hey, Cody," Brooke drawled, no doubt trying to come off as sexy. Wearing the tiniest tank that barely covered her tits and didn't even offer the innuendo of it to her midriff.

She was gorgeous, no question, but something soured in his stomach when he looked at her standing next to Wagner's daughter.

"Hey, Brooke." He tried to keep looking at the dark-haired beauty, wondering what the fuck was wrong with him when his attention kept trying to slide to the blonde at her right.

"How's it going?" he asked, going for cool and casual.

Brooke groaned. "Terrible. I'm being a good sport and going out to the stables with Hailey since she thinks she needs to spend half her life with the beasts."

Cody took the opportunity to look at Hailey.

He'd never officially met her, only knowing her name by the mumblings of the hands.

"You like horses, huh?" he couldn't help but ask her.

He already knew she did. It wasn't like he hadn't been stupidly tracking her every movement over the last two weeks when she'd been out on the grounds.

He didn't know what it was about her.

What had him intrigued.

Probably the fact that she was forbidden, which was seriously fucked.

She was clearly innocent and sweet, the way she kept down casting that ice-blue gaze, her cheeks pinked, continually shifting on those dusty cowgirl boots.

He needed to leave it at that.

Hailey let go of a self-deprecating laugh. It was throaty and sounding of something that hit him entirely in the wrong way.

Like a low lash of seduction.

"I think you could say it's required of me," she said. "Formed somewhere in my DNA."

"I can see that," he told her.

"And I hate horses." Brooke wound her arm through Hailey's and tugged her close, trying to win back Cody's attention.

"You don't hate them…you're just scared of them." Hailey's voice was encouragement.

"Whatever you want to call it, just know I don't want to be anywhere near them, so you know I must love you if I'm willing to go out there with you." Brooke feigned a shudder, though Cody saw there was real affection for her friend. "Which means she has to go with me to the party at the river tonight. Are you going to be there, Cody?"

He'd avoided them since the night he'd hooked up with Brooke there, though he found himself nodding right then. "Yeah, think I'm going to be."

"Good." Brooke tucked Hailey's arm a little closer. "That means we'll be seeing you there."

Cody couldn't help but look at Hailey then. Take her in. The way she blushed and seemed to want to disappear into her friend's side.

Not a chance.

Because with that energy radiating off her?

She was the only thing Cody could see.

⤬

"Ma?" Cody knocked at the screen door just as he was pushing through and stepped into his childhood home.

It was late afternoon, and Dakota was home for the summer from college and would be at work downtown at the bakery, and his youngest sister, Kayla, would be at dance class.

But his mother's car was parked out front, and he'd wanted to pop by to check on her.

Silence held fast, though there was a disorder to it, the kind he always felt like a kick to the gut whenever he came in and his mother was distraught.

He had a sixth sense about it.

In tune.

He just knew when she was struggling since it'd been his job to look out for her. To take care of her. To help her the best that he could.

For so long of it, he'd been a kid, not really able to contribute all that much.

But that was about to change.

"Ma," he called again, and his chest clutched when he heard the telltale sounds of her crying.

The muffled sobs that she always tried to keep buried.

He followed them down the hall and to the bedroom at the end. His heart that felt like it was being crushed got obliterated when he pushed open the door to find her on the floor, hugging her knees to her chest.

"Ma." He was on the floor in front of her in a second flat, scooping her up and into his arms.

He sat down with her on the side of the bed. "What's wrong?"

She tried to hide the evidence. To swat away the blotchy mess that scuffed her cheeks raw, like she'd been at this for hours.

"It's okay, Cody. Just give me a minute." Her voice was hoarse from the sorrow.

"Not leaving you."

"Cody." She whispered it, slowly shaking her head. "You're always trying to take care of your mom."

She said it gentle, her eyes lighting in that affected way she'd always watched him with.

He squeezed her tighter. "That's right. That's what I'm supposed to do."

Saddened surrender filled her voice. "No, sweetheart, you're not, and I've been far too much of a burden for you. I hate that for even a minute of your life you thought you had to sacrifice. That you lost a day of your childhood."

His head shook in ferocity, his arms bands around her thin body. "Nothing is lost if it's given to you and my sisters."

A sob tore out of her at his words, his mother succumbing to something that Cody couldn't see. Something different than had been there before.

He pulled back so he could study her tear-stained face. "What's going on?"

Her mouth tweaked down on the side. "I tried so hard, Cody. Tried so hard to make everything work. To balance it. I'm so sorry."

Fear bottled in his chest, and the question ground off his tongue. "What does that mean?"

Hesitation brimmed around her before her shoulder drifted up to her cheek. "I have to let go of the house. I know this is the last place we had with your father, but—"

Anger surged, not really at her, but at himself that he hadn't recognized it or realized how much trouble she was in.

"You told me you were set."

"I was…for a while. But with Dakota in college and now Kayla going in the fall…" She paused then said, "Something's got to give."

Cody gave a harsh shake of his head.

She'd been hiding it, trying to play it that she was fine without his help.

Little did she know he'd been saving.

"I can help, Ma. I have an extra five thousand dollars that I've stocked away."

Her bleary gaze traced over his face. "I can't accept any more money from you, Cody."

"Please."

She set her hand on his cheek. "Honey, you are amazing and wonderful and I'm so grateful, but that isn't going to be nearly enough. I need to let it go."

"How much do you need?" he demanded it.

"Way too—"

"How much?" It boomed through her room. When she cringed, he softened his voice. "How much, Ma? I'm not a little kid you need to protect any longer. I need to know."

Her attention dropped to her lap. "I took out a big loan on the house a couple years ago. It fell behind and the house has gone into foreclosure. The only way I can recoup anything is to sell it."

"How much to get it back in standing?"

Her gaze dipped. "Sixty thousand."

"I'll get it."

"No—"

"I'll get it. I don't know how, but I'll get it." He pushed to standing and tipped up his mother's face.

Horrified embarrassment lingered there, like she was to blame when she'd given everything for them. "I'll get it. I promise."

Then he walked out, having no idea what that really meant.

Chapter Thirty-Four
Cody

I WAS DRENCHED IN SWEAT, AND MY TEE CLUNG TO MY SKIN AS the sun blazed down from the bluest sky. No clouds or coolness were to be found. I drove the shovel deep into the earth, grunting as I shifted to use my boot to ram down on the sides to dig it in deeper.

Wry laughter rolled from behind me. "You look like you're taking out whatever happened to you last night on that dirt."

I tossed a glare over my shoulder. Matthew stood with his hands on his hips, smirking down at me where I was in a hole that was about three feet deep. We'd used the Bobcat to dig most of it out, but we'd gotten down close to some pipes, and we needed to do the rest by hand to make sure we didn't hit one.

The last thing I needed was to cause a huge fucking leak.

"And you look like you're standing around like a lazy prick when you could be helping me dig this hole."

Two guys on our crew hadn't shown today, and I was down here doing it myself since the rest of the team was working on the mold for the pathway in front of Cabin 6B that was going to be poured tomorrow.

Turned out it was the exact kind of day that was going to piss me off.

I was completely on edge. Raging on the inside and trying to keep it tamped, riding a thin line that warned I might snap.

My head fucking throbbed like a bitch, and my face was so swollen I was lucky I could see out of my right eye.

Matthew's brow arched. "I thought we were past all the manual labor?"

"The day the boss decides he doesn't want to get his hands dirty is the day the business goes to hell." I grunted it as I pitched the mound of dirt in my shovel up onto even ground.

"Looks like you got more than dirty, Cody. You look like you were about five seconds from needing that hole for yourself because someone was close to putting you six feet under."

Fury blistered through my blood.

I'd been able to keep it partially under control last night. Giving it everything not to lose it in front of Hailey, even though I'd been half mad when I'd fucked her.

Fast and quick and hard, terrified it might be the last time I would get to touch her.

I'd seen it in her eyes. The fear of fully letting me in. Thinking she was responsible when I deserved any ugly thing coming my way. I should have known Karma wouldn't let me get by so easily.

"It was just some punk who jumped me at a bar."

The half-truth was going to have to suffice.

Matthew laughed like any of this was funny. "You might look like shit, but I'm betting that guy is worse for the wear."

Not yet, but he would be.

"He caught me by surprise then took off. It was over before I even knew what happened," I said, focusing my agitation on the shovel that I drove deep into the ground.

"Well, damn. Hope the fucker tripped as he was running around the corner." Matthew was all lightheartedness, making it a joke, like I normally did, too.

I couldn't find it in myself to find the humor in it.

Not when I knew what this meant for Hailey. What was riding on it.

"I'm sure he'll get what's coming to him," I said, tossing the dirt up onto the pile.

"No doubt. So, you want my ass in that hole, huh?" he said, shifting gears, gesturing to the pit I was making.

"Nah, go check on the rest of the team and make sure they have those molds correct. They need to be set before anyone leaves this afternoon."

Honestly, I didn't want the company. I wanted to stew in the outrage. In the wrath that was coming.

"Alright. Just holler if you change your mind."

"Will do," I told him.

Matthew strode down the pathway in the direction of where the rest of our guys were working, and I turned back to the task at hand, praying by the time I finished I'd have come to some sort of solution.

A resolution.

It was damned hard when I had no idea how to handle a scumbag like Pruitt.

He struck me as a weaselly prick, and I was ninety-nine percent sure the actual person who attacked me wasn't him but rather someone who'd been sent to do his bidding.

Nothing but a twisted fuck who had so much control and power that he could send someone to commit a crime without much of a worry.

Hailey and I had talked this morning on the way to work about going to the police, what our options were.

She'd asked for a little time. Needing to figure out how she was going to handle this.

I turned back to spear out another shovelful when I felt a shadow cover me from behind, blocking out the rays of light though it did nothing to blot out the heat.

My stomach clutched, and I slowly shifted around, fighting the way my ribs wanted to cave in when I saw the man standing over me.

Douglas Wagner.

Surprise scuffed from his mouth when he saw my busted to shit face, and he shook his head, though it wasn't quite in disbelief. "Trouble follows you wherever you go, doesn't it?"

I scoffed and went back to shoveling like my stomach wasn't sick at the sight of him.

"And I wasn't even asking for it this time." I injected as much irony into it as I could, even though the statement wasn't necessarily true.

I had asked for it.

Had asked to stand for Hailey.

No doubt, this asshole was going to be none too happy if I claimed it.

"It's a lifestyle that breeds those things." His tone was the same as it'd been all those years ago.

Condescending.

Disgusted.

"I'm not that same kid any longer."

"That doesn't mean you're a different person."

I drove the shovel straight into the ground and rested my arm on the top of the handle. Agitation clamored through my nerves, though I forced myself to remain calm as I stared up at Hailey's father. "And what exactly are you implying?"

He didn't hesitate. "The same thing I was saying then. Stay the hell away from my daughter. She has enough going on in her life without you making it worse."

Scorned disbelief rattled in my chest. "Your daughter is a big girl. She can make those decisions for herself."

"My daughter is grieving. Looking for something…anything… to make her feel good."

I bit down on my tongue to keep from spouting off just how good I actually made her feel.

"I'd suggest you don't prey on that," he added.

Anger screamed, running hot through my veins. Still, I managed a semblance of composure, though the words were rough. "That's quite the accusation to make."

He stepped forward so he completely blocked the sun. Placing me in his shadow. "If it fits."

"You don't know anything about me." I couldn't help but spit it.

"Maybe not everything, Cody Cooper, but you know I know the one thing that counts. You aren't good enough for my daughter. Not then, and sure as hell not now."

He didn't give me a chance to respond. He turned his back and stalked down the walkway in the direction of the stables.

I grabbed the shovel and rammed it into the dirt, gritting my teeth, barely able to breathe.

I might hate him for it, but I knew every word he spoke was God's honest truth.

Chapter Thirty-Five

Hailey

"MOMMY, MOMMY, MOMMY! YOU HAVE TO WAKE IT UP right now! Today is going to be the very best day of my whole entire life, and you have to get up so we can get ready!"

I peeled an eye open where I was face down on my pillow, lost to the most restful sort of sleep. The kind you could only experience after you'd been kept up for hours being worshipped, your body sagging from the exhaustion of bliss, then you fell asleep in the same arms that had taken you there.

Arms that had held me until morning.

Sure.

Strong.

He'd done it every night this week, keeping me floating on this plane of ecstasy I'd had no idea even existed.

My body was lodged somewhere between depletion and exhilaration.

A hypnotizing satisfaction that ran bone deep.

But I didn't have time to revel in it right then.

Not when my little girl was currently bouncing on her knees at my side and yanking at my arm.

"Get up, Mommy! Mr. Cody is already up in the kitchen makin' us the best breakfast because he said we really gotta have our energy if we're going to play with the horses today, and I'm so very excited!"

Forcing off the fatigue that wanted to suck me back under, I shifted around so I could push up to sitting.

My fingertips brushed down my daughter's precious face. "You're excited, huh?"

"Yes! I get to see the horses, and I get new friends! I think it's really a very special day."

Paisley had texted two days ago to confirm the barbecue she was planning so the kids could meet. I'd told Maddie about our plans last night.

Soft laughter rolled out, love pulsing against my ribs.

This was what I wanted.

For my daughter to find sanctuary.

A place where she was protected and surrounded by friends.

People who adored her.

Home.

"I think it's going to be a really special day, too."

I glanced around at my bed. The covers were rumpled and twisted.

Cody would have slinked out sometime before dawn the way he'd done each morning since I wasn't ready to explain to my daughter why he was sleeping in my room.

I didn't want to confuse her.

Didn't want to set her up for any disappointment or pain, even though I knew that was exactly where I had myself.

Lost to the words he'd issue with his lips pressed to the side of my head. Lost to the way he'd murmur praises into my sleep in the seconds before he'd sneak out my door.

Don't know how I got so lucky, waking up next to you.

You are the most incredible woman I've ever met.

Gorgeous. Sexy. Kind and strong.

I'm going to be right for you.

I fought the fizz of guilt that churned in my stomach.

I would never. I promise you, Brooke. I would never do that to you.

I pushed it down into the crypt I kept for her, praying that one day that sick feeling would evaporate.

I didn't want to look at Cody and feel shame. Not for the way I felt.

But how could I forget her? That promise? What had happened? And it was because of me.

Maddie jumped to her feet, jostling me all over and tugging at my hand. "Hurry it up, lazy pants."

I cleared the roughness from my throat and pasted a smile on my face. "You know we're not supposed to be at my friend's ranch until three o'clock, right?"

"Um, yeah, Mommy, which means we gotta get ready!"

It wasn't even quite seven, but I relented and let her haul me out of bed.

She had ahold of my left hand, dragging me across the room. With my right, I did my best to try to sort out the bedhead I was sure to be sporting considering the way Cody had been fisting it last night.

She led me out into the main room. Rays of sunlight streamed in through the windows, ribbons of gold threaded with hope looping through the space, the warmth so distinct it hit me like an embrace.

Like I was walking straight into a mesmerizing dream.

And that's what it felt like—a dream with the man standing in the kitchen, wearing sweats and a fitted tee, his feet bare, his rugged face so handsome with his short beard and his harsh brow.

He tilted me that smirk he always met me with. The one that tied my stomach in a thousand jittery knots.

Maddie beamed as she presented me like a gift. "Look it! I got her for you, Mr. Cody, because you said you needed her real bad."

"You want me, huh?" I wheezed it, barely able to speak.

I was hanging onto Maddie's hand like she was the lifeline when I was so close to getting swept away.

"That's right, I do." He said it low and smooth, and his head was cocked to the side as he crossed the three steps it took to bring him to me. There was no hesitation in the action, just a glint in those golden eyes as he reached out and grabbed me by the cheek and dipped down to kiss me.

Close mouthed, though it sent shockwaves trembling through my body.

My heart battered at my ribs and my spirit was dislodged from the place where I'd tried to keep it protected.

From where she swayed beside me, Maddie giggled, both embarrassed and joyed in her precious, innocent way. "Are you kissin' my mommy, Mr. Cody?"

And I realized it was the first time he'd kissed me in front of her. The first time he'd touched me in front of her.

Well, other than the secreted, covert brushes when he was sure she wasn't paying attention.

His hand slid down to curl around the side of my neck, his big fingers splaying wide as if he was holding the whole of me.

He turned his gaze down to my little girl. "Do you mind if I give your mommy kisses?"

Maddie shrugged. "I guess you probably should if you love her."

The air was suddenly thick. So damned thick that there was no chance of getting it into my lungs, my chest squeezing and my pulse going erratic at the thought.

Cody looked back at me, and he brushed his thumb across my flesh, his regard both tender and acute.

Uncertain and sure.

I shivered beneath it.

His teeth raked his bottom lip before he seemed to come to a conclusion, and he pulled away to pick Maddie up from under the arms and tossed her into the air. She squealed in delight, screeching as she flew before she frantically curled her little arms around his neck when he caught her.

"You caught me," she gasped as if there was a chance he wouldn't have.

"Of course, I caught you, Button. That's what these arms are for. Holding you and your mother up. Taking care of you. Because you and your mom are important to me."

Cody glanced back at me when he said it, repeating a semblance of the words he'd spoken earlier that week. Words that tried to hook into the most brittle places hidden inside.

"Really important?" Maddie peeped.

Cody set her on the island, his hand on her leg to make sure she was safe. His attention swept between the two of us, and his voice lowered when he said, "The most important, Maddie. You and your mom are the most important to me."

"Good, 'cause I think you're really important, too."

"Is that so?"

"Mmhmm." She beamed that smile, blonde, wild ringlets bouncing around her chubby cheeks. "And it's a really important thing to know that I'm really very hungry right now."

A rough chuckle scraped from Cody's throat. "What am I goin' to do with you, Button?"

"Keep me?"

Affection bound the room. So intense I was nearly shredded by it.

Mixed in it was the unknown. That dark thing that would crowd in at the edges of Cody's aura and clot out the easiness in his spirit. The part of him I wanted to seep into, too.

Cody poked Maddie's belly, trying for light, to break out of whatever demons that held him trapped.

Squealing, she grabbed at his hand. "You got me, Mr. Cody!"

Emotion gripped him, the words a coarse, ragged grumble. "Nah, Maddie. Think you got me."

⌒✳⌒

Country music played from the speakers and dust flew behind Cody's truck as he barreled down the dirt road that led to Hutchins Ranch. We'd already traveled more than forty minutes, winding through the forest as we'd left Hendrickson and made it into Time River, before we'd hit a straight two-lane road that had taken us across flat plains where the vegetation had become sparse.

The blue sky wide open above us.

We'd made the right off the main road and onto a long dirt drive, and we climbed a high hill.

Once we hit its peak, a valley opened below. The mountains that hugged Time River rose up high in the distance, and at its base we could see the river that snaked through.

The landscape was breathtaking. Awe-inspiring in its beauty.

A staggering ranch was sprawled out between, tucked in the safety of the valley. Trees grew up on the fringes and green, grassy fields stretched on for miles. A ton of buildings, barns and stables and cabins, were situated in every direction.

At the far end was an enormous house that rose out of a copse of trees, its pitched roof stretching toward the heavens.

"Wow." I didn't even realize the admiration had slipped between my lips.

Cody chuckled from where he drove.

I looked that way, and my breath was stolen all over again.

He wore his cap, jeans and a tee, a tattooed arm stretched out where he held onto the steering wheel.

He tossed a grin my way. "Caleb's the richest man in Time River. Even richer than your dad."

He wagged his brows with his pestering, and I tried to process that Cody had brought my father up at all. The disquiet I'd been carrying flared.

"You probably shouldn't go around telling my father that," I played along anyway, not sure where this conversation was going. Besides, my father might have been a shrewd businessman, but he honestly wasn't all that proud. I doubted he cared all that much about who was making more money than him.

But what he did care about was me.

The easiness in Cody's demeanor dampened. "I'm not sure there's a whole lot I'm going to be telling your father, Hailey."

I bit down on my bottom lip.

There it was.

That speck of misgiving that lingered from our past.

I knew how my father had felt about Cody.

I could still hear his warnings that he'd given me back then, and it wasn't like he'd stopped implying them once I'd returned. As if I were a child who wasn't smart enough to make her own choices.

I gripped my phone on my lap like it could erase the messages I'd ignored from him that had started coming in mid-morning.

Dad: We need to talk.

Dad: Where are you?

Dad: Don't act like a child, Hailey. I know you're getting my messages.

We'd had an argument when he'd stopped in to see me at the stables the day after Cody had been attacked. He'd looked me point-blank and told me to stay away from him. He had told me I was being foolish and any daughter of his would open her eyes.

Hurt had slashed through my insides, and I'd told him he didn't have a say, and if he was going to toss demands around like he had the right to disparage Cody and disrespect me? Then he could stay away.

The thing was, I had been foolish for years, and he hadn't had the first clue.

My voice turned earnest. A promise. "There isn't a thing you need to explain to him."

Reaching across the seats, Cody threaded his fingers through mine and gave them a slight squeeze. "Nah, neither of us need to explain ourselves."

Then Cody wavered, his teeth working at the middle of his bottom lip, his hand tightening on mine like he was the one who needed to cling to me. He kept his voice low, trying to protect innocent ears. "But you should know I got into a bit of trouble when I was working for your father. There's a reason he hates me."

I felt myself pale, the vague warnings he kept giving me rising to the forefront. "What kind of trouble?"

Cody looked to the rearview mirror, at my daughter who was watching out the windows.

I got it.

His reluctance.

I squeezed his hand back. "It doesn't matter, Cody. That was a long time ago, and this is now."

Could I claim that? Make it true? Stand in it for every obstacle and barrier that worked to keep us separated?

The promise I had made?

This guilt?

Give in and let go?

Is that what Cody wanted? Is that what we were headed for?

I inhaled around the disorder, putting it aside. "I need to figure out this other situation, anyway, then we can deal with my father."

"Sounds like a plan to me." Relief coated Cody's tone.

"What kind of plans you got, my Mr. Cody?" Maddie piped in from the backseat.

She said it like she'd had no clue what we were talking about, her voice eager and excited, the way it'd been the entire trip, though she'd finally settled down over the last ten minutes since the ride was taking longer than she'd understood that it would.

Cody glanced at her through the rearview mirror. "The plan is we're about to introduce you to some new friends, and you're going to have a blast."

"I love that plan!" she yelled.

Cody chuckled, and he squeezed my fingers some more as he glanced over at me. "What do you think of that plan, Hailey? Do you think we're going to have a blast?"

There was a tease to it. A gentle ribbing. A nudging toward what was hanging out in the periphery waiting on me to let go.

I shifted to look between him and my daughter. "I think it's going to be the best day ever."

"Now that sounds like a solid plan," Cody said.

"Yes!" Maddie shouted, throwing a little fist in the air.

Dust billowed behind us as Cody drove his truck down the dirt lane that wound through the outbuildings of the ranch, and he eased all the way around to park next to another large truck and a white Volvo with a Time River Market & Café logo in the back window.

"Are my new friends already here?" Maddie asked, squirming and yanking at the straps of her car seat.

"It looks like everyone is just getting here, don't you fret, Button," Cody told her.

"Then let me out!"

"I've got you, little one," he promised.

He hopped out of the driver's side and moved to open the back door. He leaned in and unbuckled Maddie then swooped her out and into his arms like he did it every day.

Like he was happy to do it.

Like he was purposed to do it.

Nerves thundered my pulse.

This was so different.

So new.

And it felt so good and right and I was terrified that I was setting us both up for destruction.

Because I was sure this kind of breaking would be the unbearable kind.

Because my heart ached just looking at the two of them.

But I didn't want to let reservations get in the way.

I didn't want to hide or shutter.

I wanted to open myself to this—whatever it meant or wherever it was going to lead.

Was it selfish though?

Bringing him into this?

We'd already seen exactly what happened when I did, the fading bruises on his face proof of that. But he'd sworn that he wanted to be here for us, and I had to trust in that. Believe in him when for so long I'd stopped believing in anyone.

Cody came around the back of the truck with Maddie hooked to his side. Her little arms were wrapped around his neck.

"Hurry it up, slow poke! I got friends to meet."

Cody widened his eyes. "That's right, hurry it up, slow poke."

"Someone's awful anxious."

"Me!" Maddie threw her arms high, and affection was rushing wide, radiating from both Cody and me.

Reaching out, he took my hand and brushed my knuckles across his lips.

"I'm so glad you're here," he mumbled there.

Affection bound my chest in a fist.

"Me, too," I whispered back.

It was foolish, but I was.

I wanted to be here.

With him.

He led us behind the few cars that were parked in a row toward the gathering of people on a sprawling lawn that extended out from in front of the mansion.

He didn't let me go as we walked below the rays of the sun, though Maddie wiggled to get down.

The second her feet hit the ground, the child beelined in the direction of a group of kids who were playing beneath a giant tree on the far side of the lawn, wild curls billowing behind her as she went.

Her voice carried as she sang, "Hi! I'm Maddie. Are you my brand-new friends?"

Cody chuckled as we ambled along. "There isn't a shy bone in her body, is there?"

"Not even one," I told him.

"She is something, Hailey." His voice went low.

My ribs clenched around my hammering heart. "She's everything."

His hand tightened on mine. "You both are."

Everything pulsed.

Squeezed and sped and made me weak in the knees.

I tried to clear it away when Paisley suddenly stood from one of the chairs that surrounded a patio table beneath a couple of big blue umbrellas.

"Hails Bells, get your cute butt over here."

"I'm already on my way," I called back.

She was all grins, though I watched her attention dip to where Cody had his hand wound in mine.

How much had changed since I'd met him.

There was no question left that we were together.

Dakota and Savannah shifted around.

Shock widened their eyes, and an uncertainty rippled through the hot air.

Cody didn't cringe or shirk.

He just pulled me closer and leaned in to kiss the top of my head, muttering, "Prepare yourself for the inquisition."

All the women scrambled to their feet.

Dakota, Cody's sister, made it to me first.

Nerves swallowed me whole.

She pulled me in for a tight hug. "Hailey, it's so good to see you again."

Her voice was kind, and there was no missing the sincerity of her welcome, though I could feel her peeking at her brother from over my shoulder.

I pulled away in time to see Cody lift his hands out to the sides, feigned offense written in his countenance. "What, you didn't miss me?"

"Now why would I miss you?" she taunted.

Cody scoffed, his temperament back to teasing. "Only because I'm the best damned brother you could ever have."

"The only brother I have." Dakota was laughing under her breath when she stepped up to hug him.

Lifting her off her feet, he swung her around. "It's good to see you, little sister."

Her tone softened. "It's good to see you, too. Are you coming to family breakfast at Mom's in the morning? We didn't see you last weekend."

Cody's attention slanted my way. His expression was searching, tender and sure and somehow fierce.

The ground trembled beneath my feet.

"Yeah, but I'm going to have a couple extras with me."

Apprehension flew, and I shifted uneasily, twining my fingers together at what didn't seem quite an invitation but more like a statement.

Dakota looked my way. Something close to surprised glee lit in her smile. "Ryder told me, but I wasn't quite sure I could believe it."

Her regard might have been on me when she said it, but I was pretty sure she was talking to Cody.

"Believe it, little sister," Cody told her, though he was looking at me, too.

"Okay, you two stop hogging my Hails Bells, I haven't even gotten a hug in yet." Paisley slipped in front of me and hauled me in for one of her raucous hugs, squeezing me like I was also one of the *most important* people in her life.

I honestly didn't know how to process it, being alone for so long and then suddenly surrounded by these incredible people who made me feel like I'd come back to the place I belonged.

Like there'd been a spot reserved for me.

Like they'd known how badly I needed friends.

That I needed to understand the significance of that again after I'd shunned the idea of it because entertaining the possibility had been too painful.

"I can't tell you how happy I am that you're here. I missed the crap out of you," Paisley said.

"It's only been a week."

"Well, I'm still missing you from all the years you were gone." I could feel her smile behind the statement, and I couldn't help the discordant, affected laugh.

"You're ridiculous," I whispered.

"No, I just know when someone is special, and all the special people belong with us. You know, because we're amazing."

"Facts," Dakota said.

Savannah was shaking her head when she stepped forward for a hug, too. "These two might be full of themselves, but in this case, I think I'm going to have to agree with them. You must be extra special to turn this guy's eye."

She glanced at Cody, and he gave me one of those slow grins as he said, "Ah, this one is special, all right."

Heat blasted my cheeks. "You all better be careful. This is liable to go to my head."

"Right where it belongs, baby. Claim it. We do." Paisley tossed an arm over my shoulders.

A giggle slipped out, and Paisley gestured with her chin toward the children where they were playing tag under the big tree. "Let's go meet all the kids. It looks like your little one slipped right in."

I glanced that way. Maddie was laughing hysterically, her arms stretched out in front of her as she chased a little boy with blond hair so light it was almost white.

My chest tightened at the sight. "I'm pretty sure you're stuck with her."

"That is the plan," Paisley said.

Cody took a step toward us, eyes raking me, searching for whatever I might need. "I'm going to grab a beer and see what the guys are up to. You good?"

"I'm great." I didn't have to search all that deep inside myself to discern it was the truth.

He reached out and touched my nose the way he often did Maddie. Butterflies swam in my stomach.

God, I was done for.

"Good," he murmured in that rough voice. "That's the way I want it."

Without saying anything else, Cody turned and started across the lawn, his round ass hugged perfectly by his jeans. There was no looking away as he wandered over to where Caleb, Ryder, and Ezra were standing around a barbecue, watching as Caleb grilled something that smelled sweet and delicious.

I didn't realize I was just staring like a weirdo until Paisley suddenly shook me, cracking up as she leaned in close. "That man is smitten, and I think someone else might be, too."

Flustered, I waved her off. "It's new."

Dakota's warm brown eyes widened. "This is my older brother we're talking about. I'm not sure if you know much about his past since this is *new* and all, but one thing I can tell you is he has never once shown up at any event with a woman."

"Exactly, which was why I was trying to warn you off him on Saturday. You clearly didn't listen." Paisley wound me around and started us in the direction of the kids.

Dakota and Savannah took up my other side.

"I'm going to have to say I'm glad she didn't," Dakota said. "I've never seen my brother look like that in all my life. That man is on his knees for you."

"Oh, bet he's a whole lot more than just on his knees for her." Suggestion lined Savannah's words.

More redness flamed.

Cackling, Paisley jostled me around. "Oh my God, look at her. It looks to me like Cody isn't the only one who's tripped. Head over heels, baby."

"I don't think we're quite there yet." I forced it out, needing to be pragmatic about all of this.

"Ha, you might not be there yet, but that man is already doing laps around you," Paisley said.

"Panting, completely out of breath." Dakota nodded, grinning like mad. "Or maybe she has him panting for entirely different reasons."

"I bet that man does love you up real good." Paisley leaned around, her green eyes dancing with the scandal.

Amusement wound with the mortification. "Um…am I supposed to answer that in front of his sister?"

Dakota linked her elbow in mine. "Hell yes, you are. There are no secrets between friends."

Friends.

"You might as well go ahead and dish it," Savannah said. "These two hounded the crap out of me when I first started hanging out with Ezra, demanding every detail. It's only fair."

Dakota hip checked her. "You know you love it."

Everything about Savannah softened. "I do. I love every second of it."

Tenderness billowed between the three friends, wrapping around me, prodding at me to fully let go.

To grasp onto the truth that this was worth it.

Whatever it cost.

Whatever risk I was taking.

Whatever turmoil I had to struggle and fight to get through to the other side.

It was worth it.

To give my daughter the chance at a normal, beautiful life. It was worth it.

Just like she was experiencing right then.

Maddie squealed as she copied another little girl who was doing cartwheels across the lawn, though Maddie fell onto her butt each time she attempted to do one, giggling the whole time.

A little girl with messy brown hair and giant chocolate eyes turned course when she saw us, skipping in our direction. "Mommy! We got a new best friend, and her name is Maddie, and she even likes horses as much as me and Olivia do! We have to take her to the stable so I can show her my favorite horse, Mazzy."

Paisley leaned in and murmured, "That one's mine," before she released me and knelt in front of the little girl. "We will definitely show Maddie your horse."

"Yay!"

"Yes!" Maddie clambered up behind her along with another little girl, the two of them jumping high at the news, though it was Maddie's excited voice that filled the air.

"I get to see horses, and I got so many brand-new friends, and they're so very nice, Mommy, and this is for sure the biggest blast that I ever had, just like my Mr. Cody said I was going to have."

Affection pounded, and I stood there feeling overwhelmed.

Overflowing with the magnitude of my little girl's joy.

"I'm so happy you've already met new friends," Paisley said to my daughter. "I knew you, Evelyn, and Olivia were going to hit it off."

"We hit it off a lot." Maddie gave her a big nod.

Paisley let go of a soft laugh as she stuck out her hand. "I'm Paisley, one of your mom's old friends, and I'm Evelyn's mommy."

Madison shook her hand. "It's so very nice to meet you, too. Thank you for inviting me over to your house and letting me have so much fun."

"It's my pleasure."

Maddie giggled like crazy. "No way. I got all the pleasure."

"You are just adorable, aren't you?" Paisley murmured.

I didn't pretend not to agree.

Paisley stood. "Okay, so let's do some introductions." She touched the little girl's head who stood beaming up at her. "Like I said, this is my Evelyn."

I gave a small wave. "Hi, Evelyn."

"Hi!" she sang.

"And this sweet one right here belongs to Ezra and Savannah… my niece, Olivia. And those two ragamuffins running the yard are their twins, Owen and Oliver."

Two white-haired boys who couldn't be more than four or five were currently racing across the lawn, little feet pounding the earth, their laughter floating on the warm breeze.

At the bar last weekend, Savannah had told me about how she'd met Ezra last summer, how he'd insisted she move into their guest house, and how she'd fallen in love with both the man and his three children.

I could feel her love wash the atmosphere.

A tiny boy who was probably three came tottering toward us, and he lifted his arms to Dakota. She swept him up, snuggled his sweet cheek to hers, and smiled my way. "And this is my little man, Kayden. Can you say hi to Mommy's new friend, Hailey? She's a *really good* friend of your uncle Cody's so I'm pretty sure you're going to be seeing her a lot."

She smirked at me.

I choked out a laugh.

"Hi, *Haywee*." The tiny boy reached for me with precious, chubby fingers.

I reached out to touch them, and that was it.

My heart burst.

Paisley knocked into my shoulder with hers, though this time, there was no tease to her words. "Welcome to the family."

Chapter Thirty-Six
Cody

"WHAT THE FUCK HAPPENED TO YOUR FACE?" RAGE jumped into Ryder's demeanor the second he saw me. Yeah, I knew that one was coming.

"What the hell, man?" Ezra wheezed it when he turned around, his hand cinching down on the can of beer he held.

I took off my cap and anxiously squeezed at the brim. "Had a little run-in with a punk after I left Time & Tap Tavern after I met you the other night." I issued the words in Ryder's direction.

Ezra jumped in, spitting with enraged disbelief. "Looks to me like you had a hell of a lot more than just a run-in. From where I'm standing, looks like you landed somewhere in the area of getting your ass beat and needing an ambulance. And this went down in my town, and you didn't think to tell me?"

Unease wobbled through my consciousness. "I had it handled."

Incredulity pulled into Caleb's expression, and his attention swept between me and the steaks he was flipping. "And what's the other guy look like?"

I blew out the strain. "Don't know. He took off before I could get a look at him."

Ezra hissed. "I'm not sure that I'd describe that as having it handled. You didn't get anything on him? And he just took off? Did he rob you?"

I could feel Ezra spinning, the badge he wore coming out, dude Sheriff through and through.

I scuffed my palm over the top of my head, and I warily glanced at where Hailey was being introduced to the kids. Joy emanated from her, the girl so fucking stunning where she stood beneath the shade of the trees with the little flecks of light making their way through.

I turned back to my crew.

"Think it's more complicated than that."

A disturbance rolled through them, and I saw the second Ryder came to awareness. His mind traveled right back to what I'd told him that night. When I'd warned him about what Hailey might be up against.

"Hailey's ex?" The two words ground to dust. In an instant, my best friend was a toil of turbulence.

"Like I said, I didn't get a look at the bastard, but I'd bet my life it was him, or at least someone he sent to shake me down. Scare me off. Whoever it was said I had one chance and said he'd recommend I use it to run."

I couldn't tell them there was another option.

That this might be on me.

Karma finally swooping back to end that borrowed time I'd been living on.

"Fuck." Ezra rubbed a massive paw down his face before he planted his hands on his hips. "Why the hell didn't you come to me?"

"Hailey is trying to figure this shit out for herself right now, and I didn't want to get in the way."

"Figure it out for herself? That's dangerous, Cody. You know that."

While I agreed with Ezra, I had to respect her wishes.

She was the one who'd told me to stay away while she was dealing with this bullshit, and I was the one who'd insisted I wasn't going anywhere. But at the base of it, I wanted her safe. I hated the idea that motherfucker might be out there lurking. Waiting for an opportunity to hurt her.

"We discussed it, and she said she needed time to decide what she was going to do. I can't blame her for that."

"Because she's afraid of him?" Ezra pushed, his own protectiveness swelling high.

Fury coiled my insides. "Maybe…but she's working a plan. She said she wants to get him out of her life rather than making the situation messier than it already is."

Ezra stared across the space where our girls had gone to watching the kids play. "I don't fucking like it."

"I don't like it, either. But we're holding right now. Besides, I'm not one-hundred-percent it was that fucker, anyway."

Intuition screamed that was a lie.

Ezra took a single step toward me. "If anything else happens— even a fucking whiff of the guy—I want you to call me. You can't ignore this, Cody. It's reckless."

I hesitated, and he pressed, "Promise me."

"Yeah, man, I promise."

"That, or Cody and I can handle that bullshit together." Ryder vibrated with hostility.

Ezra pointed at him. "Don't even think about it. Everyone here has been through enough bullshit—enough danger. You all have families to worry about, so don't go and do something stupid." Then he cracked a grin. "Though I know with the two of you, not doing something stupid is basically impossible."

I let go of a chuckle. "You wish, asshole. You just can't wrap your little head around mine and Ryder's special brand of brilliance."

Ryder laughed, and Ezra shook his head as he mumbled, "Dicks. The lot of you."

Then he was back to studying me in contemplation. "And here you show up with the woman and her little girl. Hand-in-fucking-hand."

There was a question behind it.

"That's right." Exactly where I wanted to be.

Ryder let go of a dark chuckle. "Told you, Ezra…fucker's whipped."

"That's right," I told him, too.

No longer was denying it.

Flipping a steak, Caleb glanced our way. "Called it Saturday night. Dude was sporting a heart on the entire time."

My brow shot for the sky. "A heart on?"

"Yup." He smirked. "For the first time you weren't just thinking with your dick."

"Oh, I've been thinking with that, too."

"But it's that other beating part that counts," he pushed with a jut of his chin.

And I said the same thing I'd been telling all of them.

"That's right."

❧

Darkness rained from the sky, covering the earth in a quiet, stilled peace. Stars were tossed across the expanse, so thick out here in the middle of nowhere that it created a silvered haze that twisted through the heavens, like glittering vapor that swirled and coiled into a beauty unlike any other.

I glanced over at Hailey.

Well, all except for her beauty.

Hers was unrivaled.

It was the kind that kicked me in the gut and knocked me upside the head. The way this woman had infiltrated every fiber of my being.

Shifted it around.

Knitted it into something better.

She had drifted to sleep about ten miles back, which I was pretty sure had a whole ton to do with the fact that I kept her up 'til nearly dawn every night.

Sweet little Maddie had fallen asleep basically the second we'd strapped her into her seat, her day spent playing on the ranch, running and chasing and laughing.

I'd even taken her for a short horseback ride out on the land, Hailey at our side on her own horse, the three of us exploring.

We'd come back and shared the delicious barbecue dinner that Caleb and Paisley had prepared, and my sister had capped the night off with one of her chocolate cake concoctions that had nearly melted my mind it was so damned good.

But *this* was what really melted my mind.

Obliterated everything I thought I knew.

The two of them with me like this was exactly where they'd always belonged.

At my side.

My family.

The arrow of truth speared through me.

So fucking staggering I struggled to get the next breath into my lungs that felt like they'd just collapsed.

But it was the truth.

That's what they'd become.

My family.

My reason for breathing which was a complete mindfuck considering it hadn't been that long ago I'd been promising I'd never give myself to anyone.

Not when my past lurked like phantoms behind me. One misstep, and they'd catch up. That shady agreement I'd made that I'd carried, and here I was, breaking that oath that I'd made to myself.

That time stamp on my chest that was meant as a reminder of where I could never go.

But she was worth it.

She was worth it.

Didn't care what it cost, even though I was going to give it my all to end the mess I had myself in. To find a way to fully give myself to the two of them because they deserved all of me.

Not the twisted, mangled pieces that at any moment could completely splinter apart.

I made the last turn into Time River, and I pulled into the gas station off Manchester and stopped in front of a pump. There wasn't a soul around, that stilled quiet hovering.

Hailey stirred when I shut off the engine, and those crystalline eyes flickered open to look across at me, though she was clearly still out of it.

"Just going to fill up before we make the trek to Hendrickson. Go back to sleep."

She gave a small nod and curled back up, a contented sigh slipping from between her plush, full lips. I couldn't stop myself from reaching out and tracing them, though I saw no point in resisting when touching her was the only thing I wanted to do.

My spirit clutched.

God, what had she done to me?

Blowing out a sigh, I cracked open my door and pushed out, and I dug into my back pocket to get my wallet when a black car turned into the lot.

Its headlights were blinding as it wound around the pumps and pulled in by the curb near the air compressor.

A prickle of unease skittered across my flesh, lifting the hairs at the back of my neck into spikes.

I didn't know what it was, but I was instantly on guard, watching it in my periphery while I swiped my card, flipped the lid and unscrewed the gas cap, then situated the nozzle.

The car just sat there idling, while a rash of shivers rolled. I stuffed my hands into my jeans' pockets and leaned against my truck, all casual like, though I kept watch.

A minute later, the door to the car finally snapped open, so fucking slow.

Agitation blistered, and I straightened in the same second the bastard rose from his car.

Wearing gray slacks and a light blue polo and this expression on his face that claimed he had the right to be there.

Tall and thin, but Pruitt didn't vibrate with the kind of power Ryder did, and I was surer than ever that he wasn't the actual one who'd attacked me on Tuesday.

Still, rage thundered, a ferocious pounding that licked through my veins.

A firestorm.

An eruption.

I barely kept myself from storming across the space to snap his neck when I spat, "What the fuck do you think you're doing here?"

That was right when a stir of energy blasted through the air, and the passenger side door of my truck swung open and Hailey flew out.

She rounded to the front of the truck so quickly I had no chance to stop her before she was halfway across the lot, though I did my damned best to get there.

I'd made it to her by the time she stopped midway, and I stood a foot behind her, ready to attack if this motherfucker even inched in her direction.

Hailey's hands clenched and unclenched, her breaths ragged, her horror palpable.

She angled his direction, her words shards of animosity and hate. "What the hell do you think you're doing, Pruitt? Did you follow us here?"

"I need to talk to you."

"You need to talk to me?" Her voice was half frenzied, an accusation and incredulity. "Here? At the gas station? Twenty minutes from my house?"

"You're never alone for me to find a better opportunity." He sneered it, glance cutting to me.

A growl got free of my chest. "Guess what, asshole, she isn't alone now, either."

The scrawny prick scoffed, lifting his chin, tossing his arrogance all over the place. "I'd advise you to stay out of this."

Scorn ripped up my throat, and I took a menacing step forward. "Yeah, well that's not going to fucking happen."

Hailey put a hand out toward me, asking for a minute, before she turned the full force of her revulsion on him. "I want to know how you knew I was here. Did you follow us all the way to my friend's house?"

"My daughter is in that truck."

It wasn't lost on me that the asshole didn't answer the question.

Derision whipped from Hailey's mouth. "Don't use her as an excuse. You and I both know she doesn't mean anything to you, and I will no longer let you use her or myself for your selfish purposes. Just leave, Pruitt, leave while you still can."

She lifted her chin in what was a clear warning.

A gauntlet thrown.

Questions and dread spiraled through my being. I wanted to demand that she tell me what the hell that meant. What she was holding over him. If it put her in danger. To *trust* me.

But this definitely wasn't the time or place to do it.

So I remained towering off to her side, leaving no question for this bastard what was going to happen to him if he even thought of trying to get to her.

"Don't make threats you can't keep, Hailey." He issued it like she was pathetic. One to be manipulated.

"You said the same thing when I told you I was leaving you." She lifted her head higher with the challenge, and damn it all, if I didn't want to give her a high-five and celebrate because my girl was fierce and strong and so goddamn brave, but it was clearly not the time for that, either.

Disdain filled his voice. "I chose to let you go to give you space. To give you time to come to your senses. You took it too far, Hailey."

"No. You are the one who took it too far, Pruitt." She tried to keep the trembling out of her voice. "You sent someone to attack Cody? I want to know. I want you to tell me the truth."

The sound he let go of was mocking. "If only I could take credit. Now get our daughter and get in the car before you regret it."

"You can be sure I regret it." Her words tremored. "I regret every moment I've ever spent with you. Every day. Every hour. Every second. You won't get one more."

The scumbag's jaw clenched, and I could feel his fury sizzle in the air. His eyes darted between her and me, his overinflated ego unable to accept that she was standing up to him.

I stepped closer and casually tossed an arm over her shoulders, even though I was shaking like a bitch, so goddamn close to cleaving apart. "That'd be your cue to get the fuck out of here. If you hadn't noticed, she doesn't want you any longer."

I raised my brows, taking him back to that day when I'd kissed the hell out of her.

A show that had changed everything.

Wrath quivered through his body, so violent I could feel it rupture the air. He warred like he was contemplating coming at me, though the asshole finally thought better of it and stepped back to jerk open his car door.

He stood on the inside of it, glowering at us, his jaw so tense I didn't know how it didn't crack. "I'm finished playing games, Hailey. This was your last warning."

He slipped into his car and slammed the door shut, and he left a trail of squealing tires as he sped across the lot and out onto the road.

I curled my arms around Hailey as we watched him go, holding her close while the night pulsed around us in hot, sticky coils.

His car roared as he flew down the street, and I held her like that until his taillights disappeared and the sound of his engine faded away.

It wasn't until then that Hailey sagged against me, fisting those sweet hands in my tee. "I'm so sorry." She whispered against the spot where *time* was stamped in the middle of my chest.

I pulled her even closer and murmured against the crown of her head. "You don't have a thing to be sorry for, Hailey. It's my honor to stand for you."

Chapter Thirty-Seven
Cody

Twenty-Four Years Old

CODY LEANED BACK AGAINST THE TRUNK OF THE GIANT TREE hidden in the recesses of Wagner Ranch, his eyes closed where he sat beneath the shade that did nothing to keep him from feeling as if he were getting burned at the stake.

Distraught.

Throttled by grief and the loss that he knew his mother was going to feel if she lost the house.

He'd put out feelers from one end of Colorado to the other, basically begging for extra jobs, even though he was already stretched thin. When that hadn't panned out, he'd gone to the bank, praying on the few good acts that he'd committed in his life that he might be able to get his own loan, which he knew was foolish as shit, getting a loan to pay for a loan, but drastic times called for drastic measures.

The woman there had looked at him with regret when she'd told him he didn't have the assets to back it up.

So there he sat, helpless, pressing the heels of his hands into his eyes and trying to blot out the distress that consumed him. Hoping beyond hope that some sort of magic might befall him.

He froze when he felt the shift in the air, that stunning energy that always stopped him in his tracks beating into him from afar, making his heart hemorrhage and his pulse run rampant.

He slowly dropped his hands away and peeled his lids open to find her standing there.

Just off in the distance holding some kind of plastic container.

Crystalline eyes taking him in with this sort of worry that made him want to weep.

Or maybe he already was, the way he had to hurry to brush off the wetness that had slipped down his cheeks.

He'd thought he was secluded enough that no one would find him where he'd sneaked off to eat his lunch, but there she was.

A dream manifested.

He'd been having them the last month.

Dreams.

Forbidden ones.

Thoughts of her.

He knew it was fucked up that he had a thing for the rancher's daughter.

Especially since she was shy and timid and so clearly innocent, not to mention he had to be at least six years older than her.

It sure as hell didn't stop the way his guts twisted whenever he saw her, though.

Hesitantly, she edged forward, like if she did it quiet enough, she wouldn't disturb the tormented bubble he was in.

Or maybe her sole intention was to pop it.

One thing he did know was she was a disturbance, all right.

Honey-streaked hair was twined in two of those braids at the side of her head, the girl tall and thin, though there was something about the insinuation of her curves that promised she was getting ready to bloom.

But it was that sweetness that emanated from her that bowled him over each time. This vulnerability she seemed eager to shuck.

She wore a pair of light blue corduroys and a matching country tank with fringe along the neckline.

Her steps were slow as she approached, coming closer and closer.

He sat there tacked to the tree, unable to move.

"Hey," she finally whispered as she eased closer.

"Hey." It was a coarse rasp, the emotion clotting his throat making it difficult to speak.

"Am I bothering you?"

He couldn't stop the tugging at the edges of his lips. "Nah, darlin', pretty sure there isn't a chance your presence could bother anyone."

Redness pinked her cheeks, and she kept peeking at him as she came to settle on the ground off to the side of him, facing the same direction.

For a bit, the two of them just sat staring off into the thick woods that held them like a shroud.

"I saw you earlier…and you…looked upset." She chanced it, each word hesitant and filled with question.

He choked out a laugh that wasn't the least surprised. "You always notice, don't you?"

Uncertainty wound in her posture. "I shouldn't, but I do."

He knew what she was referring to.

Brooke.

Brooke who he'd made that *mistake* with two more times in the last month. Being a fucking idiot and allowing lust to grip him. Or maybe he was just doing everything to drive a wedge between him and Hailey since he knew there was no chance in hell he could ever have her.

Now that? That would make him a monster.

He knew it.

But he felt like a piece of crap, leading Brooke on the way he had, but she kept promising she was only looking to have as much fun as she could before she left in September for college.

This thing was no strings.

A fun fling.

But it wasn't feeling fun to Cody, anymore, and he'd promised himself that he wasn't ever going to touch her again.

It felt…wrong.

They sat in the silence for a little while before Hailey shifted to peer at him, her knees drawn to her chest. "Do you want to talk about it?"

Air huffed from Cody's nose, and he picked at a blade of grass below him. "Not sure it's something you would understand."

"Try me."

He exhaled heavily, peeking at this sweet girl he should definitely tell to go on her way.

But he liked her there.

Liked her presence.

Liked the way she soothed a little bit of the ache lighting a path through his body.

"Just someone I care about is having a bit of trouble and, as hard as I tried, there doesn't seem to be a damned thing I can do about it."

Her expression dimmed, and she looked out at the peace of the scenery that whispered around them. "I'm sorry," she murmured.

"Me, too."

She chewed at her plump lip, so damned shy and timid all while being this bright shining light that beamed, no chance of the radiance she emitted being contained by her reticent shell.

Yeah, this girl was getting ready to bloom.

He was sure of it.

"I brought you something." She passed him the plastic container that she'd set on the ground beside her.

He couldn't help but grin. "You brought me somethin'?"

Eager as all fuck, he peeled off the lid.

Inside sat a big heaping pile of strawberry shortcake.

His stomach rumbled right as his chest tightened.

"Did you make this?" He couldn't stop the wonder from filling his voice.

More heat splashed her cheeks, and she shrugged a shy shoulder. "It wasn't a big deal. I just…saw you eating fresh strawberries with your lunch a couple weeks ago, and I thought you might like it. That maybe…"

She was looking at him then, her eyebrows puckered together in hope. "I thought it might make you feel better."

Cody took the plastic fork that was tucked inside the container and dug it into the concoction. Through the whipped cream and sugared strawberries and down to the shortcake at the bottom.

He groaned when he put it in his mouth, the sweetness hitting his tongue and his heart doing that stupid thing it liked to do whenever she came around.

"You like it?"

His chuckle was rough. "Do I like it? Best thing I've ever tasted."

And that was saying a lot because his sister was shaping up to be a damned good baker. Dakota loved to bake things to make people feel better, though, and he wondered if it wasn't the same for Hailey.

Pride flamed on Hailey's face, and she rubbed her palms up the fronts of her thighs.

He took another bite, licking at the fork. "See. I already feel better."

Modesty had her looking away. "I'm glad," she whispered.

She seemed reluctant to push to her feet, but she did, the girl standing over him.

Appearing an angel who'd been sent to assuage his failure.

Awkwardly, she gestured in the distance. "I should go. Brooke will be wondering where I am."

Disappointment pulsed in his spirit. "Okay."

She started to walk, though she hesitated then shifted to look back at him. "Brooke is wonderful. You're lucky you have her."

Without saying anything else, she turned and hurried back up the path she'd come from, Cody watching her go, regret thick in his throat.

"Fuck," he muttered, shaking his head, though he sat there and ate every bit of that strawberry shortcake.

This was for the best.

Hailey chalking his and Brooke's non-relationship up as something that counted.

Once he was finished, he packed up his things and wandered to his truck to put his lunch pail inside so he could get back to work.

He startled when a presence came up to him from behind, then he let go of an easy smile when he saw the ranch manager standing behind him, acting cool and casual though he was praying to God he hadn't caught him sitting next to Douglas Wagner's daughter.

Brent was tall and fairly muscled, though not close to Cody's size. He was maybe in his mid-forties and had been pretty chill since Cody had started working on the fencing project.

"Hey, Brent. What's up?" Cody asked.

A question lifted Brent's brow. "Heard you need to make some quick cash."

Hope jumped into Cody's system. "Now that I am, brother. You know of something?"

"Sure do."

"Good because I need a lot of it."

Chapter Thirty-Eight
Cody

"ARE YOU SURE YOU WANT TO DO THIS?" HAILEY ASKED IT from where she sat in the passenger seat of my truck, staring out the window at the modest house tucked in the middle of Time River.

My childhood home.

"What?" I asked her, needling her a bit since I could feel the frazzled nerves zinging through her body.

The woman had itched the entire way over here.

Hailey swiveled her attention to me, those eyes the color of the river washing me through, so intense as she looked me straight. "Take me in there."

Reaching out, I set my hand on her cheek, and I brushed my thumb across the apple. "Now why would I not want to take you in there?"

Hailey lowered her voice to keep it from her daughter who was anxiously waiting in the back. "Don't you think this has all become too much, Cody?"

"Nah, darlin', it's not close to being enough."

"Cody."

Hailey was still warring with it, her spirit dampening after the verbal altercation with Pruitt last night. Once she'd gotten back in my truck, she'd been quiet on the way home, almost distant, like she was looking for a way to put the walls back up between us when there was no chance that they could stand.

Not when she was meant for me.

Not when this was the way it was supposed to be.

I unclicked my belt. "Come on, all the most important people in my life are in that house which means you belong there."

I let that resonate, the truth that's what they'd become.

Maddie had no issues agreeing. "Yay!! Get me, my Mr. Cody!"

I slipped out of the truck, though I ducked my head back in to meet Hailey's uncertain gaze. "You'll see, Shortcake."

I shut my door then opened Maddie's, the kid kicking her adorable feet like it would propel me to get her unfastened faster. Since I wasn't in the game of disappointing my Button, I flew through the locks and swung her up into my arms.

Loving the weight of her.

The feel of her.

My heart pounding in the type of contentment I never thought I'd feel.

By the time we rounded the other side, Hailey was stepping out, and I took her by the hand, kissed across her knuckles, and gave her one of my best smiles.

"Prepare yourselves for the best breakfast you've ever had. You know Dakota runs the most delicious café within a thousand miles, and my mother taught her everything she knows."

A fresh round of nerves rattled through Hailey.

I chuckled, and I leaned in so I could whisper at her ear. "Are you nervous to meet my momma, Hailey Wagner?"

She looked up at me. "I don't want to be. I don't want to be afraid…of anything. But it doesn't change what's going on."

I nuzzled my nose in her hair. Filling my senses with the scent of strawberries and cream. "Let's just be, Shortcake. See where this thing takes us. Don't start pushing me away now."

"I just can't stand the thought of putting you in harm's way." She barely uttered it loud enough that it broke the air, the woman guarding her daughter, her worry given only to me.

I didn't say anything as we traipsed up the walkway to the two steps that led up to the front door, though I stopped right as we made it to them.

Turning to face her, I curled my arm around my girl's waist, her daughter tucked between us, right where she belonged.

I didn't quiet my words. Just issued, "I'm where you are, Hailey. Rest on me, just for now."

Her nod was wary though I felt her melt into me, and I reached out to open the door, but it flew open before I got the chance.

My baby sister Kayla stood in the doorway, her mouth gaping and her brown eyes wide.

Oh my God. I don't believe it. Her lips moved, but no sound came out.

A rough chuckle scraped out of me. "Believe it."

"Hi!!" Maddie lifted her sweet hand at my sister who stood there stupefied since I'd never brought a woman anywhere near here before. Had never even considered it.

And there I stood with an arm looped around one and her little girl held tightly in the surety of my arms.

Kayla finally gathered herself from where her composure had toppled to the floor and placed a giant smile on her face. "Hi. You must be Maddie who I heard all about."

"You heard about me?" Maddie said in that adorable voice that twisted through me. Each word like branches tangling in my spirit.

Permanently rooting themselves.

"I sure did…my big sister Dakota is here, and she said she got to meet you yesterday and I was going to be so happy to meet you today."

"Are you happy?" Maddie asked.

Kayla laughed. "Very happy."

But it was the presence coming from behind her that pummeled me, the soft sound that escaped my mother's lips as she saw us standing there.

She pressed her hand to her mouth like she could cover it, that love that had forever radiated from her pulsing through the space.

Then she rushed forward. "You must be Hailey and Maddie. Welcome to our home."

But I knew what she really meant.

She was thinking *welcome home*.

The exact same way as me.

Chapter Thirty-Nine

Hailey

N O MATTER HOW HARD I TRIED TO KEEP IT CONTAINED, the giggle erupted from my throat.

Not a chance of stopping it.

"You did not," I accused, looking at Cody who was slung back in the chair where we were all gathered around the table that rested on one side of the kitchen. Dakota had just told me about the time he'd put blue dye in her body wash.

"Don't look at me that way, darlin'. You can be sure she deserved it. Payback, baby."

He sent an evil gleam that was nothing but a tease at Dakota who sat across from us, snuggled up to Ryder who was chuckling under his breath.

"I absolutely did not," Dakota defended. "I walked around looking like an Oompa Loompa for a week."

"Oh, pretty sure you did deserve it," Ryder rumbled, giving her a little jostle. "You were the one who stole our clothes where we'd left them on the bank of the river. We had to ride our bikes back through town, completely buck."

"Okay, but why were the two of you skinny dipping together?" I asked through my laughter.

Annoyance took to Dakota's face. "Because Saley Thompson and Kendra Stevens were there with them."

"Jealous." Ryder mussed up her hair.

She sent him a flirty grin. "Of course, I was jealous."

"So, this was all about Ryder and didn't have a thing to do with me?" Cody stretched those tattooed arms out in that playful arrogance he loved to wear.

"I thought everything was about you?" Kayla razzed as she took a sip from her coffee.

"Well, most things are about me since I make quite the impression, but in this case, it seems I was unjustly targeted."

I laughed at the ping-pong match of ribbing that had been played around the table during breakfast, though I nestled deeper into the comfort of the atmosphere.

No hostilities or hate.

No fear or dread.

Just love and support, the way it was supposed to be. The anxiety I'd been feeling all of last night and this morning had nearly evaporated as I'd sank into the mood of this place.

As if Cody felt my thoughts, he slung his arm over the back of my chair and curled a hand around my opposite shoulder to bring me closer. The man slanted me the softest grin.

Another promise that I belonged.

And I felt like it—like I belonged. Like I could slide right into this peace and become a part of it. As if there wasn't a threat lingering outside these doors.

With Cody, it was so easy to pretend like everything was just fine.

I had to remember to be careful. I had no idea how this was going to pan out. How it was going to end. If I'd remain standing.

Guilt tried to climb up through the questions, that sticky sensation that refused to let me go even though I kept trying with all of me to cut those bindings free. Praying that Brooke would forgive me. That she would understand.

That she wouldn't look at me with the same betrayal as she'd looked at me with that night.

Cody tugged me tighter, likely feeling the way my nerves ticked my muscles into tension as I warred with the tumult of my thoughts.

"All of you were nothing but trouble, always out wreaking havoc on this town." Cody's mother pointed between Cody and Ryder, then Dakota and Kayla. "Each in your own way. I had my hands full with all of you."

There was no anger behind it.

Warmth spread in my chest. Cody's mother, Patricia, or Pat like everyone called her, had welcomed me in a way I should have expected with the way Cody had talked about her.

His praise and adoration for her unending.

Still, I felt unsettled by it, by how close they all were. A tight-knit web of safety and protection, and I knew I was dragging disorder into the middle of it.

Pulling her son into something that he shouldn't have to face.

But he remained solid at my side. Impenetrable. Refusing to leave.

"Who me?" Cody grinned. "Never caused a lick of trouble in my life."

"And someone is straight delusional," Dakota said, tilting me a wayward smile, like we were thick as thieves.

The oldest of friends.

"I have what's called self-esteem, Dakota."

"You mean a big, fat ego?" she tossed back.

"Cocky Cowboy." I nudged him, playing too, and he pulled me even closer and went to tickling my side.

"Oh yeah? Say it now?"

I was cackling, flailing all over the place, this feeling spreading through me unlike I'd ever felt before.

Joy.

Joy.

Joy.

His smile went soft as he slowed, just the same as everyone else's at the table as they watched us.

I tried to smooth out the disorder, to tame the redness on my face and the feeling that was bursting from my soul.

I wasn't sure I could.

Not when Cody placed a big hand on the top of my thigh and grunted, "Might be cocky, but I'm your cowboy."

God.

What was he doing to me?

I chewed at the inside of my lip as I caught his mother peeking over at us, and the same thing was blazing from her, too.

Joy.

"Can we go outside and play now?" Maddie came bouncing in from the living room where she was playing with Dakota's son, Kayden.

The adorable little boy was right behind her, flapping his arms in the air. "I wanna swing, my Daddy Rye-Rye!"

Ryder didn't hesitate, he stood. "Then let's go, little man."

My foundation cracked nearly all the way through when Cody stood, too. "Come on, Button, let's go outside."

Cody swept my giggling girl into his arms, peppering kisses all over her face as he carried her out into the heat of the summer day.

I just watched, unable to look away from the hope that radiated back, mine banging into his and the man emitting it right back.

A hand suddenly was on my wrist where I had it rested on the table. I looked to my right to Cody's mother who sat between me and Dakota. She brushed her thumb over the back of my hand and whispered, "I'm so glad you're here."

Emotion clutched, and I could barely force out, "I am, too."

✦

"Wait a minute," Maddie said, a sweet demand of excitement. "You got my favorite *and* your favorite?"

Maddie squealed it as Cody cut a big piece of pumpkin pie where he stood at the island of my kitchen later that evening.

He shook up the can of whipped cream and squirted a giant mound on top, swirling it up into a perfect peak.

He'd swung into the grocery store on our way back from his

mother's house earlier this afternoon. It was amazing that after everything that had been happening that we had found solace in the day, but it'd been there, this serenity that had lulled.

Respite.

"That's right, Button, I got both our favorites," Cody said, glancing down at her where she stood peering up at him.

She threaded her fingers together and lifted them up under her chin, her mouth stretched so wide that she showed off all her tiny, gapped teeth, ringlets bouncing around her cherub face. "You remembered all the really important things about me, my Mr. Cody?"

Devotion flooded the room, and I could feel his spirit swim.

He tapped at her nose. "How could I forget when you and your mom are my most important things?"

Her giggle was light, not quite grasping the magnitude of what he was saying, and she scrunched her shoulders up to her ears. "I like being that."

"I like you being that, too," he told her.

My spirit thrashed, and my grandmother leaned in and whispered from where she sat on a stool beside me, "Yeah, I bet you like being that, too."

I did.

So much.

And I was so afraid of accepting it then losing it.

"Get on up there," he told Maddie, gesturing to the stool on my opposite side.

Maddie climbed up, and she sat on her knees as Cody set the pumpkin pie in front of her.

He shifted to look at my grandmother. "What about you, Lolly? Do you have a favorite?"

"I wouldn't mind a piece of that pumpkin pie."

"On it."

He prepared hers the same way as he'd prepared Maddie's and set it in front of her.

"What about mine?" I asked, playing coy.

Cody set his big palms on the countertop and leaned my direction, that smirk that slayed me through firmly planted on his face, voice a coarse glide of arrogance and greed. "You get yours later, Shortcake."

Redness splashed my cheeks and heat blistered across my flesh. Anticipation had me shifting on my seat.

Lolly chuckled as she dug into the mountain of pumpkin pie and whipped cream on her plate, her grayed eyes gleaming as she looked between the two of us. "Yeah, I sure do like the way that reputation looks on you."

She lifted her fork and prodded it in Cody's direction. "You be sure to keep it on her."

Cody grinned. "I plan to."

⌒⋆⌒

"Your mom was right…you're nothing but trouble," I told Cody where I stood leaned against the island while he finished the dishes from our dinner and the dessert Lolly and Maddie had eaten, finally getting him alone after we'd tucked Maddie into bed and Lolly had retreated to her room. "I can't believe you said that in front of my grandmother."

He sent me a smirk from over his shoulder as he placed the last dish into the dishwasher. "You can't believe it, huh?"

"Okay, I can because like I said, you are nothing but trouble."

"You don't seem to mind all that much." Suggestion wound into his teasing tone, though those golden eyes raked me from head to toe, devouring me where he stood.

I clung to the counter behind me. "I guess I don't."

Turning around, he grabbed a towel and dried off his hands, never looking away from me as he tossed it to the counter and he rumbled, "Good because I'm ready for *my* favorite thing."

"What's that?" It quivered out of me.

"You."

He came for me, the ground trembling with each big step. His expression vacillated between that easy arrogance and the hunger that rippled through his muscles.

He diverted course and ducked into the refrigerator to pull out the big bowl of strawberry shortcake he'd already prepared, tucked the can of whipped cream under his arm, then grabbed a spoon.

I started to move around to the stools before his command hit me from behind. "Think what I have planned for you needs to take place behind closed doors in your room, darlin'."

A needy shiver rolled down my spine. He hadn't even touched me, but I already was shaking.

The ground kept rolling as he followed me into my room, and chills lifted on my nape as he walked right behind me, his breaths brushing across the bare skin of my shoulders and my exposed neck since I was wearing a sundress, and my hair was in a braid that I'd twisted into a halo on top of my head.

He dipped in and pressed his lips to the sensitive juncture where my neck met my shoulder. "Close that door and lock it."

"You're awful bossy tonight." I went for flirty. A tease when I was positively vibrating with need.

One look from this man and I was already coming undone.

"You might call it bossy, but the only thing on my agenda tonight is making you feel good. Cherished the way you are. Can't help it if I'm going to derive a whole ton of pleasure from it for myself."

I could feel his smile against my skin, and I shifted to shut and lock the door as he walked the rest of the way into the room. He set the bowl and whipped cream on the nightstand before he turned around to look at me through the muted light of the room.

A shockwave slammed me.

Energy bounding and inciting, dense as the tension curled through the space, climbing the walls and crawling the floor and twining up through the center of me to tie me in knots.

The power of this man standing there, rippling strength and volatility.

Radiating that sweetness, too, that goodness that gushed out of him like a river. The man so different than I'd conformed myself into believing.

When I'd stowed him away as a bad memory.

He wavered for a moment, his intensity blazing in the room. "Can't tell you what it meant to have you at my mother's house today, Hailey.

That's a sacred place to me. Never thought I'd want to bring someone there. Make them a part of it. And that's exactly where I want you to be."

"And I was afraid of going there because I was worried I might want to stay."

"That's what I want, Hailey. I want you there. With me. Not sure I can imagine my life without you in it anymore."

The truth of what we'd become tremored around us. A threat that both of us were precariously perched on the edge. This heart so close to no longer belonging to me.

"Come here, Shortcake…let me show you just what you mean. Going to make you feel so good tonight…and just like I promised Lolly, I don't plan to ever stop."

There was no hesitation.

I moved.

Drawn to him in an inexplicable way. The way I'd always been. No control over the lure that pulled and persuaded.

He stretched out a long arm and dragged the chair from the small desk that sat against the wall between the room and the bathroom, and he turned it out to face me.

"Sit."

I complied, no reserves, no restraint.

That didn't mean I wasn't shaking like an old washing machine that had been set off-kilter.

Balance lost.

Cody dropped to his knees in front of me.

Need cracked.

A thunderbolt of energy that whipped through the room.

He grabbed the bowl of strawberry shortcake, that slyness riding back to his face as he drove the spoon in deep then came out with a heaping mound. "Open."

Flavor burst on my tongue as he pushed it deep into the well of my mouth.

The tart of the fresh strawberries and the sweet of the cream and the texture of the shortcake all mixed with the impact of the man.

The whole of it made me moan.

Cody growled as he withdrew the spoon and placed it into the bowl.

"What that sound does to me, Hailey. Your voice has become my song."

His eyes traced my jaw, my cheeks, my brow. "What this face does to me. This face that has become my landscape."

A hand clamped down on my waist. "And what this body does to me. This body that's my playground. My sanctuary. My haven."

He set the bowl on the floor, and he dug his fingers into the dessert, forgoing the spoon.

I trembled when he lifted it and pressed two big fingers into my mouth.

"Suck," he told me.

I did. Gladly.

"Good girl," he murmured.

He reached around me and slid the zipper down the back of my dress.

Chills flew as he nudged it down, and I shifted so he could drag it under my bottom, and he knelt as he fully twisted it free of my ankles.

Leaving me bare except for the tiny slip of satin that covered my aching center.

"So fucking stunning, darlin', stealing my breath the way you do."

My nipples hardened.

Diamond peaks.

He went in for another scoop of the dessert, smearing the whipped cream over my left breast before he sucked the pebbled tip into his hot mouth.

Pleasure zipped through me, lighting up between my thighs.

I whimpered and wiggled on the chair.

"So good," he said. "So sweet. You're the treat, Hailey Wagner."

Then he leaned up high on his knees, fingers deft as he plucked out the pins in my hair, carefully, watching me the whole time as he untwisted the halo and unwound the braid until the long locks of my hair drifted down around my shoulders.

"Look at you. An angel I could never deserve. I'm on my knees for you. I'm going to need you to spread yours."

Whimpering, I complied, hands clinging to the edges of the chair like I might float away, my stomach twisted as I watched him dig around for a whole strawberry in the bowl.

One side of his delicious mouth tweaked up as he dragged the tip of it over the scrap of my underwear.

My hips arched from the chair. "Please."

"My sweet, eager girl. I'm going to give it to you, darlin'. Don't you worry."

"You're teasing me."

He chuckled a low sound that tumbled through me like greed. "It's going to be worth it."

Cody hooked his fingers in the band of my underwear, and I drove my heels into the ground and lifted from the chair so he could get them free.

Shivers raced as he slowly dragged them down my legs, his gaze eating me up as he did.

My knees quaked as I sat there fully naked.

"Spread them wide," he ordered, and I obeyed. A short gasp ripped up my throat when he repeated the motion with the strawberry, though this time he was dragging it through my center.

Then he lifted it to his mouth and sank his teeth into the red-fleshed fruit, chewing slow as he watched me through the dancing shadows of my room. "Yeah, my girl is the sweetest treat."

I mewled a desirous sound, the man spinning me into disorder, no foundation left.

No fortitude or rationale or the thought of what waited for us outside these walls as he was pushing to standing and peeling off his tee as he went.

Need grappled through my insides as I gaped at the magnitude of the man. At that packed, bare chest with the designs rippling over muscle, his stomach flexing and bowing with strength as he stood right in front of me.

It was me who was reaching for the buttons, tearing through them like a fiend, because I wasn't sure I could take the playing for a second more. "I need you," tumbled from my lips.

"You got me, Hailey." There was something about the way he said it as he swiped his thumb over my lip, gathering a bit of the whipped cream that remained there and sucking it into his mouth.

A roll of thunder curled through me, rocking through the place that I'd tried to keep protected.

Gaze fierce, he shoved down his jeans and underwear.

His cock popped free, enormous and hard and pointing for me. I leaned forward and licked the tip.

Cody grunted. "Vixen."

"I want to be everything for you." It was out before I could stop it.

"You already are, darlin'," he said as he shucked the rest of the way out of his jeans.

The man bold and bare.

That fortress that promised to stand for me.

He grabbed the can of whipped cream and pushed it to my mouth. "Open."

He sprayed it inside before he bent down and stroked his tongue between my lips.

A buzz lit in my body. Bliss streaking.

His touch and his sweetness and his command.

He ate me up, licking deep into my mouth, moaning as he did. "Strawberries and cream."

My nails raked his chest. "I need you, Cody."

"You've got me," he murmured back, then he took me by the hand and pulled me to standing, though he shifted me around to face the chair. He took me by the outside of my right thigh and propped my foot on the chair, then he smoothed his palm over my bottom and squeezed.

Desire rolled through me on a violent wave, and I pushed back into his hold.

"Needy girl," he murmured at the back of my head before he thrust two fingers into my body. "Is this pussy ready for me?"

"Yes," I rasped.

He drove them in and out before he eased back and took both my butt cheeks in both hands. "How about this ass? Is it mine, too?"

"Yes."

I was half mad with lust.

Needing him anywhere.

Everywhere.

Cody was suddenly on his knees behind me, lashing his tongue from my clit to my ass, swirling and lapping as he ate me up again.

He started swirling the tips of his fingers around my clit as he licked at my backside.

I jarred forward, consumed with the sudden sensation.

Flickers of that bliss lit inside me, flames that lapped, threatening to burst into a forest fire. I held onto the back of the chair as he continued his perfect assault.

"Cody." His name was a petition.

Everything I wanted.

Everything I needed.

Him.

Him.

"I want to feel my cock in that tight ass, Hailey. Want to take it. Claim it. Make it mine. You okay with that?"

My hair whipped around me as I was struck with a frenzy of greed, my nod erratic as I pushed back. "Please."

Cody stood, and I whimpered at the loss. He took the step back to the nightstand and pulled open the drawer, taking out a condom and the bottle of lube he'd tucked in there at the beginning of the week.

I was beginning to understand why it was strawberry flavored.

I watched him from over my shoulder where I was basically bent in two, clinging to the back of the chair with my hips tipped back in a plea.

He groaned. "Never seen a prettier sight. That ass in the air and that face peering back at me. So damned perfect, Hailey. Every curve. Every angle. I'm going to memorize every inch of you."

He flipped the cap to the lube and squeezed it down the cleft of my ass before he was licking me again, working me into a frenzy.

I gasped when he stood, covered himself, then pressed the head of his cock to my hole, trembling and trembling as I waited for him to take the place that I'd refused to ever let Pruitt touch.

Cody had touched me there a bunch of times this week, with

that lube, pushing his fingers inside as his cock had been fitted in my pussy, each time driving me out of my mind.

But this was different, and I saw it too, the way Cody's jaw was held rigid, those eyes aflame and his care pulsing out as he smoothed a big hand down my spine.

"You tell me if it's too much, Hailey. Do you understand?"

My nod was rabid.

He gripped me by the hips. And it probably was a little too much, the man enormous, the pressure and sting of him as he slowly nudged himself inside making me writhe and gasp and choke.

"Are you good?"

"Yes. Please." It was chaos dripping from my tongue. "Cody, please."

I couldn't stop the tumble of need.

He grunted in restraint as he took me and took me until he was fully seated, until I was rasping and my thighs were trembling and a bead of sweat was gliding down my back.

"Fuck me, darlin'. You don't have a clue what it feels like taking you like this. How good this ass feels fisting my cock. So tight you're going to knock me the fuck out."

I couldn't process all the sensations, the way it felt like I was dying a little, in the most perfect, mind-bending way. This dark, decadent bliss that curled around me in drugging waves, the way it felt like too much and too little, like I was never going to be the same.

I tightened my hold on the chair while I looked back at the man from over my shoulder.

At his rugged features that had gone severe.

His jaw fierce and his lips plump.

Every inch of him vibrating with possession.

And that's what I wanted.

I wanted to be his.

So I told him, "Fuck me, Cody, and don't you dare be gentle with me."

Chapter Forty

Cody

MY FINGERS TREMBLED WHERE I HELD ONTO HER HIPS like they could keep me from losing all control.

This woman pure fire.

An inferno.

My demise.

My recovery.

My awakening.

I smoothed my palms over the fullness of her luscious ass that my dick was currently buried in balls deep.

The girl a clutch of heat that burned through the center of me.

My stomach was in knots and my jaw was clenched so tight I was sure I was going to crack a tooth as I tried to manage the urge to take her wild, and there she was, begging me to do it.

She was the one who rocked back, demanding it. "Fuck me like you want to, Cody. I'm yours. Take me."

A groan got free, and I sank my fingers into the lush pillow of her cheeks, spreading her wide, watching as I withdrew, nearly losing consciousness at the sight as I slowly drove back in.

Hailey moaned a delirious sound, and her head rocked from side to side, all that hair whipping around her, sliding over her shoulders and gliding down the gorgeous curve of her back.

I started to move in her in long, deep strokes, taking her ass as I kept her spread wide. "Look at you, darlin', taking me like this. Such a good girl, taking my cock in that sweet ass. You were meant for me, weren't you?"

Possession wound me tight as the words tumbled from my lips, and my stomach tightened as pleasure prowled up and down my spine like a beast.

I started taking her harder.

Fucking her the way she'd begged me to.

"You were meant for me, weren't you? Say it, darlin'. I want to hear it chanting from your mouth." I drove harder, bucking into her, fingers burrowing deep into her flesh.

"Yes." Hailey wheezed it, pushing back, urging me on.

Stoking the flames that erupted into a flashfire.

"Tell me, Hailey. I want to hear you say it." I couldn't stop the commands. This feeling washing over me that was close to manic.

This girl was mine.

And I wanted her that way.

Forever.

No matter what circumstances might be waiting for us in the very near future.

"Do you feel it? The way you were made for me?" I grunted.

I reached around her so I could play with her swollen, needy clit, and she was rocking back, breaths panted as I spun her into a puddle of desire.

But what set me off was my name that chanted from her tongue.

"Cody. Cody."

I felt it when she splintered.

A flash of electricity that blistered across her flesh, girl giving way to a full body glow. She started throbbing all around, breaking apart as an orgasm tore through her like a storm that had come from out of nowhere.

One stroke later, and that storm whipped through me, too.

A pounding of devastation.

A pummeling that left sheer obliteration.

Rapture taking me whole.

The blinding kind, the kind that knocked you right off your feet and sent you spinning, a tornado that whipped and whirred and left you nothing but ruin.

On a shout, I came, grasped by the shock of bliss.

A whorl of ecstasy, my dick pulsing with greed.

We both were gasping. Writhing as I curled an arm around her waist and held her through the aftershocks.

I slumped forward and pressed my nose to the nape of her neck, inhaled her.

Strawberries and cream.

My arms tightened around her to keep her upright since her knees had gone weak, and I murmured at her sweat-slicked skin. "You, Hailey Wagner, are my favorite fucking thing."

Chapter Forty-One

Cody

"YOU LOOK FUCKING GOOD ON THAT HORSE."

I kind of loved it that Hailey still blushed as she rode up on the brown mare. There shouldn't be a lick of modesty left in her since I'd spent all last night worshipping that delicious body, and she sure as hell wasn't acting shy then.

But there she was, those full cheeks pinked, all kinds of sweet, though the rest of her looked sexy as sin.

Rich blonde locks weaved in honey and maple struck beneath the rays of sunlight that speared down through the leaves of the trees that towered on the property, the woman wearing tight cowgirl jeans, red boots, and one of those fancy blouses she always wore to work.

She peeked each direction to make sure no one overheard, and her voice slipped into a giggle. "You'd better watch yourself. You're going to get me fired for fraternizing with the hot contractor."

I grinned as I leaned against the backside of the main stable where I'd been waiting for her, one boot kicked up against the wall and my arms crossed over my chest.

"Hot contractor, huh?"

That adorable smile pranced across those full, full lips. "Are you begging for compliments, Mr. Cooper?"

"Ah, we're back to Mr. Cooper?"

"We are at work."

"Well then, *Mr. Cooper* is definitely begging for a few compliments, and in case you needed clarification, he is definitely game for a little fraternizing."

I pushed from the wall when she got near enough, and I took hold of the horse's bridle, giving the beast a pat to her neck as I stared up at the woman who never failed to steal my breath.

"Is that so?" Hailey seemed fully game to play.

"Come down here and I'll show you just how game I am," I told her.

She giggled again, and she glanced around before she let me take the reins and accepted the hand that I extended to help her down from the horse. The second her boots hit the ground, I edged her back against the wall, leading the horse behind me.

Pinned, Hailey bit down on her bottom lip, blue eyes peeping up at me from beneath those long, long lashes. "Just what do you think you're doing, Cody?"

"Fraternizing." I murmured it before I dove in to take that delectable mouth.

Her shiny lips were sweet, and her tongue whispered of purpose.

I curled my free arm around her waist and angled in, devouring her mouth while my entire being sank into her spirit.

Yeah, kissing Hailey Wagner was definitely my favorite thing to do.

The way it felt like I was both floating and my feet were firmly planted on the ground for the very first time.

Moaning, I pressed myself deeper against her.

From behind, the horse whinnied.

Hailey flinched like she'd just remembered where we were, and she pressed those sweet hands against my shoulders. Her face was flushed when she looked up at me. "You keep it up, and you're going to traumatize poor Starlight."

I chuckled. "Nah, that was approval."

"Really? And what exactly was she saying?"

"Something along the lines of 'git it.'" I rocked my hips into hers.

Laughter rolled out of Hailey. Her smile was unstoppable.

Fuck, I liked it.

I liked making her happy, and if I could, I would keep this exact same expression on her face forever.

"What?" she asked as she searched my features, a slight frown pinched between her eyes.

"Just thinking what a lucky bastard I am."

A soft puff of air escaped her nose. "I think I'm the lucky one."

We stayed like that for a moment.

Gazing at each other.

Relishing in what this meant.

Finally, she gave me a slight nudge.

"I'd better get Starlight back to her stall. It's going to be feeding time, then I need to get to my meeting."

I sent her the best pout I could manage. "Don't like that you're not coming home with me."

She had some kind of administrative dinner tonight inside the lodge.

Her fingers fiddled in the fabric of my shirt. "It'll only take a couple hours, then you can pick me up and take me home, and I'll be sure to make it up to you."

I let the smirk climb to my mouth. "Oh, darlin', you'd better watch yourself because I'm going to hold you to that."

"You'd better," she said.

I was shaking my head as I stepped away and passed her over the reins.

Yep, no question I was fuckin' whipped. Couldn't stand the thought of being away from her for even a second.

"Text me fifteen minutes before you think you're wrapping up, and I'll head out."

"Okay. Give Maddie a kiss for me."

"You know I will...I'll probably have to give Lolly one, too." I winked at her.

Amusement shook her head. "Oh God, don't give her any ideas."

"I'm pretty sure Lolly's ideas are all her own." I backed away slowly, hands stuffed in my pockets as we swam through the lightness.

Through this thing that felt so right.

The confession threatened to work its way free of my tongue. Because I knew it, looking at her, that she was it for me.

"I'll miss you," I told her instead of admitting it.

Hailey lifted her hand in a small wave. "Be careful."

"Always." I turned on my heel and followed the path around the side of the stables and down to the parking lot in front of the maintenance building. My team was already gone for the day, having wrapped up another pour earlier this afternoon.

Pride filled me as I thought of the progress we'd made. The project was coming together nicely, the first group of cabins already to about twenty-five percent completion. We'd be here the whole summer, but we were more than on track, and the work that had been done was fucking gorgeous.

I wasn't too humble to admit it.

I waved at Tyrek who was locking the front door of the maintenance building before I strode across the dirt lot to where my truck was parked on the far side facing a dense thicket of woods.

My boots clomped on the loose dirt, and I clicked the locks, glancing left and right to make sure there wasn't anyone lurking about before I pulled open the driver's side door.

I went to hop inside.

I didn't know what it was that stopped me.

What made me hesitate a beat.

A tacky awareness slicking over my flesh.

I didn't have time to process it.

No time to step back or just fucking run.

Not before an explosion so fucking loud and disorienting erupted in a gulf of flames.

A detonation of heat and fire and power that blasted me back.

There was no way to stop it or prepare for it.

No way to even contemplate the pain as I flew.

There was nothing at all as my entire world went black.

Chapter Forty-Two

Hailey

I LED STARLIGHT TO HER STALL, SMILING THE WHOLE WAY, MY lips tingling from the meaning I'd felt behind Cody's kiss.

I opened the gate and removed her bridle, whispered my love to her, before I started back out.

A scream tore out of me when I was suddenly rocked by a thunder so intense that the ground shook violently beneath my feet.

A sonic boom that echoed through the air, rattling the metal of the stalls and tossing the entire world into disorder.

My hands shot out to steady myself against the gate.

My knees weak and my heart hammering as bolts of confusion and anxiety shot through me as the ground tremored and rolled.

An earthquake.

A volcano.

A rendering of peace.

I gasped and tried to orient myself, to process what I'd heard.

To make sense of what still trembled through the atmosphere.

Shouts rose up from all around, in the distance and some coming from a couple ranch hands who ran past me down the aisle where they tossed the door open at the end in search of what had happened.

My head spun, and I swallowed around the tumult that had me in shock.

Gathering myself enough to focus, I tuned my ear to the shouts and voices that were coming from outside.

Not an earthquake.

An explosion.

Oh God.

It was an explosion.

Panic erupted in my senses, and I slammed the stall gate closed, latched it, and went running in the same direction as the other hands had gone, flying out through the door to the disorder happening on the other side.

Shouts.

Mayhem.

Chaos.

Voices penetrated from all around, rising through the smoke that clouded the air.

"Someone call an ambulance."

"Stay back!"

"We need an extinguisher."

I faltered for only a beat, my heart in my throat as my gaze raced to where the commotion was coming from.

To the lot near the maintenance facility.

Then I was running.

Sprinting.

Hemorrhaging.

My heart bleeding out when through the haze of smoke and dust I saw Cody's truck.

Consumed in flames.

"Cody, oh my God, no, Cody."

I ran as hard as my feet would take me, my boots pounding the ground, the world falling away around me.

People were gathered around, though a few were holding them

back, keeping them away from the heat that I could already feel blasting my face.

"Cody!" I shouted it through the terror that ravaged, and I barreled through the wall of bodies. "Cody!"

Arms curled around me from behind. "Stay right here, Ms. Wagner. It's not safe."

I flailed and tore at Tyrek's hold, my chest bowing as I warred to break free. Screams ripped out of my lungs. "Cody! Where is he? Let me go! Please, let go."

Two men were on the opposite side of the truck, about eight feet out, kneeling around something I couldn't see.

But my soul knew.

"Cody." I whimpered it that time.

A siren bleeped from the fire station that was only a mile down the road, and the whirring sound of it curled through the heavens as it started our direction.

"Cody."

It was mayhem then.

The fire trucks and ambulance that pulled up, firefighters and paramedics descending on the scene, pushing everyone back while employees scrambled and swarmed to see what the clamor was about.

While I felt my heart shatter out in front of me.

Chapter Forty-Three
Cody

Twenty-Four Years Old

CODY SAT IN HIS TRUCK BENEATH THE SHADE OF THE TREE. Waiting.

His guts in a knot of shame and desperation.

How many times had he heard the sayings? Proverbs and inspirations and pretty words inscribed on plaques about the lengths a man would go to for his family? He doubted much those sentiments extended to what he'd succumbed to. The immorality he'd been driven to.

But he had no other choice, and he was close. So close to getting his mother out of the hole she was in, and he was determined to dig her out of it even if he ended up buried.

It turned out Brent was running an illegal gambling ring based at the horse track here in Eddings, a small city a little more than an hour from Wagner Ranch. He'd used his connections at the ranch to give him an in. Using it as a cover.

The guy was dirty. As dirty as they came.

And he was using Cody to put pressure on those who hadn't made good on their bets.

Cody tried to justify his actions by saying these guys had it coming to them. It wasn't like they were innocent. It wasn't like they weren't out pilfering away their families' security with their addiction to money. With their greed. With their stupidity.

Cody kept telling himself that over and over as he waited for any sign of movement outside the accountant's office where he was hidden at the far side of the small back parking lot that accommodated three cars.

There was only one sitting there.

A white BMW that he'd confirmed the idiot drove the night before when he'd followed him to his house, keeping his distance, fucking sick to his stomach at what he was supposed to do.

It didn't matter that he'd already done it close to fifteen times. He was sure he was never going to get used to it.

The only thing that kept him moving was his mother's grief that was wound in his spirit. Her tears in his hands. That promise he had made to his father as a little boy playing through his head on repeat.

And he was going to keep that promise.

So he slipped from his truck when he saw the back door swing open and the middle-aged man come waltzing out without a clue. Dressed in slacks and a button-down, confidence oozing off him in waves.

Cody came up behind him just as he was opening the driver's side door of his car, and he had him by the wrist. He was locking his arm behind his back and pinning him to the frame before the man even noticed he was there.

Shock blistered, a beat of succumbing, before the man flailed and tried to break free as he roared, "What the hell? Do you know who I am?"

"Yes, I know exactly who you are." Cody grunted it at the man's ear, and he wrenched his arm back farther until he let go of a howl of pain. "A *good friend* of yours sent me."

A cold chill rolled through the man, like he was just then catching on that this wasn't some kind of robbery. This was about what he owed.

"You didn't think you could just ignore his calls, did you?" Cody warned it, cool and low.

Fear radiated from the asshole who winced in his hold, dude about to piss his pants as he floundered all over his words. "I…I already talked to him. We came to a deal. Just ask him."

"Ah, see, I know you're lying because I just talked with him this morning, and he told me you didn't keep your end of the deal. You were to have fifty g's in his pocket by last night. He already let that day go by once. It's not going to happen again."

"I…I…please, I'll get it, just…don't hurt me." Guilt constricted Cody's body as the man spluttered all over the place.

Begging.

Pleading with Cody not to be the monster he was paid to be.

Cody forced him down onto his knees.

Bile rolled his throat as he leaned down to issue the vitriol to the back of the man's head. "You don't have it by midnight tonight, things are going to get ugly. I'd suggest you take this as a friendly warning because you aren't going to get another."

Cody nearly gagged when he clocked the guy on the side of the head, sending him slumping forward, knocking him clean out. The punch was softer than the one that he could have delivered, though. Softer than the one he was supposed to.

He fucking prayed the message would be enough. That this fucking idiot would come through. This guy who had three little kids at home and a wife who probably had no clue her husband was bartering away his life. Putting them all in danger.

Because it was becoming clear what Brent was capable of, and Cody was hoping to God that it wouldn't come to that.

The only thing he did know as he strode back for his truck, hopped in, and peeled out from behind the building and onto the road was that he was done. This was the last job he was going to do. He had enough to pay off his mother's debt, and he sure as fuck wasn't in this to get greedy.

He'd done his duty.

For his mother.

For his sisters.

To his father.

Now, he had to get out of this before it completely warped who he was. Before the demons that had already slithered their way into his soul weaved themselves any deeper. Before the shame grew to something he couldn't stand beneath.

Because those scars were already there, marking his insides, the depravity that he'd risen to.

No more.

No more.

Because being this monster was someone he refused to be.

⌒✳⌒

He felt the presence crawl over him from behind. Not the bright, shining one he'd come to crave. Not those blue eyes that washed him in warmth and that sweet smile that knitted his heart in comfort.

Nah.

This one was malignant.

Corrupt.

"You did good. Payment came in as expected," Brent said, as casual as could be, as if he were commending Cody for finishing the fence rather than having threatened and assaulted.

Rather than having incited discord and fear.

Disgust prickled the fine hairs at the base of Cody's neck, and he ground his teeth as he drove the hammer harder against the nail, fitting the railing to the support pole as he struggled to rein in the shame and dread that gathered like devastation in his being.

Cody turned, hating the face that grinned back, this guy's persona so fucking fake Cody couldn't stand looking at him, kind of the way he was starting to hate looking at himself in the mirror.

Brent passed him the envelope that contained a fat wad of cash for the last five jobs he'd done, including the one yesterday. Five more men Cody had terrorized.

It was the last ten thousand Cody needed.

The promise he'd made his father bashed against the reproach, and Cody reached out and took the blood-tainted money. There was no fucking way on earth he could bring himself to say thank you.

Brent just kept looking at him with that smug look on his face, and Cody itched, feet shifting in discomfort. He gestured to the fence, voice rough, "I'd better get back to it."

"Think that's going to have to wait, I have something more important for you to handle."

Cody gave a harsh shake of his head. "I finished what we agreed on. Job is done."

"Well, see, the thing is, Cody, I'm going to have to ask you for one more favor. I have someone who's become a problem, and I need you to take care of that problem."

Foreboding rolled through Cody's being, and his flesh slicked with sweat. "I'm going to have to pass."

"Nah," Brent said, still grinning. "You're going to have to see it through. Instructions are in your truck." Brent clapped him on the shoulder like they were old pals, sending him a wink before he strolled off with his hands stuffed in his pockets.

⌒✳︎⌒

Cody sat in the driver's seat of his truck.

Terror rolled down his spine as he stared at the two items that had been in the manila envelope.

The first was a picture of a guy he'd shaken down about a month before. One he'd beaten for owing a hundred grand.

The other item was a gun.

It didn't take all that much to discern the guy hadn't paid up.

Cody trembled like a fucking earthquake, a ball of razors rolling his throat as he tried to swallow, as he tried to breathe, as he tried to process the disaster that he'd gotten himself into.

He'd promised he'd help his mother, no matter the cost, and Cody was realizing just how steep that cost might be.

Because the decision he made was likely going to land him in a shallow grave. But there was no fucking chance he'd stoop to this level, so he sucked all the fear stampeding through his insides down, and he shoved the contents of the manila envelope back inside, and his gaze rose through the windshield toward the enormous cabin in the distance.

Sickness lined his guts, that terror clamoring, his end in sight. He could almost feel his time running out, the hands on the clock of his life coming to a mangled standstill.

But his fear wouldn't stop him. He'd accepted it. What this was coming to.

So, he strode up the long walkway made of decorative rock and around the side of the massive house to the separate entrance to Douglas Wagner's office that was attached at the far side.

His hand was a dead weight as he lifted it to rap at the door.

He'd barely talked to the man, Brent being his point of contact, and confusion littered the guy's expression when he opened the door to find a frazzled Cody standing there. "Can I help you?"

Sweat poured down Cody's back. "I need to speak with you, sir."

Douglas Wagner's frown deepened. "Of course. Come in and have a seat."

Except Cody couldn't sit as he confessed what he'd been involved in. As he told the man about the betting ring that Brent was heading. The shakedowns. What Brent was now asking him to do.

Cody set the evidence on Douglas Wagner's desk.

The man had gone pale, blanching in disbelief. Weak, he sank down onto his brown leather office chair, the picture in his hands, his voice ragged as he peered up at Cody. "And this was Brent who got you involved? Brent who runs my goddamn ranch?"

Regret carved into Cody's words. "Yes, sir."

Mr. Wagner nodded through dismayed acceptance. "I see."

Then it was anger that surfaced, as if he'd had to work up to what this really meant. Standing, he scuffed a hand over his face before he was glaring at Cody. "I'm going to deal with this through a friend of mine at the Feds, but I need it quiet. I can't have this scandal marring the reputation of the ranch. As for you…"

Cody couldn't stop shaking as the man stared at him in repulsion. "I'm disgusted that you got involved in this to begin with, but

I am grateful that you came to me in the end. So, here's what's going to happen...you're going to get in your truck and drive off my ranch. You're going to turn your back and act like none of this ever happened and thank your lucky stars that I'm not turning you in, too. Beyond that, I don't want to ever see you again."

The man steeled his voice. "Not here on my property, not in this town."

He leaned in closer to prove a point. "And if I ever catch you talking to my daughter again which you can be sure I've noticed the way you've been doing? I'll make sure you won't have the capacity to make that mistake again. Stay the hell away from her. Do you understand me?"

Cody's nod was a jolt of relief.

"Good. Now get the fuck out of my face so I can deal with this mess."

Chapter Forty-Four

Hailey

I'D HEARD THAT IT ONLY TAKES ONE EVENT TO REFORM THE entire shape of your life.

One moment to construct a different mold.

One second to reconfigure the truth of what you knew.

I trembled in the aftermath of it, my mind trying to process the catastrophic incident from earlier this afternoon.

My spirit screamed with the horror of what I had brought to this town.

With what I had caused.

With what I had done.

"Would you stop it?" Cody rumbled.

"No, I won't stop it." I could barely speak around the rawness of my throat.

"While I appreciate your fretting, darlin', I can promise you it isn't necessary."

I inhaled a shaky breath.

I couldn't calm down.

Couldn't soothe the dread.

Couldn't assuage the fear that he could have been killed.

He could have been killed.

Because of me.

Because of me.

"I think it's very necessary." I choked out the words as I tried to help Cody from the front seat of my Durango. It wasn't like I could support the weight of the man, but God, I was going to try.

Cody eased out onto his feet, sporting a grin like this wasn't a big deal and he hadn't spent the last six hours in the ER being treated and observed. "I barely got a scratch."

Disbelief left me on a shaky exhale as I tried to hold onto his wrist that didn't have any bandages on it.

"Barely a scratch? You have stitches in four different places, bruised ribs, a cracked collarbone, and a severe burn on your arm."

Shattered glass had been imbedded all over his body, impaling him like darts as he'd been sent rocketing back like an arrow. The explosion had burned him, his hair singed, and it'd scorched his forearm and hand that had been closest to the truck, and they said it was likely he'd suffer some permanent hearing damage.

It'd been his saving grace, though—the fact that he hadn't been inside the truck when the explosive had gone off. I had to believe Pruitt knew I was supposed to have been attending a meeting this evening. That he somehow knew that I wouldn't be leaving with Cody that evening.

But how?

Grief crawled around in my chest, slithering like a snake, the sensation sticky and gross.

Tears pricked behind my eyes.

I fought to hold them back.

"And they shot me full of something that made me feel just fine." Cody tossed another grin at me as we ambled up the walkway and onto the porch.

He'd left the hospital against medical advice since they'd wanted him to stay overnight for observation. But he'd refused, insisting that he needed to be home with me and Maddie and Lolly, which only made me worry more.

I stayed right at his side, hands fumbling as I tried to keep him steady, even though he was standing just fine.

But what if he hadn't been?

Sorrow bound, clotting off oxygen. I wheezed around it.

"If I went tumbling onto my ass right now, Hailey, I'd be taking you down with me," he teased. "I wouldn't stand so close if I were you."

"Liar," I muttered under my breath.

We crossed the porch, our footsteps thudding on the wooden planks.

We stopped in front of the door, and I tipped my face up to him.

"Liar," I whispered again.

Confusion pinched his brow.

"You would absolutely be standing right here, holding me up, if the tables were turned."

Understanding dawned, and his smirk softened, his smile going so tender that I ached. "Of course, I would, darlin'."

"Then don't ask me not to stand by you."

I turned and unlocked the door.

It was close to midnight, and it was silent inside.

Maddie had gone to sleep hours ago, having no clue there'd been any issue, while Lolly had texted me incessantly until about ten when I'd finally convinced her Cody was okay.

If only I could convince myself of the same thing.

Cody had demanded that I not call his family. He wanted to be the one to do it. To be able to go to them and tell them he was okay without them running to the ER terrified.

I'd tried to argue and tell him they would want to know—that they deserved to know—because they loved him.

Loved him fiercely.

But he'd asked this one thing of me so I had to respect it.

We kept our footsteps quieted as we stepped inside, and I deadbolted the lock behind us.

Anguish fisted my spirit.

The truth of what this had come to. That reshaping. The reforming.

A conflict of what I wanted and what I had to do.

This was exactly what Pruitt wanted, though, wasn't it?

He wanted me terrified. He wanted me bent to his will. And he didn't care what it cost to force me into that position.

Cody's boots scudded on the floor as we trudged across the great room, my thoughts so heavy that I could barely see.

I realized my breaths were heaving from my lungs in short gasps by the time we made it into my room, agony claiming my existence.

I dropped my attention to the floor in an attempt to gather myself.

To hold it back.

To rein in the spiraling.

The door clicked shut behind us, and I turned to Cody who stood facing me.

The bathroom light was on, and it shed enough light on him that I could plainly see he was battered.

His hair black from the smoke and the fire, his jaw red from the burn.

His shirt was tattered and torn and filthy with soot.

A bandage covered his left forearm and ran down to the back of his hand, and there were little bandages covering the spots where he had gotten stitches.

Agony swept through me. Wave after wave.

How could I have let this happen? How could I have been so selfish that I'd invited him into my life? Knowing the danger?

"Shortcake." He murmured it through the ghosts that played through the room.

I curled my arms over my chest like it could hold together the pieces that were fracturing apart.

"Don't call me that."

It was a plea.

A plea for him to turn and leave.

For him to see that he should run.

He had his whole life out ahead of him, and I'd nearly been the one responsible for cutting it short.

"Now why would I go and do that?" he rumbled in that low voice.

Moisture blurred my eyes, an excruciating burn running up my throat. "Because you need to leave. Let go. I can't ask you to keep putting yourself on the line like this. You could have—"

It croaked off.

I couldn't say it aloud.

Cody took a step forward, and the floor shook beneath my feet. "But I didn't."

I blinked against the pain. Against the riot that thrashed at my chest.

"Maybe this is payback, Cody. Punishment for the sin I'm committing. You need to get away from me. Before it's too late."

A scowl compressed every line on his handsome face. "What are you talking about?"

I couldn't contain the tears, and they slipped hot and fast down my face, the guilt I'd been trying to suppress finally breaking free.

"Brooke." Her name dropped from my tongue like a boulder of regret.

Surprise sent him blinking. "Brooke?"

I squeezed my arms tighter across my chest. "She loved you, Cody. She loved you, and she wanted to be with you. She saw us that day... the day we almost..." I cut off, the words jagged and barbed, sticking to my lips. My breaths cleaved, so harsh they ripped and slayed.

"She saw us." I whispered it that time. "I promised her I would never do that to her. That you and I were only friends and that was the only thing we were ever going to be. But she was so upset...so upset..."

I gasped it, my arms squeezing so tight like I could keep the mangled mess that was my heart confined within the gaping of my ribs. "She never would have gone into that corral. Never. She was terrified of those horses. I know she..."

I couldn't fully give it voice. Her death had been ruled an accident. But I knew. I'd always known.

"Fuck, Hailey." Sorrow rippled from Cody, and he took another step closer. "I can't believe what you're saying, but if she did, you've got to know that wasn't your fault. None of this is your fault."

"It is, Cody. She went running out that night. I…I didn't stop her. I thought she needed time to cool off, and once she did, she'd understand and forgive me. Forgive me for wanting you because God knows how much I did, and Brooke knew it, too."

A sob tore out of me. It was the first time I'd ever admitted it aloud. The first time I gave voice to the horrors of what I'd believed.

I'd held it for years. A dirty secret that had haunted. What had driven me to a place I never should have gone.

Massive arms wrapped around me, and Cody pulled me tight against him, his breath a whisper across my hair, as quiet as the words he confessed. "If that was anyone's fault, then it was mine, darlin'. Mine and mine alone."

"You told her you loved her. How could you say that and not mean it?" The question was pocked with soggy, gasping tears.

Cody froze, and his arms went rigid. Regret pilfered from his nose. "I didn't, Hailey. I never told her that. Would never lie about that. If I tell someone I love them, I fucking mean it."

Sobs kept erupting.

Uncontrolled.

Unchecked.

I wanted to accuse him of being a liar. But once I'd opened the box where I'd stored away the memories, it came flooding back.

Brooke had wanted him to. She'd wanted him to love her.

But he hadn't. It had been clear.

I'd chalked him up to being a player.

Toying with both of our emotions.

But that wasn't him.

"It broke my heart, too, when you were with her." The revelations kept coming, the stress of the day pushing me to my breaking point. I was no longer able to contain what had been brewing for years.

His regret doubled, and those strong arms pulled me tighter, his voice splintered pieces of gravel. "I'm sorry. I'm fuckin' sorry for hurting you. I couldn't touch you, Hailey. Couldn't. Not when you were this sweet, innocent girl my gut warned me I would wreck."

He inhaled a shattered breath. "Because I wanted you in a way that I knew wasn't right, and I'd be a bastard to touch you, so I did everything in my power to stay away from you. It was hard, though, every time you came around, shining so damned bright when I was in the middle of this shit that I knew was going to ruin my life."

He was injured, but he kept drawing me closer, like there was no chance he could get close enough. I clung to him, too, my consciousness spinning. "What shit, Cody?"

Shame filled his sigh, though he didn't let me go. "My mother was going to lose her house. I couldn't let that happen. The Wagner Ranch manager at that time heard I was looking to make some extra money and he offered me an opportunity. The guy was crooked, Hailey. Running illegal bets down at the horse track over in Eddings. I didn't know it when he offered it, but I was hired to shake guys down when they didn't pay up."

Alarm blared in the back of my mind.

Cody felt it, and he somehow hauled me closer.

"He was a bad guy, Hailey. Really bad. I didn't realize just how bad until I was in too deep. After he'd already given me enough money to pay off my mother's debt. After I'd already taken the money and given it to her..."

"What happened?" I almost begged it.

A shiver rocked down Cody's spine. "There was this guy who'd gotten a couple beat downs. Owed a shit ton. Refused to pay. Brent came to me with an extra hundred grand to take care of the problem."

Horrified disbelief slammed me on a rogue wave. "Oh my God."

Cody's throat rolled heavily as he swallowed. "It's why your father hates me. I went to him for help, and I confessed what was going on. He called a friend at the Feds to take care of Brent and break up the ring he was running. He told me I got a free pass since I'd done the right thing and come to him, but he warned if I ever showed my face anywhere near him or his family again, he was going to see to it that I never had the capacity to make that mistake again."

He sucked for the air that had gone missing. "It was the day I left, Hailey. When I came to tell you goodbye because I couldn't leave without doing it. Then I turned my back and buried my head and kept my nose clean for the last six years, always looking over my fucking shoulder for the day those crimes were going to catch up to me. Worried that someone who knew me then was going to come back for me. That, or your father would finally turn me in."

"Cody." I whimpered his name. "But you're here. With me."

After every warning.

After every danger.

He pulled back, his thumb tracing beneath the hollow of my eye, the gold of his gaze flaming in the muted light.

"Told you that you're worth it. Whatever the cost, Hailey, you're worth it. If anyone has Karma coming their way, it's me, Hailey. It's me. So drop this bullshit that you're in any way responsible for this."

He was wrong, though.

Pruitt was my responsibility. Cody had nearly been killed because of him.

I blinked through the tears that wouldn't stop falling. "Pruitt isn't going to stop until I give in."

"Pruitt can go to hell."

"This isn't some drunk guy at a bar throwing fists, Cody." I begged it. "Pruitt is dangerous, and he won't let anyone get in the way of what he wants. I should have realized the lengths he would go. I should have run far away, hidden where he could never find us. I never should have come here."

Cody pulled back and cupped both hands around the sides of my face. "Fuck that, Hailey. You're right where you belong. With me."

"I won't be responsible for you getting hurt any more than you already have been."

Cody gave me the slightest shake of his head. "It's too late for me, darlin'."

He kept staring down at me, both thumbs brushing my cheeks.

Energy thrummed.

Pulsing and compelling.

That connection writhed in the space.

Demanding to be acknowledged.

"It's too late," he repeated. "I'm already gone. Already done for. Already yours."

"Cody." His name shuddered off my tongue.

Begging him to stop.

To see reason.

His thumbs swept over the moisture that wouldn't stop falling, voice rough when he murmured, "I'm in love with you, Hailey. So in love with you that there isn't a piece of me left that doesn't belong to you."

My lips parted on a shattered exhalation.

Cody just held me tighter, his nose dropping close to mine. "I've made a million mistakes in my life, but standing here, with you? For you? That's not one of them. Because when you love someone the way I love you? You don't bail when things get rough. You stand closer to them in their battles. You pick them up when they fall. You carry them when they can't run. You love them with all you've got because they are the very meaning of *time*. Because you and Maddie are the reason I'm living it. You are the sun setting and the sun rising. Every minute. Every second. Every fucking beat."

I swayed beneath the power of his words.

Beneath the power of his touch.

His hand slipped down to the side of my neck, his words harsh and sweet. "You got me, Hailey. You've got all of me."

"Cody." I rasped over his name.

The emotion I'd been trying to hold back burst free.

Got loose of the sacred place I'd tried to keep it shored.

Where guilt had lived.

But it couldn't thrive there anymore.

"I love you, Cody. I love you so much, and there is a piece of me that always has. I tried not to, to deny it, to ignore what I always felt, but I don't think there was a way to stop myself from falling in love with you."

Playfulness kicked up at the edge of his mouth. "Well, I'm pretty impossible not to love."

I choked over a soggy laugh, and my chest squeezed as I gazed up at his rough, masculine beauty.

At his battered face and his flawless heart.

"You're right. It's impossible. It's impossible not to love you."

His expression intensified. "You're it for me."

I gulped around the love that rushed. "Good because I won't let you go."

Because of it, I knew what I had to do. I was terrified of it, but I couldn't let Pruitt get away with his cruelty. Couldn't let him continue spreading his wickedness in the world.

He needed to be stopped.

And it was time we were free.

"Now that we got that cleared up." Mischief played across Cody's face, sparks flickering like greed in those gold-flecked eyes, right before he crushed his mouth against mine.

This kiss was searing.

A mark.

A brand.

A claiming.

I wanted it.

I wanted him written all over me.

On every inch of my body and in every recess of my heart.

But I was also brutally aware that he had almost died today.

"We can't," I urged against the force of his kiss.

Cody pulled back, still holding onto both sides of my face, mouth cocked in that smirk.

"Oh, but we can."

Chapter Forty-Five
Cody

THERE WAS NO AMOUNT OF PAIN THAT WOULD KEEP ME from her right then. No agony that would stop me from touching her because the true agony would be not getting to spend this life with her.

I'd thought I was going to lose that today. Thought my past had finally caught up to me, and my time had ended. I'd thought I wasn't going to get to ever kiss her again. Touch her again.

Hold her until morning the way she liked me to do. The way she'd curl up in my arms and whisper her need for me in her sleep.

I'd thought she'd never get to hear it—that she'd never know just how goddamned much I loved her. How this heart now beat for her. And I'd almost never gotten to hear her say it back.

Confess those words that had washed through me like a cleansing.

Purifying all the wrongs I'd ever committed.

I love you.

I love you.

"I don't want to hurt you." Concern weaved through her brow, but I could taste the way her need filled the air. Her fingers digging into my shirt. Heat licking in a slow dance between us.

"The only thing that could hurt me right now is not getting to have you, though you might have to be the one who's doing all the work." I let the tease play into the words.

Let them wind as seduction.

Hailey nibbled on her upper lip like she was envisioning all the ways she could make that happen.

"All the work, huh?"

"Yup."

"Hmm..."

I brushed my thumb over her lip before I leaned in for a kiss, taking her mouth slow, relishing in this woman.

The words rolled up my throat, soft and adoring. "You are the meaning of this life."

She inhaled them, taking them on as her own, and she breathed hers back into me. "You are the hope that I'd been missing. The light when my faith had gone dark."

Our kisses were slow.

Our mouths moving in time.

In sync.

Treasuring each other.

Her touch was soft and careful.

Mine was reverent, palms gliding down her back and riding up her sides.

Holding her face.

Her neck.

Carefully, she peeled up my shirt, and I edged back to help her, trying not to wince which was fucking impossible since every inch of me throbbed like a bitch.

None of that mattered.

The only thing that mattered was her.

"You are a piece of me I was terrified to admit existed," she whispered as I leaned down and she peeled the fabric over my head.

Eyes the color of that river swept over me in the shadows that played across her room.

She reached out and gently brushed her fingertips down the center of my chest. "The first time I saw you all those years ago…from all the way across that field…I wanted you. Wanted something I'd never wanted before."

She kept skimming those fingertips over my flesh.

Soft.

Adoring.

Healing.

"I thought it was physical. That thing called attraction. But maybe it was all of you, Cody Cooper. Maybe my spirit already recognized you. Because in all those years, I could never forget you."

"There was always something that ached at the back of my mind every time I thought of you," I told her.

She peeked up at me. "You thought of me?"

"How could I not think of you?" I asked it as I started to work through the buttons of her blouse, and a wisp of a sigh fluttered between her lips when I pushed the material back.

She wound out of it and let it drop to the floor just as I was taking her enormous tits in my hands.

I brushed my thumbs over the peaks of her nipples.

Whimpering, she pushed harder into my touch. "Cody."

"I know it, darlin'. I feel it, too. You and me were supposed to be."

I knew she felt some guilt over it. Could feel the minute flinch that my words brought. Her confession still rolling through the air and kicking me in the guts.

I was having a difficult time imagining that Brooke might have done what Hailey implied. That she'd purposefully taken her life. That it wasn't some tragic accident.

Brooke had told me she got who we were to each other. That she agreed there wasn't anything real between us. That it'd been just as we'd established at the beginning—a fling and nothing more.

Apparently, she'd led Hailey to believe something else.

I needed Hailey to know there would never be anyone standing in the middle of us.

"You are the first person who has ever really made me feel anything, Hailey. The first person who made my heart beat faster. The first person who's ever kept me up at night."

"And you are the first person who has really stood for me. You are the one who makes me feel safe. Cherished. Loved," she whispered back.

"Because that's exactly what you are. Cherished and loved. I love you so fucking much, baby. Never thought it would happen. And you… you changed everything I knew." I reached around and unclasped her bra as I said it, and I dragged the silken straps down her arms.

A hiss slipped from between my teeth. "So fucking stunning. This face and this body and this heart. You turned me inside out, Hailey."

"It's you who changed everything, Cody. I think it was you that brought us here. I think you were calling us home."

"That's right, darlin'. You were the one I was waiting on all along."

I tugged at the button of her jeans. "And no matter what, I'm going to be right here. With you. We're going to take this bastard down."

Fear flashed through her features, the dread that hovered around us in the periphery, waiting to consume. It didn't have any place with us tonight, so I swooped down and captured her mouth, refocusing her attention on the things that were right.

Tender hands roved my body, and she carefully unbuttoned my jeans as I kissed her with all the passion bottled inside.

What had built for years, shored up for this time.

For her.

Hailey shifted me to sitting on the bed, and she climbed down in front of me. She worked the laces of my boots.

"Have to admit I like the sight of you on your knees for me." I tried my best to make it come out a tease, but it was hard holding onto that right then. Not with the way the energy thrashed and lapped.

Tugging one boot off, she quirked me a soft grin. "I've been on my knees for you since I was eighteen."

"Don't worry, honey, you've got me the same. On my knees. Motherfucking smitten."

Redness lit on those cheeks, and I traced the spot while she un-laced my other boot. Once she got it free, she angled up so she could peel down my jeans.

She took my underwear with them as she went.

I lifted up to help her drag them off my legs.

A static charge zipped through the room.

Me sitting there bare and so goddamn hard I couldn't see.

"You're so beautiful," she murmured, which was fucking ridiculous because I was all scars and roughened skin and years of working out in the sun, and she was pure, unblemished beauty kneeling in front of me.

"Only thing I care about is being right in your eyes, Hailey."

"You already are, Cody. You are the only thing I can see."

She wrapped a hand around my dick, fisting me as she gave a hard stroke.

Pleasure prowled my spine. "Fuck me, baby, just that sweet hand could send me over the edge."

Who knew such an innocent smile could also come off as wicked, and those plush, full lips twisted in seduction as she kept stroking me. "Good because I'm already halfway there just looking at you."

"Well, *half* is not going to do, now is it? How about you strip the rest of the way out of those jeans?"

"You want me to strip for you, huh?" She played right along.

"Yeah, do it real nice."

Hailey pushed up to standing, backing two steps away, bare from the waist up.

A river of that warm blonde hair cascaded around her, teasing tendrils I couldn't wait to fist.

Tits pert and peaked and perfect.

She leaned over to pull off her boots and the thick socks she wore with them, and she wiggled her toes as she stood there staring across at me, unsure of what she was supposed to do next.

"Don't be shy, darlin'. You're mine, remember?"

She swayed those hips back and forth, slowly rocking her head from side to side, her hand riding up her abdomen and over her breasts until she was winding a hand up in her hair.

"Hell yes, just like that," I grunted.

The button was already undone on her jeans, and she slowly turned around in a lust-inducing dance. She hooked her thumbs in the waistband and barely wiggled them down, giving me a tease of just the cleft of that glorious ass.

I growled. "Temptress, aren't you?"

"Never, I'm only doing what my man asked me to do."

She peeked at me from over her shoulder when she said it, the razzing written all over her face while desire dripped from every inch of her body.

"You really are my match. Signed and sealed." Need barreled out with the statement, and she slipped those jeans lower, exposing the lace of her panties.

"That's right. We're a perfect fit."

Fuck me.

She was teasing.

Playing.

Tantalizing.

Maybe because she wanted to ignore what was looming around us, too. What we were going to have to face.

But not tonight.

Tonight was for us.

"Then get that hot ass over here so I can show you just how perfect a fit we are. I want that pussy on my dick."

Heat sparked at my words, and she shimmied the rest of the way out of her jeans before she turned to saunter over, peeling those undies down as she came.

She wound them off her ankles at the last second before she was standing right in front of me.

Bare.

So fucking stunning my heart tripped.

I pushed my fingers between her thighs. "Already dripping for me."

At the contact, Hailey whimpered, then she lightly pushed at my shoulders. "Lean against the headboard."

My brows rose at her command. "I see who's in charge tonight."

She shrugged a delicate shoulder. "You told me I was going to be the one doing all the work."

"I like the sound of that, but I'm going to like the feel of it even better," I told her.

Flames licked in the room as I crawled backward up the bed, re-adjusting the pillows so I could fully lean upright on the headboard.

Hailey stood at the side.

A vision.

A goddess.

My sweet Shortcake who'd turned all vixen.

Blonde hair falling all around her as she crawled onto the bed.

I grunted when she came to straddle me.

She hesitated. "Am I hurting you?"

My fingers clamped down on one of her lush hips. "Only pain I'm feeling right now is the need to get inside you."

Hailey braced herself with one hand on the headboard before she lifted up and aligned my dick at her center.

A flash of hesitation brimmed in her gaze as she hovered there, my dick bare, and my throat nearly closed off as she slowly sank down onto me.

Taking me skin to skin.

Claiming me in her own way.

Because we both knew from here on out it was only going to be the two of us.

No barriers left.

Her walls throbbed as I filled her to the brink of breaking.

Her thighs shook as she fully seated herself.

So hot and tight that I nearly blacked out at the feel of her.

"Perfect fuckin' fit, you and me. The way this pussy hugs my cock. You were made for me, darlin'. Carved for me. *It* for me. And I was created for you."

A shaky breath left her as she adjusted to me again, both hands coming to my shoulders, eyes brimming with the love that could no longer be contained. "There was a part of me that always knew it. I felt you like a piece that had gone missing."

I brushed back a lock of soft, silky hair. "No more missing, Hailey. It's just you and me. Now ride me, darlin'. And don't you worry about being gentle."

Hailey lifted up and sank back down.

Friction blazed.

Spreading like wildfire through my veins.

She did it again, a little harder that time.

A little faster as she began to ride me.

"You feel so good," she whimpered, her nose brushing mine, her breaths shallow as she rocked.

"You are paradise."

My heaven.

My escape from the chains.

She started taking me harder, whispers and moans slipping from her mouth as she spun her perfect pleasure.

Knitting me in ecstasy.

She leaned in closer, the words barely a breath. "And you are my home."

"That's what I want to be, darlin'. Your home. Your safe place. Your everything."

"You are, Cody. You are."

Devotion pummeled me like a fist to the head.

The truth that this was it.

"Need it harder, baby. Don't be shy. Wreck me."

I already was.

Done for.

Destroyed.

Greed filled her gaze, and I nearly died at the loss of friction when she slowed then stopped, but then I was dying all over again when she languidly shifted around.

This time in the best way possible.

The woman giving me a view of that round, sumptuous ass as she straddled me facing away.

A greedy groan tumbled around like rocks in my chest. "You really are trying to wreck me."

"You asked for it." She sent me a saucy grin, though it was affection in those eyes, and I knew I was the luckiest bastard alive when she sank back down.

Her cunt fisted me in its tight, wet grip, and she gasped out at the change in position.

I had to grit my teeth not to burst apart at the blinding bliss that streaked through my body.

Intensity shivered around us, tiny lightning bolts in the room, that energy whipping and whirring, this connection unlike anything I'd ever shared with another.

I wrapped an arm around her front and fisted the other up in the fall of her hair, and I pressed my lips to the back of her neck. "I love you, Hailey. You got me. All my days. All my tomorrows. Every night and every morning."

"Every second," she murmured.

I could feel the charge in the air. The sense that everything was going to combust.

Crackles lit on our flesh. Pinpricks that sparked and flamed and whipped.

I ran my fingertips across her back, following the chills that blazed a path across her skin.

Puffs of need left her on wisps, and she started moving again, taking me in slow, measured strokes, my hand bound in her hair and her back brushing my chest as she rocked.

And it felt like we'd become one entity.

One body.

One mind.

One existence.

Our souls meshing.

Our worlds colliding and crashing.

In the aftermath, we'd become something brand new.

I let my hand wander down her belly so I could get to her engorged, needy clit.

The woman wound in desire, need escaping her lips with every roll of her hips.

Heat flared the second I touched her, and I swirled my fingers around that sweet nub.

Hailey began to gasp and writhe, the two of us rising, our spirits lifting, this pleasure gathering the strength of a thousand suns.

I pushed my mouth up to her ear. "Let go," I grunted.

Hailey sank back into my hold and she whispered, "I already did. I'm yours. My heart is in your hands."

I felt her orgasm hit. Spasms lit her up. A full-body glow as she whimpered and writhed.

Her cunt throbbed around my dick as she sucked me even deeper, and that ball of bliss that had wound inside me snapped.

She squeezed me as I came, and I poured and poured into her, this rapture going on and on.

Forever.

Because that's what this was.

Forever.

We both were panting as we hovered high.

Lifted above this reality to a place that was all our own.

I pulled her closer, and I wrapped both arms around her as I pressed my lips to the cap of her shoulder. "I can't wait to spend my life loving you."

She barely shifted to look back at me, that gaze spearing me through. "Good. Because I give every single one of my days to you."

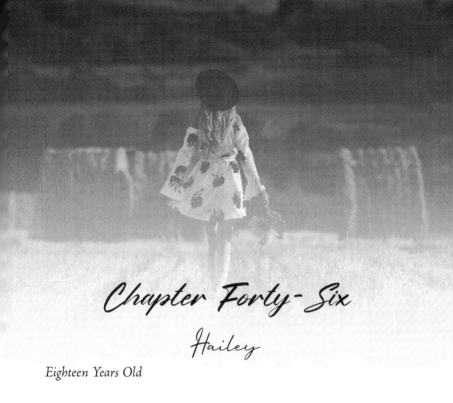

Chapter Forty-Six

Hailey

Eighteen Years Old

HAILEY WAS OUT IN THE STABLES, METHODICALLY brushing the mare's coat. The day was fading away, the light in the massive stables going dim and tossing a stilled peace through the space.

This was her favorite time of day. When most of the hands had finished their jobs and had gone back to their cabins or left the property if they lived offsite. The horses fed and quieted as the bright light melted into ambiguity and the vague, innocuous shadows came out to play.

Hailey continued to stroke the brush down the horse's side, and the sweet girl gave her a chuff as Hailey pressed close, loving her with attention.

She shouldn't have smiled when she felt the presence emerge from behind. The way it took her whole and surrounded her like an embrace.

Brooke would hate her if she knew the secret fantasies Hailey kept of Cody Cooper.

The way she dreamed of him at night and sought him out far too often during the day.

She'd spent the entire summer sneaking out to catch glimpses of him, purposefully placing herself in his vicinity, too often ending up at his side and under the bath of those warm, honey-kissed eyes.

A tingle spread across her flesh, and she peeked back at the man who'd invaded her senses. Sparked her desire and curiosity. A man who'd never even touched her, but she couldn't stop from imagining the way it would feel if he did.

"Hey." His voice was rough where he was hidden in the shadows, so low she knew he was keeping her a secret, too.

"Hey." She whispered it as she fully turned.

Dread clenched her chest when he stepped forward and into a spray of light that slanted in from an open door in the distance.

His expression was contorted in an apology.

That same grief she'd seen him wear so many times that summer etched deeper than before.

Stark and distinct.

Cody glanced over his shoulder, undoubtedly worried someone might catch them. When he found it clear, he slowly moved through the gate she'd left open.

Energy ricocheted through the enclosed area.

Powerful and dark.

Her heart pumped with something she barely understood. With something she didn't quite comprehend.

"I wanted to tell you goodbye." It was coarse coming from his tongue.

He was so handsome it was hard for her to speak. "Are you done for the day?"

Mirthless laughter rolled from his throat, and he shoved his hands into his jeans' pockets. "No. I'm done here, Hailey. With the job. With the ranch."

Anguish jumped into her consciousness.

Sharp and gutting.

That tightening in her chest twined so tight she felt a piece of herself break.

"Oh." Her teeth clamped down on her bottom lip as she fought the moisture that instantly burned at the back of her eyes and raced the length of her trembling throat.

"Fuck," Cody grunted when he saw what was so clearly written on her face. She couldn't hide it. Not right then.

He crossed the three feet that were separating them, and one of those big hands she'd been dreaming about came to her face. He cupped her cheek, his thumb stroking along the hollow of her eye. "Don't cry, darlin'. It fuckin' kills me to see you sad."

She shouldn't be.

She had no right to be.

Sad.

But she tasted that sorrow like a bitter pill.

A tear streaked free, and the words were dropping without her permission. "I don't want you to go."

An emotion passed across his face that she couldn't discern. "I don't want to go, either."

Hailey got brave, and the brush in her hand dropped to the ground as she curled both hands into his tee. "Then stay."

His forehead dropped to hers. Pain poured from his being. She'd gotten good at reading him. When he was torn or sad or struggling. And he was struggling right then.

Just as she had been since the moment that she'd first seen him standing across that field.

Struggling with what she felt.

His aura was all around her.

Spice and cedar and earth.

She wanted to slip into it. Disappear. Give herself over to something that called to her like she'd been missing a piece of her soul and it had finally found its way back to her.

Insane since this man could never belong to her.

He shifted a fraction.

Their mouths were so close to touching.

His breaths pulled into her lungs the same as hers were given to him.

A war went down in his eyes, and his hand curled tighter on her cheek when she whispered, "Cody."

"I can't do this, Hailey."

She was jarred back when he suddenly pulled away with an agonized groan, and the man turned and stormed out without giving her an explanation.

Shaken, Hailey watched him go, that piece of her she was just recognizing splitting in two.

But it was the pained gasp that echoed from the other side of the stables that broke Hailey's heart.

Brooke stood across from her, and she could barely make her out where she was hidden in those shadows, though she could clearly see the betrayal that was slashed all over her best friend's face.

"Brooke." Hailey croaked it.

Brooke's only response was to run, her feet pounding in the opposite direction of where Cody had gone. It took half a second for Hailey to come to her senses, to realize what she had done, and she took off after her, slamming the stall gate shut and racing to catch up.

By the time Hailey made it out to the far end of the stables and into the encroaching night, Brooke was in the distance, running toward the house.

"Brooke!" Hailey shouted behind her. Her boots crunched on the leaves that littered the damp ground.

Brooke ignored her, and she increased her pace, flying up onto the massive front porch and tearing through the door.

Hailey pushed herself as fast as she could go, clambering through the rambling house and up the stairs to her room.

Guilt splintered through her when she found Brooke dragging her bags out from under Hailey's bed.

"What are you doing?" Hailey begged.

Brooke swatted at the tears that rolled down her cheeks. "What does it look like? I'm leaving."

Brooke ripped open the top two drawers of the dresser that

Hailey had given her to stow her things while she stayed there for the summer, and she wadded up two armfuls and shoved them into the suitcase she'd tossed onto the bed.

"No, please don't go."

Brooke scoffed an aggrieved sound. "And stay here with someone who is supposed to be my best friend and instead would betray me like this? I don't think so."

"Brooke…" Hailey surged forward. "Let me explain."

Brooke's laughter was bitter as she stormed across the room to the dresser and gathered up another wad of clothes. "Explain what? That you're fucking the guy I'm in love with? After you know how I feel about him?"

"No, of course not—"

"You can save it because I don't want to hear it. I saw everything I needed to know."

"Please, Brooke…just listen to me. I didn't…" Hailey tried to grab Brooke's hand to stop her. "I would never. Cody and I are just friends."

The second Hailey said it, she knew it was a lie.

Brooke whirled on her. The treachery Hailey had cast was emblazoned in her features. "I saw, Hailey. I saw, and I know."

"Brooke." Shame blistered through Hailey.

Brooke zipped up her suitcase, dragged it to the floor, and hurried across the room. Only she stopped in the doorway and looked back at Hailey. Tears blurred her gorgeous face. "You broke my heart, Hailey. I would never do something like this to you."

"Brooke—" Hailey started to rush back across the room, but Brooke stopped her with the shattered belief written in her expression. "Just leave me alone, Hailey. Leave me alone. I never want to see you again."

Brooke turned and walked out, and Hailey crumbled.

Shame dropping her to her knees.

How could she have done this to Brooke?

To her best friend?

To the one person in the world who had ever really been there for her?

She'd make it right. Apologize. Grovel. Beg. Never look at Cody Cooper again. The way she never should have done in the first place.

She'd find a way.

She'd find a way.

"I promise," she muttered at the vacancy of her door. "I promise, Brooke, I will make it up to you."

Hailey awoke groggy, the hour early, the wispy night still clinging to the earliest hours of the day.

She immediately reached for her phone, going directly to the thread labeled *Bestie Brooke*.

Hailey had sent at least fifteen texts last night.

> **Hailey: Please, come back.**
>
> **Hailey: Can we talk about this?**
>
> **Hailey: I'm so sorry.**
>
> **Hailey: I admit it, I've had a crush on him, but I never acted on it. Only because I care so much about you. I never wanted to feel the way I do, but I couldn't stop it. Please understand.**
>
> **Hailey: You mean so much to me, and hurting you destroys me.**
>
> **Hailey: Please, Brooke, talk to me.**

Agony curled through Hailey's guts when she found all of them unanswered, the same as the phone calls she had made.

Weary, she dragged herself out of bed. She was still wearing the same clothes she'd had on last night, and she shoved her feet into her boots, needing to get out of her room before the walls closed in on her.

Brooke would forgive her. She had to. She just needed to give her time. She'd make her understand.

She prayed for its truth as she let herself out the front door and moved down the long trail toward the stables in the distance. The sky was still darkened, just hinting at gray, a smattering of stars still littered overhead.

Which was why she wasn't sure how she even noticed the shape off to her left, in the covered exterior stalls where the stallions were kept during the summer.

The lump that disfigured the normally flat ground.

She slowed as she squinted, trying to make the shape out, and then she was moving in that direction.

One step.

Then two.

Then panic shocked through her nerves and sent her flying into a frenzy.

She ran for the stalls.

Toward the fence that Brooke had sworn she'd never go close to.

And it was her name that was tearing up Hailey's throat.

"Brooke! Brooke!"

The stallion whinnied, agitated, tromping around the confined space.

But the lump in the middle didn't move.

"Brooke!" Hailey screamed it, terror lighting her through. "Brooke!"

Hailey was scaling the fence and throwing herself into the stall, not caring that the stallion was in there.

Because Brooke was, too. Unmoving, her limbs bent at odd angles. Blood everywhere from where she'd been trampled.

Hailey skidded onto her knees, and she gathered her into her arms. Agony raked from her chest. "Brooke! Brooke! Please, oh God, no, please!"

She hugged her best friend to her chest, rocking her, wailing, besieging toward the sky, "No! Please, no!"

Chapter Forty-Seven

Hailey

DAYLIGHT BARELY CRACKED AT THE HORIZON, THOSE FIRST bleary rays that lit at the edges of the earth and covered it with a feathery haze.

I gazed over at the man who was long asleep, his head rested on the pillow, his arms still firm around me.

They'd been firm around me since he'd finally succumbed to the exhaustion and the pain meds they'd given him for his injuries.

The man had held me until morning.

Refusing to let go.

Even in the depths of slumber his arms had been unyielding.

Sure and strong.

And I knew it was time that I was strong for him.

Taking in a steeling breath, I carefully unwound myself from his hold and slipped out from under his arm that had to weigh as much as a tree.

I froze when he stirred, distorted discontent filtering from between his lips as if even in his slumber his soul had recognized I was no longer at his side.

I breathed out a sigh when he settled back in, then I pushed from the bed and tiptoed around the room to gather my clothes from the floor.

I dressed as quietly as I could, then I glanced back once more at his sleeping form, my chest squeezing in a swell of devotion.

Then I crept out the door.

Silence swam through my house since Maddie and Lolly were still asleep. I grabbed my purse from where I'd dropped it on the floor next to the front door last night and let myself out into the waking day.

It was beautiful out, those last cool moments of the night hanging on before the sun would fully take to the sky.

I didn't wait around in the peace of it.

Not when that's what I was fighting for.

Peace.

The true fullness of it.

I rushed to my SUV and hopped in. Anger sprang to my chest when I put the key into the ignition. I didn't hesitate to turn it over. I knew Pruitt didn't want me dead.

He wanted me pathetic and afraid.

Destitute.

Subject to his will and his hand.

He just didn't mind hurting the ones I cared about to get me there.

I backed out of the driveway, my hands shaking as I put it in drive and headed through my small neighborhood.

When I pulled out onto the two-lane road, I floored it.

⌒⁕⌒

A quiver of unease rolled through me as I lifted my hand to the door of the quaint house that was nestled in a family neighborhood in Time River, the trees high and the lawns manicured.

My fist rapped against the wood.

Even though the sun was steadily climbing into the sky, I shivered.

Apprehension ripped down my spine.

This was it.

There was no turning back.

It seemed like it took forever before movement finally rustled from behind the door, and the curtains swished on the window.

One second later, metal screeched as the locks were disengaged.

Savannah stood there with her daughter Olivia in front of her, a hand set over the little girl's chest.

Concern twisted up Savannah's face as she studied me. "Hailey? What are you doing here?"

"Hi, Miss Hailey! It's so good to see you. Did you bring Maddie with you? I love that I got to meet her, and me and my cousin Evelyn had the best time with her. We think she should always be with us."

Emotion clotted my throat, and I turned my attention to the little girl. "She's not with me right now, but I promise we'll get you both together to play again soon. How's that sound?"

"That sounds great! I'm going to make her a special invitation for you to take with you so she can come to my house and play on my playset!" She looked up at Savannah. "Is that okay, Mommy?"

I could feel the dread dripping from the woman as she ran a tender hand down the back of the little girl's head. "That's fine. Why don't you run and do it really quick so I can talk with Ms. Hailey?"

"On it! Stay right there, I'll be right back," Olivia peeped, and she disappeared back inside.

Savannah turned back to me, the same question I hadn't been able to answer coming low from her tongue. "What are you doing here? Are you okay?"

"I need to talk to Ezra."

She glanced around like she was looking for a threat before the terror was rolling off her tongue. "Ezra just got word from the station about what happened at Cambrey Pines yesterday. Is Cody hurt? Why didn't you call us?"

Guilt climbed up my throat, and in a bout of disquiet, I twisted my fingers. "Cody insisted that we didn't call. He wanted to be the one to tell everyone himself."

He'd known they were going to be distraught, just like it was clear Savannah was right then.

She blew out a sigh. "Well, the second Ezra heard about it, he was in his truck and heading to Cody's house."

Distress buzzed in my being.

"What is it?" she pressed.

"I really needed to talk to him. In private."

A frown pulled across her face. "Are you in trouble?"

I wavered, attention dropping to the ground because I'd carried this secret with me for so long.

Welcome to the family you didn't know you had.

The memory of what she'd whispered to me as she'd hugged me as we'd been leaving the ranch on Saturday twisted through my mind, and my heart thudded.

Because I trusted her, and it was time I stopped hiding.

Stopped hiding in plain sight.

"I am, and I need Ezra's help, but I need to do it without Cody knowing because I don't want him getting more involved than he's already been. I can't cause him any more danger than I already have."

She looked over my shoulder like Ezra might appear there. "He left twenty minutes ago. You probably passed him on the road as soon as you left."

Anxiety billowed. "Okay, well…can you call him and let him know I need to talk to him? Cody is at my house. Tell him to check in with Cody, and not to leave until I get there. I'll talk to him outside."

"Of course." She hesitated then reached for me, taking my hand. "Is there anything I can do to help? I hate this, Hailey. Hate that I can feel the fear rolling off you."

My head shook. "It's just time I stood for what's right, and I'm going to need Ezra's help to do that."

She breathed out the worry. "Okay. But I'm here. Whatever you need."

I squeezed her hand back. "Your friendship is enough. I'm so grateful for it. For all of you. For making my daughter and me feel like we belong."

"That's because you do."

Footsteps pounded from within the house, the clamor growing louder with each eager thud.

Olivia was suddenly pushing back in front of Savannah, an eager smile on her face. She rocked back on her heels as she handed me a piece of paper that was folded into a small square and had a bunch of pink tape and heart stickers all over it.

To my new best friend Maddie was scrawled in the middle.

"Would you please give this to Maddie, Miss Hailey?"

My heart clutched as I accepted it. "Absolutely."

"Go on and get your hands washed for breakfast," Savannah told her, though I knew she was making an excuse to get me alone.

"Okay, Mommy! Bye, Miss Hailey."

"Bye," I whispered, and she ran back into the house.

I looked up at Savannah. Care and worry vibrated from her.

"I'll text Ezra right now and let him know you're on your way."

"Thank you."

Throwing her arms around me, she hugged me tight. "Always and anything, Hailey. Just…be careful and text me later."

"I will."

She nodded against me, reluctant to let me go.

I finally turned and jogged back down the sidewalk that cut through the middle of their yard to my Durango that was parked at the curb.

I was quick to hop in, started it, and whipped a U-turn in the middle of the street. I wound back out of the neighborhood and hit the road that led back to Hendrickson.

My heart was lodged in my throat as I traveled.

The beat of my heart palpable there.

Anticipation and dread thick.

The forest grew up on all sides.

Dense and deep.

The rays of the rising sun blipped through the leaves of the trees, flashing above me as I drove beneath.

I wound through the desolate woods, anxiety gripping me in a vise as I raced to get back to my house.

Suddenly, I was hit with that sense again. The creepy vibe that slithered over my skin as I took the curves of the deserted, winding road.

Alarm pooled and sweat slicked my flesh.

On instinct, I glanced in the rearview mirror.

The car behind me had come from out of nowhere, trailing me at a distance.

Flashes of metallic black and the glimmering of glass striking in the rays that speared through the leaves.

The same car that had freaked me out all those weeks ago.

The same car Pruitt had been driving when he'd followed us to the gas station this last weekend.

Panic surged, my throat closing off, and I pushed down on the accelerator.

Though this time, it didn't stay back and match my speed.

It increased, gaining on me so fast it made me dizzy.

I pushed my SUV harder, flying around the corners, heart hammering out of my chest as I drove as fast as I could.

I took a sharp curve.

And the car behind me?

It flew around me, taking it sharper and cutting me off.

A scream ripped out of me as I slammed on my brakes.

My SUV went into a skid, and my back tire hit the dirt shoulder of the road.

And I couldn't control it.

Couldn't stop my car from fishtailing one direction then the other.

Couldn't stop its slide as it careened off the steep embankment on the side.

My eyes were frozen wide as fear tore through my spirit as my SUV flew through the underbrush.

Bouncing and jarring and out of control, heading directly for a giant tree.

I screamed when I slammed into it. Metal ground and glass shattered as the Durango twisted around the trunk.

Pain splintered up my left side.

The airbag deployed, and my skin felt as if it were being singed as I smashed against it.

An instant later, the bedlam quieted, just the hum of an engine fan melding with the ringing in my ears.

Disoriented, I fought for my senses, to ward off the shock that wanted to hold me hostage.

I fumbled to get my seatbelt undone, and I could barely get my hands to cooperate as I struggled to get the door wrenched open.

A daze clouded my mind as I staggered back up through the woods.

But it was horror that consumed when I made it out through the break in the trees.

Because Pruitt was glaring at me from across the distance.

And he wasn't alone.

Chapter Forty-Eight
Cody

I JARRED AWAKE TO THE POUNDING AT THE FRONT DOOR, confused as I blinked into the murky light that covered Hailey's room. The covers were rumpled beside me, and I didn't have time to grumble about the fact she wasn't there to wake up in my arms before another round of battering railed at the door.

That was right about the time a call started buzzing from my phone where it rested on the nightstand.

Ezra.

Shit.

No doubt, I was about to get clobbered for not calling the dude yesterday to let him know what had gone down, and I wasn't so sure that statement was in the metaphorical sense. He was bound to be pissed.

But the last thing I'd needed was my mother rushing down to that hospital terrified. Thinking she was going to lose another man in her life.

I needed to show up at her door, whole and alive, and tell her myself.

Blowing out a sigh, I scrubbed a hand over my head, trying not to wince at the blister of pain that throbbed from every inch of my bruised body. The good stuff they'd pumped me full of yesterday had long since vacated my system, and I would be a liar if I said I wasn't hurting.

Instead of grumbling about it, I thanked fuck that I was still standing.

That these legs could carry me from Hailey's bedroom and toward the front door that was getting battered again, the damn thing rattling on its hinges.

I was looking around, wondering where the fuck Hailey was if she wasn't in bed, my chest stretching in a bid of worry when she wasn't already there to answer the door.

"Hailey?" I called, figuring Ezra banging at the door had woken up the entire house, anyway.

Footsteps pounded, but it was Lolly who made it to the end of the hall at the same time as I was peering through the peephole to verify it was in fact Ezra.

"What's going on?" Lolly muttered, her face still bleary from sleep.

"Don't worry, Lolly, it's just Ezra, one of my best friends. Pretty sure he caught wind of what happened yesterday afternoon."

"Well, you'd better let him in before he busts that door down and wakes up the entire neighborhood."

I undid the locks and Ezra barged in the second I turned the knob, the giant of a man storming into the house raring mad.

"What the fuck, Cody?" he demanded the second he saw me. In a flash, his attention had skated over my frame, categorizing my injuries.

One second later, he was crushing me in his arms in some kind of bear hug. "Fuck, are you okay?"

"Yeah, man, I'm okay."

"Good, then I'm going to kick the crap out of you for not calling me," he said as he stepped back, eyes scanning me again. "What the hell happened?"

"Was getting in my truck at the end of the day. I opened the door and everything went boom."

Fury gritted Ezra's teeth. "This Pruitt bastard?"

I pushed a shaky hand through my hair. "Likely."

"Shit," Ezra spat. "I'm going to get with the Sheriff of Hendrickson, and we are going to nail this fucker."

"Yeah. We have to take this monster down. Before he gets to Hailey."

That sent my gaze roving, and another bite of unease rolled through me when Hailey still wasn't standing by my side.

"Do you know where Hailey is?" I asked Lolly.

Her head barely shook. "I just came out of my room to see what the commotion was about."

Ezra sighed. "I'm not sure what's going on here, Cody, but Savannah just called as I was pulling up out front. Said Hailey had been at the house and needed to talk to me. She's on her way back here."

Trepidation thudded deep. "Why the hell would she leave without telling me?"

I didn't know who I was asking.

Ezra.

Lolly.

Myself.

The only thing I knew was things weren't sitting right. The energy this morning felt off.

Our rhythm off beat.

It climbed from the depths of me and into my consciousness, a warning that had started to blare.

"Do you know what it's about?" I pinned Ezra with the question.

His exhalation was heavy. "I'm not even supposed to be saying anything to you since she asked to talk to me in private, but no, I don't."

That trepidation spiked. Daggers of unease.

"Fuck," I rumbled toward the floor.

"I'm sure it's about what happened yesterday. Her ex. I'm sure she's blaming herself right about now," Ezra surmised.

"None of this is her fault." Lolly's voice was haggard, worry flooding out on her raspy voice.

Both Ezra and I swiveled her way.

Terror colored her features, so heavy and distinct. Different than I'd ever seen in her before.

"I knew neither of them would let her go." She whispered it like a secret.

That alarm blared louder, a siren that screamed in my ears and ricocheted through my being. "What are you saying, Lolly?"

She looked sick. Her skin pallid and green. Fear throttling the overabundance of life she always exuded. "Pruitt and her father."

Uncertainty pinched my brow, dread gathering fast and overflowing my senses. "Her father? What are you talking about?"

I tried to keep the desperation out of my voice, but there was no stopping the way it whipped from my tongue.

She wrung her frail fingers. "I love him, love him so much, and God knows I tried hard to raise him right, but my son still turned out a bad man. And I was hoping beyond hope that once Hailey came back here, he'd see the error of his ways. Hoped with all of me that he'd changed."

A wave of foreboding crashed against my spirit. My throat thickened as my mind whirred through her implication. Wrought with the insinuation of her suggestion.

The past spun. A blur through my mind that was becoming too clear. "What do you mean?"

The words were gravel.

A plea.

Lolly blanched, and I stood there staring as horror and grief slashed across her weathered face.

Her chin trembled when she spoke. "Hailey marrying Pruitt wasn't an accident. I knew what Douglas had in mind the first time I saw that slimy weasel standing in his office. I knew he was going to force them together. Knew what he was planning. Knew they both were crooked. Wicked to the core. Only someone who is truly evil would pull someone that was as sweet and innocent as Hailey into their schemes."

Sickness coiled in my guts, and awareness hovered like a drone carrying weapons of mass destruction overhead.

"The illegal gambling. Your son was involved?" My question scraped the room.

Lolly tugged her robe tighter as if it could act as a shield. "Involved in it? He's the mastermind. The ringleader. Always one step ahead at keeping his name clean, pinning the blame on those running his dirty deeds. Pruitt is just another of his minions. He'd told me he'd given it up. That he was going clean. He promised."

She choked around the new wound that had been inflicted.

"Obviously, it was a lie, but there is no way my son can continue to hide the way it has tarnished his soul. And I won't pretend like I don't know the extent of it for a second longer."

Horror jumped between us when I met Ezra's eye.

A second later, I was turning on my heel and rushing for the room where I'd left my phone. I snatched it up and dialed Hailey's number.

It rang four times before her voicemail came on. "It's Hailey. Leave a message."

A sinking sensation came over me. One that had me feeling like I was getting dragged to the bottom of the ocean.

Clutching my phone, I rushed back out of the room. "She didn't answer."

Ezra was trying her again before I finished the sentence, and he gave a minute shake of his head when she didn't answer his call, either.

Panic surged, pumping fast with the beat of my blood. "We need to find her. Get to her before someone else does."

That was the second before a scream reverberated from Maddie's room.

My eyes blew wide, and I ran around Lolly and down the hall, throwing Maddie's door open.

Rage blistered.

A forest fire.

Maddie thrashed in a man's hold who'd torn her out of bed, the fucker wearing all black and a ski mask.

This wasn't happening. I wouldn't let this happen.

"You motherfucker." I didn't give myself time to process what I was doing. I simply hurtled across the room.

400 | A.L. JACKSON

He lifted his hand and pointed a gun my way. He popped off a shot right as I dove for the floor.

Maddie screamed.

Screamed and screamed.

And my goddamn heart shattered at the sound.

My sweet little Button.

The one who beamed all her adorable, innocent light.

I couldn't let this happen to her.

And I fought harder, reaching out to get the bastard by the ankle just as he angled the gun down.

"Freeze!" Ezra's voice banged through the room, and that point-blank shot didn't come for me.

It was lifted and fired in Ezra's direction.

The fiend kept shooting as he backed out.

Gunshots rang out across the room.

I prayed to God Ezra took cover because there was no chance that he could fire back. Not with the piece of shit using Maddie as a shield. He kept firing the whole way as he jumped back out the window.

And the shots...they just kept coming...just the same as the pain that burst in my body.

Chapter Forty-Nine

Brooke

Eighteen Years Old

THE SUITCASE BOUNCED ON THE STEPS BEHIND HER AS SHE hurried downstairs. Tears blurred her eyes and blades of hurt gouged her heart into a mangled, mutilated mess.

It sucked so bad when you loved someone so much and they didn't love you back. It sucked even worse when that person was in love with your best friend.

Brooke had known it the whole summer. Had known it in the way Cody had watched Hailey like she was an untouchable angel that he admired from afar.

She choked on a tiny sound when she hit the bottom landing and the thought slammed through her aching mind.

Cody wasn't wrong. Hailey *was* an angel.

Brooke knew that, too.

She knew that Hailey had watched him the same way, though she had tried to pretend as if she were unaffected. She had tried to be supportive and encouraging while Brooke had thrown herself at a man who so clearly didn't return her feelings. A man she had told lies to, assuring him that the fling they were sharing hadn't meant a thing when she'd wanted it to mean everything.

She knew.

She knew.

But that didn't mean it wasn't agonizing. It didn't mean that seeing Cody embracing Hailey the way she'd longed for him to embrace her hadn't cut through her like a dull, cold knife.

It was that pain that drove her through the quickly darkening house and out onto the front porch where the sky was stretched in a wispy gray, the west edge only tinged in pink.

There, she stopped, trying to catch her breath.

To see through the disorder the sight of Cody and Hailey had stirred her into.

The slap of betrayal clashing with the smack of truth of what Hailey had said.

Hailey would never intentionally hurt her, and if she was being logical—rational and real—she'd admit that Hailey had been in the same type of pain every time she'd had to watch Brooke slink into the darkness with Cody.

God. Why did life have to be so complicated? She'd only wanted to have a fun summer with her bestie before she left for college, and now they were here.

Both in love with the same man.

Her phone started buzzing in her back pocket. Hailey, no doubt. She'd answer her later. When she wasn't so upset. When the sting had faded.

Right then, she just needed to find a place to lick her wounds and come to terms.

Because she didn't want to leave town like this next week.

With this ache or the riff stretching between her and her best friend.

Inhaling a shaky breath, she swiped some of the tears from her face and wheeled her suitcase across the porch toward the side steps where she'd parked her car.

She slowed when she heard hushed voices carrying from the

direction of Mr. Wagner's office that was tucked just on the other side of the wall, a man she'd taken to calling Dad over the summer since hers sucked and Hailey's had been kind enough to let her stay there.

The two people talking must have been standing outside the office door.

She wavered when she heard the angered displeasure that reverberated from Hailey's father when he normally spoke gently, and her feet quieted to nothing as she tried to decipher if she should keep walking to her car and surely interrupt the intense conversation or stay hidden until it played out.

"Asshole seemed desperate enough. He came through on every job I gave him the entire summer. Passed every test. Thought he was going to be game." The voice sounded familiar, and Brooke struggled to pinpoint who it was.

"Yeah, well, he's not, and this has now become a very big problem," Douglas growled. "Cody Cooper cannot be out there knowing what he knows. He goes to ground."

A block of ice slipped down Brooke's spine. Shock and confusion confounded her senses.

No. There was no way Hailey's father was saying what she thought he was.

She had to be mistaken.

Fear tumbling through her, she edged closer to the wall, concealing herself more, her heart battering at her chest.

"I sent him away saying I didn't want to see him on the property again, told him to keep his mouth shut or else I was going to turn him in. I believe he's afraid enough of that happening that he'll stick to it for a bit. I want you to disappear from the ranch for a couple days and then take care of it, and do it clean," he continued.

"The guy has a reputation for partying."

Brooke finally recognized the second voice.

Brent.

The ranch manager.

"I'll make it look like he had too much to drink and took a little dip in the lake and didn't make it back out."

"Good. I don't want any ties to this ranch. Make sure it's done far away from here."

"I know the drill," Brent said, so casual, like this happened on the regular.

Terror shivered through Brooke, and she pressed herself tighter to the shadows that spread across the wall, locking her throat to stop the cries that wanted to erupt.

They were going to kill Cody.

Oh God, they were going to kill Cody.

Why? What did he know? What had he done?

She had to stop this. Warn him.

"That's why you're the one person I can count on," Mr. Wagner said. "After this, I want you in Austin to keep your eye on Pruitt. I want to know I can fully trust him before I send my daughter there."

"Yes, sir. I'll text you when it's done and I'm on my way to Texas."

"Good. Be safe."

Be safe?

Be safe?

Brooke wanted to screech it, unable to comprehend what she'd heard. Nausea curled her stomach and fear saturated her skin. She pressed to the wall, petrified when footsteps started to thud on the wood planks, coming her way.

She pressed her hand to her mouth, praying to cover the sound of her breaths as Brent rounded the corner and started across the main porch. Her eyes were wide in horror as he passed.

She didn't dare inhale until he had fully made it down the main porch steps and strode to the work truck parked in the distance, didn't move a muscle until he started the truck and whipped it around in the dirt.

Then she sagged, her shoulders slumping as she stumbled forward to watch his taillights disappear down the driveway. Both relief and horror clawed at her insides.

Then her stomach toppled over when she heard the regret in the voice that came from behind. "Ahh, Brooke, I wish you hadn't heard that."

Chapter Fifty

Hailey

I SQUINTED THROUGH THE DAZE AND THE DUST THAT BILLOWED through the morning air.

My mind and spirit trapped on an out-of-control tilt-a-whirl.

Spinning.

Spinning.

Spinning.

"Get in the car, Hailey." The man I'd adored for all my life, one I'd held on a pedestal, the one I'd believed good and right and caring, opened the back door of the black Mercedes where it sat off to the side of the road about fifty feet away.

My father.

His tone was grim and his expression was hard.

My knees wobbled. The world canting, the sky a spiraling vortex overhead.

Pain splintered through my body, the very real one that burned up my left side and the one that felt like my heart had been pulverized.

Crushed.

No longer recognizable.

"I gave you plenty of time to come to your senses, but you've run out of it," he said.

I blinked, immobile, frozen. Still trying to process that my father had actually run me off the road. Trying to process that he was here. That he was doing this, whatever brutality it was he intended.

A shriek ripped free when a hand suddenly latched onto my wrist and jerked me forward.

Pruitt.

Vileness oozed over me in a slick of depravity as he pressed his mouth close to my face, and I felt the barrel of a gun press up into my ribs. "It's time you listened."

"Bring her here before someone comes by," my father ordered, and Pruitt dragged me forward as I thrashed and flailed, my sense of fight or flight finally coming back to me.

I intended them both.

Pruitt tightened his hold.

Painfully wrenching down on my wrist, so hard I knew it would bruise.

"Watch yourself," my father warned, his attention on Pruitt, as if he were suddenly concerned for my well-being.

I would have laughed at the absurdity of it if I wasn't currently gulping through the fear.

Pruitt gritted his teeth, though he loosened his grip a fraction as he continued to haul me toward the car.

I fought him harder, my boots skidding on the loose gravel, arms flailing as he shoved me into the backseat.

One second later, a car came around the bend.

I screamed, begging for someone to notice, but it blazed by without having any indication that anything was wrong.

But it was.

It was wrong.

So wrong.

Everything.

Everything.

Pruitt pushed me into the middle before he crammed in beside me, and my father rounded the front and got into the driver's seat. He eased back onto the road.

"How could you do this?" The words were croaked and bent in two, my eyes on my father's cheek that was reflected in the rearview mirror.

The muscle ticked, and he glanced up, eyes meeting mine. "I've always had bigger plans for you, Hailey. You just weren't ready to take them on yet. You were too soft. It was Pruitt's job to guide you. Mold you into who I needed you to be. He didn't do the best job of it."

Disgust barreled through me, sickness gliding through my veins as awareness began to seep into my consciousness.

Pruitt flinched at my side, barely contained anger vibrating from his flesh.

Hatred.

I could feel it. The way he hated my father.

Hated that he was in control.

I blinked again as my mind spiraled through the information that I'd gathered on Pruitt.

His crime ring went deep and dark.

Illegal gambling. Racketeering. Money laundering.

Murder.

I'd had an inclination that there might be someone above Pruitt. That he wasn't at the helm.

And it was my father—my father who was in control the entire time.

All the worry I'd possessed, the way I'd been scared to go to the authorities because I was worried his connection with Pruitt might somehow implicate him when he was innocent.

Except he wasn't innocent.

Nausea crawled over me like a physical sickness, my flesh going clammy and my mind getting warped.

"What do you want from me?" It would have been a whimper if there wasn't so much spite behind it.

Pruitt leaned in and ran his nose down the side of my cheek. Vomit pooled in my mouth.

"Do you not understand it yet, Hailey? You've always been my prize. My gift for bringing my father's world into your father's. You are the key to this merger. I told you that you were mine. I take over once your father is gone. And without you? This whole deal falls apart. You wouldn't want that to happen, now, would you?"

He dragged the barrel of the gun up the top of my leg.

Shivers crawled like a thousand spiders skittering across my skin. Poisonous.

Toxic.

"I won't go anywhere with you." I spat the words, though they were soggy with horror.

Pruitt slung an arm around my shoulders, and he crushed me against him, his mouth at my cheek.

"See, now that's where you're wrong. I'm taking you home. Where you belong. Don't worry, I already had one of my guys swing by that hovel where you were staying to pick up our daughter. He took care of that hick who thought he could have what is mine at the same time. Two birds and all of that."

Cody.

Agony tore and ripped.

I thrashed against Pruitt. "No."

No.

God, no.

Please.

Pruitt tsked, taunting, "You know, your dear daddy here has been trying to get rid of Cody Cooper for years."

My father's jaw clenched, and his hands flexed against the wheel.

"Ever since Cody discovered the ring in Eddings. Of course, he had to call that execution off when your friend happened to overhear the plans and it became far more important to silence her than it was to go after Cody. He couldn't have two *accidental* deaths so close together, now, could he? Especially since each of them could be tied to the ranch?"

Another shot of grief rang out.

Bullet after bullet piercing my soul.

Brooke?

Oh God.

What was he saying? My father...he...

I spluttered over the gutting disbelief. The shattering sorrow that surged and swept and overcame.

Pruitt grinned and his dark eyes gleamed. He knew exactly what Brooke had meant to me. He was the one who'd comforted me after her death. Wrapped me up and promised to make me better. And now he was taunting me with the truth of what had really happened.

A sob ripped from my lungs.

Unstoppable.

The pain unbearable.

Brooke.

Cody.

I rocked, unable to sit still beneath the atrocities that ravaged me like the squall of a hurricane.

"Personally, I think your father never should have allowed Cody to live, but he's always been a little on the soft side," Pruitt continued, completely casual.

"We kept an eye on him for years, waiting for him to step out of bounds. And he finally did. Don't worry, though, sweetheart, I made sure to put an end to that problem." Pruitt's mouth was at my ear, his voice turning vicious. "He had to die just for the fact that he touched you."

"No!" I screamed it. "I'll kill you."

Pruitt laughed and sat back in the seat, his easy words tossed at my father. "Maybe she's more like you than we thought. I guess it's a good start."

Chapter Fifty-One
Cody

EZRA CAME RUNNING BACK UP THE ROAD JUST AS I WAS lumbering out the front door. His gun slack at his side and regret on his face. "He got away."

Rage boiled my blood, and I gritted my teeth against the agony as I stumbled down the porch steps.

Worry cut into Ezra's brow as he ran my direction, and he shouted, "Just sit, man. I called for backup. An ambulance will be here in five."

"Yeah, that's not going to happen," I said as I shuffled down the walkway, leaving a trail of blood behind me as I went.

The shot that had struck the outside of my thigh had saturated my sweats, and I had my hand pressed to the one that had hit low on the left side of my abdomen.

"Fuck, Cody, you need to sit." Ezra tried to stop me when he got to me, panic whirring around him, and I shrugged him off as I headed toward my truck.

"Have to get to them."

"We're going to, I promise you, but we need to get you taken care of first."

I spun on this guy who was more a brother than a friend, my hand flying out to his shoulder. I squeezed it in emphasis. "Don't ask me not to fight for them, Ezra. You were in this exact position not that long ago, and there was not a goddamn thing in this world that could have stopped you from going after Savannah. From protecting her. Don't ask me not to do the same."

"But you've been shot. Were almost killed yesterday. You can't—"

"I might be bleeding, Ezra, but they're the blood in my veins. They're the ones who've made me whole. And if something happens to one of them? That's what would be the end of me. That's what would destroy me."

Ezra's exhale was heavy, his nod slight as he came to acceptance. "Fine, but I'm driving, and you're staying in the truck and going to let me do my job."

I didn't take the time to argue with him, I just hobbled as fast as I fucking could to his SUV and slipped into the front passenger's seat just as he was hopping into the driver's. But it was Lolly yanking at the back handle that had him pausing.

"Lolly," I breathed. "Fuck. Go back inside."

"Open the door, both of you. Those are my girls, too. And I won't sit idle until we have them back."

Ezra looked at me in reluctance, and I winced, every inch of me on fire, and I gritted through the words, "There isn't any use arguing with her. She's as stubborn as they come. And we need to go. Now."

Ezra unlocked the door, and Lolly was shouting as she hopped in, "Get to Wagner Ranch. There's no chance my son isn't involved in this."

Ezra tore out of the neighborhood with his lights flashing, on his radio giving instruction for any deputies in the area to be on the lookout for the black SUV that had been peeling up the street when he'd rushed out to try to stop the intruder.

To proceed with caution as it held a four-year-old little girl who'd been abducted.

My guts twisted in a vicious knot as he gave her description.

Maddie.

Maddie.

And Hailey.

Felt like I was being asphyxiated as we traveled. Oxygen ceasing to exist. That aching knot in my gut promising they had her, too.

The hour it took to travel to the deep woods outside of Langmire where the ranch was located was the longest hour of my entire fuckin' life.

Time moving as slow as the gnarled hands of the clock imprinted on my chest.

Frozen, that moment that had marked me burning like a bitch.

The moment I'd believed I'd started living on borrowed time. Sure that one day the mistakes of that summer were going to catch up to me.

They finally had.

But I'd had no idea how twisted and entwined those circumstances were going to be.

When we finally made it to the turnoff, Ezra took the right onto the long, single-lane road at a clip, wheels skidding and peeling out as he hit the dirt. He punched the gas hard as soon as we'd righted, the engine roaring, and another police cruiser came flying in right behind us.

"Please be here, please be here." The words barely made it from my muttering lips, praying to God that we were in time. That they hadn't already taken off with the two of them. That I wasn't too late.

Because I didn't know this motherfucker Pruitt's intentions. Didn't know how Douglas Wagner could have been so callous that he'd send some assassin-clad villain to kidnap his own granddaughter.

Didn't know anything but the truth that I would chase them to the ends of the earth. I wouldn't stop until they were safe in my arms. Until Pruitt and Douglas had gone down, even if it meant I went down with them.

"They will be there," Lolly said from the back. Her angst roiled in the cab, a deep-seated grief that spiraled and shook.

"They're going to be okay," I grunted, not sure exactly who I was promising.

"Fuck." A low roll of dubiety dropped from Ezra's lips when an SUV came into view, coming at us from the opposite direction.

Flying fast and kicking up a storm of dust behind them.

A black bullet speeding our direction.

"Is it the same one you saw taking off from Hailey's?" I could barely squeeze the question from between my lips.

"Yup," Ezra said.

The asshole didn't slow as the lights and sirens came at him.

He accelerated.

Dread and disbelief whipped through my insides as this monster gave way to a dangerous game of chicken.

"Hold on," Ezra ordered, his voice calm, but I could feel the tension radiate from his pores as he slammed on his brakes and cut hard to the right. Our SUV skidded, dust flying and the cab jostling. My heart vibrated a manic beat as we came to a quick stop sitting sideways across the road, fully blocking it from the SUV that was still barreling our way.

The cruiser behind us did the same, though they went left. The two vehicles came to a rest completely obstructing the road and shoulders, trees rising up high on each side to create a full blockade.

There was nowhere for them to go.

My eyes were wide as they just kept coming.

No care for the lives that were hinged inside that metal box. No care for themselves. No care for us.

They weren't more than fifty yards back when the fucker finally slammed on his brakes, skidding hard and coming to a screeching standstill about forty feet away. Both front doors flew open at the same time as Ezra was out on his feet, using his door as a shield with his gun propped in the opening between it and the windshield.

"Hands up!" Ezra shouted.

Douglas stepped out of the passenger's side, and he did lift a hand, only that hand wielded a gun. Brent, the motherfucking ranch manager who'd gotten me trapped, stepped out from the driver's side, holding up what was likely the same gun he'd shot me with earlier.

"How could he?" Lolly croaked from the backseat. "Shameful. Wrong."

"Toss the guns to the side and get onto your stomachs on the ground," Ezra shouted.

"I'm afraid I'm not going to be able to accommodate that," Douglas called back, his voice firm and confident, like he was in control and Ezra was subject to his command. "We have a plane we need to catch."

Fucker had gotten so used to getting away with this bullshit for so long that he held no fear.

But the bastard should be very, very afraid.

"You don't, and I shoot," Ezra called back in warning.

I could see the two officers from the cruiser behind me were also out of their cars, crouched and angled, ready to fire.

The back door suddenly opened and Pruitt slid out, dragging Hailey with him. He had her back to his chest and a gun was pressed to her temple.

My lungs fucking collapsed.

I could hear her whimpering. Crying as she flailed in the barbarity of his arms. Those eyes that were the color of the river so wide.

Bottomless and toiling with terror.

A blister of fury snapped across my skin, the blood boiling in my veins overflowing, bubbling out from the bullet holes the monster had left in my body.

Hands shaking, I pulled out the handgun I'd grabbed from the small gun safe I'd stowed in my duffle under the bed when I'd gone into Hailey's room to get my boots.

I'd known all the way to my guts that I was going to need it.

I'd known it was going to come to this because I sure as hell wasn't going to allow Ezra to be the one to stand in the line of fire for me.

Not when he had three kids and another baby on the way.

Cranking open the door, I stepped out. A swell of lightheadedness nearly dropped me to my knees. I'd lost more blood than I'd thought.

Or maybe it was just the blinding rage that made it that I couldn't see straight.

I could see the gasp rip out of Hailey when she saw me.

Energy slashed through the air.

The connection thrumming.

Her relief and my desperation.

Pruitt frowned in surprise and loathing.

Yeah, I'm not dead yet, motherfucker.

Ezra's shouts filled the air. "Do not get out of the truck, Cody! Stay inside!"

But I wouldn't sit there and do nothing.

I'd made a lot of promises in my life.

Ones to my father.

Ones to my mother.

But the one I'd made Hailey blared.

A siren in my soul.

I wouldn't let him hurt her or Maddie.

I angled up to the front of the SUV just as Brent edged to the side of the door, douchebag aiming at me. I popped off a shot in his direction before he got the chance. Scum toppled to the ground like the pile of shit he was.

It was enough of a surprise to make Pruitt let his guard down for one second, and Hailey, that fucking brave, amazing girl, took the opportunity to ram her elbow into his gut. A jolt of pain burst from his mouth just as she broke out of his hold, and she turned to fight him while Ezra started yelling, "Get on the ground! Get on the ground!"

It was the trigger that sparked the chaos.

Pruitt began to fire, as did Douglas, and Ezra and the other officers were shouting. Shots sounded from every direction.

Smoke and dust billowed, and urgency pushed me out around Ezra's SUV.

Sweat slicked my skin, fear pounding my bones to dust.

But it wasn't fear for myself.

It was for the two girls who deserved a magical life. Every moment and every hour and every good thing this life might have to offer.

"Get down, Cody!" I heard Ezra shouting it, but I couldn't take it in.

Douglas curled into a ball at the side of the SUV, his hands going to the back of his head like that was going to protect it, and I kept moving toward Pruitt who was reaching down to grab a fistful of Hailey's hair to drag her back to standing.

He stalled when he felt me coming, and he lifted his gun, spitting, "I warned you to stay out of our business."

A figure suddenly stepped out of the woods behind him. Lolly barefoot and wrapped in her floral robe.

Dread covered me like I'd fallen through the cracks of a frozen lake. What the hell did she think she was doing?

"It's already over, Pruitt. You might as well give up now because there's not a chance you get my granddaughter. I won't allow either of you to destroy her. She won't live like me and her mother had to."

She was holding a rock in her left hand.

"Now step away from my granddaughter."

When he started to whirl her direction at her voice, she swung it, clipping him in the side.

"Lolly!" I shouted it, a warning, a plea, and I started running that way. But I couldn't make it to her before Pruitt spat, "You stupid bitch."

Then a single gunshot rang out.

It was loud, penetrating the air in a cloud of obliterating darkness. A total eclipse. A hollow echo that reverberated through the heavens just as the woman dropped to the ground.

A toppling of color and life and belief.

Hailey screamed from where she was on her hands and knees. Screamed and screamed as she started to crawl for her. "Oh my God, Lolly! No, Lolly!"

Pruitt started to turn back around to get to Hailey when two more shots rang out. One from Ezra and one from another officer.

Pruitt jolted backward as each penetrated his chest, and the gun slipped from his hand as his body hit the ground right next to Lolly.

Gathering the last strength that I had, I stumbled forward. I made it to my knees behind Hailey the second she made it to her grandmother.

And I wrapped my arms around her as she began to weep.

Chapter Fifty-Two

Hailey

"LOLLY, OH MY GOD, LOLLY."

Torment ripped through my insides, tearing me to shreds as I struggled to gather Lolly in my arms. Lolly who was gurgling and choking.

Frantic, I pulled her against me, her head cradled in my lap. "Lolly. It's okay. I'm right here. You're going to be okay."

The words toppled out. Pleas of desperation.

Her grayed eyes that were wide in shock softened when they focused on me, and I ran my hands through her hair. "I'm right here," I whispered again.

Strong arms circled me from behind.

Cody.

Cody who I'd thought I'd lost.

Cody who was here. Cody who had stood for us. Cody who had been willing to give everything.

Cody who wrapped me up and pulled Lolly closer to us.

Holding us in the sanctuary of his massive arms.

He peered down over my shoulder at Lolly who was bleeding in my arms, her name constantly falling from my tongue. "Lolly. Lolly."

The faintest smile pulled at the edge of her mouth, her love surrounding me, so real and alive.

"You're going to be okay," I begged her.

She clung to my hand, and she pressed the back of it to her lips, her words barely audible. "I am, Hailey. I am okay. Because this is the only thing I wanted in this life—the one thing I promised to see through—to see you free. And that's what you and Maddie are. Free."

"Lolly." It was a garbled cry, and I held her closer as her eyes drifted up to Cody who held me tight from behind.

"I knew you were strong enough." It cracked, and her mouth curled into a weak semblance of one of her playful grins. "Take care of my girl. In the bedroom and out. And don't you dare forget all the important things."

"I won't," he promised, his voice raw.

Her eyes came back to me. "Don't cry, sweetheart. I will always be on your team."

A wail burst out of me when I felt her spirit float away.

"Lolly! No, Lolly, no!" I hugged her to me, just as fiercely as Cody hugged me.

Sobs ruptured as I rocked and rocked her.

Sirens blared all around us, a disorder that passed in a garbled haze. A stampede of footsteps and frantic voices bounced off the trees as more officers and an ambulance arrived on the scene.

Somewhere in the chaos, my father was shouting, spouting more lies as he was being cuffed.

"I didn't know, Hailey. I didn't know what Pruitt was involved in. I didn't…"

Maddie's little cries lifted from where she was in the back of the SUV that was now surrounded by officers, Ezra's voice calm and soothing as he tried to assuage her fear. "You're safe, Maddie. It's over."

Two paramedics were suddenly kneeling in front of us. "Ma'am, I need you to let her go."

How could I? How could I let her go when I wanted to hang onto her forever?

Cody held her close to us for a few seconds more before he pressed his lips to the top of my head and murmured, "Let go, Hailey. She's gone. Maddie needs you. Can you stand?"

My nod was weary, but I could.

I could finally stand.

But Cody?

He could not.

Chapter Fifty-Three
Cody

I BLINKED MY EYES OPEN TO THE MURKY DARKNESS OF THE room, though the sun might as well have been blazing in through the window with the power of Hailey's presence that burned in the small space.

Through the haziness, I searched, and I found her curled up in a big pink pleather chair that sat next to the hospital bed where I had to be hooked up to at least ten different machines, the quiet beeping and the soft heave of her breaths the only sound in the room.

It was sometime in the night, I realized, and flashes of what had gone down came battering back into me.

Maddie getting kidnapped.

The shots that had punctured my flesh.

The shootout on the drive to Wagner Ranch.

And Lolly.

Lolly.

Grief wrapped me in ten-thousand-pound chains.

Bows of sorrow and relief knitting me in a vise as I gazed at the woman who was right there, still at my side, safe and whole and undoubtedly cut through by the torment of what she'd lost. Of what she now knew.

As if she felt the weight of my stare, those blue, blue eyes opened to me. They were bold and bright in the night.

A gasp wheezed from her when she saw I was awake, and she bolted off the chair. In a flash, she was standing over me, my hands wrapped in hers.

"Cody." My name broke on her lips.

"Shortcake." My voice was rough and filled with regret. With shame and apology.

Her words fell frantic. "I was so scared. I thought…I thought…"

I lifted my arm, awkwardly since I had tubes stuck in my wrist, and I cupped her precious face. I gazed up through the torment at that beauty that never failed to knock me from my feet. "I told you I wasn't going anywhere."

The frenzied edge bled into softness, and she reached out and ran those tender fingers through my hair. "I knew you would find us."

"I'm sorry that I didn't do it sooner. That I didn't do it better. That I didn't get to—"

"I'm the one who's sorry, Cody. Sorry that I dragged you into all of this."

"I was in it long before you know, Hailey. I—" There was no more hiding or denying it. I'd no longer carry that disgusting secret.

She pressed trembling fingers to my lips. "I know, Cody. I know everything. I know what you got involved in that summer. And I also know what you tried to stop. Why you left so suddenly."

She splayed that shaking hand right over the clock imprinted on my chest. I pressed it closer to me, the pressure allowing me to feel the beat of my heart against her hand.

"I got this tattoo marking the moment your father told me I could never set foot in Langmire or see you again. Broke my fucking heart walking away from you that night. Never knew I could feel that way about anyone, even though I never even had you," I confessed.

"It broke mine, too," she whispered.

Ghosts played through her expression, and I could tell that she was struggling, words on her tongue that she didn't know how to release.

"What is it?" I pressed.

"My father…he killed Brooke when she overheard him giving the order for Brent to kill you."

Hailey's grief banged against the walls. Heavy and harsh. A tear got loose of her eye, and I gathered the moisture with my thumb.

That fucking monster.

I still couldn't believe it.

Couldn't believe that one man could be so dirty.

That he could be so vile.

"I'm so goddamn sorry, Hailey. I'm so sorry for every single thing you've been put through. I wanted to protect you from it all."

"You did." She sniffled. "He's the one to blame. He's the one who orchestrated everything. Set it all into motion. I hate him, Cody. Hate him for stealing the most important people from me. Brooke. Lolly."

She choked over that, a sob ripping through the desolation.

Agony thrummed. Sorrow suffocating.

She held tighter to my hands.

"And he tried to steal you, too. But he can't have you, Cody. Not when you're mine."

She inhaled a quivering breath, and another tear fell. "You saved us."

"I think Lolly did a lot of that saving, too." The words were gravel. Awe and grief.

Wistfulness danced through her features, her face soaking wet as she nodded. "Yeah. The two people who ever truly loved me came for us. Stood for us. Fought for us."

"She was so damned brave…just like you." I murmured it.

"Says the man who suffered three gunshot wounds for us." The softest tease played in her soggy words.

My thumb brushed her cheek. "I would have taken them all."

Her throat bobbed heavily when she swallowed. "I know you would have."

"And I'll be standing for you for all my days, Hailey. For as long as these feet will carry me. Well, just as soon as I get free of this mess."

I wiggled the hand that had the tubes and wires stuck to it, giving her the slightest smirk, trying to find some light in the darkness that hovered in the room.

A promise that she was going to be okay.

Hailey let go of a watery giggle. "I think you would even then."

"Yeah, you'd like that, wouldn't you? Me hauling off down the hall, ripping these tubes from my arms, wearing this hospital gown with my bare butt on full display out the back."

"It is a nice butt," she said, sniffling through a laugh.

I stared at her through the dense, laden silence.

A thousand emotions banged between us.

Hurt.

Grief.

In the middle of it was hope and relief, and even as hard as it was going to be, I knew we were going to be okay.

That this was a new start.

A new beginning as we rebuilt after the devastation.

I wiped a few more of the tears that fell from her face. "Come here, darlin'. I need to feel you next to me."

She hesitated. "You're hurt."

"And you are the only balm I need."

Hailey wavered for only a second before she carefully crawled up onto the small bed and tucked herself into my arms. My soul was soothed the second she rested her cheek on my chest.

Inhaling, she sank into my hold. For a few moments, we lay there in both pain and content. Our worlds shaken, new wounds that slayed, while I was sure a million others were being healed.

"How is Maddie?" I finally asked, the question low.

"She was scared but uninjured."

I swallowed around the lump in my throat. Around the regret lodged there. The horror of finding that deviant in her room and being unable to stop him. "Where is she?"

I felt Hailey's smile seep through the hospital gown to my skin.

"Your entire family was here all day. Ryder and Dakota. Ezra and Savannah. Caleb and Paisley. Kayla. *Your mother.*" Reverence filled the last.

My chest clutched, and Hailey snuggled closer like she felt the weight of my shame. No question, by now, my mother knew what I'd done. The lies I'd told her about where I'd gotten that money.

"Your mom held your hand the entire day while Maddie and I were in the emergency room being observed. She spent the day praising you for being brave. For fighting for us. For fighting for them. She loves you, Cody. And when Maddie was released, she took her home with her to rest so I could stay with you."

"Only thing I want is to be right for all of you."

Hailey scratched her nails through my short beard. Tenderly. Soft scrapes of love. "You're more than right, Cody. You're everything we needed. Our missing piece."

"Good to hear, darlin', because you aren't getting rid of me."

A bit of that lightness weaved through the atmosphere, and I could feel those plush lips twitch. "Cocky Cowboy."

Grinning, I fiddled with a long lock of her hair. "Well, I guess since I'm your cowboy and you're going to be getting a whole lot of my cock, then it fits."

Hailey rolled those sweet, beautiful eyes. Eyes that swept and flowed and rippled with crystalline beauty.

My sanctuary.

My home.

Snuggling in deeper, she murmured, "I'm going to hold you to that, you know."

A rough chuckle skated out. "All too happy to oblige, Shortcake."

"I didn't think you'd mind."

"Nah, don't mind a bit."

She drifted after that, exhaustion weighing her down, finally free of the shackles that had held her chained. No question, it could fuck a person up when the two men who should have loved and protected her with everything they had instead had kept her prisoner to their wicked games.

But it was over.

It was over.

And having her tucked up against me that way? With her heart beating in sync with mine? Her breaths even and her body whole?

I swore that the hands on the clock tattooed on my chest started to tick again. Because I was no longer living on borrowed time.

No.

I was living for them.

I laid there wide awake, breathing her in while she slept in my arms.

Inhaling her aura.

Strawberries and cream.

And I held her until morning.

Just like I was going to do for the rest of my life.

Epilogues

Hailey

COUNTRY MUSIC PLAYED FROM THE SPEAKERS AND DUST flew behind Cody's truck as he barreled down the dirt road that wound through the deep woods outside of Time River. Blips of blue sky flashed overhead as we traveled beneath the soaring trees that touched the heavens.

The windows were down, and the wind gusted in, whipping my hair into a disorder, while still managing to wrap me in the greatest sense of peace.

I looked over at the man who sat in the driver's seat, wearing jeans and a dark-blue tee and a cap with those soft locks peeking out the bottom and curling around his ears. Tattooed arms stretched out, the bulky muscle flexing and bowing beneath the intricate designs as he held onto the steering wheel.

My gaze caressed his profile. His strong brow and chiseled cheeks, his rugged jaw covered by a beard that he had let grow a bit thicker.

My breath hitched at the sight of him.

It seemed it didn't matter how many times I looked at Cody Cooper. He was forever going to have that effect on me.

"Is this it? Are we almost there yet?" Excitement rang from Maddie's voice where she sat in the backseat buckled in her booster, and she tried to push up higher so she could see out the windows.

Cody glanced at her through the rearview mirror as he slowly followed the bumpy, uneven dirt road that was little more than a path carved out by truck wheels. "One minute more, and we'll be there."

Squealing, my daughter threaded her fingers together like she was issuing a prayer. "I can't even wait," she shrieked. "I'm pretty sure this might be one of my favorite days in all of forever. What do you think, my favorite Mr. Cody? Is it going to be one of your favorites?"

Affection pounded from his spirit, and he chuckled. "Yeah, Button, pretty sure it's going to be."

At that, he tossed a glance my way. Creases deepened at the corners of his eyes as he set his delicious mouth in one of those grins when he found me just staring at him, and he reached out and squeezed my thigh with one of those big hands. "Though I have to admit, every single one of my days are my favorite."

Warmth heated my cheeks. My heart throbbing full.

Yeah, every single day had become my favorite, too, even though there were moments that were incredibly difficult. Moments when it felt like I might splinter apart from how badly I missed Lolly.

My love for her was so great that it physically hurt, and agony would spear through me like the piercing of an arrow whenever I thought of her.

When I thought of how fiercely she'd loved us. When I thought of the sacrifice she had made. When I thought of what she'd been willing to give in order to offer us safety.

There were also moments when I reeled, my spirit in turmoil over the truth of who my father was.

The truth of what he had tried to tie me to.

The truth of what he'd done to Brooke.

What he'd done to my *mother*.

We'd discovered evidence in the diary that Lolly kept that my father had also been responsible for my mother's death, the car crash orchestrated when he'd found out that she'd had plans of leaving with me.

It bore such sick similarities to my situation that I still couldn't fully process it.

He was currently awaiting trial for a multitude of sins. Sins that would put him behind bars for the rest of his life.

Pruitt was dead, as was Brent.

God, it was all so much, and I could spiral in it if I allowed myself to, but my grandmother didn't give us her very last moment for me to dwell on that. On the loss. She gave us this chance, so I refused to squander even a minute of it.

Cody weaved the truck through a thicket of trees before it broke open to a clearing.

A vast clearing of five acres.

Rolling fields covered in high grasses and wildflowers.

Time River ran through the far side of the land before the mountains rose up behind it. So gorgeous I was losing my breath all over again.

"This is it?" Maddie screeched.

Cody slowed his truck to a standstill and put it into park. "Yup, this is it."

"We're home!" she shouted, her little hands moving in a frenzy as she pushed the button to release herself from her booster and scrambled out the back door.

"Someone's excited." Cody rumbled his amusement.

"Can you blame her?"

"Nope, not one bit. I'm excited, too." He leaned over the console and pecked a playful kiss to my nose. "How can I not be when I think of all the fun we're going to have here?"

A seductive tease wound into his voice, and he didn't give me time to respond before he grabbed the cardboard tube where he'd had it tucked next to his seat and opened his door. "Come on, darlin'."

He stepped out, and Maddie took his hand, and she bounced backward as she dragged him farther out into the meadow.

Purple wildflowers grew up around them, the mountain behind, the green foliage and the beauty of the trees.

Breathtaking.

Simply because it was the two of them at the center of the picture-perfect scene.

She beamed up at the man who'd changed everything.

The one who cherished.

The one who adored.

The one who teased.

He looked back at me with that smirk on his face and hollered, "Get that cute butt out here, Shortcake."

"Yeah, get your cute butt out here, Mommy!" Maddie parroted.

A short giggle rolled out, and I stepped from the truck and slowly wandered in their direction.

My life.

My everything.

Maddie let go of his hand and tromped over to the area where the dirt had been cleared. Lifting her hands over her head, she spun in a circle.

"Is this where our new house is going to be?"

After that fateful, horrible day, we'd never gone back to Hendrickson. Cody had been in the hospital for two days, and once he'd been released, we'd gone to his mother's so he could fully recuperate.

It became apparent quickly that I couldn't bring myself to return to my rental house without Lolly waiting there for us when we returned.

Couldn't stomach taking Maddie back to the place where her greatest trauma had occurred, that room no longer a sanctuary after it'd been poisoned and tainted, and we felt like Cody's house would likely be too close of a reminder, as well.

So, we'd been staying with Cody's mother over the last three months as we dealt with the physical and emotional aftermath of what had happened. Maddie and I had both been seeing counselors for our grief and the wounds that littered our hearts and minds.

During that time, Cody's mother had become a mother to me.

Her care and love profound.

Even though I'd been grieving Lolly and Brooke, coming to grips at why I'd never had the chance to really know my own mother, the summer had still been magical.

Falling deeper in love with Cody as our truths had been fully exposed, our secrets revealed, our trust given. Falling in love with his family who had become my own.

Both Paisley and Caleb and Dakota and Ryder had been married during that time, and Savannah and Ezra's wedding was coming up next month.

We'd spent so many days and evenings with them.

Loving and living and learning.

Laughing and teasing and finding the place where our hearts were made whole.

Maddie surrounded by her *best cousins* who she adored.

Cody and I had decided we wanted to raise Maddie close to them, and Cody had brought me out here last month on a Friday evening and stood me right in the spot where Maddie was currently spinning and asked me if I wanted to make this place our home.

When I'd cried and whimpered a soggy, *Yes*, he laid me down and made love to me on the bank of the river then promised we were eventually going to christen every inch of the land.

I couldn't wait.

He'd been working on the plans ever since with the intention of building the gorgeous cabin himself with those big, beautiful bare hands.

"Sure is. And your room is going to be right over here." He moved to the spot where her room would be at the back of the house and lifted his hand above his head, his palm parallel with the ground. "But a little bit higher because it's going to be on the second story. What do you think about that?"

"I think I like it!" She jumped like she could reach that very spot.

"And I'm thinking those walls should be pink," he mused like it was just occurring to him though I was pretty sure he'd likely already picked the color out.

I swore the sun shined out of her eyes. "Because pink is my very favorite color, and you know all the important things about me?"

He ran his hand over the top of her head. Adoration flooded from his being. Devotion distinct and unending. "That's right, Button. Because I know all the important things about you. I know them because you and your mom are the most important thing to me."

She took his hand again, swaying at his side while she gazed up at him in that sweet, sweet hope. "Because you love us, right?"

And if anything could bring this rough, rugged man to his knees, it was my little girl. Because he knelt in front of her and brushed a wild ringlet from her face and whispered, "That's right, Maddie, because I love you."

Then he turned those honey eyes on me and said, "With every part of me."

Cody

One Year Later

It was just after nine that night when I stepped out onto the back porch. Rain was pouring down, a deluge from the sky. It was a summer storm that had built for the better part of the afternoon, the clouds gathering high and thick, before it'd finally unleashed its fury just as the sun had begun its descent toward the horizon.

I fucking loved storms.

Loved the energy.

Loved the blinding flash of lightning before the crack of thunder followed.

Loved the way the earth smelled afterward, like it was promising something brand new.

It made me think of that night a little more than a year ago when I'd been driving back to my house with plans to kick my boots up on the railing of the porch and toss back a couple beers as I took in that storm.

Instead, I'd found my drenched, hot as fuck new neighbor running through the rain.

My new neighbor who'd held my past and my future.

Popping the cap on the beer bottle, I sank down on the wood

rocking chair. I kicked my boots up on the railing, just the way I liked to do.

A satisfied sigh pilfered from between my lips as I sank into the comfort.

Into the beauty.

Into this life that I never could have anticipated.

We'd moved into the cabin two months ago. A cabin I'd built myself.

Blood and sweat, but there hadn't been a single fucking tear.

Not when I was cherishing every second that I'd been given.

My chest squeezed. For so long, I'd thought I'd been living on borrowed time, and it just turned out my life had been set to pause.

Waiting on her to return to me.

From behind, the screen door opened then clattered shut.

Hailey's presence washed over me.

Wave after seductive wave.

Strawberries and cream.

All things sweet.

Sex and sin.

My heart's completion.

My perfect match.

Her footsteps were light as she shuffled across the porch, and I blindly reached out for her, even though I would be able to find my way to her in the pitch of dark.

She eased around the chair and slipped onto my lap, and the woman shifted to her side and curled up against me. I wrapped my free arm around her and tugged her close.

The rain fell around us, a soft, constant pattering at the roof. A whinny echoed from the barn where we kept three horses, one for each of us, though I supposed I'd have to add another soon.

"Is my Button asleep?"

I could feel the press of Hailey's amused smile. "After she read the same chapter to me four times."

A light chuckle rumbled around in my insides. "She read me the same one at least seven times before you took over."

"She's pretty proud of herself that she can read it." Hailey shifted so she could tuck her face up under my chin, and she pressed those full lips against my throat. I inhaled the warmth of her breaths.

"Seems right. I'm pretty proud of her, too."

So proud.

My little girl was as smart as a whip. Funny and kind. The life-beat within these walls.

Satisfaction swam like we were suspended, floating on a tranquil breeze.

Quiet contentment.

A blanket of ease.

"I'm so happy," Hailey finally whispered, so low I felt it inscribed on my skin rather than heard it with my ears.

I set my beer onto the porch beside me then splayed my hand over her protruding belly.

I felt my little boy kick.

Joy ricocheted back at the connection.

"So fucking happy," I muttered low.

I dipped in for a slow, lust inducing kiss.

You know, since it turned out that kissing Hailey Cooper was my favorite thing to do.

I nuzzled my nose into her hair, breathed her in. We stayed like that for forever, me sipping at my beer and my girl in my arms. When the rain tapered off, Hailey stood and took my hand, and I followed her back into our cabin.

It was rustic, all exposed woods and rugged stone, a perfect blend of luxury and comfort. Large enough that we'd have plenty of space to fill the rooms but small enough that we'd never lose touch.

Humble enough that we'd never forget how we got here.

I followed her upstairs, and we hit the landing of the big loft that overlooked the great room below, and I started to follow her to the right toward our room before a little voice hollered from the opposite hall, "Daddy! I hear your big boots. You're forgetting something important!"

Hailey gave me an affected smile, those blue eyes on me, her nails scratching through my beard. "I'll be waiting for you," she said.

I took that hand and brushed my lips over her knuckles before I turned course and headed to Maddie's room.

A dim nightlight glowed from low on the wall, and I quietly moved over to her bedside and sat down on the edge.

My little Button beamed up at me.

"You think I forgot something important, huh?" I teased.

She almost looked contrite, though her blue eyes danced with mirth. "Well, you didn't really forget since you already gave me a goodnight, but since I wasn't asleep yet, you're supposed to give me another."

"Is that a new rule?"

"Goodnights are important, Daddy! It's how we get good dreams." She said it like I was clueless.

A rough chuckle skated out, though it rolled with affection.

"Well, you get all the goodnights, then," I said, and I started poking at her belly, making her giggle as I tickled her and sang, "Goodnight, goodnight, sleep tight, never, ever let the bed bugs bite."

She grappled for my fingers as she howled with laughter. "You got me!"

Everything slowed, the energy a quiet hum of intensity. I touched her cute little nose that she had all scrunched up. "No, Button, you got me."

I swept in and pressed a kiss to her forehead, and she hunkered down beneath her covers with her Princess Verona tucked to her side. "I love you, Daddy."

Adoration pressed hard at my chest. "I love you the most."

Pushing to standing, I eased back across her room, leaving her door cracked so we could hear her if she needed us, then I moved back down the hall to the other side of the upper floor.

I opened one side of the double doors that led into our bedroom.

Hailey was sitting up in bed and leaning against the headboard.

The sight of her punched me in the gut.

Blonde hair woven in maple and honey cascading around her stunning face in soft, touchable waves.

Pouty lips.

That body that drove me straight out of sanity. Her belly round with our kid.

But it was those crystalline eyes that would forever do me in. The way they dragged me into eternity.

Yeah.

They got me.

Every day. Every night. Every minute. Every moment.

And every single morning.

The end

Thank you so much for reading HOLD ME UNTIL MORNING! Cody and Hailey swept me off my feet, and I hope they have your hearts too!

If you haven't read the rest of the Time River series, I recommend heading back to the beginning with *Love Me Today*, Caleb & Paisley's epic love story.

Want more? I have a special FREE Time River bonus scene for you—see the whole crew at Paisley & Caleb's wedding. Head to my website to download!

About the Author

A.L. Jackson is the *New York Times* & *USA Today* Bestselling author of contemporary romance. She writes emotional, sexy, heart-filled stories about boys who usually like to be a little bit bad.

Her bestselling series include THE REGRET SERIES, CLOSER TO YOU, BLEEDING STARS, FIGHT FOR ME, CONFESSIONS OF THE HEART, FALLING STARS, REDEMPTION HILLS, and TIME RIVER.

If she's not writing, you can find her hanging out by the pool with her family, sipping cocktails with her friends, or of course with her nose buried in a book.

Be sure not to miss new releases and sales from A.L. Jackson - Sign up to receive her newsletter http://smarturl.it/NewsFromALJackson or text "aljackson" to 33222 to receive short but sweet updates on all the important news.

Connect with A.L. Jackson online:

FB Page https://geni.us/ALJacksonFB
A.L. Jackson Bookclub https://geni.us/ALJacksonBookClub
Angels https://geni.us/AmysAngels
Amazon https://geni.us/ALJacksonAmzn
Book Bub https://geni.us/ALJacksonBookbub

Text "aljackson" to 33222 to receive short but sweet
updates on all the important news.